MW01125038

RESTLESS SPIRIT

HELL HOUNDS HAREM

BOOK 1

FIRST TRILOGY

BY BRIANA MICHAELS

COPYRIGHT

DEDICATION

For the one who taught me the importance of *trust*.

CHAPTER 1

Being dead was the worst thing in the history of ever. Everly crossed the street without looking first because there was no need. If the number nine bus plowed into her, she'd just go through the damn thing without experiencing even a flash of pain.

That sucked ass, too.

One might say she was unstoppable now – being already dead meant she couldn't technically be killed, and not feeling anything meant she was invincible. Badass, right? Wrong. Everly *wanted* to feel things. Being dead was so damn frustrating.

"I'm in Hell," she insisted for the ten thousandth time. "I'm in absolutely fucking Hell. What did I do to deserve this bullshit?"

Her memory was a blank canvas regarding her life-before-death moments, so Everly truly had no idea what she'd done to deserve being stuck on earth. The whole white light show and angels singing in concert, welcoming her into the heavens, hadn't happened yet and she was seriously starting to wonder if it ever would. The closest she ever got to the big, bright light was when she danced on stage at one of the clubs in the district where she lived. And even those moments had been disappointing since no one could see her killer moves because she was a damned ghost.

Death sucked. Had she said that already?

Stomping across the street, Everly no sooner made it to the other side when she caught a glimpse of shadows moving down the sidewalk ahead of her. "Shit."

Everly stopped short and quickly hid behind a garbage bin. The black shadows she evaded on a daily basis slithered their way down the street, unseen by everyone except her. Holding her breath, she waited until those creepy things were out of sight before continuing her walk towards the scent of roasted coffee beans and pastries.

Of all the curses in the world, she managed to hit the lottery with hers. Even though Everly couldn't touch or be touched by other people, there were exceptions to every rule, right? Everly's exception was she'd become a target for the twisted and depraved creatures with hollow eyes, gaping mouths, and skin black as fresh laid tar. Those things could touch her and she could touch them.

Go fucking figure, right?

They scared the piss out of her and she tried to dodge them at all costs. The only problem was, they were everywhere. As if they multiplied in the shadows or had infected other, weaker souls like a damned plague, those crazy dark spirits practically infested the city.

No matter, Everly knew a thing or two about self-defense, and she wasn't afraid to protect herself. *Survival is key when you're dead.* Wait... that didn't sound right. Whatever, she knew what she meant.

Jerking out of her train of thought, Everly jumped and ducked when an explosion of horns honking and the distinct crash of metal on metal echoed behind her. She didn't bother turning around to see the car accident. It wasn't her business and if anyone was dead, they wouldn't see her anyway.

No one ever did.

Ghosts ignored her. The living ignored her. It was horrible and lonely and frustrating as fuck. She was desperate for attention... Okay, wait, back up, she was desperate for attention that *wasn't* from those dark things.

There was no doubt in her mind that accident was the handy work of those damned dark spirits. They were always running around causing some kind of trouble. While some of them seemed like a pain in the ass, others - like the ones that just turned the green light red and cause that nasty accident - they were much worse.

2

Scary, quick, and poisonous, that's what they were.

By the way, it was also Halloween and there was a bit of truth to the whole "the veils are thinnest on All Hallows Eve" and yada-yada-yada. But regardless of the day, dark spirits like those were out all the time – not just on holidays and special occasions. Everly had to admit though, she was excited for tonight and didn't give a shit about the danger she might find herself in at some point during the evening. This was her fifth year of being dead and Halloween was definitely the best night of the year for a ghost.

Especially since she had died in a costume.

Dressed in a corset, black leather pants, boots, a top hat, and face painted like a skull, Everly looked like a creepy, sexy, voodoo badass. A cane with a horned skull on the top completed her outfit. And yup, she walked around every day dressed like she was sexy, bad juju because didn't that just figure. Someone should really warn a girl to be careful of her outfit choices, because what you die in is what you wear *forever*.

Had she mentioned yet that being dead sucked ass?

Arriving at her first destination – Bare Beans Café - it was time to get the day started. The smell of espresso and chocolate made her all kinds of fucked up. She would kill for a cup of coffee and a chocolate pastry right about now.

Stepping into the café, Everly walked around the little tables and took a seat across from a dashingly handsome guy in a suit. She peered into his cup and sighed lustfully, "Oh yum, that's a caramel macchiato with extra whip, isn't it?"

He continued to stare at his laptop, clicking away on the keyboard. Ignoring her. Living his life like she didn't exist.

This was torture at its finest for Everly. The denial of sugar and caffeine when it was literally surrounding her was a special kind of Hell. Everly would never taste those fine flavors again, and boy did she want to. She couldn't stay away, though. Warm, gooey, baked goods and freshly brewed coffee smelled divine. It brought her comfort. "You should totally get a cinnamon roll, too."

The handsome man just kept clicking away on his laptop.

Bored, she moved to the next person. She talked to them, they ignored her. She moved on to the next table and, what do you know, those people ignored her, too. It was always the same. She could scream in their faces and they wouldn't even know it.

"Come on!" she yelled. "Someone see me!" Weaving around the tables, waving her hands and jumping up and down, she screamed at the top of her lungs for someone to see her. Then she plopped into a vacant chair, her knees bobbing up and down, while her emotions started to ride her hard.

Growing restless was something that started plaguing Everly within a few days of being dead. A burst of frustration slammed into her. Everly lashed out and upended a table, sending two teas and a black coffee splattering the walls and floor. Everyone in the shop gasped and looked around, startled and confused.

No one could see her, no one could hear her, and no one could blame her for the spilled drinks. Filling her lungs with coffee-scented air, Everly screamed at the top of her lungs. Fury flooded her system and she shook with rage. Storming out the front window, Everly left the café before she shattered the glass case of muffins and motherfucking bear claws.

It was moments like these, when death became too lonely, and being reckless and mean was too easy, that Everly seriously wondered what side of the fence she belonged on. Heaven was what she wanted but Hell probably suited her mood better.

It was no wonder so many spirits turned dark around here. They probably suffered from the same affliction: Loneliness. It would certainly explain why she was able to touch and feel them but nothing else. They were probably some kind of kindred spirit or some shit. She shivered at the thought…

Suddenly, Everly wondered just how long she had before her soul would turn as black as theirs.

Darkness settled in and the city was alive and thrumming with all kinds of delightfully wicked behavior. After her temper tantrum in the café, Everly had kept herself hidden for the rest of the day and got her head back in the game of being a woman who was going to have a good time and not spend the evening sulking.

With the moon high in the sky, she got into a better mood, gripped her skull-tipped staff tight, fixed her top hat so it sat sexily on her head, and went back into the city. First stop: The Black

Abbey Club.

It was a dump of a place with enough riff-raff and debauchery to make any respectable person's skin crawl. It also was home of some badass underground fight rings. Annnnd the DJ was amazing. Skipping past the long line to get in, not paying the cover charge, and marching right into the club was definitely a perk to being dead. Everly smacked the bouncer's fine ass as she walked right on in. He didn't feel it. Oh well.

Making her invisible grand entrance, Everly felt alive as the bass beat, filling her up with excitement. Music spoke to her soul, lighting her up from the inside out, and she figured she must have been that way when she was alive, too. Some things don't die. Her love of music was immortal.

Sauntering through the crowd, Everly smiled big and bright. Everyone was in full costume, bodies grinding, drinks pouring, people sexing it up against the back walls. She loved it here.

And that song playing right now? Oh Hell yeah. This was one of her favorites.

Everly flung her hands in the air, jumping, and grooving to Nickelback's *Burn it to the Ground*. Dancing through the crowd of grinding bodies, Everly swayed her hips, mouthing the words, and she backed up to dance with a tall, dark and fairly handsome guy dressed in a demon outfit. He smelled like aftershave and vanilla. Fucking delicious.

Demon Dude wore adorably small horns peeking out of the top of his head. Everly could only hope the size of his horns didn't correlate to the size of anything else on him, or else someone might go home disappointed later. He spun around and started dancing with a woman dressed like a vampire. They laughed, he grabbed her hips; she pressed into him and ran her hands playfully through his thick hair.

God, what Everly wouldn't give to be able to do the same to someone.

Next, she danced towards a woman dressed in a red devil outfit. So cliché, but still cute. Her red pumps made her stand five inches taller than Everly and she was swinging her arms in the air with another woman dressed like an angel.

Seriously? That's the best they could do for tonight? Ugh. Couldn't the angel have on a cracked halo or something like...

ohhhh a broken wing! And the devil girl could have at least added a set of fangs to her ensemble. This was just lazy dressing up.

Shit, Everly was thinking way too hard about this, huh?

She shook her head, berating herself for being too bitchy and picky, then began snaking through the crowd again. She noticed a gorgeous man sitting at a small table drinking alone in the back of the club. Her gaze locked on his for a hot second and she gave him her best seductive smile before turning around and getting lost in the crowd again. Not like he'd see her anyway, so why waste time on flirtatious smiles that would go unappreciated.

Heading towards the bar, Everly leaned back, resting her elbows on the bar top and tsked the idiot dressed in a cop uniform as he tried to hit on some cat woman. Everly's eyes rolled automatically, they just couldn't help themselves.

"Come on. One drink?" Officer Dumbass tempted.

Everly stuffed herself between the two of them and gawked. Cat Woman was in head-to-toe black latex with a tiny metal belt that had a fake whip attached to it. The woman's smile said she was thinking about taking the officer up on his offer.

"Don't do it," Everly urged. "He's married. I saw him slip his ring off before he came up to you."

"Come on, pussy cat. One drink."

The woman looked down at his hand. She had to have seen the white band of skin on his finger from wearing his wedding ring. "You gonna arrest me if I resist?" the woman teased.

The cop laughed and hailed the bartender over, ordering two shots of tequila. Everly waited for the bartender to deliver their order. Once they both grabbed their shots, she let Officer Dickwad put the drink to his lips, then she focused on her anger and targeted it right at him before flicking her finger out. The shot glass tilted up, flinging the drink all over his face. Bonus points came when he choked and spit out what was in his mouth all over the chick he was trying to hit on.

"My work here is done." Satisfied, Everly moved on down the line complimenting folks, bitching at others, and generally trying to have a good time socializing with herself amidst the living.

Godsmack's *Voodoo* started playing and Everly squealed. "I love this song!"

Scurrying back out to the dance floor, she used her staff as a prop to dance with. Wrapping her hands around the carved wood, she swayed seductively and sang to the horned skull mounted on top of it, pretending it was her date for the night.

Pathetic? Yes. Fun? Also yes.

Spinning in slow, sensual circles around the dance floor, Everly caught a glimpse of the man still sitting at the back table by himself. Annnnd since she couldn't be seen, acting like a fool was next up on her docket for the night. Some songs just brought out her inner stripper and this was one of them. With wild abandon, Everly began singing along while she stared at the man gazing her way. Clearly he was watching the show of bodies grinding, hips swaying, and hands groping on the dance floor.

Everly wanted nothing more than to be part of that scene, so she made herself part of it. She moved like she was the only woman out there. She danced like he was watching and liked what he saw. She bit her lip and slid her hands down her body, writhing to the rhythm of the music. This song always awoke something in her soul. She loved it. And she danced in a way that proved she loved it, too. Slow… gritty… sexy…

When the song ended, her head was down, her dark hair a curtain framing her face. She slowly looked up, wishing like hell that man was still looking in her direction.

He was.

Everly blew him a kiss and was just about to turn around and head to another part of the club when —

"Holy shit," she gasped.

The guy was still staring. He crooked a finger at her, beckoning her to come forward.

To come to him.

"No fucking way," she whispered. There was no way he was asking her to join him. He couldn't see her. No one could. To prove she was right, Everly cocked her head to the side, smiled wickedly, and pointed at her chest mouthing, "*Me?*"

She damn near fainted when he shook his head yes.

CHAPTER 2

Jack had arrived at the Black Abbey Club just after sundown and swiftly took a seat at one of the back tables. The place was packed tonight, which was typical for the underground club, but they knew to free up a table for him the minute his boots stepped across the threshold.

He'd been there long enough to have a double bourbon on ice and was patiently waiting for a second round. He was in no hurry to leave, no hurry for his second drink, either. Nope, he was too busy watching the Voodoo Vixen make her way around the entire club.

Seeing her dance to Godsmack had been hard enough, but when that siren pole danced around her staff with its ridiculous skull perched on top, Jack wanted nothing more than to be that fucking skull and have that woman's hands wrapped around his body instead of that wooden staff of hers. Watching her dance had been more intoxicating than his drink. Leaning forward, Jack smiled, mesmerized, as she dipped down low only to slide back up nice and slow, grinding her hips like she knew how to make a man melt under her heat. She was bloody fucking gorgeous. Unforgettable.

When the song ended, she blew him a kiss and that was all it took for him to want more. He crooked a finger, bidding her to join him.

"Me?" she said with that sexy mouth of hers.

All he could do was nod at that point. If he tried to speak, he knew a growl would rumble out of his throat instead.

The woman sauntered over to his table and every step she took to get closer to him, her demeanor changed. Somehow, from the dance floor to his table, she had morphed from a sexy vixen to a cautious bunny rabbit.

"You can come closer, I won't bite," he smiled, leaning back, "Unless you ask nicely."

Her eyes widened. "Holy shit. You can see me?"

"How can I not? You're incredible."

He must have said the right answer, because her face lit up like the fourth of July and she quickly plopped down, not across from him... but beside him. If he had personal space, she just entered and shattered it.

Turning her luscious body towards his, she smiled, "I'm Everly."

"Everly?"

"Yup."

"Jack," he said tightly, holding his hand out to shake hers. He watched her hesitate and then, as if throwing caution to the wind, she shrugged and put her hand in his.

The minute they touched, she gasped and immediately put her other hand on top of his. "Oh my God," she whispered, squeezing him tightly.

Just then, the waitress returned with his next drink. "Anything else I can get you?"

"That's all, for now. Thank you." Jack grabbed the glass with his free hand and took a sip. "I'd offer you a drink, but I doubt you'd be able to indulge."

Everly let go of his hand. "Are you... a psychic medium or something?"

"Nope, not even remotely close," he took another sip of his drink, eyes continuing to scan the club.

"How can you see me, then?"

"I'm special."

"Special?" she snorted a laugh. Then there was silence

between them. "Hey," she snipped, "will you look at me?"

His heart was pounding. Her voice... that desperate plea behind those words just... *Bloody hell*, he thought.

"Please?" she whispered. "Can you just... look at me again? No one ever sees me anymore."

His heart sank. No woman should ever sound so sad. But Jack knew damn well that when he turned his focus towards the woman sitting next to him, his night would be over. He would forget his purpose and that just couldn't happen yet. Not until —

"Excuse me, love," he slid out of his seat, "Stay. Here." He could only hope she would listen and obey. Praying she would, Jack wasted no time slipping through the crowd to track down his prey. Halfway across the dancefloor, he pulled out his blade and slithered through the crowd, heading straight for his target.

Each step Jack took, his prey would double it. The piece of shit target headed towards the bathrooms. Jack followed, his jaw clenching. After making sure no one else was around, Jack opened the door and saw the men's room was empty.

"Where are you?" he growled in low tones.

His answer came from up above.

Tilting his head, Jack grinned as the dark spirit – the *malanum* – clung to the ceiling, poised right above him, ready to pounce. And pounce that fucker did, too. Taking Jack down to the ground, they struggled to get at each other's throats. Jack immobilized the shrieking soul by pinning it in the head with his blade. The steel tip chipped the floor tile as it pierced all the way through the *malanum's* head. A black inky substance splattered out of its mouth as it continued to scream.

With a flick of his hand, Jack opened up the black hole – a one-way ticket back to Hell. Crouching over the shrieking soul, Jack grabbed it by the legs, ripped it free from the blade with a sickening wet popping noise, and slung it down into the dark pit.

"One down, four to go."

Straightening his shirt and cracking his neck to relieve some tension, Jack ran his blade under warm water to wash off the black ink before tucking it back into his sleeve and fixing his shirt. He wanted to look presentable before he headed back to that sinful beauty at his table. He just hoped she would still be there.

Stepping out of the bathroom, he maneuvered through the

throng of bodies and made his way back to the table. Relief flooded his system, more intensely than he'd care to admit, when he saw her still sitting there.

"Sorry about that," he said getting back to business.

"That's okay."

His gaze slid over to her then, and holy fucking hell he wished he hadn't peeked. Immediately, he grew rock hard. She was spectacular in that outfit.

"What are you dressed up as?"

"A Voodoo Priestess... I think."

His dark brows popped up in surprise. "A Voodoo Priestess wears leather pants and biker boots?"

She shrugged and her smile damn near stopped his heart. "I guess I'm more of a modern day badass Voodoo Priestess that likes a good ride on something big and powerful."

He couldn't help it. He cracked a laugh so loud his chest rumbled, vibrating the leather cushions of their booth.

Everly tucked a long lock of hair behind her ear and shrugged again, almost blushing. "So what are you?"

For a second, he thought she was asking him what kind of creature he was, then he realized she was trying to figure out his costume. One couldn't get into The Black Abbey Club without dressing up tonight, so it would stand to reason he was dressed as *something*. But black tailored dress pants, a black button down shirt, and silver cufflinks really didn't scream anything creative. "I'm a Voodoo Man."

She smirked, one perfect dark brow arching, "Really? A Voodoo Man?"

"Yup."

"You don't look like a Voodoo anything."

Jack took another sip of his drink. Every inch of his body went stiff, his heart hammering so hard in his chest it hurt to breathe. "Well, it looks like we both have different views on what Voodoo folk look like."

"Creative differences, huh?"

"Mmmm," he took another sip of his bourbon. Then he made the terrible mistake of looking at her again. Holy Hell... she was bloody fucking gorgeous.

"Soooo," Everly fidgeted in her seat as he continued to eat her up with his gaze, "What brings you here?"

The way she asked, he knew she was nervous. And slightly scared. He didn't want her to fear him, but he wasn't a liar either. "I'm looking for someone."

"Oh," she slumped in her seat and looked out towards the dancefloor. "Your date?"

"Not hardly."

"A friend then?"

"Nope." Christ, she asked a lot of questions. "I'm a hunter."

"Like a bounty hunter?"

"Something like that." Jack wasn't about to go into what his profession was, or his real reason for being at The Black Abbey. He needed to tread carefully here and treat this vixen with caution. "Tell me about yourself, Everly."

"I still want to know how it is you can see me."

"I'm sure lots of people can see you, love." He bit back what he was about to say next and put a drink to his lips instead.

"I'm dead. You're talking to a dead chick. You know that, right?"

"Mmm hmm." He went back to scanning the scene again. *Shit, another one.* "Excuse me." Jack left before she got another word in. This time, he headed up the metal staircase to the only door on the second floor. It was shut and locked.

The black spirit had the ability to slide through cracks, whereas Jack did not. Not to worry, he had other tricks. Once he got into the room, he found it was empty. Thank fuck for that because having witnesses right now would have really sucked. Eyes narrowing, Jack scanned the dark room and found his target huddled in a corner, munching on something.

Without looking to see what, or who, the *malanum* was eating, Jack snuck up from behind, pierced the back of its head with his knife, waved his hand to open the black hole, and slung the bastard down into the abyss. His quota was almost met for the night. Jack's ass vibrated as his cell went off in his back pocket and he checked the text.

17 down for me.

Chuckling, he texted back: *You did a night's work for all.*

Relax and have fun. See you in the morning.

Bloody perfect. Jack stuffed his cell into his back pocket and looked around for something to wipe his blade clean with. Not finding anything, he swiped it across his black pants and headed back down to his table again.

If she's still there, it'll be a miracle.

If she wasn't, he'd hunt her down. No way was he losing her when he had only just found her.

To his relief, Everly was still sitting there. Glaring at him as he crossed the club to rejoin her, she looked abandoned and pissed off. It made his gut twist to see her look like that. "I'm sorry," he said standing in front of her. "You wanna get out of here?"

"Why?" she glared at him with her arms crossed. "What's wrong with here?"

He shrugged, playing it cool, and held out his hand for her. "Come on, love. The night is young. Let's see what kind of Hell we can raise in this city tonight."

Her anger melted into a smile and, to his sheer and utter relief, she took him up on his offer. He squeezed her hand hard and held her tightly.

Jack had no plans of letting her go now.

CHAPTER 3

Holy Hades, this was incredible! Everly gripped Jack's hand tight and her staff tighter as they headed out of the club and into the night.

Well... sort of. She did grab his hand and her staff but she stopped short just as they hit the streets and turned left. Up ahead, she sensed a dark spirit and quickly swung her body, steering Jack in the opposite direction. "Let's go this way."

"Where to?"

"Doesn't matter."

"Thennnnn," he swung her back to head in the original direction, "let's go this way if it doesn't matter."

Her feet glued to the ground and she refused to take another step further. "I said no."

Jack cocked an eyebrow, turned to look down the street, and his face tightened. She saw his jaw clench while his eyes narrowed on her. "Don't be afraid, love. Not with me here to keep you safe."

"Look," she sighed, "This is seriously amazing and all that you can see me. Which," she jabbed a finger in the air, "I still want to know how that's possible. But I'm not going that way. You were right. You aren't the *only* one who can see me. And I don't necessarily like to be seen... by *them*."

Oh what the hell? She sounded like a lunatic. There was no way this guy was going to stick around after that sad evasion of the real truth. But damnit, she wasn't ready to let go of him yet. Not now that she finally found someone who could see and talk and *touch* her. "I don't want to go that way, Jack."

"Alright then, we won't."

They went in the direction she wanted and got further away from the dark spirits she sensed. Holding his warm hand, Everly decided to focus on that single thing. The *feel* of Jack.

He felt damn good. His hand was big and rough and probably capable of crushing coal into diamonds. Yet he held hers as if she was priceless porcelain. Firm, but gentle.

Jack looked both ways before they both crossed the street and it was then she thought of the most absurd thing. He probably looked like he was holding hands with an imaginary friend. No one else would be able to see her, so him having his hand out and fist cupped against air probably made him look dumb. Feeling bad about it, she slipped her hand out of his.

He stopped walking and stared at her. "What's wrong?"

"Nothing I just..." Everly froze in terror. "NOOOO!" she screamed and ran in front of Jack with her arms out in front of her just as an SUV was about to drive right into them.

Her scream was still tearing out of her throat when she was suddenly flying across to the street. The SUV went by, along with several other vehicles and Everly stared, slack-jawed, at Jack. He'd pinned her against a brick wall and was glaring at her.

It took her a second to put the events in order. "You just tried to save a *ghost*?"

"And you just thought you were going to be able to stop a five thousand pound metal tank with your bare fucking hands?"

Everly shrugged, "It was instinct to save you. Putting my hands out was all I had time for. All I could do."

Yeah, sure, the instinct was there, but the backup of muscle and power wasn't. Why the hell she thought she could have helped him was stupid since the vehicle would have driven straight through her and hit him a second later. Jack would have been splattered all over the road had he not moved them out of the way fast enough. Speaking of which, "You just saved a dead person, ya know."

His smile made her knees a little weak. "Instincts, love. We both have them." He tossed her a wink, then backed away from the wall to give her space to move. Too bad for Everly. She kind of liked him all up close and personal.

Ghosts really had no boundaries.

In comfortable silence, they walked down the street again. Her staff was magically back in her hands even though she'd dropped it to do the Save-Jack routine moments ago. Funny thing about being a ghost - the clothes you wore never come off, and apparently anything you were carrying at the time of death, you'll always carry.

Death sucked. Seriously. She was going to keep saying it until it wasn't true anymore.

Everly hadn't seen herself naked at all since she died. Every time she tried to take off her pants, they would just magically reappear on her ass again. She has been in the same outfit for five years and it drove her nuts carrying around the staff with a dead goat head on it all the time. Not that having the staff was always a bad thing. When those dark spirits would try to attack her, it was hella handy to have for a weapon.

Jack grabbed her hand and immediately she could feel him again. It was a shock to her system, that's for sure. "Can we go somewhere private?" she blurted.

He turned with a smirk, "How private would you like?"

Ohhh she could answer in a dozen ways. "Anywhere that it can be just the two of us."

"Can I ask you something?" Jack steered her to the right and they headed towards the residential district.

"As long as it's personal."

He chuckled, "Alright. Do you know how you died?"

Soooo, yeah, he just totally went there. "I don't know. I don't remember." Probably not the answer he was hoping for, but that's all she had to give him. Everly really couldn't remember a damn thing about dying. She just woke up dead one day.

Scary shit right there, huh? And the even scarier part was that her first day dead was also the first day she was fighting off the black spirits. They literally surrounded her and within seconds, her instincts kicked into survival mode and she'd gone batshit crazy beating them off of her.

16

It hadn't stopped since. The fight to survive and live happily dead was a constant struggle for her. The dark spirits were always around, lurking in the shadows.

"You don't remember anything about it?"

"Nope, nada."

"I'm sorry," he said softly, squeezing her hand.

"Not your fault, you didn't kill me." She stopped walking, forcing him to stop too, "Did you?"

He stared at her for several heartbeats. Pain and sorrow slowly filling in his eyes, and she hated it. She far preferred him to have the sexy come-hither look on his face like back at The Black Abbey. "No," he said in a deep voice. "I would never."

Holy Hell, he was so intense. It made her want to melt into him. Believe him.

"Oh good!" Everly shot him her perkiest smile. If he stared at her like that for much longer, she would probably disintegrate. Pushing forward, they started moving again. "So what are you apologizing for then?"

"If you don't remember how you died," they ran across the street, "it means you were ripped out of your body too fast."

"Makes sense." Really, she didn't want to talk about her death. It was old news and she was sick of the subject. "Can I ask you something?" Deflect, deflect, deflect.

"Anything." He held the lobby door open and they both entered an apartment complex.

"Where do I get one of your big knives?" Not skipping a beat, Everly headed towards the elevators and pressed the UP button. Well, she tried to press the UP button. Her fucking finger went through the control box and she cursed. It would take a lot of energy to actually push it, and she didn't want to waste a drop. But not being able to do something as simple as push a button was infuriating.

A whip of anger lashed her and she fought the raging scream trying to tear out of her throat. The only thing grounding her was Jack. She wanted to behave in front of him. He was the first person ever to see her and she wasn't about to scare him off so soon.

A coldness shivered down her spine, unnaturally. She looked at her hands, eyes growing wide when she saw the black spot on her palm. Closing her fist, she frantically tried to calm the hell

17

down. *Breathe in, breathe out.*

Jack hit the UP button and she wasn't sure if he noticed her teetering on the edge of losing control and was just being polite, or if he hadn't noticed a damn thing because he was trying to concentrate on an answer to her question.

The elevator *ding-dinged* and they stepped inside.

"So?" she pushed, "Where does a girl like me get a knife like that?"

"You sure you want to know, love?"

The elevator door shut, closing them in together with no one else around. She wasn't sure who should have been more scared - Him being trapped in a small space with a ghost who was turning dark, or her being trapped with a man who could catch and kill spirits like her with one badass blade.

One thing was certain: Someone was gonna get fucked.

CHAPTER 4

Jack tried to come up with an answer to her question. *Where does a girl like me get a knife like that?*

How the bloody hell had she even seen his knife? It was concealed, not just literally, but magically too. "What makes you think I have a knife, love?" He pushed the number seven button and ignored the lurch in his stomach as the elevator began to rise.

"I saw what you did."

Again, he didn't know how to respond. "I'm not sure I know what you're talking about."

"Then how about I give you a recap since your memory seems to be as shoddy as mine." The doors opened with another *ding-ding* and they stepped onto the seventh floor of the complex and began walking down the hall. "I saw you stab that dark spirit in the upstairs private room of the club." She held her hand up to stop him from speaking, "A girl will put up with a guy excusing himself once from the table… but not twice. I followed you and saw what you did. And I'm glad you did it. But, I wanna know how I can get a weapon like that."

Jack tried to hold back his smile. The fact that she had followed him was impressive. He should have been able to sense her and yet she'd gone completely undetected. Follow that up with

19

the idea of her wielding a blade like his, and he was turned on the likes of which he hadn't felt for a long fucking time.

"You have need of such a thing?" he asked cautiously.

"That," she poked him in the chest and ignored the electrical buzz she felt from the contact, "is none of your business."

She followed him to the last door on the left. He unlocked and held it open for her so she could go in first. Jack was a lot of things, but he was still a gentleman. Everly stepped inside the apartment and a big smile spread across her face. Jack's heart hammered in his chest again.

"Nice place you have here," she made herself at home instantly. Propping her staff against the black leather couch, she spun around and studied the layout. "Are you colorblind or something?"

"What? Uhhh no," he stuffed his hands in his pockets and moved cautiously around her.

"So what's with all the black and white then? Did you have a designer come in and decorate for you?"

"Yeah, something like that." Jack swallowed the lump taking up way too much space in his throat. He looked around the apartment. It had been a while since he was last here, and looking around the place felt strange all of a sudden. The space was the same it had always been. Open, simple. The couch was black, the carpet white, and the walls were a steely gray. Not much color really, except for the dark purple lamp, a vase, and some other little things. He never really put much thought into the interior of this place; it just was what it was. Sleek, refined, and calming – that's what he thought of whenever he was here.

Everly sat on the couch and stretched her arms across the back of it, matching the apartment perfectly considering she was dressed in all black and white herself. Jack strode over to the wet bar and poured himself a drink before sitting down next to her.

"I'm still waiting for you to answer my question, Jack."

Hell's bells, this girl wasn't going to let up, was she? Persistence was a beautiful thing… so was ignorance.

Jack took a sip of his bourbon while his gaze latched onto her amazing hazel eyes. If he answered with the truth, he worried she was going to take off and Jack wasn't ready for her to run… not yet.

Was she scared of this guy? Nope. Not at all. Besides, one of two things was going to happen with him in this apartment: Either he was going to kill her, which, um hello she was already dead so that would be pointless, and if he stabbed her with that knife of his, she'd probably try to thank him for it because she knew she was turning into a dark spirit and would need to be put down eventually. Or – and this was what she was really hoping for – he'd give her a night to remember.

It was a win-win for Everly. Truly.

She watched him take another sip of his drink, the ice clinking in the fine crystal as Jack tipped back his bourbon. His gaze was fixed on her and it was intense. Everly's mouth watered while she watched him swallow, his throat moving up and down with every gulp.

Suddenly, her attentions were elsewhere and she no longer cared about his knife at the moment. Her wish list just doubled as she watched him swirl the bourbon around in his glass. Was it spicy? Smoky? Were there hints of vanilla or caramel? Was the bourbon warming him from the inside out or did it leave his tongue tingling?

And just look at his mouth. His jaw line. His gun-metal grey eyes that looked ancient and hungry as he stared back at her. Fuck he was hot. And he was making her hot. His arm flexed a little as he swirled his glass around. And he smelled insanely delicious.

"Do you like what you see, love?" His voice was dark. Deep. Sexy as fuck.

Everly's legs rubbed together, instinctively. Yeah, she liked what she saw. She liked the way he looked. She liked that he could see her. The way he was looking at her right now, drinking her in with his eyes. She liked the way his throat worked on swallowing that bourbon. And how his tongue flicked out to lick his bottom lip.

Lord. Have. Mercy.

She wanted him. Her desire clawing its way out of her soul, eliminating every other thought, every other sense but her desperate need to touch and be touched.

"What's it taste like?" she whispered.

Jack took another sip. Savoring, teasing. "Want to taste it yourself?"

She bit back a frustrated snarl. All the desire she just felt was suddenly doused with cold reality. "I can't. I'm dead."

"Sure you can, love." He leaned over a fraction closer to her, "Kiss me and taste it yourself."

Was this a fucking trick? If it was, then it was a damned cruel one. But like the desperate woman she was, Everly leaned in and pressed her mouth to his.

Heat engulfed her, filling her up from tongue to toes. Jack's mouth was warm and soft, and when he slid his tongue against hers, Everly moaned. He tasted rich, bold, with a hint of vanilla and something smoky.

Jack reached around and pulled her in tight, one hand sinking into her hair while the other pressed against the small of her back.

Everly broke away with a gasp. "How can you do this?"

Her heart hammered in her chest. Or at least it sure felt like it was. Holy Hell, she was feeling. FEELING. *What is this guy?* She didn't even care what the answer was. It didn't matter. Jack made her feel good and that was all that mattered right now.

"I'm not like other men," he said before kissing her again, deeper this time.

She lost all her senses when his tongue dove into her mouth. He tasted like Heaven and Hell and all the things in-between that got a girl lost in ecstasy. She ran her hands through his hair. The need to have more, feel more, taste more was driving her wild. Before she knew it, Everly was in his lap, grinding against him.

He broke the kiss and cursed, "Jesus, you're —"

"Ridiculous?"

"No," he laughed, "I was going to say incredible."

She swallowed the lump in her throat, but didn't bother to climb off Jack's lap. She could feel every inch of him and didn't want to give it up. Not yet. "How. Are. You. Doing. This?"

She could still taste the bourbon in her mouth. Everything inside her grew tingly. Good Lord, this was unbelievable. Everly had spent her entire death being cut off from what Jack was now providing her.

"Do you think people come into your life at the right time, Jack?" Instead of letting him answer with words, she started kissing him again and he groaned against her mouth.

"Yesssss," he practically hissed when she squeezed the back of his neck.

Everly was behaving like a fool. She knew it, but ask her if she cared.

Jack was intoxicating and she'd been deprived of desires of the flesh for too long. A raw hunger roared within her. Her soul practically shattered when she felt his hands roam over her body.

"How are you doing this?" she groaned.

"Does it matter?"

"Nope, not really." Not right now. All that mattered was that she finally found someone with the power to make her feel the things she craved.

Ever since she died, Everly didn't have the energy – or focus for that matter – for what it took to even satisfy her own desires. It took every ounce of energy she had just to knock over a tea cup at a café. Getting herself off was impossible. She just didn't have the right combination of power and focus. She either had one or the other when it came down to pleasuring herself.

Jack grabbed her ass and stood up. Everly wrapped her legs around his waist and he carried her down the hall and into a large bedroom where there was a white fluffy king-sized bed. Bending down, he laid her on the bed. Placing one knee between her thighs, he spread her legs open. "Fuck you're gorgeous like this. All wound up with no place to go."

"I can think of a few places I wanna be."

She felt his leg press against her thigh as he let go of her waist. He was keeping some piece of him touching her, she realized. Unbuttoning his shirt slowly, he teased her with a sneak peek at his taut muscles. She licked her lips, eyes fixated on his nimble fingers making fast work of each black button. When he pulled off his shirt, she moaned her approval and he cocked his head to the side, "Your turn, love."

Before she could explain that her clothes never came off because they seemed to be stuck to her, he had already unbuckled her corset. She actually felt the air hit her skin in places that the sun hadn't shone on in several years.

"Oh my god," tears welled up but there was no time for crying right now. Jack had started working on stripping her leather pants off. She was practically trembling now. "How is this fucking possible?"

"Does it matter?"

"No," she panted, "It definitely doesn't."

Next, Jack placed a hand on each of her legs. "If I let go of you, we'll have to start over," he explained.

"Then don't let go." *Ever.* "Please." Everly didn't want to lose a smidgen of what Jack just managed to do. This was more progress than she had ever made before.

Jack growled low in his throat and he sounded like an animal. A sexy beast. "Take my pants off."

She leaned forward and did as she was told. With a little finagling, Everly slid his pants down over one helluva sculpted ass. Before she got to truly admire his physique, he dipped down and started blazing a trail of kisses up her legs, starting at her ankles and going all the way to the apex of her thighs.

"Lay back, love. I suspect it's been a while for you and I mean to catch you up on what you've been missing."

She didn't have time to get a word in before his tongue licked up her slit and an incredibly undignified moan flew out of her mouth. His chest vibrated as he chuckled, but Jack didn't bother teasing her. Well, he didn't bother teasing her with words. Instead, he plunged a finger inside her opening and she arched her back, thrusting her hips up for more.

"You're so tight," he nipped the bud of nerve endings, coaxing another moan out of her, and then he started the fastest tongue flicks imaginable. Next, he dipped a second finger inside her body.

Warm honey pooled everywhere within her. Filling her up. Overflowing.

"Don't stop," she begged, sinking her fingers into his hair and holding his head right where she wanted him. Faster and faster her orgasm climbed its way up and out and when it broke free, she flew apart. One hand on his head, the other gripping the sheets, Everly screamed his name until her throat was raw.

"Fuck," Jack said, crawling on top of her. He positioned the head of his cock at her opening. Rubbing her, enticing her. "Are you sure you want this?" He would stop right now if she wanted him to. But she didn't want him to.

"I need this, Jack. Oh God…" her eyelids fluttered as he pushed the tip in. "Please… I need this. I need you…"

She gasped when he entered her. He did it slowly. Deliberately. "Hold on to me," he said as his pace began to quicken.

Sinking her fingers into his shoulders, he rocked her back and forth, coaxing her closer and closer to another sweet release. "Come for me," he rumbled in her ear. "I want to watch you come."

Part of her wanted the moment to last a little bit longer, but the other pieces of her were already shattering apart as he brought her over the edge and let her freefall into sublime bliss.

And that was just the beginning…

Whoever this guy was – good or bad – she wasn't letting him go. Ghosts could attach themselves to things, and Everly had every intention of clinging to this man for as long as possible. The fact that she really knew nothing about him didn't even seem important.

That should have been a red flag, right?

CHAPTER 5

After several hours of what was the best sex session ever, they laid in silence with their limbs tangled and Jack played with her hair. They hadn't broken physical contact this entire time and she managed to stay whole, naked, and embrace the sense of touch.

"This feels good."

"I agree," Jack lifted her hand and playfully nipped her fingertips.

"I would trade my soul to the Devil if I could keep this," she sighed.

Jack stiffened. "What makes you think you'd have to go that far?"

"Because Heaven wouldn't feel this sinful… or this good."

He chuckled again and kissed her head.

Biting her lip, Everly debated on pushing the issue and decided, *fuck it*. She twisted up to look into his grey eyes, "Please tell me how you did this?"

"Why does it matter?"

"Because I want to know."

"What if the truth scares you?"

"Nothing scares me."

"This might," he rolled over, still keeping constant contact with her, and reached down to the side of the bed to grab his blade. He watched Everly with cautious eyes and handed over the weapon so she could hold it. "I'm not… normal."

"Hmmm… well, that's good. Normal is boring."

"Normal is safe."

Everly ran her finger over the tip of the blade, "Are you an angel?"

Her question surprised the hell out of him. "No," Jack warned, "I'm most definitely not one of those."

She bit her lip and the urge to take her mouth with his was too great to deny. Jack leaned over and captured her mouth, the fever between them grew hot again. He grinned when he felt the blade press into his neck. "Do you wish to kill me, love?"

"No," she half-whispered, "But I want to know what you are. And you keep fucking distracting me."

"Why do you want to know so badly?" He nibbled on her bottom lip and allowed her to keep the blade where it was on his neck. If she needed to feel in control of something, he wouldn't deny her the illusion.

He wouldn't deny her a damn thing.

Everly twisted the tip, nicking his skin. "Aren't you afraid?"

"No," he deadpanned. "I trust you."

"You don't even *know* me." Everly carefully maneuvered her body so she was on top and he let it happen if only to see her naked and straddling him while wielding his favorite weapon. "Tell. Me."

He ran his hands up and down her thighs, knowing she could feel his cock pressing against her core, growing harder and harder with every bit of friction their bodies made. "Why is it so important to you?"

"Because I want to know, damnit."

"*Why?*" he moved his hips, urging her to do the same. He'd give his fucking black soul up again to have her ride him right now. She was all angry and erotic and deadly. The trifecta of unholy sexiness.

"Because I want to know what you are so I can be like you."

He froze. That wasn't quite the reason he expected. "But you might not like what I am."

"That might be," she bent down and eased the blade away from his neck so she could kiss him again. "But I know I *definitely* don't like what I am right now. Being like you has to be better than being like me."

"How so, love?" He groaned when she grabbed his cock and started to stroke it between her thighs.

"I ache," she continued to stroke him, "I crave," she scraped her nails lightly over his chest, "I need," she nibbled her way down his body. Taking his cock into her mouth, she licked it slowly, as if she was savoring every bit of him she could. Wrapping her hand around the base of his shaft, she took him into her mouth and his eyes rolled into the back of his head. She opened her throat and took him down as far as she could get. His head thrashed back on pillow. Words failed him at that point. Thoughts, decisions, precautions – they vanished as she began to ride his cock again. For the love of God, this woman was insatiable.

And he fucking loved it.

How he managed to find her tonight was nothing more than a stroke of luck. Miracles weren't things he believed in. But luck? Perfect timing? Those he could accept. Jack just happened to be at the right place at the right time tonight. He didn't know what was going to happen from this point on, but he knew one thing for sure: he wasn't going to let her go.

Instincts dictated his moves now, forcing him to reach out and wrap his hands around her hips.

Flipping her over, onto her back, Jack kept his eyes locked on hers as he rode her harder and harder. A growl rumbled out of his throat and he didn't hide the sound. He wanted her to hear it. Let it rattle her soul and light her up. Another hour of pleasure and he finally came again, after making sure she was fully satisfied.

When they were too exhausted for another round, they laid in comfortable silence once more. He never took his hand off of her so she would stay whole for a little while longer. Her body heat matched his own now and that was just fine by him. He liked her this way. Going by the smile on her face, he figured she didn't want to give this up yet, either. But… all things come to an end. "We should get dressed."

"Why?" Everly twisted around to look up at him. She was drawing lazy circles around his abs.

He didn't want to say he had a bad feeling. It would have ruined the moment entirely. But something in his gut – those bloody instincts of his – were urging him to get up. Jack kissed the top of her head. "How about we go out for a little while?"

"I'd rather stay here," she said.

His jaw clenched in frustration. Every breath he took was growing more desperate, more shallow. He was losing energy keeping her whole like this. And yet… he would drain himself down to a husk to keep her in his arms just a little while longer.

That was the soft side of him talking, though. That piece of him he rarely let out to play anymore. Jack was a killer, a hunter, and a dangerous motherfucker. The hairs on the back of his neck stood on end and a chill swept into the room. In his current state of weakness, he wasn't sure what was causing it: his depleted energy, the woman in his arms, or the danger lurking around the city lately.

Maybe it was his guilt for being in bed right now with one helluva woman when he should be elsewhere instead.

Looking over at the alarm clock, he noticed it was the witching hour of night. *That must be it,* he thought. Magic was in its most chaotic phase right now. Still, time was running out and he'd spent the better portion of the night doing all the things he shouldn't.

Not that he regretted a bloody minute of it.

"Please tell me what you are, Jack."

He ground his molars together. Would she freak out if she knew the truth? Would she just accept it and roll on?

"Why is it so bloody important that you know what I am?" Angry that it was getting to the end of the fantasy- because that's what this was right? A fantasy? A cruel trick? A wicked form of magic made to haunt him more than he already fucking was? Jack hopped out of the bed and immediately started getting dressed.

Tugging on his pants and reaching for his boots, he wanted to scream. The silence in the room was bloody awful. He yanked his shirt back on and sat on the edge of the bed. Burying his head in his hands, he was perilously close to unraveling.

"Jack?" Everly ran her hand down his back, which made this moment so much worse. "I don't want to live like this forever," she said quietly.

Jack swallowed, audibly. She clung to his arm and he pushed his energy into her, keeping her whole for a little longer. He stood up, not able to escape and not able to stay. Everly went right with him, following his movements, keeping constant contact. She turned his face towards hers and kissed him. It made him roar inside.

When she broke away, it was all he could do to not yank her into his embrace. Crush her body to his, tuck her in for safe keeping so he could hang on to this moment. Her dark hair framed her face and her gorgeous eyes were heavy lidded, "I don't want to be alone anymore."

"How long," he cleared his throat, "How long have you been on your own?"

"Too long." She swiped a tear away from her cheek and it just about killed him to watch. "Tell me what you are," she begged.

"I... I don't know how to tell you. You don't... you're not..." he exhaled loudly, "bloody fucking hell, woman."

A coldness filled her hazel eyes. She was pissed and her anger shot out in an icy burst. "Fuck. You."

Frustrated, Jack grabbed a fistful of her hair and tugged, "Look at me." When she met his gaze, he stayed silent long enough to put his words together carefully. "If I tell you, your life as you know it will be forever changed. Do you understand that?"

It wasn't dramatic, it was accurate.

"Okay."

He arched a brow, "*Okay?*"

"Yes. Okay. Now tell me."

Too bad, so sad. Confession time was over before it even began. Darkness engulfed the bedroom and they were surrounded.

CHAPTER 6

"Bloody fucking hell!" Jack snatched his blade and jumped between Everly and the *malanum* creeping into the bedroom.

More and more *malanum* entered the room, hissing and screeching. They climbed the walls, the ceiling, slithered across the floor, closing Jack and Everly in on all sides.

Stupid, stupid, stupid. So enthralled with his female, he hadn't taken any of the precautions necessary to keep the apartment safe. No wards or charms had been placed on the doors and windows recently. Damn, what an idiot he was tonight.

Preparing for battle, Jack let go of Everly and she was instantly a ghost again, completely dressed and hissing right along with the rest of them. Only she was on his side. Thank. Fuck.

Trapped between the bed and the window, Jack positioned himself in front of his woman, shielding her from what was slinking towards them. "We jusssssst want her, Hound."

"Not gonna happen." Jack didn't bother with the small talk anymore. He swung out and stabbed the thing with his blade, opening up a black hole with his other hand, and slung the fucker inside. The other *malanum* began to shriek and slink away at that point, putting as much space as possible between them and the hole.

"Time to go," said another. It was clinging to the ceiling and dropped down in front of Jack to distract him while two more grabbed Everly and took off with her.

Out the fucking window.

Jack screamed as he leapt forward to snag one by the leg, but it was too slick and damn quick and got away. "NO!" Turning to fight off the others, he saw they, too, vanished and pure dread consumed him. The *malanum* would tear his woman to shreds, or worse…

Fuck, he didn't even want to go there.

Taking off to hunt them down, Jack ghosted himself. There were perks to being one of his kind and switching between forms was one of them. He ran onto the balcony and jumped the full seven floors. He landed with a drop and roll, blade out and ready.

"Where are you, where are you, where are you?" He ran down the alleyway, chanting those words as his boots pounded the pavement. His fury grew hotter with every breath he took. All his careful control blew six ways to Sunday when he heard Everly scream. Her voice echoed through the darkness like a banshee with a death song.

Bolting towards the noise, he caught up with them in an ally just a block away from the apartment. She was against the wall, holding her own against three huge *malanum*. Swinging her staff out, she stabbed one of them and used his body as leverage to spin out and kick the one advancing on her left. As Jack ran over to jump in on the action, the third *malanum* managed to knock her legs out from under her and she went down hard.

The evil bastard began to drag her off again but she twisted around, screaming for all she was worth, and managed to yank him down to the ground with her. They started strangling each other while Jack took out the other two attackers. Opening the black hole, he slung them inside, their screams growing faint as they were gobbled up by darkness.

Everly roared in fury as she wrapped her legs around the last one, strangling it with her thighs. Its long fingers wrapped tightly around her throat and Jack hauled ass to quickly snatch the bastard off of her. With a roar, he tossed the last *malanum* into the hole and closed it again.

Turning to check on Everly, he—

32

"Woahhh, easy, love." Cautiously, he walked over and tried to get her to calm down. She was crouched on all fours, panting hard, eyes wild. "Look at me." He grabbed her shoulders and she lashed out at him on instinct, hissing much like the *malanum* would.

Oh hell no, this was not going to happen. She was not going to turn into one of those bastards. If she did, there'd be nothing left of the woman she once was and he would have no choice but to —

Not. Going. There.

Jack hauled Everly to her feet and slammed her against the wall. "Breathe through it," he gritted his teeth. Fuck, she was flickering in and out while she struggled to gain control of her spirit. Pushing what little energy he had left to give, Jack shoved all he could into her, "Come on, love. Please. Try."

Try to fight it. Try to focus. Try to hold on.

Everly's breaths turned ragged. He wanted to scream in relief when she gripped his shoulders, squeezing him tight as she fought off the darkness threatening to consume her.

"Come on, girl. You've got this." Jack shoved her back, slamming her against the wall again to snap her attention to him. "Fight it! FIGHT IT!"

Her head shook violently as a silent scream began working its way out of her gaping mouth. It was then he saw that both her hands were completely black now. The darkness was spreading up her arms like sleeves. The *malanum* had bit her, clawed her, done all they could to devour and make her like them.

Jesus fucking Christ, Jack had to work hard to swallow past the lump stuck in his throat as the terrible reality of her fate came into focus.

"Help," she squeaked.

Jack got all up in her face. Pressing his forehead to hers, he penetrated her with a gaze so fierce she would not be able to look away no matter how hard she tried. "I've got you," he growled loudly, "I've fucking got you. Breathe through it. Fight it, love. You're not going to turn. You're not going to turn. You're not going to turn."

He repeated it over and over like there was a chance that if he said it enough times it would be true. He wanted to look at her arms, to see if the blackness had stopped spreading, but he didn't dare break the stare down they had going on.

Her hazels were pleading for his help and he was a Hound who delivered.

"Stay focused on me." He pressed his forehead against hers harder. He moved one arm down to her hips, while the other stayed on her shoulder, keeping her flush against the wall. "Focus on me. Lock eyes on me, woman, and don't you fucking let go. Stay with me."

He wouldn't quit. Jack kept pushing his energy into her, all the while praying in his head that it would be enough to save her.

"Stay with me," he pleaded fiercely. "Fight this. I know you can." His heart was hammering so hard he was losing his hearing. "FIGHT FOR ME!"

Everly's nails dug into his arms, drawing blood.

"COME ON!" he yelled, "STAY WITH ME." Sweat ran down his temples and back. His limbs shook. His nerves were shot. His energy was totally gone.

Not that any of those things mattered right now. All that mattered was that he didn't lose her to the *malanum*.

"Come on, love," his voice cracked.

After several minutes, Everly stopped shaking. He continued to hold her steady, encouraging her to breathe in and out slowly. Finally, she stopped snarling and groaning against the evil trying to morph her soul and was able to stop herself from crossing over to the darker side.

It was painful to watch a spirit unravel, and be so frightened, as they lost control of themselves. It was also a beautiful thing to witness – her fight, her focus, her will to not succumb to what was undoubtedly tempting her with every breath she took.

Becoming evil was easy – it felt good to live with no morals or conscience. It's freeing in a sense. Staying good involved a lot more work and even a few sacrifices now and then. Everly would have felt the pull towards evil like a shark would blood. A desire to surrender would have overwhelmed her, tempting and luring her down a darker path that would promise delights and then swallow her whole. Jack couldn't have been more proud of her for fighting back just now.

He felt her nails ease up on his shoulders. And so, he eased up on his restraint, too. When he let her go, she slumped forward and he caught her. "Easy, love. I've got you."

Jack pressed his lips to hers. His kiss was sweet and simple – nothing compared to earlier when they ravished each other. He was gentle with her now, fearing she might shatter at any moment if he wasn't careful with her. "You good?"

"Yeah," she whispered.

Reluctantly, he let her go and backed up to give her some space. Once he did, she was a ghost again and he was crazy dizzy from using all his energy.

Exhausted, Jack leaned against the wall and slid down on his ass. There would be no more attacks quite yet. *Malanum* stayed far away from the likes of him because they knew what the endgame was if they were ever face-to-face with a Hell Hound. For them to have attacked like that just now? It was against their nature, which made Jack get more aggressive.

Jack was a great many things, but above all, he was a protector. His instincts roared with the need to grab this woman and guard her properly. Bring her someplace safe and secure. Keep her close.

The *malanum* would smell that. Sense his aggression. And they would stay away for a while. *Malanum* were all about self-preservation.

"Holy Hell!" she panted beside him. "That was too close."

Yeah. That had been way to damn close, he thought. He had only just found her, to have her ripped away from him now? Or worse yet, for her to turn into the very thing he was made to hunt and send back to Hell? No. Fucking. Way.

"I need to learn how to do what you did." Her voice cut through his thoughts. "I have to know how to open one of those black holes because I can't keep fighting these things. All they do is come back." She pulled herself up and held her hand out to help him stand. "Teach me. Please. I'll beg if I have to."

Ohhh, if only begging was all it took, he thought.

CHAPTER 7

Jack tucked her in close to his chest, all the while scanning for signs of more of trouble. "We need to get you someplace safe."

"There is no safe place for me, Jack." She held out her arms and they both looked at the damage done. "I'm turning."

Yup, she was. A few more attacks and she'd be done for.

"Fuck!" Grabbing her hand, Jack yanked her further down the alley and they popped out on the opposite side of the apartment building. They needed to get out of there. Everything in him screamed to protect her, his instincts had manifested into a snarling beast with gnashing teeth and a vicious temper. It rattled its cage inside his bones, howling with rage.

Seeing her fight off those *malanum* made his head spin. He might be a hunter and a killer, but he was more than that. She needed him. Hell, she needed *more* than him.

Jack started to head back towards The Black Abbey Club again. They needed to get the fuck out of here. Fast. "Where have you been staying this whole time?"

"I haven't really stayed anywhere," she stumbled, trying to keep up with him, "I died in New Orleans and have been on the move ever since."

They crossed the street, the red traffic light glowing extra bright all of a sudden. Then the bulb blew out. Jack ignored it and kept walking. "How do you know you died there?"

"Well, I'm assuming that's the case. I don't really know since I can't remember anything. But I woke up there, dressed like this and invisible to everyone. I was attacked later that day and have been ever since then. But tonight," she started to jog in order to keep up with him, "tonight was way worse."

Yeah, he guessed so. The *malanum* tried to consume her – spiritually and literally. It was as if their only mission was to turn her. Most caused mayhem everywhere they went. They fucked with electronics, scared people, ran other spirits off.

The *malanum* Jack hunted were more sinister than that. They twisted the innocents into the worst creatures imaginable. Evil like that was contagious. Addictive. They would take a soul and poison it, warp it into one of them. Some *malanum*, if they were strong enough, were even capable of possession. It was rare, but brutal. Those vile bastards could turn a nun into a slut and convince her to fuck herself with the cross she carried around her neck. They could take a child's mind and warp it, turning a toddler into an animal. They could take a mother's soul, darken it to the point that she would drown her children in the bath tub while singing them lullabies. And that's just what they did to the living. To the dead? They killed what humanity was left in a lost soul and make it hunger for darker things like torture, violence, pain and destruction.

Evil had many faces and only one enemy: The Hell Hounds.

To become a Hell Hound wasn't easy. And to stop being one was impossible. It wasn't a life sentence, it was far more long-term than that.

"Where are we going?" Everly swapped her staff into her other hand. She was holding it like a damn javelin, as if gearing up to impale the next spirit she saw.

"I'm taking you home with me."

"But that's in the other direction!" she pointed towards the apartment building.

Jack went over to a black '69 Camaro and unlocked the doors. "I'm taking you to my other house. Get in."

She didn't bother opening the door. It wasn't like she could even if she wanted to. Instead, Everly went right through it and took a seat. Jack bit back a smile; she was being so cooperative. She had no reason to trust him. She was a fool to hop into his car and let him take her out of there.

Of course, he reminded himself, she was also dead. She could ghost out whenever she wanted to and he wouldn't be able to stop her.

Revving his engine, Jack pulled out of the parking spot and took off down the street. "How did you end up here then? Philadelphia is not a hop, skip and a jump away from Louisiana."

"I travelled either by foot or by car."

"Why did you come here?"

"I don't know," she admitted, "something just pulled me here, I guess. I can't explain it."

"How long have you been in this city?"

"About a week, maybe? Or a month? I can't keep track of time so easily anymore." She crossed her arms over her chest, hugging herself. "Why all the questions, Jack? What does any of that matter?"

He opened his mouth to answer when all the street lights blew out. "Shit," he growled.

Up ahead, just under the next traffic light, were two large *malanum* standing in the middle of the road. *Holy Hell, they're everywhere tonight!* Jack stomped on the gas, hit first gear, redlined and slammed it into second. His engine roared and he barreled towards the waiting spirits.

Everly screamed in the passenger seat and thrust her hands out, like it was going to stop the souls from hitting the car. His Camaro blew right through them. Jack slammed it into the next gear and drove faster. The engine screamed. Everly screamed. Jack smiled.

He had one mission in mind: Get her out of there.

Blowing through every red light was easy when you had the right tools. And Jack was more than equipped for this. Burning up the road, he hit the highway and didn't ease up on the gas. Instead, he coaxed that needle to creep closer and closer to the 145 mark.

"JACK!" Everly yelled.

He narrowed his eyes, focusing on his destination. "Stay with me," he commanded.

Then he drove them, not into the tunnel they were headed towards, but into the wall.

CHAPTER 8

Everly almost pissed her pants. Well, if ghosts could pee, that was. Instead, she just screamed in unholy terror as Jack swerved away from the mouth of the tunnel and drove right into a motherfucking wall.

Thank God I'm already dead. Holy Hell, the fact that she was actually thankful to be dead spoke volumes of her current situation. This has been, by far, the craziest fucking night of her life. And now she was cussing way too fucking much, which only added to her excitement because, yup, she loved cussing and it felt good and so did the energy rush she was riding and speaking of rides, holy shitballs that was fan-fucking-tastic!

They'd gone through some kind of portal. Another type of black hole. Jack slowed his car down and he looked over, tossing her one deliciously sexy grin.

"Good girl," he purred.

There was a new energy pulsing between them. She couldn't see it, but felt it prickle her skin like tiny needles. Instinctively, she rubbed her arms and was disappointed that she couldn't feel her hands on her skin.

So what was the energy dancing all over her now?

"Seriously," she huffed, "What the fuck are you, Jack?"

He pulled onto a back road to nowhere. They were on it just long enough for her to start feeling uncomfortable about being there and then an old farmhouse appeared, complete with a big red barn on the side.

"Where are we?"

"Home," he said, pulling up the driveway and parking the car in front of a large detached garage. "Nothing can touch you here. You're safe, I swear it."

Not to be all judge-a-book-by-its-big-dark-sexy-cover, but Jack didn't seem like the kind of guy who lived on a farm. He looked more like a modern high-rise with lots of windows and city lights kinda man. Then again, she'd only just met him so what did she know.

Annnnd after going through a fucking wall to get here? Everly would need to save her thoughts for processing another day because her mind had just been blown.

She immediately stepped through the car's door and gripped her staff tighter. She was running on desperation here. Desperation and something that most normal folks would call stupidity, but she would call it curiosity.

Being dead could sometimes give one a false sense of security. Like, what else could be worse than being dead?

Don't answer that. Seriously.

Jack grabbed her hand, "Come with me, love." He tugged her up some concrete steps. She noticed there was some kind of red dust all over the threshold, but didn't bother looking too closely. Standing at the front door, he sorted through his keys until he found the right one and then unlocked the door, holding it open for her to go in first.

Such a gentleman.

When she stepped inside, her immediate reaction was to smile. The house was cozy, bigger than she thought, and smelled like man. Yummy, dark, spicy, earthy, smoky man.

She got a buzz just standing there.

They were in the living room. The décor was eclectic. There was a modern leather couch, a live-edge coffee table big enough to serve a Thanksgiving dinner on, two recliners and a serious stereo system. There were also symbols all over the walls in various shades of white that showed some were old and some were freshly drawn. Nothing about this room resembled Jack's apartment.

"Follow me." His voice was suddenly soft and she couldn't help but do what he requested.

They went upstairs and she tried to look at the paintings on the wall, but couldn't quite focus on everything going by her. It was a lot to take in at once. They climbed the wooden steps that creaked and groaned from Jack's weight. Everly, on the other hand, was the sound of silence as she practically glided up the stairs. Ghosts were stealthy like that.

They went down a long hallway and he ushered her into the second room on the left. His bedroom. Holy Moly, this place smelled insanely good. Everly held her staff a little tighter. Anxiety danced along her limbs as she quickly looked around, surveying the area. "Do you live here alone?"

"No," Jack pulled his blade out, resting it carefully on his dresser before turning to her. "But the others will be a while getting back."

"Oh," she said nervously. Part of her wanted to know more, but the other part of her liked keeping Jack a mystery. Whatever. The bottom line was she was grateful she had found him and that he'd helped her so much tonight. It was stupid to trust a stranger, she knew that, but didn't care. Everly trusted him. She had no choice, really, right? Ugh. "Why are we here?"

"I don't have enough energy to keep myself out there with you, so I figured if I brought you back here, you could stay safe while I regained my strength. I'll take you wherever you want to go as soon as I'm able. Or…"

"Or?"

He pulled off his boots, "Or you could stay. If you want."

Everly cocked a perfectly arched eyebrow, "Stay?"

"Stay." Jack sauntered over to where she was and started unbuckling his belt. With a *ffffft*, he pulled his leather belt off his hips and tossed it onto the bed. Next, he got to work on his fly.

She couldn't seem to stop staring. Her gaze nothing more than a laser-focused beam of desire to be touched again. To be taken by him again.

What the hell was this guy? *Addictive,* came to mind.

Jack sucked on his bottom lip, nice and slow, and Everly mirrored the act. Next thing she knew, Everly was getting all hot and bothered again, the need for a release making her brain fuzzy.

"Easy, love." Jack chuckled, "I have to have energy to give you. Until then…"

She tilted her head to the side, "Until then… what?"

"You're just going have to watch," Jack winked as he walked right on by and headed towards the bathroom. He left the door open and started up the shower. Steam filled the room, but she couldn't feel the warmth of it.

Jack disappeared behind the glass door. Everly watched his silhouette move around behind the fogged glass. She should have felt like a creeper staring at him like this, but she didn't. Besides, he invited her to watch, to see him slather up that gorgeous body of his. It would be rude to decline his invitation.

She stepped into the shower, staff in hand. The water didn't get her wet but he sure did.

Jack leaned back and let the hot water cascade through his cropped dark hair, down his broad shoulders and chiseled abs. His thighs were long and thick, just like something else on him.

It took her a second to make eye contact, but when she did, Everly realized he had said something and was waiting for a response. "Huh?"

Jack slayed her with his next smile. He knew what he was doing, toying with her like this. "Do you like what you see, love?"

Yuuuup. She fucking loved what she was seeing. "Meh," she shrugged, "I've seen bigger."

His laugh boomed through the bathroom and she felt herself shake with the volume of it. Next, he reached down and gripped himself, stroking that long thick muscle with one hand, while the other tugged on his sac.

"Fuck," she whispered. This was so not fair. She wanted to give him the same show. She wanted to strip down and get all nice and wet and soapy and rub herself in front of him so he could watch her writhe and not be able to touch her while she orgasmed. But she couldn't. Sadly, the energy spent to feel herself took mad focus. Focus she would always lose the instant her body started to build into a tight clenching climax.

Talk about being sexually frustrated. *Fuuuuuck.*

Jack leaned forward, bracing one hand against the tiled wall, the other still stroking his big cock. He trapped her between the wall and his muscular, tattooed body. This guy was an extra special flavor of sexy that was raw and savage and beautiful.

"Come for me," she heard herself say. "Keep your eyes on me, Jack. And come for me."

He ground his molars together, his gaze on fire as he focused on her. His breath became shallow, until he was practically panting. One grunt, two grunts, and a deliciously deep moan later, Jack found his release. She half-expected him to close his eyes and get lost on that beautiful fast ride to bliss, but he didn't. Nope. He'd done what he was told and kept his eyes locked on hers.

Which made it soooo much worse.

God... damn... to see a big man thrust himself into ecstasy like that? It was, by far, one of the hottest looks she had ever seen on a man.

Everly wanted to kiss him. Eat him alive. Go down on her knees and suck his dick and lick his balls. Score his back. Climb up that big torso, wrap her legs around his waist and ride him into a hot fucking frenzy. She ached to feel him inside her again. Needed him like she needed to save her soul.

Jack bent down to kiss her, his mouth a hair's breadth away from hers. Then he smiled with these adorable little crinkles on the sides of his eyes that made him look older than he probably was. Before she could say a word, he stepped back and did another quick suds and rinse. Turning the water off, he opened the shower door and grabbed a towel.

He left her in the bathroom and headed back out to his bedroom. "You coming?"

Not yet, she thought angrily. But she was going to be soon. Hopefully.

CHAPTER 9

Jack knew she was good and worked up. Ghosts were resilient things. And so was he, for that matter. Lighting a few herbs and sticks of incense around his room, he let the energy of the house soak into his skin. He could feel the rejuvenation kick in almost immediately. And thank fuck for that. If he didn't get his hands on his woman soon, he didn't know who was going to snap first – him or her.

With a broad smile, Jack stood naked for her pleasure and waited for her to join him back in his room. Appearing in his doorway, she looked like a pissed off woman on a mission and, Holy Hell, that was a hot look on her.

Just when he was about to grab a handful of that luscious ass of hers, Everly shocked the shit out of him by screaming in his face. Next, she spun around with her staff and managed to knock half of what was on his dresser onto the floor.

"WOAH!" he put his hands up and grabbed the damn goat skull, ripping it out of her hand. "What the fuck!"

Everly was positively seething. "I can't do this."

What. The. Hell.

"Talk to me," he didn't dare touch her. No matter how bad he wanted to.

"You want me to talk to you? Okay. Fine." Everly sat on the edge of his bed and glared at him. "Then talk to ME. I want to know what you are, Jack."

He sighed and leaned against the dresser, crossing his arms over his broad chest, not bothering to care that he was still naked. "I'm a Hell Hound."

"A Hell Hound."

"Yup." They stared at each other for what felt like a god damned lifetime. "I died once. Just like you. Only I wasn't ready to go. I was, however, ready to do anything possible to make sure I didn't fucking crossover to the other side."

Everly seemed to calm down. "I'm listening."

"Hell Hounds have the ability to go between the living and dead worlds. We have one purpose."

"And that would be?"

"Kill the evil souls that escape Hell. The *malanum*."

"The things I'm running from. What I'm becoming?"

Jack nodded slowly. "I gave my soul to the Devil for a second chance at life. I serve Lucifer."

"Soooo, the black hole is?"

"Hell, love. The prison all forms of evil reside in."

She whistled low. Yup, she was actually fucking impressed. The fact that she wasn't running for the hills screaming at the moment told him two more things about her: she believed him and she accepted his truth.

"So you hunt them down," she said slowly.

"I do."

"Easy job considering they practically threw themselves at us tonight."

"That's never happened before." Everly cringed, catching his meaning. "But the *malanum* won't come near this place. It's why staying here will keep you safe because they wouldn't dare come close to this house or the Hounds living here."

"So how did they —"

"Get into the apartment earlier?" Jack shrugged, "That's not quite the same place as this one is." He left it at that.

"How do I become a Hound?"

Jack's surprise wasn't hidden. "Uhhhh..." How did he explain this next part to her?

Everly stood up, "I'm not really asking the right question." She moved over to him and traced a transparent finger down his chest. He shivered at her cold touch, desperately wanting to grab and heat her body up with his. "What I meant to ask was..."

"How can you sell your soul?"

She nodded and bit her lip.

"It's not so easy, love. First, you have to offer it. Then it has to be accepted. Then..." There was so much that had to happen afterwards.

"Are you saying my soul isn't good enough?"

"What? No, that's not it."

"Then what's the problem? I can fight them. I'm not afraid. I can sense them like a blue tick hound dog. I have since the day I died. Plus my soul is damned already."

"What makes you say that?"

Everly moved away and shrugged as she turned her back on him. "It just is."

"No," he spun her around, "Why do you think that?"

"I've seen hundreds of people die, Jack. I've been everywhere... seen so much since I became," she swiped her hand down her body, "this." Everly started pacing around, growing restless again. "When everyone else dies, they have this happy look on their faces and then they just vanish." *But not me*, was what she wanted to say but didn't. "And the bad ones? I've seen them vanish, too. Like they knew where they were going the whole time and once they died, they were looking forward to the trip south."

Jack's mouth turned up into a slight smile. "You're right," he took a few steps closer, "they do look forward to it. Until they get there. Then they see how awful it is and will do whatever they can to climb out. Escape."

"That's why you're here?"

"Mmm hmmm." Jack chanced another step closer to her. "I get to live. But I live to serve. And when the Devil calls, I answer."

"It sounds like a decent living."

Jack couldn't help the cold-hearted laugh that burst out of him. "You have a very deranged view of life."

"Then you don't have a very clear view of death, Jack." Everly took her top hat off and tossed it to the bed. It instantly made an appearance back where it belonged. On her. "So what would be worse? Spending a limited amount of time dead and being hunted, in a constant fight with your own soul because it's being ripped down the middle between good and evil only to eventually turn anyway because heaven didn't want you and hell doesn't know you're here? Or spending an eternity being useful and at least fighting off the shitheads preying on the souls of the innocent? I mean, I could seriously go on and on, but the bottom line is this: it's my soul and it's my choice. Either you help me get into Hell or I'll find a way in there myself. What's it going to be because I can promise you one thing," she shoved a finger and put enough energy into it that she poked Jack in the chest, "I'd rather be the hunter than the hunted."

Jack stood there, slack-jawed.

"Well?"

"Okay," he grumbled. "Fine. Yes. I'll take you."

All that anger and fear and frustration she'd been rocking blew away and she smiled. "Seriously?"

"Seriously."

"Let's go. Now." She held her staff and thumped it on the floor.

Jack's body stiffened. Then he turned to get dressed. She was the only person he ever met who actually looked forward to meeting Lucifer. Tugging on his pants he couldn't help but smile.

He was almost looking forward to bringing her to Hell, if only to see the Devil's face when he met her.

CHAPTER 10

Everly followed Jack down the steps of his home and into the basement. Okay, this was starting to get creepy and stupid again. Who knew what would be in Jack's basement. She was surprised to find herself grateful to be dead – if only to ensure that false sense of security she clung to, lately.

The basement was just how she expect it to be - cold, bare, boxes stacked up against the wall to her right. A punching bag, some weights and a bench, along with a big mat to her left showed that he and the other Hounds living there liked to work out.

Jack seemed nervous. At least, that's what Everly thought when he continued to keep his head down. Everything about this night seemed so fucking crazy now. It was undoubtedly the longest night of her death, that's for sure.

Jack took out his key ring and shuffled through them to find the right one. Everly's gut clenched as her mind raced with all the ways this was a very stupid no good bad fucking idea. She had no clue what was behind that door. For all she knew, he kept dead bodies in there.

Oh but wait, this was apparently the doorway to Hell, wasn't it? Good God, she must be insane.

Jack inserted the key into the padlock and placed his hand on the door the same time he turned the knob. "Come on, love. Let's get this over with."

He held the door for her but she didn't budge. Her feet refused to move forward. There was nothing beyond that doorway that she could see. It was just… nothing.

No, she thought, *not nothing… it was black. A black hole.*

Panic slammed into her and she took a step back. "I thought…" the rest of her words fell away. She was scared shitless to go in there.

"Did you think it was going to be different?" Jack held his hand out.

"Well, yeah, actually. This," she shoved her staff in his direction, "looks exactly like what you threw those souls into. How do I know —"

"That I'm not tricking you and throwing you into the dark pits of Hades, too?"

She bit her lip and was suddenly super self-conscious about her arms having turned already. It wouldn't be all that surprising if this was a trick, would it? She was turning into the very thing he said he hunted. So why not give a girl the greatest night in all her death only to trick her into Hell to be miserable forever.

Will you walk into my parlour? Said the Spider to the Fly. Everly eyed up the blackness beyond that door and then shot Jack a suspicious glare. He was standing there, patiently waiting for her to make a move.

The choice was hers: Walk in and face whatever was beyond that black air, or get out of here and spend the rest of her death days fighting the inevitable.

I'll take door number one. Rounding her shoulders, Everly had some serious white knuckle fever with her staff as she took one step, then two, then three more towards the door.

"After you, love."

Everly didn't bother to look at him. She just focused on moving her damn feet and getting to her final destination. It was the one place she always feared would claim her sooner or later… *Hell.*

Okay, so Hell looked nothing like what she thought it would.

It was clean. Quiet. Nice marble floors and toasty little fires in beautiful sconces lined the walls.

Seriously, where were the screaming bodies? The torture devices? The big balls of flaming agony and bottles of blood?

This place smelled like leather and spice with a bit of chocolate. She could have sworn it smelled like fresh baked brownies. Everly gasped when Jack grabbed her hand and gave it a small kiss. "This way, love." His voice was soft and deep and she noticed he seemed on edge again.

"I'm in Hell," Everly was in awe with everything they passed. Big gilded mirrors, small tables with fresh red apples, and... was that a fully stocked bar?

Jack pulled her further down the hall. Every open door they passed had voices beyond them but she couldn't see anything in the rooms. Finally, they made it to a set of double doors with huge handles made of bone.

Everly tried to smile, truly she did, but she'd have to pick her mouth up off the floor first to do it. Jack opened the door and stepped aside so she could enter the colossal-sized room with only a chair sitting in the back. Once the door shut behind them, Everly decided being scared didn't matter anymore. She was all in now.

"Jack, what are you doing here tonight, it's Hallow—" Lucifer stopped, mid-sentence, and stared at her. His eyes flashed an eerie glow. "What do you have here, Jack?"

"Meet *Everly*."

Lucifer's gaze darted to Jack and he raised an eyebrow. "*Everly*," he said cautiously, "How very nice to meet you."

She was going to shake hands with the devil. She was going to... okay, so yeah, he had a huge hand and thick fingers, and he kinda reminded her of The Rock, which probably meant she had just lost her damn mind thinking shit like that at a time like this.

Lucifer stared at her hand as he shook it. He saw the black there. She saw it too. Soooo... this was awkward. Lucifer cleared his throat, "And to what do I owe this pleasure, my darling?"

"She wants to be a Hound, my lord."

Lucifer's stoic expression never changed. He was soooo careful to keep whatever he was thinking close to his chest. For some reason, it made Everly feel better. It was good to feel like she might actually have a chance here, even if it was only in her head.

"Leave us," Lucifer ordered Jack.

"But—"

"Leave. Us."

Lucifer didn't make a third repeat. Jack spun on his heel and shoved open the door with a curse.

"Tell me, darling, how long have you been dead?"

"I'm not sure. Maybe five years?" Was this an interview? She could handle that. Keep things pleasant. Upbeat. Positive.

She wanted to put her hands behind her back so he wouldn't keep staring at the black on her arms, but Lucifer kept their handshake intact and placed his other big baseball mitt of a hand on top, sandwiching her dainty one. "You are infected by the disease."

"Evil is a disease?"

"How can it not be? It spreads, thrives, and cannot be eradicated."

Yes, she supposed he was right. "Well, then I'm infected. And I want to be cured."

A smile curved his mouth and he dipped his head down so close to her face she had to fight not to back up. "You want to be *cured*?"

"Yes."

"And you think I can do that?"

"Yes. You can take me. Take my soul. Make me better."

"I'll make you different."

"I'm fine with that. I want to be a Hell Hound." She suddenly found herself wanting nothing more than to be a Hound like Jack. Any other needs, big and small, vanished and all that remained was a burning desire to Be. A. Hell. Hound.

"Have you any fighting skills?"

"Yes," she said with a little more oomph. "I managed to keep those dark spirits away from me since the day I died."

"Mmmm," he glanced down at her blackened arms, "And how has that worked out for you?"

"Just fine," she gritted out. "Evil isn't what plagues me."

"Then what does?" He let go of her hand and started making circles around her like a wolf before it attacked.

"I can't feel. I can't be seen. I can't be heard. I've turned into a nothing."

He paused his predatory rotation. "And a Hell Hound is what

you want to be?"

"Yes." She spun around as he continued to walk circles around her. No way was she giving the Devil her back. "I can sense them coming. I can fight them. If I had the right tools, and you made me like Jack, I could be a great asset to you." She cleared her suddenly dry throat and quickly added, "Sir." Or should she have said, your lordship? Master? Hot sauce? How does one address the devil to get on his good side?

Lucifer laughed. "It takes a lot more than tossing a twisted soul down a hole to be a Hell Hound."

"I've got what it takes."

"Do you?"

"YES!" she stepped forward, her one hand a fist, the other gripping her staff.

"You'll have to fight things far bigger than you. They're strong. Powerful."

"I can do that."

Lucifer took off his shirt and spread his legs shoulder-width apart. "Prove it."

Everly had just stepped right into the spider's trap.

Oh. Shit.

Everly was panting and sweat dripped down her spine. She felt alive and exhilarated. Going head-to-head with the Devil himself was more fun than it should have been. She moved around him in slow circles and they danced with fists and legs and snarls and pent up fury. He was taking it easy on her. Had to be. It was a mercy she used to her advantage.

Hey, it wasn't every day a girl got to tango with the Devil. She was going to make the most of it.

"Are you not afraid?"

"No," she smirked. "I feel good here."

Lucifer's dark brow arched as he parried and swung, jabbed and blocked. "How did you die?"

"Don't know," she ducked as his big fist thrust out, almost nailing her jaw.

"Where did you die?"

"New Orleans," she went down low and tried to kick his leg out. The Devil moved so fast, he was almost a blur, and then he was right behind her. "Shit!"

He put her in a choke hold and hissed in her ear. "Why did you tell Jack your name was Everly?"

Her mouth dried up and she couldn't speak. Not because he was choking her, but because she was scared shitless. How did he know her name wasn't really Everly? "I don't know my name!"

"What game are you playing, woman?" Lucifer started to drag her across the room and her feet could do nothing but skid on the floor. Twisting as hard as she could, she bit into his biceps. Lucifer let her go with a chuckle. "You always did play dirty."

Everly checked herself. "What do you mean by that?" Her heart hammered in her throat, "Do I... Do we know each other?"

"Do I look familiar to you?" his face was stern, but his eyes were soft around the edges. He wanted an answer and she was afraid he wouldn't like what she was about to say.

"No," she took a step back. "I don't know you. But..." she looked around the room, "I feel happy here."

Lucifer's shoulders dropped a fraction of an inch, hands falling to his sides. Slowly, he walked up to her and she didn't back away, no matter how badly she wanted to. Surprisingly, he cupped her face in his hands and rubbed his thumb over her mouth.

She didn't move. Didn't breathe. Didn't blink. Oh God, was he going to kiss her? That would be weird, right? Or would it be exciting?

Fuck, fuck, fuck. He stared at her like he was debating something and then, "You will go to the Hounds and will not come back until you have answers for me."

The air rushed out of her lungs. "Does that mean I'm one of them now?"

His brow furrowed as if her question confused him. "Go with my ladies first. They will see you are cleaned and ready." He turned and walked away.

Everly didn't have time to process what just happened. She was already being led away by Lucifer's Ladies. A million questions ran through her head, but none were asked.

She was taken away, brought into another chamber, and

shoved into a gigantic flame.

Jack waited anxiously in the hall and couldn't stop pacing. Finally, the door opened and Lucifer nodded for him to come back in.

With a huge exhale, Jack walked into the room, eyes scanning the place for the woman he'd brought into Hell, and his breath hitched when he saw she wasn't there.

"She passed."

Oh thank God. Jack tried to not drop to his knees in relief. *She passed.* Those two words meant everything to him right now.

Lucifer knew what a huge deal this was. More than most. "Where the hell did you find her, Jack?"

"In a club, dancing." Running a hand through his short, cropped hair, he wanted to howl but didn't. This was far from over. "Where is she now?"

"Going through the transformation. Again."

Again.

Yeah... this was so far from over. Holy fucking shit. Jack had to concentrate on not letting his knees buckle. "The *malanum* hunted her, Luce. Every day. Every fucking day. They almost won."

"But they didn't." Lucifer calmly walked over to a small table that had a decanter and four empty glasses on it. He poured two drinks and handed one over. "She's still got that mean thigh grip."

"You fucking fought her?" Jack gripped his glass so tight, it almost shattered.

"I had to make sure."

"I wouldn't have brought her here if I wasn't sure."

"You might have been looking with the wrong thing. The eyes see what the heart desperately desires. You knew that or you wouldn't have brought her here first."

True, Jack thought. But still, she had been through enough tonight. She'd taken it all like a champ, but Hell's blades, she wasn't at her best and she just went head-to-head with the Devil and won him over?

Pride swelled in Jack's heart. *Atta girl,* he thought. "What happened to her?"

"I can't be sure," Lucifer took a long sip of his drink. "But something seriously fucked her up. She was down to almost nothing. A wisp."

That would explain why it took so much of Jack's energy to make her touchable, at least. "She told me she doesn't know how she died."

Just before Lucifer could say anything more, Everly stepped back into the room looking whole and slightly off kilter.

"There she is," Lucifer grinned and her cheeks blushed when he came over and kissed her hand. "Bet you feel better now, yes?"

"Yes," she said quietly.

Jack could only gawk. Getting her body back to the way it should be meant getting cleaned up and transformed back into a body of flesh and bone. All that face paint she'd been wearing was washed off. She also changed her clothes. Gone were the leather pants and corset. Now, she was in a pair of jeans and a black tank top.

As if she was unsure of what to do with having two free hands – because she no longer had her staff either – Everly rubbed her thighs before settling on stuffing her hands in her back pockets. Her eyes darted from Jack to Lucifer. "When do I start?"

Lucifer laughed. His voice, deep and booming, made the air feel like one great big vibration. "Easy, darling. Let's get you settled in first. Fighting can wait for another day."

"Then where should I go?"

Jack took two steps towards her. "With me, love. You come home with me."

"I'm staying with you?" Her eyes softened in relief.

Jack smiled, he couldn't help it. Seeing her face light up made him so damn happy. "Yeah, love. You're staying with me."

Lucifer cracked Jack on the back, a silent *You Got This* from the big man himself. "Tell your Hounds she'll get there."

Her eyes sparkled, "Ohhh, do I get to meet the rest of the Hounds now?"

Jack could only bite back his next words and nod. Yeah.... This was going to fucking hurt.

CHAPTER 11

It was early morning by the time they left Hell. Jack was never more relieved to be home. Never more nervous either.

Voices in the kitchen verified that, yup, the guys were home and at least two of them were making breakfast. Jack felt his woman's arm jerk. She was instantly on guard, as if the sounds were intruders and she was ready to defend her territory.

"Easy, love." He grabbed her hand and kissed it. "That's your pack up there." Yeah... *your pack*, he thought. *Fuuuck*.

Jack went up the steps first. This wasn't going to go well. The least he could do was soften the blow somehow. Be a buffer.

Kalen and Eli were in the kitchen – Eli was cooking omelets, Kalen was cleaning blades after a night of hunting.

"Hey man! When did you get back?" Eli tossed some mushrooms into the egg mixture. "You want some?"

"No thanks," Jack reached around behind his back, squeezing his woman's hand, "I'm good. Turn that burner off for a moment, Eli."

"What's up? Why are you so nervous?" Eli turned off the burner and turned to stare at Jack. With a once over, he frowned, "The fuck is wrong with you, Jack?"

There was no sense in prolonging this. But... shit... he didn't know how to explain last night to anyone. His heart slammed into his chest. Bloody Hell, this was a bad idea. He should have done this differently. Now it was too late to turn back.

"Jack," Eli practically barked. "What gives, Hound? You alright?"

Without a word, Jack moved to the side and kept a wary eye, not on Eli, but on Kalen as their woman peered out from behind his body.

"Hi," she said nervously.

That was it. That was all she said to silence two of the world's best killers.

Jack heard Eli curse and but didn't look at him. He was still keeping his eyes on the angry beast growling at the kitchen table. Kalen was going to take this the hardest. Jack knew that, so he was prepared for anything at the moment. Kalen would think it was a trick. He'd most likely act accordingly.

"Holy... shit," Eli's spatula hit the floor and he froze, stunned. "Is this..." he gripped his head with disbelief, "Is this fucking real or some kind of voodoo magic?"

"It's real. She's real," Jack grabbed her hand and wasn't sure if he was reassuring himself or her as he rubbed his thumb over her knuckles. "I found her last night."

Kalen trembled at the kitchen table. A darkness filled his eyes, glassing them over and making him completely unreadable.

"This is Eli and that's Kalen, love."

"Hi," she said again, "It's nice to meet you."

Kalen's eyes grew even darker. "She doesn't know us?" His voice sounded deadly. "What is this, Jack?"

The Hounds didn't say a word. "Ummmm," she said nervously, "Maybe I should just go and —"

"Which one of you dickheads used the last of the shampoo and didn't bother replacing it?" The fourth Hound waltzed into the kitchen with perfect timing.

"Annnnnd this is Tanner, love. The last Hound in the pack."

Tanner pulled the same stunt the other two had when he saw her. He froze for a solid five seconds. Then Jack watched Tanner do what Tanner did best - make the move no one else had the nerve for.

Tanner dropped the empty bottle of shampoo in shock. One

heartbeat, two heart beats annnnnd, "Sara?" Tanner's voice was a little more desperate than a prayer. "SARA?" he repeated with more *oomph*, then he took the six steps to get to her. Cupping her face in his hands, Tanner crushed his mouth to hers and kissed her like she was his salvation.

Well, at least one of them was taking this well, Jack thought.

"SARA?" Tanner said, just before kissing the ever loving shit out of her. And Holy Hell could this guy kiss. He pulled away and pierced her with incredibly blue eyes, leaving her breathless and tingly.

That was probably rude, right? To kiss another guy in front of a guy you'd just spent one awesome night with? Oh man… this was just weird. Even weirder was, she wanted to do it again. Mr. Blue Eyes kissed like she was a star he orbited around. A girl could get addicted to that kind of passion.

"Sara," Tanner whispered. Even at a whisper, this guy's voice was so deep it would make Barry White sound like a soprano. "I can't believe this," Tanner bent down, going in for a second round of kissing her senseless.

"Easy, boy." Jack pulled on his shoulder and Tanner backed off with a whimper.

She looked around the kitchen, slightly embarrassed. All the excitement and anticipation she had just moments ago, burned to ashes when she realized she was a big – and most likely unwanted – surprise to all of them.

God, just look at the way the man at the table was glaring at her. Kalen, a huge mountain of a man with a sleeve tattoo of Celtic designs held a huge knife in one hand, his other was balled into a fist. Then her gaze sailed over to Eli, a man with tufts of dark, curly hair and big brown eyes. Then she looked back to Tanner, the naked sun god with eyes bluer than the ocean.

These men… these *Hounds* were not what she was expecting to come home to. Jack was devastatingly handsome enough with his military looks and sharp jaw and killer abs, but now she was going to live with three more just like him? Damn… She'd moved up in the world. Or was it, she'd moved down? Geographically speaking Hell was as low as you could go, right? Whatever. That's not the point. The point was she just bit off more than she could chew and it was obvious she was missing something here. They were scared, angry, shocked and freaked out just looking at her.

And they called her Sara.

CRACK! She jumped back as the kitchen table snapped in half and, with a pang of hurt, watched Kalen storm out the back door.

"Let him go, Hounds," Eli said, not prying his eyes off Sara. He slowly moved closer to her, and then turned to Jack and said, "You've got some serious explaining to do, Hound."

"I know." Jack grabbed her hand and tugged her into the living room. Tanner and Eli followed. She could feel the tension roll off each of them and she decided to stick as close to Jack as possible.

After sitting down in the living room, no one spoke for several heartbeats. The air chilled as they awkwardly sat there and stared at each other. Funny, she spent her death being so hell-bent on getting someone to see her, now she had three sets of eyes on her and wanted nothing more than to be invisible.

"What happened, Sara?" Tanner pinned her with those baby blues.

"I'm... I—"

Jack stepped in, "I found her at the Black Abbey Club."

"I'm..." Jesus, she couldn't find her words. "I'm..."

"Why didn't you come home? Where the FUCK have you been?" This coming from Eli. He sank to his knees in front of her, those big brown eyes of his searching her face for answers she couldn't give.

"I... I—" She couldn't make words. She couldn't breathe, either. Someone had sucked all the oxygen out of the room.

Tanner angrily ran his hand through his blonde faux hawk. "Do you have any idea how worried sick we've been? We thought you were DEAD!"

"Tanner," Jack glared, "She *was* dead."

She watched the two new guys pale considerably. "I..." damn her mouth! Why wouldn't it work?! "I..."

Okay, this was too much and she didn't know what to do besides fight and scream and that wasn't going to help her at the moment. She wasn't about to attack a room full of men who were staring at her like she was the answer to their long said prayers. And to know Jack hadn't said a word to her about this – not even a warning – just pissed her off even more.

Jumping to her feet, she was ready to bolt. "I can't be here. I don't know what this is… I don't understand…"

Tanner grabbed her hand, "Beautiful, please, hang on a sec."

"No," wrenching her hand free, she turned and glared at Jack, "You tricked me. This is some kind of fucked up trick." Now she was good and mad. "Is this like a psychological Hound hazing thing? Lucifer couldn't beat her in the test so we're going to try and break her mind? Is that what this is?"

Eli's eyes widened as he turned to Jack. "You already took her to see Luce?"

"I took her to be sure." Jack's control and calmness felt like a new kind of threat. Like that low, steady growl a wolf has to warn you to not fucking move or you'll get bit. "I wasn't going to put you all through this if it was a false alarm."

"It's her? This is really real?"

"Yeah."

"Holy shit," Eli stood up, "Sara," he reached out for her, as if he wanted to pull her in close and hold her tight.

She backed away more. "Don't touch me. Don't any of you fucking touch me." She needed to get out of here. Now. None of this was making any sense. She hadn't been saved, she'd been tricked. This was some kind of horrible, awful, crazy nightmare. "I've got to get out of here."

"You can't leave," Jack said quietly.

"I can and I will." Marching over to the front door, she placed her hand on the door knob and opened it up only to see it was just white space. "Where is everything? Where is the world?"

"Right here, trying to get away from us," Tanner mumbled.

She ignored the compliment. Or was that an insult? She couldn't figure anything out anymore.

"We go off grid so we can rejuvenate, love. You're stuck here with us."

"For how long?" She didn't need to be a mind reader to know the answer written so plainly on each of their faces.

Forever.

CHAPTER 12

Without the ability to leave, she locked herself in Jack's room, yelling that she wasn't coming out unless they agreed to let her go. Until then, they could all kiss her ass.

Ohhhh if only she knew how happy taking her up on that offer would have made them.

The white space she saw wasn't an illusion or a trap. It was because her Hound senses hadn't fully kicked in yet. She was too weak right now, which was all the more reason they needed to keep her close and protected. Her Hound magic would revive the longer she stayed with her pack, but that was going to take time. Not that any of them got a chance to explain that to her before she slammed the door in their faces.

Eli sat on the coffee table, elbows leaning on his knees. "Seriously, Jack, you gotta explain this."

"I found her at Black Abbey early last night while hunting. She was dressed in battle leathers, her favorite corset—"

"The one with the knife inserts?"

Jack nodded, "Yeah, and her face was painted as a skull. She had on my old top hat and a staff with Georgie's skull on top of it."

"Shit," Eli mumbled.

"She was dancing to Nickelback," this time he looked at

61

Tanner. "Burn it to the Ground."

Poor guy almost slid off the couch. That was their song. Tanner and Sara were the only ones in the house who liked that band. No offense, but Nickelback was like the musical version of cilantro. You either loved them or hated them. Coincidentally, Tanner and Sara also loved cilantro.

"She didn't recognize me." Jack leaned back and rubbed his neck. "She was a fucking ghost. Literally. Only she had no energy at all. I didn't sense her. I didn't even know she was there until she caught my eye dancing."

"She loves to dance," Tanner mumbled.

"I can only assume she must have willed me to look at her... otherwise I'd have never seen her there. I got her to come over to my table. We talked. She was so fucking happy that someone could see her." Jack cleared his suddenly dry throat, "I thought it was a trick. Kept thinking someone was fucking with us, or that maybe I'd finally lost my mind. I just couldn't bloody believe she was there, right in front of me. Then I touched her and she turned solid just for a moment and *hope*," he exhaled a ragged breath, "I felt hope for the first time in ages."

Eli scrubbed his face and Tanner stood up and started pacing.

"Denial had me second guessing everything in the club. I abandoned her twice to hunt *malanum*, thinking she was some kind of diversion, all the while praying that it wasn't true. Both times I returned, there she was, still waiting for me. And she'd actually even followed me the second time. I didn't even sense her..." Jack sighed. "I brought her to her old apartment," he shook his head slowly and looked at Eli, "She didn't even recognize it."

"Jesus."

"She calls herself Everly."

"Fuck."

"She doesn't remember how she died."

"Fuck, fuck."

"Her tats are gone, too."

"And you know this how?" Eli glared.

"How do you think?" The only way to see down her spine was to take that corset off. And there was no sense in explaining why he'd do a thing like that. "I brought her here, too. She didn't say a word the entire time. She doesn't know this place."

Tanner slumped on the couch and buried his head in his hands. "We gotta get her to remember. We gotta get her tats back on. And we gotta figure out how she died and who did it so we can fucking kill them."

"One thing at a time, Tanner." Eli stood and looked towards the kitchen. "We need to work on Kalen first."

"Rock, Paper, Scissors?"

"You two go," Jack ordered, "I'm going to see if I can talk our girl off the ledge."

"I can do that," Tanner argued. "I'm always the one who—"

"Forget it, Hound," Eli started steering Tanner out of the living room. "She's not going to go to anyone but Jack right now. One of us trying to talk to her is just going to freak her out more. She found him. There was a reason he was there at the right place at the right time. Let's you and I just be happy she's back and go check on Kalen."

The two Hounds left and Jack climbed the stairs to explain things to Sara.

He just hoped she hadn't found his stash of blades in the closet. He had a feeling if telling her the truth didn't cut him in two, she sure as hell would.

Sitting on the edge of the bed with her knees bobbing up and down, her energy was all over the place, much like her thoughts. In her hand, she held a quad blade and wasn't afraid to use it or any of the other fun toys she found hidden in Jack's closet.

Yes, she snooped.

She wanted answers and searched his room to find something that would help her figure this crazy shit out. A picture. A letter. A clue of any kind that she could use to piece this puzzle together. But it wasn't a puzzle at all, was it? Hell no, this was a goddamned clusterfuck of epic proportions.

A knock on the door broke her focus off the picture that hung above his bed. It was a painting of a skeleton couple – one male looking dapper, the other a female in a lace dress. They were sitting at a table for two, one sipping from a tea cup, the other pouring poison into a glass.

"May I come in, love?"

No. Yes. She didn't know.

Jack made the decision for her by opening the door and then shutting them both inside his room. Maybe he didn't know what to say or maybe he didn't know what to say first, but as he stalled out, she fiddled with the quad blade and stared at the floor. "I didn't know my name. I made up Everly because it seemed like a beautiful name."

Jack sat on the edge of the bed next to her and focused on their reflection in the mirror across the room.

She sniffled. "How do I not remember anything?"

"I don't know, love." He sighed. "I thought for sure this was some kind of trick when I saw you in that club. I seriously thought you'd been sent to destroy everything we've worked so hard on."

"Soooo you slept with me to get the upper hand?"

"No, love. I slept with you because you really were our Sara, and," he moved around until he was squatting in front of her, "I couldn't stand it a moment longer. I needed to touch you. Feel you again."

She wasn't going to melt. No matter how desperate his voice sounded right now, she wasn't going to let herself fall for him any harder than she already had. "Annnnd at what point did you know I was your Sara?"

"When I saw you dance. And then fight." Jack rubbed her legs in an attempt to calm her down and get them to stop bouncing, or maybe it was because he just wanted to touch her. Either way, she wasn't complaining. "Give us a chance, love."

"A chance to what?"

"Show you who you are."

Sara gave him the stink eye, "And what? You're okay with that guy, Tanner, just plowing me over and kissing me?"

"He's yours."

"*Mine?*" That just sounded.... Oh never mind how that sounded. "So then what are you?"

"Yours, too." That answer was presented with a killer smile. "We're all yours, Sara."

"All mine? You mean, even the spatula guy?"

"The sp—" Jack chuckled, "Eli? Yeah, him too, love. Most

definitely him, too."

"And the one who smashed the table and hasn't come back inside since?" She had watched that one from the window earlier. That big guy was outside the barn, chopping wood like his life depended on every swing of his axe.

"Kalen's also yours."

This just sounded unreal. "He didn't seem happy to see me."

"Don't let his actions fool you," Jack's voice was low and dark and velvety. "He has trouble expressing himself sometimes."

Sara crossed her arms around her chest and almost cut Jack with the quad blade in the process. "Sorry."

"Don't be. Keep it. Do whatever you have to so you feel safe. Here and out in the field."

Out in the field. The battlefield. The world. Sara's head felt like it was going to explode. "I'm a Hound."

"Yeah."

"Have I always been one?"

"You've been a Hound for a lot longer than a day, let's just leave it at that for now."

So what Lucifer told her during her "interview" was true then. Did that mean the other things he'd said were true, too? Sara bit her lip. She didn't want to talk about it right now. Didn't want to think about it, either. "Soooo, you're saying to keep armed with whatever I want. I'm a Hound. My name is Sara. Annnnd I have my own pack of Hell Hounds?"

She would have fallen on the floor if she wasn't already sitting – that look on Jack's face blew her away when he said, "Abso-fucking-lutely, love."

With that, he cupped her cheeks and brought her in for a kiss that had her groaning against his mouth. When he pulled away, he winked. "Give us time, Sara. And we'll show you."

Just before he was about to walk out the door she fell for it, "Show me what?"

"That you're our girl."

That seriously shouldn't have sounded as good as it did.

CHAPTER 13

Refusing to come downstairs, but not wanting to stay locked up in Jack's bedroom any longer, Sara decided to venture out. She knew they were all keeping their distance, giving her some space so she could deal. Trouble was… she was having trouble dealing.

Not that she was at all disappointed with what she knew so far, it was just a lot to take in. And… well, damnit, she was wound up tight as a drum with a serious need to get pounded.

It didn't feel like she was any different now in the lust department than she'd been when she was a ghost. The overwhelming need to touch and be touched hadn't relented in the slightest now that she was a Hound. If anything, it intensified.

Now, she was both alive and dead. She had a body, warmth, hunger and blood pulsing in her veins. Yet she could tell, just by the familiarity of being a ghost, that she could easily turn her form into something similar to a spirit. She was the best of both worlds.

Not in a hurry to ghost out anytime soon, Sara meandered down the hallway quietly. And yes, she still had a blade in her hand but had swapped the quad blade for a more practical one – a tactical double blade folding knife. Not gonna lie, she kinda felt like Batman carrying it around.

Padding her bare feet down the hall, she could hear the guys talking in the kitchen and smell something insanely delicious. Her stomach growled and she placed a hand over her belly, forcing it to shut the fuck up. She wasn't going down there. It would be awkward.

Sneaking into the bedroom next to Jack's, she found herself in a space that was all black – black bedding, black furniture, and black throw rug. It was about as monotone as it could get with one exception: the painting above the bed.

It was a sunflower, painted bright as the sun itself, that looked like it was exploding with bits of petals and pollen splattering all over the canvas.

Fucking gorgeous, that's what it was.

Sara was still staring, mesmerized by it, when someone came up behind her. Reflexively, she spun around and held the double-blade out and pressed it against the neck of the intruder.

"Easy, Beautiful," Mr. Blue Eyes purred. Tanner, this was Tanner the kisser.

Well now she felt overly paranoid and foolish. Still, she was a woman trapped in a house with four guys from Hell. A girl's gotta keep her guard up, right? Even if they all claim to be devoted to her.

"I... I just was..."

"Snooping?"

"A little."

Tanner chuckled and waited for her to remove the blade from his neck. He could have easily disarmed her or at least taken a step back to get out of harm's way, but he didn't. Nope, instead, he just penetrated her with those incredibly blue eyes and waited for her to make the first move. "I don't know who this is harder for, us or you."

She pulled the blade away. "What do you mean?"

He walked around and grabbed a shirt from his dresser drawer. When he gave her his back, she noticed a line of symbols going down his spine. To stop herself from touching them, Sara fiddled with her blade instead.

"We've spent five years mourning you, Sara. And then you show up out of nowhere," he stuffed his head in the shirt and yanked it on, covering up some serious muscle. "And I'm sure you have so many questions you can't think of what to ask first so you just aren't asking any."

Yup, that just about summed it up.

"We're going to figure this out, okay? And we're going to get us back to… well, *us*." He turned towards his dresser again and grabbed a pair of socks next. Plopping down on the bed, he continued to get dressed while she stood there. "You were looking at the painting when I came in."

"Yeah," her voice cracked.

"Did it… maybe spark a memory or something?"

It hadn't done anything but make her feel lost in the excitement – as if she was the flower and something had detonated and blown her apart. "No. Should it have?"

Tanner shrugged. She knew he wanted to say something but was holding back. When he stood, she gasped and felt terrible. She'd cut his throat with her knife. "You're bleeding."

"Meh, it's just a scratch." He looked at his reflection, tilted his head back and swiped the blood away with his thumb. "You've done worse."

Then that dirty dog snapped his eyes to hers and she watched him suck his thumb clean. Her gaze narrowed in on how perfect his mouth was, how sharp his jawline was, how nice his tongue could lick… With a wink, he left her alone in his room and shut the door as if to keep her there. With him. For later. Some strange piece of her thought that was a pretty damn good idea, too.

Holy Hell Hounds, what has she gotten herself into?

CHAPTER 14

Jack was in the kitchen. Since Kalen seemed to be in no hurry to come in, someone needed to finish cleaning and sharpening their combat knives, so he figured he'd get to it.

Eli was cooking burgers on a cast iron grill pan. Cheeseburgers were one of Sara's favorite foods. Right up there next to jambalaya, cheese pizza, and fried pickles. So yeah, they all knew this meal was being cooked with her in mind.

"You say she has no recollection at all?"

"Nope."

"Of anything?"

"It's all a blank, apparently."

"What did Lucifer say?"

"He gave us time off to set her straight. Her tats are gone from her spine. We need to get them back."

Eli stiffened before flipping the patties again. He was grilling inside and they both knew why. If Kalen smelled burgers, he'd likely go into overdrive and chop down the entire barn once he ran out of timber. He'd think they were celebrating and living it up with a BBQ when really they were taking the first steps to ignite Sara's memories.

Jack knew this wasn't going to be easy for any of them but

what the hell else could he have done? Hiding Sara until she was back to her old self wasn't right or fair to anyone. Jack had managed to keep her to himself for a measly seven hours and it nearly killed him inside to do even that much because he knew it was wrong to hide her from his Hounds.

They'd spent the past five years mourning her. Trying to hunt without her. Trying to move on with their lives with her no longer there.

And they'd all failed miserably.

Kalen's acceptance of this being real was going to take time. He was a wounded animal who approached things like hope with a considerable amount of suspicion and caution. He would come around eventually, but forcing him right now wasn't a good idea.

Jack grabbed another knife – the last one on the table – and started sharpening it. Music began playing in the living room, Staind's *It's Been Awhile*.

Fucking Tanner strolled into the kitchen seconds later. "What?"

"You know what." Eli said without looking up. "This shit's depressing."

"And also a favorite of hers."

As if they needed the reminder? Fuck, they had spent five years trying to forget that she loved music, would dance around the kitchen, could take down any number of *malanum* on her hunt nights and howl for more. They'd spent five years *not* eating her favorite meals. Changing the radio channel when her favorite songs played. And don't think for a second they could stand being in her city apartment with her scent clinging to the walls and the sheets.

"If we can surround her with all the good old stuff, maybe it'll spark a memory." Tanner slumped into a chair and scrubbed his face with both hands. "I'm desperate here, Hounds. I can't fucking sit back and do nothing."

Tanner never could.

The day Sara had gone missing, they stripped New Orleans looking for her. They were ruthless in their pursuit to find her. Tanner had snapped after the third day of that hunt. Gone was the happy-go-lucky Hound he was known to be. The man was an animal. Savage.

It took them a solid year to get Tanner to smile again. To get him to calm back down and focus on the reason they'd all been given a second chance at life. So, like any wounded Hound whose heart was busted, Tanner and the others poured their all into their job. It was work, rejuvenate, work, rejuvenate and work, work, work.

Why would they live life? What good fucking reason would they have had to go out and have fun?

In their eyes, Sara was gone and with her went all their passion for anything. Everything.

Sara was the pack's center. The heartbeat. The motherfucking soul. She was all that was good and wild and fun and passionate and addictive and –

"Fuck," Jack cursed. Maybe Tanner was right. Maybe playing her favorite songs would spark her memory. "Put on Metallica next. Nothing Else Matters."

Tanner popped up on his feet, "I'm pulling out her old playlists."

"Good. Put it on repeat," Eli sighed. "And turn it up."

Eli flipped the burgers because it was either that or he was going to go upstairs and stalk Sara until something miraculous happened. Grabbing the lettuce and other stuff from the fridge, he made quick work of putting together a plate of add-ons. And he'd carefully selected only the best tomatoes to thinly slice.

Shinedown's *Simple Man* started playing and all the air rushed out of him. This was their song. Their. Fucking. Song.

"I love this song," Sara said from the doorway.

It took Eli a second before he could turn around and face her. In that time, Jack was up and holding a chair out for her. They'd already replaced the table Kalen broke earlier with one of the spares they kept in the barn. Broken furniture around here had become a common thing after Sara had disappeared.

Tanner popped the top off of a beer and placed it quietly on the table in front of her. No one said a word. What could they say? The pain felt fresh, too fresh, and hearing her voice was a balm they all probably wanted to slather on and never wash off.

Eli had to swipe his face clean before he was able to spin around and put the platter of lettuce, tomatoes, pickles, onions, and jalapenos on the table. "I hope you're hungry," his voice was wayyyy too soft and more controlled than usual, "I've made cheeseburgers."

Her smile would have knocked him to his knees had Eli not already been expecting the reaction. And he couldn't fucking stop himself from what he did next. "Fuck woman," Eli grabbed her cheeks and pressed his head against hers, "I've missed you so fucking much it still hurts to breathe."

Eli tried to stop himself from kissing her, figuring she wasn't ready yet. So imagine his surprise when he felt her chilled hands reach up and grip his arms. They both locked onto one another, neither saying a word and that kind of silence screamed volumes. Clearing his throat, he broke away and got back to toasting the Kaiser rolls.

Getting over Sara was the hardest thing he ever attempted to do. Or so he thought. Eating dinner across the table from her when she didn't have a clue who he was anymore? Infinitely worse.

This. Was. Hell.

CHAPTER 15

They were giving her space, but she didn't necessarily want that anymore. She didn't know what she wanted, actually. Oh and that music? Each song that blasted through the big speakers was one of her favorites. Which was odd, but not really, she supposed. If they were her Hounds, then then they should certainly know what songs she liked, right?

It just dawned on her: They pied-pipered her out of hiding with a killer playlist. And what sealed the deal and got her all the way down the stairs and into the kitchen? Red Meat. Oh the humility.

Sara's stomach growled and she was starting to feel a little nauseous. She figured eating something would boost her energy up for whatever happened next.

One word bounced around in her head like a ping-pong ball: HAREM.

Each of their scents triggered things deep within her – A hunger she suspected would never be satisfied. And how could it? They were Hell Hounds, crafted by Lucifer's hands to do his bidding. A certain amount of wickedness would be included in their making, right? A thirst that would be hard to quench. Sara looked at Jack, then Eli, then Tanner. She swallowed as a thought occurred to her: No touch would be deep enough. No taste would linger on her tongue long enough. Closing her eyes, the glorious image of Jack naked and thrusting into her body had Sara breaking out in a sweat.

Quickly, she shook the lust out of her head. This whole situation was so crazy. What if none of this fantasy was true? What if they were the bad guys and saw an easy target? Or maybe it was the truth and she needed to chillax and take this one step at a time with them.

Good God, she was a mess. Sara snatched the beer from the table and chugged the whole bottle in one long pull.

"Thirsty, love?" Jack's eyes glinted with humor.

She didn't bother answering. Tanner slid over another fresh one and she didn't even thank him for it. She just chugged. Next, Eli plated the food and served her first. Because why not, right? She was the only lady here, after all.

The. Only. Woman.

"Mmmm, looks great, Eli. I'm starving," Tanner reached for the ketchup and poured it all over his hand-cut fries, saturating them.

Monster.

"How can you do that?" Sara asked. "You've just—"

"Ruined them," she and Tanner both said at the same time.

They laughed at their jinx and Eli placed a tiny bowl next to her beer, like he knew she wanted her ketchup separate so she could control the ketchup-to-fry ratio for every bite she took.

Okay, this was just weird.

Sara stared at the bowl and it made her feel…

Pushing away from the table, she jumped up and Jack immediately did the same. Eli was already standing and Tanner sat back and watched her start to seriously unravel.

"I… I can't do this. I'm so sorry." With that, she bolted out of the kitchen.

"I'll go," Tanner offered.

Jack stopped him. "Let me do it."

Sara might have made it back to Jack's bedroom but she hadn't escaped anything at all by coming up here. She couldn't escape a Hell Hound on the hunt. And Jack, going by the growl behind her, was leader of the pack and he just found his prey.

"I'm sorry," she mumbled.

He stepped into his bedroom and closed the door with a quiet *click*. "It's us who should be apologizing, Sara. Not you." Instead of getting closer to her, he leaned back on the door and crossed his arms. "We're just trying to do whatever we can."

"To help me remember. Yeah, I guessed that."

"Can you blame us?" He pushed away from the wall and took two paces towards her. "It's been hell without you, love."

Tears welled in her eyes and when she looked at him, it was as if he didn't have a choice. His body moved while his mind blanked and he just rolled with instincts. Clutching her to him, Jack tilted her head back and pressed his mouth to hers.

Sara grabbed the back of his neck, holding him in place while her other hand had a good grip on his shoulder. His tongue swept against hers and he swallowed her moan like it was the elixir of life.

All bets were off when she made that guttural, lusty sound again.

He practically tore her tank top off. Dipping his head down, Jack licked his way towards the clasp of her bra and with a flick of his fingers, had that sucker off in one smooth move. She sank her fingers into his hair, guiding him towards one of her breasts. He sucked one into his mouth, tonguing her hard nipple, grazing it with his teeth before moving to the other one.

"I feel lost," she whispered, clutching his shoulders when he took her other breast into his mouth.

"You're home, love." With that, he ran his hand down her back, directly over her spine, trying to summon those tats to reappear. She arched into him, moaning again. "You fucking drive me wild," Jack purred in her ear.

"Is that a good thing or a bad thing?"

"You tell me."

His control was gone. Unfastening her button and fly, Jack made quick work of getting Sara out of her clothes she looked so delicious in, and then he pulled his own shirt off.

"I feel like I'm going crazy." She was already leaning back on

75

the bed like an open invitation.

"Do you trust me?" What a fucked up time to be having this conversation. He was halfway to naked and she didn't reply immediately. Jack froze, his pants pulled down to mid thighs.

Sara's eyes were focused on his chest.

"Look at me, Sara." She obeyed, her gaze shooting up to his gun-metal grays. "No one in this house will hurt you. Not ever. Is that understood?" He was alpha male with how he said this. Anything less wouldn't do. "If you want to stop. We stop. End of story."

But fuck, he hoped she'd say yes. It felt like forever since he last tasted her. He knew her too well for her to hide her needs from him. He could read her like a book and knew all the telltale signs of what Sara wanted, when she wanted it, and how she fucking needed it.

"Do you want this, love?"

This could have been a whole lotta things – *this* as in him. *This* as in his cock that had its own damn heartbeat right now. *THIS* was actually them. All of them. Did she want this? Did she want them? The farm? The life? The love that came with her Hounds?

THIS is too small a word for his meaning.

Sara bit her lip. "I want… too much, I think."

"What do you want most?" He didn't dare yank his pants off. He would stand there all day if he had to. Erect, ass out, heart on his sleeve. She needed to know what she wanted. Even if it was knowing what she wanted for just the next hour or so. "Tell me what you want, Sara, so I can make it happen."

They stared at one another and fuck him to Hell and back, those hazel eyes of hers were filled with all the things he had spent five years trying to forget about. He could do nothing but stand there and wait for her to say something. If he made a move, in any direction, he would likely crumble into dust.

Jack had spent his mourning time building one helluva wall between him and everything else. Sara was the only one with the chisel.

"I want to be me."

His brow lifted, silently asking her to elaborate.

"I don't want to be Everly or Sara or a Hound or a woman. I just want to be a Me."

76

Okay, he had no fucking clue what that even meant.

"Kiss me," she murmured.

"Is that a direct order, Me?"

Annnnd that was the moment his old Sara peeked out. "Yes. Jack. It is."

A Hell Hound obeyed the orders of their leader. Jack obeyed immediately.

Sara couldn't believe what she was doing. Stress made one do some crazy shit and this was definitely C-R-A-Z-Y. All of her was on fire and screaming on the inside. All sensible thoughts burned away in flames of unbridled desires she'd been trying to snuff out since... hell, since she woke up dead five years ago.

Were all Hounds so insatiable or was it just her? Did it even matter at the moment?'

As Jack got out of his clothes and stood before her, rock hard and steady, she thought, *Nope. Nothing else matters.* Nothing else but this moment and this feeling and this guy.

She didn't want to talk, so she didn't. As the music blasting through the house pumped her veins with something indescribably wonderful, Seether's *Remedy* started playing next and all Sara wanted was to feel Jack's hands on her. And his mouth. And everything else he had to offer.

"Spread your legs."

She spread 'em.

Jack dropped to his knees. Hooking her thighs under his arms, he pushed her back. Then that Hound used his tongue for something far more pleasurable than talking.

Sara dug her fingers into his hair, grinding her body against his mouth until she was close to screaming. Sensing she was close, Jack pulled off her, gripped her ankles and flipped her onto her stomach so fast her head spun. Sara bit her lip when she felt him climb on top of her from behind.

"Spread your legs, love."

She didn't. Not at first. Jack was going to have to work for it if he wanted her so badly. She didn't just take orders. She fucking gave them, damnit.

He groaned at her defiance and licked, from the base of her spine to the nape of her neck, with a long drag of his velvet tongue. That pretty much acted as a key to unlocking her because Sara gave in and spread her legs.

She felt the heat of his cock rub against her. He bit down on her shoulder as he rubbed the head against her core, and holy shit was she wet.

"Bloody hell, love. You're killing me slowly here."

Sara lifted her head and turned to face him. "Then do something about it." She ground her backside into him.

With a growl, he gripped her hips, forced her back down on the bed, and slapped her ass. "I'm waiting."

"Waiting for what?" Sara gripped the sheets when he ran a hand down her spine again. Shit, she was so worked up she began to shake.

Jack nibbled on her ears before nipping her shoulder blades, coaxing another moan from her. "For this." Jack drove into her in one swift, long, push. Burying himself as deep as he could get, they both cried out.

Sara gripped the sheets tighter and he placed his hands over hers, entwining their fingers together. Then he pulled out of her nice and slow before working his way back in. The push and pull felt exquisite and painful and good and overwhelming. *Deep. So damn deep.*

Jack lightly bit her neck and her eyes rolled in the back of her head. This was about control and with the noises he was making in her ears, Sara knew Jack was close to losing his.

"Stop."

He halted, mid-thrust.

"I want to flip over."

Jack pulled out, turned her over and got back to business before she could even catch her breath.

"Watch me," she panted. "Watch me as I come."

Grasping the nape of his neck, forcing him to look, Sara reached down to the space between them and started making circles around the tiny bundle of nerves demanding attention. It was a work of a moment before she was flying apart with her orgasm.

"EYES. Sara." She'd closed them, riding that wave of bliss, but at Jack's command, they flew open and locked on his. "That's right, love. Let it go. Let it all fucking go."

Sara screamed. She let loose her pleasure and pain and frustration and sorrow and guilt and passion and fury. When she ran out of air, she sucked in another lung full and Jack quickened his pace and lifted one of her legs up so he could drive into her as deep as possible. "Again."

Sara's finger never left that button of hers. She rubbed faster and harder as Jack's hips turned to pistons.

"I'm watching, love. Show me. Come again. Now."

Damn if her body didn't obey. How was this even possible? The next wave of pleasure ripped her defenses wide open and Sara flew apart with another throaty roar.

Like a possessed woman, she was dripping in sweat, her one hand still down between them, the other had let go of Jack's neck and was now clawing the sheets. Her body arched, head thrashing back into the mattress and she squeezed her eyes shut as a third wave slammed into her.

A cool breeze snapped her attention towards the doorway. Tanner and Eli were there, both rigid and glaring at her.

"Not. Now." Jack barked.

Sara's eyes latched onto Eli's and she had a split second to catch the hunger in them before the door shut again. Jack snaked a hand behind her head and crushed his mouth to hers just as he found his own release. The noise he made was quite possibly the most glorious sound in all the world.

Sara might not have known her past, and she wasn't too sure about her present, but she sure as fuck knew her future.

She was gonna have more moments like this.

CHAPTER 16

Eli and Tanner went back downstairs to sit at the kitchen table. It was the furthest point away from what was going on in Jack's room without venturing outside and having to come up with some sorry excuse to give Kalen for being on his sacred ground.

Soooo, they both just sat there and stared at the juicy burgers and hand-cut fries and garden salad because neither of them had an appetite now. Not for food, at least.

Tanner frowned. "We can't be mad she chose him."

Eli tapped his thumb on the table, "I know."

"He's just giving her what she needs."

"I know."

"Hell, I can't even try to get myself mad. I'd cut my own arm off and beat myself with it if it made her that fucking happy."

"I know."

Tanner, who was lightning in a bottle, started bouncing his leg up and down. He ran a hand through his faux hawk and stared at the floor. Then his leg started bouncing double-time.

"Chill, Hound." Eli knew he was wasting his breath. Tanner never chilled. He was the chaos to Jack's control. The storm to Eli's calm. And the explosion to Kalen's fire. Tanner was the energy that made your head spin.

This farmhouse wasn't big, but it wasn't small either. At least, that's what Eli would have said before five minutes ago when they heard Jack and Sara upstairs. Jack's roar as he orgasmed rattled all the windows in the house.

Eli closed his eyes. The image of Sara's face while she was lost in the throes of passion were tattooed on the inside of his fucking eyelids. God damn, she was beautiful like that. All fire and heat and blazing glory.

God, how he's missed her.

Some piece of him still rejected the possibility that this was seriously happening. That Sara was really here and they were all a unit again. A true pack.

Shit, how many times had he woken up after her disappearance and could have sworn it was all just some bad dream. That he could go down the steps and she would be in the kitchen wearing one of his t-shirts, pouring coffee, and laughing it up with Tanner because he was a rooster who got up at the crack of dawn every morning.

How many nights had Eli come home after a hunt, taken a shower and sworn he could hear her laughing down the hall at something Jack was saying. How many times did he go down the aisle at the store and stop in front of her brand of shampoo and force himself to not pop the top and take a whiff of the sweet stuff?

And how many times had he accidentally set a place for her at the table?

Life without Sara had been an endless nightmare where no matter how fast he ran, how hard he fought, or how loud he screamed, Eli couldn't wake the fuck up.

Now here she was, in Hound form, and he was scared that if he moved too fast or even sneezed too hard, he would wake up and realize this was just another terrible nightmare. He didn't think he'd survive it if that was the case.

Eli kept his eyes closed and focused on the image of her. Jack wasn't the lucky sonofabitch because he'd made love to her just now.

Eli was.

Sara always loved having one of them watch. And Eli had just witnessed her fly apart. She allowed that. Allowed him into her moment when she so desperately tried to displace herself if only for a little while.

And when their eyes locked onto each other? God damn, Eli could have sworn his heart had stopped beating. He heard nothing but her pleasure as she made those delicious noises. He saw nothing but her body writhe and arch and dig into the mattress. He smelled nothing but her arousal. And he felt that gaze of hers sear him from the inside out.

He couldn't wait for Sara to find her memories. Until that happened though, Eli was dead set on making some new ones with her.

Sara laid on her back, nothing more than a puddle of lust on Jack's bed.

"How are you now, Me?"

Sara's mouth quirked into a smile, "Okay."

"Just okay? I should try harder next time then." Jack playfully nipped her belly as he positioned himself next to her.

Sara tilted her head so she could see him better. Jack's jaw was set and he was staring at the ceiling with one hand on her thigh, the other bent under his head. "What are you thinking, Jack?"

"I'm thinking of what I want to do to you next."

She wasn't about to deny that she'd been thinking something along those lines herself. "Can I ask you a dumb question?"

"No such thing as dumb. And shoot."

"Is it... was it... always like this?"

Jack turned to look at her, "You mean with us?"

She nodded.

"No," he sighed and settled his head back down on his arm. "It was much better."

Better? How the hell could it be better than this? She was almost afraid to ask. Fortunately, Jack answered before she even had a chance to open her mouth.

"You were... *are*... by far the most insatiable woman on this green earth. We used to joke that you were hell-bent on breaking us."

She blushed. "And none of you minded sharing me?"

Reaching over, she grabbed the shirt Jack wore earlier and put it on. With a sigh, she collapsed on the bed again because getting dressed took too much effort.

"We're Hounds, Sara. We're a pack. To be with one of us, you're essentially with all of us. Everything we have and are, we share as one."

"Including me?"

"Yes, Me."

"And I was okay with that?"

"It was your idea."

Sara rested her thigh on top of his as she replayed the moment Eli and Tanner busted down the door and saw her and Jack together.

God, Eli was something fierce. She'd pinned her sights on him in the midst of Jack destroying her senses. That one look said it all – Eli wanted a taste. She could sense his hunger as clearly as she felt her own. There was no envy in his expression. Just a burning desire and something far more potent… like understanding.

Holy Hell. I actually have a harem.

"We better go downstairs. Eli went through a lot of trouble to make dinner and I'd hate for his hard work to go to waste." Jack slapped her leg and then sat up, "Come on, love. You need to keep up your strength. Food's going to help with that."

"I feel too tired to move." That was the truth, too. Jack had been rough and relentless and magnificent, but now she feared her legs were Jell-O.

"Alright then." He hopped off the bed and kissed her one last time before leaving her alone in his room. Moments later, Jack, Tanner and Eli returned with room service.

"If Me can't come down to the food. The food can come up to Me." Jack handed her a plate before he plopped down with his back against the headboard and the other two Hounds sat on the edge of the bed.

Sara felt her cheeks redden again. She'd spent five years hoping for a smidgen of this attention from someone. And now, here she was, being doted on by three incredibly sexy Hell Hounds.

If this was what it was like to be a Hell Hound, then it was a life worth giving her soul to Satan for. She had no regrets. Biting into her burger, Sara groaned with appreciation.

"Glad you like it," Eli winked digging into his own meal.

Sara sat in the warm bed, basking in her after sex glow, biting into the burger that was cooked to perfection even if it had grown cold at this point. She looked around and thought, *It's good to be Me.*

CHAPTER 17

Sara turned to Eli. "How did we meet?"

"Tanner, how about you and I get going on the dishes." Jack grabbed Sara's plate and Tanner took Eli's.

"Thanks," Eli nodded and waited for them to leave. "You truly don't remember anything?"

Sara shook her head.

Jesus, how was this possible? Eli wasn't even sure where to start. Leaning forward, he rested his elbows on his knees and focused on the scuff mark marring his right boot. "I was a soldier in the war." Before she could ask which one he answered, "The second world war."

He heard her breath hitch. Maybe it was because that was a dismal fucking war or maybe it was the realization that he'd been a Hound for longer than she thought. Either way, his time as a Hound was nothing compared to some of the other pack members.

"I'd joined the war, determined to stop at least some of those Nazi fuckheads myself. I was in the air with so many other planes. We were like flying ants. The cloud cover was thick that day, which didn't help matters. An enemy plane came up behind me, firing so much that I was certain my aircraft looked like Swiss fucking cheese. I knew I was going down. I wasn't going to make it, so in a last ditch effort, I veered to the right and slammed my plane into his. We crashed into a field and I totally prepared to kiss my ass goodbye with the landing. The side of my plane was already on fire, between that and the engine smoking and shot to pieces, it was a matter of seconds before I was barbeque."

Eli scrubbed his face. He hated thinking about that day. "I wasn't fucking ready to die. I wasn't... *ready*. I crawled out of the plane after it crash landed in a field. The adrenaline pumped so fast in my veins, I didn't even feel the metal piercing my leg. I ripped my helmet off and crawled on my belly away from my plane before it exploded. Betsy. Her name was Betsy."

Fuck he hated this...

"And then, out of nowhere, something bit my back. Twice. Turns out, I'd been shot by the man I tried to take out before we crashed. How he managed to survive as well was beyond me. He ranted in German as he stumbled over to me. We fought, punching and kicking at each other, bleeding all over everything. He spat in my face. I pulled my knife off my belt and slit his throat just as he shot me one more time in the heart."

"Oh my god." Sara's voice was as frail as Eli felt.

"I still wasn't ready to die. I just wasn't fucking ready." Silence took over the room for a few minutes. "And then I saw you. Hovering over me in black leather pants and your hair pulled back tight and out of your face. I thought you were the angel of death, coming to sweep me away. Then you were gone."

He swallowed the lump in his throat. "I bled out on the field with the Nazi on top of me. We were both soaked in blood and hate and the mess that came with war. Then darkness took me and before I knew it, I was someplace else entirely, looking into the eyes of the Devil himself."

"So... where was I?"

"Right next to him. You just pointed at me and said, 'That one' and Lucifer brought me into a room and started interrogating me. The rest, as they say, is history. I became a Hound, I fell in love, I now live to protect the world from nasty evil fuckers, and I've never regretted my choices."

"So was I a recruiter, then?"

"I wouldn't say that. But you had the Devil wrapped around your little finger. You wanted your own pack and he gave you one.

Except, you wanted to pick your own Hounds and took your time doing it."

"There's never been anyone else in our pack, our harem?"

"There was only ever us in the pack. And we didn't become your harem until much, much, later."

"Is every pack like us?"

He laughed. "Not even close." Eli turned to look at her, "You built your own pack by your standards and then one by one, just as you selected us, we fell for you and you fell for us."

Sara bit her bottom lip. Damn, what he wouldn't give to lean in and suck her lip into his mouth, lightly graze it with his teeth and tug it just a little.

"I'm glad I found you. All of you."

That seemed like a strange thing to say, considering she didn't remember them at all. "Why's that, baby?"

"I hated being on my own. Fighting those evil souls all by myself. It was hard and lonely and exhausting."

Eli stiffened, "What are you saying, Sara? That you fought them recently?"

"I've been hunted by them since the day I woke up dead, five years ago. It was the reason I went to Hell with Jack. To sell my soul and be a Hound so I'd have all I would need to put those dark spirits back where they belong." She smirked, "Guess some piece of me already had the memory of how to fight them. I just thought it was instinct."

Eli's blood ran cold. Jack hadn't mentioned she'd been chased by their enemies. "Did you ever... was there ever a time that they..."

"That they got me?

Eli shook his head, his protective instincts raging within.

"I was already starting to turn dark when Jack found me." Sara swallowed and stared at her hands. "My hands and my arms were turning black."

Eli pulled her in close. "Oh my God, Sara."

His mind was reeling. They could have lost her. Lost her on a whole new level of awful. That she was a ghost was tragic enough, but that she was turning into their enemy? Turning into a *malanum* meant her form would morph and her mind would warp. She'd be nothing more than a vile, wicked, corrupt creature with no morals and a thirst to spread her evil. It would have only been a matter of time before one Hound – either from their pack or another – would send her to Hell.

Actual Hell. The prison side, not Lucifer's private chambers.

Eli's face tingled with panic. *Close. That had been too close.* Why hadn't Jack mentioned this part of the story to them?

Oh he knew why. Because Jack was forever trying to protect the pack from their own damn demons. He would likely live forever without telling the rest of the pack that Sara almost turned because it didn't matter now. She was found. She was back. She was safe.

She wasn't the enemy.

"You okay?" Sara asked, pulling out of his grasp.

Nope. He wasn't okay. "I'm fine."

"You don't look too good. Maybe…"

The door opened and a huge box stepped in with Tanner arms and legs. "I got this out of the basement. It's some of your clothes, Beautiful."

"Oh," Sara shifted to the edge of the bed and stood up.

"I'm gonna check on Kalen." Eli got up to leave.

"Watch it." Tanner warned, "Jack's with him right now."

Eli knew what that meant and nodded his head. As he bumbled down the steps, he couldn't figure out if he was more grateful to have Sara home or relieved that he hadn't been the one to find her as a wisp turning into a *malanum.*

Eli could accept a lot of things, go through a lot of shit, but if the timing had been a little bit different and his Sara had turned into his sworn enemy? As a Hell Hound he would have had no choice but to open up a Hell hole and send her into that dark place to suffer for all eternity. And if that had happened?

Eli would have jumped in right behind her – in a motherfucking swan dive.

CHAPTER 18

Kalen was in the barn, splitting wood. He saw Jack approach cautiously. Smart bastard. With an axe in his hands, Kalen was desperate to split things – wood, skulls, whatever. He already chopped enough wood for two brutally cold winters and had no intentions of stopping any time soon.

"Put the axe down, Hound."

Kalen continued to swing down on the log he was working on.

"Talk to me." Jack kept a safe distance. "Come on, Hound. Say something."

Kalen couldn't talk. He had no words. Kalen was a beast of emotions and none of them were pleasant.

Jack growled, "Will you at least speak with her?"

Kalen gave no response. And, damnit, he just broke the handle of the axe. Tossing it to the side to fix later, he walked over to a wall and snatched another.

Jack was fuming. "You're not being helpful here, mate."

Yes he was. Kalen staying outside and far away from what was in the house was definitely being helpful, because if he went in there now he'd be nothing but destructive, which would be very *unhelpful*. See the difference?

Jack shoved his boot against a big log. "Are you going to sleep out here too?"

"Maybe." Kalen wasn't going into that house even if a tornado hit.

"Sara needs you, Kalen. Just like she needs the rest of us."

Sara. Kalen growled low in his chest. He wasn't taking Jack's bait. "I'm sure she's doing fine without me."

"I beg to differ."

"Then perhaps you didn't hear the same noises I did about an hour ago."

Jack ran his hand through his hair and cursed. "Come in and talk with her."

One swipe of his head, that's all Kalen was capable of doing to let Jack know his answer was a big fat no. When he went back to chopping more wood, Jack left him alone and he couldn't have been more thankful.

Sara.

When Kalen saw her standing behind Jack earlier, Kalen thought he'd been poisoned. That some no good piece of shit had spiked his drink when he went out hunting earlier and he was hallucinating her. The fear of it either being true… or untrue… caused him to snap.

Being a Hell Hound took more than a blade and a chase. It meant blending in. Keeping eyes open at all times. It meant submerging into the crowd and being able to spot the target, find the shadow in the darkest recesses, and eliminate it. He was good at that – eliminating the threat.

Actually, Kalen was good at a lot of things.

Coping wasn't one of them, though.

He's seen a lot of shit in his time. Been through a lot, too. Being a Hell Hound made him deadly, but also paranoid over the years. And tonight took his paranoia to a whole new level. Never has something unraveled him the way Sara's sudden reappearance had.

Sara.

They all thought she was dead. She certainly vanished off the plains they could travel in, which was no small feat.

Sara.

The air punched out of his chest. It was too hard to breathe.

Too hard to think. Kalen shook his head until stars burst in his vision and then found his focus again. The wood. Chop the wood. Cut, split, stack the goddamn wood.

One could never tell when a cold snap would come and they were going to need a lot of wood for winter. The old farmhouse was drafty. Heating it was a pain in the ass. Regardless, Sara had insisted they buy the old house because she'd fallen in love with it, much like she fell in love with her Hounds – imperfections and all.

Sara.

Yeah, Kalen needed to heat the house. Chop the logs. Split 'em, and stack 'em.

Sara.

Kalen swung his axe again and again and again.

Sara. Sara. Sara.

She was seriously here. No amount of drugs or poison could replicate a hallucination with such precision.

Sara always was perfection. And now she was back. With them.

Kalen swung his axe again, taking all his anger out on the poor defenseless log. Where has she been this whole time? How did she find them? Did she know what happened?

The axe fell again, splintering the wood and cutting off Kalen's thoughts. Reality was staring him down, closing him in on all sides. Kalen swung down again while one, single, screaming thought ate away at his mind: *Would Sara forgive him for what he did in New Orleans?*

Tanner handled Sara's clothing as if each and every piece of it was made of fragile material. One move too quick and they'd disintegrate. Carefully, he laid them out on Jack's bed. He made a pile of jeans. Another of t-shirts. A pile of tank tops. And there were also a few sweaters and some socks.

"No underwear?"

"You never wore those," Tanner didn't even bother to hide his big cheesy smile. "There's another box downstairs with your heavier winter clothes and fighting stuff, but I thought these could do for now."

"You kept all my stuff in the basement?" That must've been the pile of storage boxes she saw when Jack brought her down there earlier.

"We couldn't part with it." Tanner stuffed his hands in his pocket and stared at the small wardrobe on Jack's bed. "It was hard enough putting it all in boxes. None of us were willing to donate or burn your things. We just couldn't let go."

"Hey," she reached for his hand. It was then she realized his palms were clammy and he was trembling.

Tanner exhaled uncomfortably. "This still feels too crazy to be real. I'm scared to blink too hard and you'll be gone again."

She didn't know what to say or do. It was such a surreal feeling to have no memory of anything, to live with a strange, emptiness. And yet, being here with the smell of these Hounds and the sounds of their voices and the touch of their hands and the looks in their eyes had made her feel like she was where she belonged.

This pack was her home.

"I understand what you mean." She tucked some hair behind her ear. "Part of me feels like I'm hallucinating this whole thing and the other part of me doesn't even care so long as it doesn't stop."

Tanner beamed a smile so big it warmed her to the bone. "Exactly."

"So where is my room? We can go put these things away and give Jack his bed back."

"You don't have a room here."

"What?"

"You don't have your own bedroom, Sara. You slept with one of us every night. Or sometimes we'd cram into one bed together."

"Like a big puppy pile?"

"Which," he chuckled, "Is just what you'd call it."

Sara looked at the size of Jack's bed. Yeah, sure, it was king-sized, but how on earth would four grown men plus her fit?

"We didn't mind getting tangled." Tanner shrugged as if knowing what she was thinking. "If you want, I can put your stuff away for you."

"I can do it."

"No, let me. I don't mind." Tanner turned and went into the hall for one hot second and came back in carrying a much smaller box. "How about you just spend some time looking through this stuff?"

"Okay," her answer was as cautious as his voice sounded.

Leaving her to open the box alone, Tanner shoved a few things into one of Jack's drawers, and then left with an armful of clothes to redistribute into various bedrooms.

This. Was. Crazy.

But not as crazy as what she saw when opening that smaller box. The first thing in it was a photo of all five of them at the beach. Sara was wearing a red bikini and sitting on Eli's shoulders. Jack was standing next to them in a pair of black trunks and aviator glasses. Tanner was giving Kalen bunny ears. They looked so... happy.

This was my life?

She carefully placed the frame on the bed and dug for the next object. It was another photo. This one was much, much older. A black and white snapshot of her and Jack. She was wearing a dress that flared out, her hair in victory curls and her one leg bent out as she leaned on Jack's shoulder about to kiss his cheek. Jack was serious as a heart attack in a suit, a wicked grin on his face, his jawline sharp as a razor blade. He had a smile that made his eyes crinkle on the edges. Sara ran her hand over the photo, caressing it, feeling all bubbly and warm inside.

The next thing she pulled out was stiff and rough - A small canvas painting of a village.

Something stirred in her. A panic. Sweat bloomed across her forehead and she quickly shoved the thing back into the box. Whatever memory that painting was trying to invoke, she wanted no part of it. Not today, at least.

Stuffing the other two pictures back into the box, she quickly closed it and rubbed her sweaty palms on her legs.

Getting up, she looked out the window and saw how dark it was now. The light in the barn let her know Kalen was still out there. The shadows of the moon and the light from inside were the only two ways she could judge the distance between him and her. It was about one hundred yards.

Or one hundred lifetimes, give or take.

Her return to this strange house and these incredible men were not what she expected when Lucifer gave Sara her life back.

He cleansed her soul of the evil that threatened to possess her. He told her that she was safe again. A Hound again.

But she wasn't whole again.

Not yet, and it wasn't for lack of trying on the guys' part. God knows they were doing all they could to help her, no matter how futile it seemed today.

No, the void she felt now was entirely different than what she dealt with while being dead for the past five years. This void felt worse, it cut soul fucking deep.

Sara suspected Kalen, the one Hound who was doing anything but be in the same house as her, might have something to do with that.

CHAPTER 19

"You didn't say she was almost one of them." Eli's words practically bitch slapped Jack. "You can't keep shit like that from us."

"It was irrelevant by the time I brought her home to the pack."

"That doesn't matter, you should have told us. What else aren't you saying?"

Jack's jaw was set and he pushed past Eli and grabbed a beer from the fridge. "Doesn't matter now. She's safe. She's here and she's not going anywhere ever again."

"And what's that supposed to mean?

"It means she's not going out on her own ever again."

Eli barked a laugh that was anything but warm. "And you know just how Sara will act when she hears that new law, *Alpha*."

Alpha was more of a kick in the balls than a true title. They all knew Sara called the shots in the pack. And when she disappeared, Jack took over. None of them complained because they all didn't want to say what they were really thinking – no one could take her place. Not in leadership. Not in comfort. Not in any fucking way.

Jack took the reins again tonight. He made a decision to keep Sara's condition when he found her to himself. He should have known that was a mistake. This house held no secrets. It's what made them such a good pack. Trust, above all else, was necessary to run a tight and strong pack.

"She can't leave without one of us. At least not until she's back to normal or," well, shit, "Back to her old self."

"What does that mean?"

Jack took a long pull from his longneck and motioned for Eli to take a seat. "Her instincts to fight are there. Last night she fought with that same fire she's always had."

"So what's the problem? That's a good thing, right? That her memory of combat moves were still there proves her memories must be in there somewhere."

"She'd been using those learned Hound skills every day to survive the *malanum*." Jack leaned in and his voice dropped to a snarl, "Every fucking day, Eli, they hunted her."

Eli sat back in his seat, a low growl rattling out of his mouth. "How is that possible? She's a Hound. They should have been running away from her the second she was within sight of them."

"Precisely. But they didn't. She told me they'd been gunning for her ever since she woke up dead in New Orleans."

"How did Luce not sense her and come for her? Or at least tell us where she was?"

"Maybe he didn't know." Maybe. Maybe not. "Either way," Jack took another swig, "she was under constant attack and held her own for five long years."

"That's our girl," Eli smirked.

"She was turning when I found her."

"She told me."

"God damn, Eli," Jack scrubbed his face and sighed with exhaustion, "I can't close my eyes and not see her arms black as pitch. At one point, she was snatched right out from under me. Flung out the window and dragged into a bloody fucking alley."

Eli's fists clenched tightly as another loud growl rolled out of his mouth.

"She fought them like an animal," Jack continued, "and then she damn near lost control and turned into one of the *malanum* right before my eyes."

"Shit."

"I don't think I've ever been so scared in my life. To have been so close to losing her in the worst possible way?" Jack pounded the rest of his beer and Eli got up and grabbed two more from the fridge and handed him one. "I just wasn't ready to say that part to you guys yet. It wasn't that I was keeping it to myself... I just..."

"Wasn't ready to relive it so soon."

"Exactly."

Silence fell over the kitchen. They could both hear footsteps moving around above them. Eli shook his head, "Tanner is so wound up, he's gotta give her some space."

"Yeah, and that'll happen the day pigs fly."

More silence. More swigs of beer. "How's Kalen out there?"

Jack shrugged, "He's his usual closed off self."

"Is he ever coming back inside?"

"Doubt it."

"Hmmph." Eli rubbed the back of his neck. More silence. "It's killing me to not go up there and keep my eyes on her at all times."

"I know what you mean. My brain is screaming to chain her to me so nothing can happen to her ever again."

Eli nodded. "I think that chain Kalen uses to drag logs is in the shed. Should I get it?"

They both started laughing.

"Ummm, guys?" Sara's voice cut through their nervousness.

"Heyyyy," Eli stood and made his way over to her. He stopped short of scooping her into his arms and squeezing tight.

"You alright?" Jack asked from the table.

"I'm pretty tired."

"I bet, love."

"Sooo," she looked around, "where should I sleep?"

Eli and Jack responded at the same time. "With me."

CHAPTER 20

She wasn't sure what to do and didn't want to upset anyone, so Sara chose to sleep in Jack's room. For now, he felt the most familiar to her and she didn't think she was ready for the whole bed hopping thing yet.

"Make yourself comfortable, love." Jack followed her up to his room and she noticed he deliberately ignored the box she'd placed on the floor, the one that was stuffed with photos and other things she hadn't looked at yet.

He got busy remaking the bed, which might have seemed foolish to some since she was about to get back into it and mess it all up again, but getting into an unmade bed just didn't feel right. Did he know that about her or was he that way too?

Hell, Jack even fluffed the pillows and rearranged them. What a Hound.

Sara looked out the window again. "Is he going to stay out there all night?"

"Kalen's got his own issues to deal with, love. Don't take it personally."

How could she not? Tanner's first reaction when seeing her was to kiss the ever-loving hell out of her. Eli's composure crumbled with one look. And Jack? He'd been nothing more than an overprotective guard dog since they met at the club – who, incidentally, couldn't keep his hands off her. Not that she was complaining.

But Kalen? His reaction had been far from the welcome home she received from the others. He destroyed the kitchen table and had done about a week's worth of wood cutting in one day.

One long, full, exhausting day. Holy Hell, she was beat.

Jack grabbed the edge of the sheets and even gave her turn-down service. Patting the pillow, his voice was quiet and calm, "Come on, love. Rest yourself."

She obeyed. Her energy spent completely. He tucked her in, too. Kissed her on the mouth quick and sweet and not at all how she expected. Then he did another unexpected thing: He turned to leave.

"Where are you going?"

He halted, bracing his arm against the door jamb. "I thought you'd want the bed to yourself. It's been a rough time, love. I don't want to smother you."

"Then don't smother me."

He nodded as if to say, *Alright, goodnight.*

"Lie here with me, Jack?" Sara tried to not sound too pathetic. "I spent five years being alone with no one but me. Five years, Jack, of fighting and screaming, and being a lonely, miserable little thing." So much for not sounding too pathetic. "I'm glad you found me when you did."

His voice dropped to a whisper, "So am I, love."

"Then lay here with me. Lay here so that when I sleep, I know I'm safe and when I wake, I know I'm not alone. That this whole thing isn't a dream."

She might as well have pulled an invisible rope that connected the two of them with the way he moved towards her. "I've got you, Sara." He climbed into the bed and didn't even bother to kick his boots off or get under the covers. His only thought was to get to her and hold her and that's just what he did.

"I want to remember," she turned and cried into his chest. "I want to remember everything."

"You will. It's just going to take time, I think."

He smoothed her hair and kissed her head. "Go to sleep, Sara. Tomorrow, we'll see what we can do to help you more."

She wrapped her arms around him and buried her face in his chest. Filling her lungs with the scent of her Hound, she was almost starting to feel peaceful. The bed dipped down behind her. "I'm sleeping in here, too. I can't stand a wall between us tonight."

It was Tanner. She smiled as he snuggled up next to her and buried his face in her hair. "It's been too long, Beautiful. I can't just pretend I haven't died a little each day without you. You're just going to have to deal with my snoring."

Jack's laugh grumbled low in his chest. Turning his head to look behind him, Sara, too, popped her head up and they both stared at Eli. He was leaning against the door, arms crossed over his chest, face masked to hide his fear of being rejected.

"Oh for fuck's sake. Come on." Jack scooted over and so did the other two. Eli pushed away from the wall and went over to Tanner's side of the bed. He laid down, just like the others – fully dressed and above the sheets.

He and Jack stared at each other for a long moment. They've been together too long to not be able to "almost" read each other's minds. Jack would take the first watch, Eli the second, Tanner the third.

With Kalen out back, and knowing he probably wasn't going to be able to sleep either, plus the wards up as their house was still off grid, Sara was safe.

And they were going to make sure she stayed that way.

Kalen came inside long after midnight. The house was dead quiet and he knew they were asleep somewhere. Probably all in one bed. There was no way any of the Hounds were going to let Sara out of their sights now. They would never take the risk of losing her again.

His hands ached. Blisters, raw and busted, did nothing to overshadow the pain he felt in his back, head, and black heart. He wanted to fall into bed and sleep for a week but he wasn't going upstairs yet. What if he ran into her somehow? Or worse, what if he went by whatever room she was in and he saw her sleeping.

She was so beautiful when she slept.

All her hard exterior - the fight in her eyes, the war paint, the sweat and violence she rocked on a daily basis when they hunted, always melted away when she slept. He used to say she looked like an angel of small death - A beautiful, deadly, creature with soft curves and doe eyes and hair that was thick and smelled like strawberries.

And she always held someone while she slept. Sara would grip one of her Hounds tight like an anaconda so they couldn't slip out of the room at any point. Not that any of them ever wanted to escape. But she, even in her dreams, held her Hounds close.

Oh God... Kalen looked down at his arms. He swore he could feel her. Would have bet his life her hands were clutching his arm right now. He knew the feel of those long fingers of hers, with her painted red nails and calloused palms from throwing blades into their enemies during hunts. He knew how she squeezed him tight as she dreamed, and would loosen her grip when she woke.

Jesus, how many times had he gone through this? Kalen had suffered from Phantom Sara Syndrome for five long years. Always, he felt her press against his body, clutch his arm, run her hand down his spine. But it was never true. His denial and guilt were forever taking his psyche for a ride that always ended in a crash landing.

Kalen blinked again, still staring at his arm. His lungs ceased taking in air. She wasn't with him. She was upstairs holding another. She was safe and sound and warm and alive and...

Sara... He wanted to see her. Touch her. Feel the warmth of her cheeks.

Sara... Kalen's stomach flip-flopped. He was turning into a wreck again. Guilt did that to a guy. And Kalen rocked a lot of guilt.

He shook his head. Fuck that, he wasn't going to risk seeing her. Her sudden reappearance was enough to break him, another run-in this soon would destroy him completely.

Instead, Kalen went down to the basement to blow off more steam. His hands were raw from the four axes he'd burned through. Not willing to stop, he wrapped his hands before another grueling work out. Nothing like some heavy lifting after a full day of strenuous wood cutting to land a guy in the zone of pure exhaustion with no hope of recovery for a few days.

He didn't need a spotter. If the weights were too heavy and

crashed down to strangle him with the barbell, he didn't care. He deserved death for what happened five years ago. Kalen had just been patiently waiting for the Universe to give him his punishment.

Sitting up to adjust the weights, he noticed two boxes were missing from the basement. And yeah, he knew which two they were. Kalen was the one who put the boxes down here to begin with. Stacked them up nice and neat. Made sure he could see them no matter where he was in the basement. There was no need to label what was in them. He memorized their contents the day they were placed inside those cardboard coffins.

Thirteen boxes were all she had. Thirteen. And seven of them were shoes.

God, how she loved a solid set of combat boots.

His chest tightened.

For five years, he has come down here every day to work out. And every time, he counted those boxes. Did a silent inventory of everything in them. Then he lost himself in a memory of a random outfit or object that was tucked away. He had survived on the ghost of memories of his Sara. He never learned to let go.

Shit, he couldn't even let go of his own life when he died. Even as he drew his last breath, he fucking clung to what was left of his life. Then he was lucky enough to become a Hound. Lucky enough to have Sara. Lucky enough to have a pack. A second chance. A purpose.

Now he felt like his luck had run out.

Kalen laid back and began his reps. After those, he did curls. Then sit ups. Then he went to the punching bag and made it his life's mission to hit it hard enough to knock the sand out. Drain that leather bound sack dry until it was as hollow as he felt.

Finally, when his bones were too weary to lift his fists again, Kalen dragged his sorry ass up the steps. He prayed for blindness to make his walk to his bedroom easier. The bedroom doors were all shut, thank God. Slowly, he lumbered into his room and pulled out some new clothes to change into after he took a shower. Pulling open the top drawer to grab an undershirt, all the air whooshed out of him.

Some of Sara's clothes were put back where they... *fuck him*.... where they belonged.

With a shaky hand, Kalen pulled a t-shirt of hers out, and

pressed the soft, gray v-neck to his nose. He inhaled deeply, filling his lungs with nothing but the woman he lost, and dropped to his knees. Rocking back and forth, Kalen clung to his piece of Sara and wept.

CHAPTER 21

Sara woke up tangled in sheets and men. Not a bad way to start the day, really. Unable to move more than a wiggle, she was pinned under them. All their arms wrapped around her body made Sara feel like a butterfly trying to bust out her cocoon... or chrysalis... or whatever the fuck.

"Hey, baby." Eli kissed her forehead and was the first to move off the bed.

Tanner stretched and yawned big enough for his jaw to crack, then he nuzzled against her side again, wrapping his arm around her waist and pulling her in close to him. "Morning, Beautiful."

Jack's eyes were pinned on her and then he cupped her face and kissed her. "I still can't believe it."

She knew what he meant. She couldn't believe it either.

Eli stretched with a groan, "Get up, Tanner. We've got work to do." He had to slap the Hound's head twice to get him moving.

"Can't we have one day of rest?" Tanner begged.

"There's no rest for the wicked, Hound. Move it." Jack rolled out of bed next.

Sara sat up, clinging the sheets against her chest. "What work needs to be done?"

"Well, for starters, love, we need to see how much of your

training is still in your head. With what I saw the other night, a good bit of it's there. We need to make sure you're ready to fight and also re-teach you how to summon a Hell hole for when we're out in the field again."

She sat up straighter. "Are we hunting tonight?" The eagerness in her voice shocked her.

"No," Eli answered. "You're not fighting until we are sure it's safe for you to go out."

"Why wouldn't it be safe? I'm a Hound."

"And you always have been, love. But that didn't seem to deter our enemies from going after you."

"Wait, what?" Tanner's head snapped up, his disheveled hair made him look like a young rebel. "What the fuck, Jack?"

"It's a story for later, Tanner."

"No, it's a story for now." Tanner hopped out of bed and poked Jack's chest, "Don't you fucking keep shit to yourself."

Eli broke the two Hounds apart before it got ugly, "I'll fill you in while you help me make breakfast. Sara, why don't you jump in the shower and get ready for the day."

"Alright."

The men left the room and Sara stretched her limbs before sliding out of bed. Rummaging through her drawer in Jack's room, she grabbed what she wanted and headed down the hall to the one bathroom.

Yup, this house only had one bathroom.

The door opened on its own just as she was about to turn the knob and she found herself face to chest with Kalen.

"Sorry. I didn't realize anyone was in here." She clutched her clothes to her chest and tried to look Kalen in the eyes. *Look at me. Look at me, damnit.* But his gaze fell everywhere but on her.

Like he was at risk of being contaminated with a plague, he leapt away from her and moved down the hall as fast as possible. She watched him go.

What the hell is his problem?

Figuring that was an issue for another day, Sara went into the bathroom, closed the door and realized there was no lock.

Dropping her clothes on the counter, she shimmied out of Jack's t-shirt and caught a glimpse of herself in the mirror.

Oh man, did it feel good to see her reflection and not have a skeleton face stare back at her. The makeup artist was seriously skilled with a brush to make her look so damn sinister, but even though it had been an amazing work of art, that didn't mean she missed it one bit this morning. It was nice to see the real woman, for once.

Standing back, she stood in front of the mirror and did an evaluation of her body. *Not too shabby*, Sara thought. Slightly lean and toned, she guessed it was from working out to keep in Hound-shape before she died. Oh and all the hunting. Talk about a cardio workout. Running to or from those evil spirits was nothing short of a marathon.

Leaning into the mirror, the woman staring back looked like a familiar stranger. How weird was that? She didn't remember what her face (without the painted skull makeup) looked like. Her lips were full, cheeks a little hollow, her eyes looked tired.

"Hi, Sara." She waved at her reflection then turned her focus to more important things. Like getting squeaky clean.

Sara pulled the shower door open and turned the faucet on. Getting the water good and hot, she stepped under the spray and let it warm her bones and soothe her muscles. Tilting her head back, Sara let the water sluice down her body and saturate her hair. There was one bottle of shampoo, no conditioner, and a bar of soap that had about three days left to it.

This was not going to work. Where was the body wash? Her apricot facial scrub? Her strawberry scented conditioner? WHERE WAS THE RAZOR!?

Holy shit. She remembered! Her razor used to sit on the ledge, just behind the conditioner. And the aloe shaving cream was below that, laying on its side so it wouldn't leave a rust circle. And her body wash? It was should have been in the far corner.

She remembered!

With a squeal of delight, Sara snatched the shampoo and did a quick lather and rinse. Shaving her legs could wait for another day, this was big new and she wanted to share it NOW! Hopping out of the shower, she wrapped her body in a towel and didn't bother to get dressed. Remembering something like this made her feel like she was gaining ground. Getting a grip on life. Rushing, she half-slid, half-ran down the flight of stairs and crashed into Jack as she bolted into the kitchen.

"I remember!" Panting, Sara spoke with some jazz hands, "I totally remembered where my shampoo sat in the shower. And my razor and my fruity face scrub! HA! It was APRICOT! Am I right?"

Jack's dark brow lifted and she saw him try to hide his humor. "Eli?"

He flipped pancakes and smiled.

"Tanner?" she spun around and tossed her hands up in the air, "Seriously, will someone fucking say something here?"

"For the love of all that is unholy, love, please grab your towel before breakfast gets burned and we're forced to eat you instead."

Sara, in her excitement and hurry to share her news, had let the towel slip and she was standing in the kitchen completely naked.

Damn her jazz hands.

Eli tried to not stare but why fight it? Sara standing naked, dripping wet, in the kitchen no less, demanded his complete admiration. And his cock's full attention.

That woman was built for sin. She had tight breasts, round hips, and an ass that beckoned for a good spanking. He held his spatula firmly, thankful he hadn't started using it yet, and turned the burner off.

Breakfast was no longer going to be bacon and eggs. It was going be Sara with a side of fuck yes and maple syrup.

It didn't help matters any when she bent down to retrieve her towel, either. Nope, that only caused the Hounds to growl. Jack and Eli started closing in on Sara, wolves moving in on their prey, and Tanner made sure she couldn't escape the kitchen.

"What… what are you guys doing?"

"Having breakfast," Tanner smirked.

"Breakfast is over there," she pointed to the stove.

"Not anymore it's not." Eli began slapping the back of the spatula against his hand. Then he thought how much better it would be to smack her ass with his hand and nothing else, so he tossed the utensil over his shoulder and took two more paces closer towards his meal.

Sara's cheeks blushed and she tried to pretend she was scared. But they all knew better. They knew their Sara better than she knew herself. And oh how true that was now. Regardless of her memory situation, the Hounds knew when Sara was pissed, scared, happy, and aroused.

"What's the matter, love?" Jack teased from behind her. "Can't play with the big dogs?"

She was practically panting already. Ass bumping into the table, she was unable to stop Jack from tugging her hair, tilting her head way back and kissing her. Meanwhile Tanner bent over and suckled one of her breasts into his mouth and Eli went for the gold. Sinking to his knees, Eli was face-to-face with a delicacy he had craved for five long goddamn years. Tanner leaned her back so she was on top of the table and proceeded to graze her nipple with his teeth.

"Put your legs on Eli's shoulder, love. And spread them." Jack was standing by her head, smiling wickedly.

Eli winked. "Relax, baby." He dipped his head down and licked her folds with a long drag of his tongue.

The guttural moan did nothing but encourage Eli to do it again.

She smelled like them. Their soap, their shampoo, their scent was all over her.

"Spread them further, Sara." Jack leaned across the table and kissed her upside down, then rumbled in her ear, "Fuck you taste good in the morning, love. And Eli's going to enjoy every last drop you have to give, before Tanner gets a taste."

"Mmm hmm," Tanner worked one breast with his mouth as his hand sailed over to the other and pinched her nipple.

"Oh God," Sara's eyes fluttered closed and she grabbed Eli's head while Tanner worshipped her upper half.

"I bet you taste like juicy citrus on a hot summer day." Jack's warm breath tickled her ear and shot pleasure straight to where Eli was currently flicking his tongue. "And I bet when you come for us, it's going to taste so sweet and thick and divine, Eli's going to make you come again and again until you can't move because he'll want all he can get."

Sara's pants turned into guttural noises again. Her body arched and Tanner groaned against her skin. "Move," he said to Eli, then Tanner dipped a finger into her hot center right along with Eli's finger.

Sara clawed the table.

"That's it, Hounds, nice and slow. I want to see how long we can make her last until she begs." Jack held her face in his hands, his eyes narrowed in with laser focus and he watched her lose herself to their touches. He watched her come undone, piece by piece, and smiled when she screamed out in pleasure with all they were doing to her.

"Again." Jack commanded.

Eli shoved her further up the table and Tanner pulled his finger out, and licked it clean. "Fuck, you taste so good."

Sara tried to focus on Tanner, but her eyes fluttered closed again as Eli brought her to the edge of ecstasy for a second time. "Don't stop," she whimpered.

"Easy, Eli." Jack's command had Eli slowing down his pace and withdrawing completely.

"NO! NO! NO! NO!" Sara smacked the table top in protest.

"You're begging already?" Jack tsked. "Sara, Sara, Sara."

"Don't you... fucking... Sara me!" She tried sitting up so she could properly snarl at the lot of them, but Tanner held her down and brought her attention to him.

"Fuck, I love it when you get mad." Tanner crushed his mouth to hers while Jack held her hands up and over her head. Eli dipped back down and picked up where he left off and it was a matter of seconds before she was teetering on the edge again.

Someone slipped his finger inside her warmth and dragged it along her g-spot. That was the end of the world as she knew it. Sara roared as her orgasm spilled over in a long and glorious wave. Tanner swallowed her noises as his tongue swept against hers, penetrating in the same rhythm as whoever finger was inside her.

"Again." Jack's one word had them all back to business.

At this point, Sara was so lost in pleasure she was grappling for anything to hang onto. Jack's hands found hers and she squeezed them while Tanner suckled on her breasts and Eli continued to move his sinful tongue.

Jack watched the Hounds wring every last drop of pleasure from her body. When they were finished, Sara was spread out on the kitchen table, breaths ragged and legs weak. She watched, with heavy lidded eyes, as Eli walked over to the pantry and grabbed the maple syrup.

"What's that for?" she panted.

Eli popped the cap off and smiled, "Second Breakfast."

CHAPTER 22

Sara's second shower of the day was more for a reset than anything else. Breakfast was never eaten. At least, not by her, and she now had remnants of pleasure and maple syrup residue all over her body. Including places she never thought to put that sweet stuff.

And ohhhhh they'd done a fantastic job of licking her clean. Sadly though, she wasn't able to turn the tables and use the sweet stuff on them. This, they told her, was the pleasure they sought after this morning – her cream on their tongues, her moans in their mouths, her body in their hands.

Who was she to deny them?

The Hounds couldn't seem to get enough of her and the feeling was mutual. It was as if they were all making up for lost time.

Did being a Hound mean you not only fought evil and brought them back to Hell, turned from corporeal to something like a ghost, *and* have a libido of a teenage boy all the time, or were they an extra special breed?

Lathering up, Sara tried to work quickly so the others could jump in the shower and still have hot water when she was through. Taking two showers already made her feel guilty. The hot water heater probably wasn't that big. Closing her eyes, she let the water sluice down her body in a final rinse.

"*I love your hair,*" Jack said reaching up and running his hands through it. "*And the smell of this conditioner drives me insane.*"

Sara's eyes popped open. She was alone in the shower but...

Holy shitballs, she had a flashback. As if the past was nothing more than pollen in the wind, she tried to capture it somehow, get more of it before the memory drifted away. Squeezing her eyes again, she tried to concentrate on just Jack's voice...

"*You hate strawberries.*"

"*I don't hate them on you. You smell like summer.*"

"*You smell like a farm animal.*"

"*Well, scrub me up, love. What did you think I was in here for?*"

"*You and I both know what you're in here for, Voodoo Man.*"

He grumbled in her ear and pulled her close. Their naked bodies were slick with soap and hot from something more than the water. He smacked her ass and hoisted her up, pressing her back against the wall.

Sara's eyes popped open moments later. She was breathless. Absolutely... breathless.

Grabbing another towel, she decided to keep that memory to herself. If they were going to get anything done today, then running back downstairs for a repeat performance wasn't going to get the job done.

Drying off, she yanked on her jeans, bra and a navy blue t-shirt. Padding barefoot down the hall, she stopped at the top of the steps and descended those suckers nice and slow. Her body was weak in all the right ways, but that wasn't a good thing when you have a bunch of Hounds around. They'd use such a weakness for their gains...

How did she know that?

Instinct.

When she reached the bottom, Sara made her way into the kitchen again and tried not to stare at the table where she had just been breakfast. Instead of having a seat next to Jack, she went over and poured herself coffee. Black, of course, just like her eyelashes and her soul.

Okay, it might have been a little too soon for the black soul joke considering how close she had come to being a serious big problem if Jack hadn't found and saved her the other night. Her hero was currently organizing some badass looking blades on the table. Tanner was nowhere to be seen, and she could see Eli out back, walking towards the barn.

"Sooo, what's next on today's agenda, Voodoo Man?"

Ohhh his smile was a killer one when she called him that. It made her all fluttery inside.

"Reflexes, love." Jack ran his hands down the line of knives and selected one. He tossed it right at Sara.

She caught it.

"Holy shit," she gasped, shocked that her natural instinct had been to reach out and grab the damn thing.

"Nicely done." Jack scooped up a bunch of blades and asked for her to head outside with him.

It was freezing out, but she figured whatever they were about to get into, she would warm up in no time. Sara's curiosity spiked when they headed for the barn. Eli was in there already, waiting. He greeted her with a sly smile.

"Where's Tanner?" she asked.

"With Kalen, hunting."

"Ohh," she looked around, "I thought Lucifer said no more going out until things were taken care of with me."

"That meant no hunting for you, love. The rest of us Hounds must hunt. We cover this district alone."

Eli grabbed some blades, "Ready?"

"Always," she teased.

Jack placed the rest of the daggers on a wooden table. Large enough for twelve people to sit around, it was varnished and lovely. Sara's eyes slowly spanned the rest of the barn. Wood carvings were all over the place and mismatched furniture in various stages of completion were against the wall. She ran her hand over the edge of the table, "Did you make all this?"

"Kalen did."

Sara looked over at Eli, "This is incredible." She had a feeling Kalen had also made the table he'd broken inside as well as the replacement one.

Jack looked around, "It keeps him busy when he isn't fighting."

"Which is a good thing," Eli tacked on.

"Okay," Sara clapped her hands together, "Sooo, what are we doing in here?"

"Reflexes and hand-to-hand combat." Jack reached behind him and yanked off his charcoal grey Henley, tossing it onto the table. Why, oh, why did men have such a knack for making stripping out of a shirt so fucking sexy? "We want to see if your memory loss is limited to just events and people, or if it includes all the skills you've gained as a Hound."

"Sounds logical," Sara walked over to a cleared area where she saw targets nailed to the walls with tons of cut marks. More were nailed to the ceiling, because, yes, she knew first hand that the evil souls, the *malanum*, could climb walls like spiders if they wanted to.

Her back was turned to them but she heard the *shing* of metal fly through the air. Sara caught the small blade with her right hand without turning around.

"Good," Jack said. "Very good."

Sara spun around and slung the small blade at Eli. He moved a fraction to the left and let the dagger fly past him and nail a target on the wall. "Nice."

Okay, Sara was totally feeling badass.

During the five years she'd spent as a ghost with no name, Sara always had quick reflexes and killer aim. But she didn't have the right weapons to fight off what always chased her. These blades? Hell, if she'd had just one of them during her time alone, she'd have done so much more damage to those sneaky fuckers that hunted her. She was all too grateful to be back where she belonged, even if she didn't have her memories back yet.

If it came down to remembering a picnic at sunset or how to toss a quad blade without cutting her own fingers off, she'd choose the skill over the sandwich any fucking day.

Well, unless it was tuna. Man she loved tuna sandwiches.

Okay, okay, okay. Enough with the daydreaming, it was time to get down with the badassery.

Time, she might have to make new memories. But time she didn't have, if she was going to be a true Hound again and go hunting. And make no mistake, Sara was plenty eager to get back out there and toss those bastards that haunted her day and night right back to Hell where they belonged.

After a few more rounds of slinging blades, they moved on. Now, Eli was pulling out mats for hand-to-hand combat exercises.

114

Sara braced on bare feet, no longer cold with the way her blood was pumping. "Can I ask you a question?"

"Shoot," Jack encouraged.

"Were any of you with me the day I died?"

The two men looked at each other before Jack eased out of his fight stance. "Yeah," he glanced at Eli again, "Kalen was."

"So, does he know how I died?"

"No," Eli stepped onto the mat, "You two were in New Orleans together. Just the two of you. The rest of us had to stay back to hunt here."

"Well then surely he knows what happened to me, right?"

Jack swallowed and she noticed he wouldn't look at her. "He called us and said you'd gone missing. That was it. You just... vanished, Sara."

"We called in all the Hounds. Everyone went on a hunt for you."

"But everyone came back empty handed." Jack's eyes became vacant, as if he was reliving the moment he got the call from Kalen saying she was gone.

"Kalen doesn't speak about it, at all." Eli moved closer to her.

She reached out instinctively and grabbed Eli's arm. "Well I'm found now. You don't have to worry."

No one's smile reached their eyes. Eli looked like a deflated balloon, Jack looked like he was still seeing ghosts, and Sara? Well, Sara had a thought pop into her head that she seriously didn't want to say out loud. For the rest of the day she couldn't shake it off, either.

Was Kalen the one who killed her?

CHAPTER 23

They spent the next seven hours either pairing up or combating two-on-one. By the end of the day, Sara was ready for a cold beer and warm bed. Waltzing in through the back door, they ran into Tanner. Guess Kalen was either out hunting still or avoiding them in some other way. Sara didn't even want to ask.

"Hey, Beautiful," Tanner leaned in and kissed her. No tongues or heavy petting, just a simple Honey I'm home kiss. "I'm thinking of ordering Thai for dinner. That sound good to you?"

Jack laughed, "Take him up on it, love, he's a horrible cook."

"But…" her brow furrowed, "how will we get delivery? Don't you need to go through that black portal thingy to get here? And what about the grid?"

Jack shook his head, "The portals are only shortcuts for Hounds to use when traveling across the country. It saves us time, but aren't necessary. And we're back on grid, love, so anyone can come here."

"Oh," she said slowly. There was still so much to relearn… damnit.

"Soooo, are we getting Thai or what, Beautiful?" Tanner's smile was insanely big. It literally brightened the room.

"Thai sounds good," she nodded.

"Awesome, then we can veg out and binge watch some

shows."

Oh man did that sound amazing. After her long day, Sara was too tired for much else anyways. "What do you all want to order?"

"We've got to take the next shift, love. It's just you and Tanner tonight." Jack and Eli kissed the sides of her neck and left the kitchen.

God, was it seriously this easy to be with all of them?

It was only her second, no, wait, *third* night now in a house with four men and they all moved like a well-oiled machine together. Like the daily comings and goings were effortless.

Still felt surreal though.

"You're both going out? *Now?*" Sara's concern was written all over her face. She was dog tired and figured they must have been too. And now they were going out to hunt for the night? That seemed risky. They should rest up. Eat something, at least.

Jack and Eli brushed her concerns off and headed out. "No rest for the wicked, love, so there's no rest for us either. See you in a few hours."

Distracting her, Tanner grabbed a take-out menu and opened it up on the counter for her to choose what she wanted for dinner. As encouragement, he said, "I'm getting a number four, six, two eights and a seventeen. What are you gonna have?"

Sara's eyebrows popped up, "You're eating all that yourself?"

"Well, I'm trying to keep a slim figure, Beautiful. Otherwise I'd also order two fourteens and possibly a twenty," he leaned in and looked at the menu, "Yeah. Definitely the twenty."

Holy Hell. Tanner wasn't a Hound, he was an eating machine. Sara bit her lip to keep from busting out laughing. "I'll take the twenty and you can have some. And the six. Plus..." she ran her hand down the menu and tapped over a picture, "two of these, please."

"Atta girl. Fuck, I love your voracious appetite."

She blushed. It just couldn't be helped.

He pulled his cell out and jerked his head towards the doorway, "I'll order, you go shower and get something comfy on."

"No way," Sara argued. Tanner had black guck and sweat and grime all over him. Certainly, he would want to clean up before she did? He looked way worse than her. Blood, grease, black gunk, sweat – he had a lot going on. What the hell did he do out in the field tonight? Wrestle *malanum* in a mud pit? Tar and feather a few of them before tossing them back into Hell? And where was Kalen? Was he still out there, fighting… on his own? Sara's heart sped up. "What about Kalen?"

She wasn't sure if she was ready to run into him again so soon after her little niggling feeling about what might have happened in New Orleans. But she also couldn't help herself from worrying about him, too. It just felt like a natural thing to do.

"He's staying out," Tanner shrugged, "Won't be back till dawn, I expect."

"Was he always like this?"

"No," Tanner left it at that. "Go on," he smacked her ass.

"I'm not showering before you," she glared.

The two of them had a stare down.

Thirty five minutes later, there was a knock on the door. Tanner was upstairs – because yes, she won the staring contest and he took a shower first - and he flew down the steps in a pair of sweats, no shirt, and his hair still dripping wet. "Fuck! Coming!"

Tanner loved the word fuck. He said it way too often for it to not be his favorite word.

Sara didn't have a chance to get the door, Tanner beat her to it and paid for the delivery.

She crossed her arms, "I could have gotten the door, Tanner."

"Nope. Not on my watch." He was being protective of her. They all were. Part of her loved that they cared so much, the other part still couldn't figure it out. She watched Tanner's muscles bunch up as he took all the bags and paid, and she had a great view of his sculpted back and ass – Tanner's, not the Thai Delivery Dude's.

Damn, but those tattoos going down his spine were wild looking. They were some kind of series of symbols or odd lettering that she couldn't translate. Beautiful, though. They matched the tattoos on Jack's back, she realized. Before Sara could get a closer look, Tanner spun around to place the bags of food on the hand-carved coffee table.

Oh dear lord, his nipples were pierced. How had she not noticed that before?

"Looks delicious," she said, maneuvering around the couch to have a seat. Annnnd she definitely wasn't talking about the food.

The two of them made quick work of pulling out all the

containers and diving into their dinner. Working all day had been fun, but exhausting. Earlier, Sara stayed too busy with her Hounds to even notice they skipped lunch. That too-busy-to-eat nonsense turned into if-I-don't-eat-something-immediately-I'm-going-gnaw-my-arm-off starvation. Opening a third container, she grabbed her fork and dove in. This stuff smelled amazing. And was that... Yes! Fresh chopped cilantro! Sara shoved a forkful of noodles into her mouth and groaned with happiness.

"What do you want to watch first, Beautiful? I thought you might want to catch up where we left off on Game of Thrones, which has only gotten more fucking ridiculously awesome."

"Oh I KNOW! Can you believe how the last season ended?"

"Wait, you watched it?"

"Mmm hmmm," she said around a mouthful of vegetable pad Thai, "Fucking Little Finger."

Tanner's face fell, "How did you watch it?"

Okay, why was he upset over this? "I watched them in some woman's house in Georgia when I was travelling. Took her six days to get through them all and then I caught the last season in an apartment in Virginia. Totally worth haunting that old bitty with sixteen cats to watch it, too. I can't wait to see where the story goes next."

Tanner's container rested in his lap. "You... travelled?"

Sara shrugged and took two more big bites of food. Jeez this stuff was delicious. "I woke up dead in New Orleans and didn't stick around. Way too much was going on there. And something kept yanking on me. Something in my gut said to keep moving. So I did. And I didn't stop until I landed here."

"And then what did you feel?"

"Better?" no that wasn't quite right, "I mean, I was still restless, but I knew to stop running."

"What were you running from, Sara?"

Hell if she knew but she figured it was "The souls chasing me all the time, I guess. Not that it was any better here since they still hunted me."

Tanner put his food back on the table. Next, he took the container out of Sara's hands and placed it on the table too. He even took her fork. Before she could protest and snatch her dinner back, Tanner scooped her up and put her in his lap. "I can't believe you've been alone all this time. How did we not find you?"

"Jack said you all had a hunt for me."

"We did."

She gulped, not knowing why she was even asking this but, "When did you stop looking for me?"

Tanner ran his finger down her jaw line, his eyes softening. "Who said we ever stopped?"

With one hand massaging the back of her head, the other spanning across her lower back, Tanner kissed her nice and slow. It was the kind of kiss that started soft and sweet and built momentum until they were nothing but greedy, needy beings on the sofa.

"Fuck, Sara." He pressed his forehead to hers, "This doesn't feel real."

"Tell me about it." Nothing about anything felt real lately.

Tanner ran his hands up and down her back, and she felt him press lightly on her spine, much in the same way Jack had before. A cool trail of *something* trickled down her vertebrae. He buried his face in the crook of her neck and started nibbling the spot just under her ear.

"You and Jack have the same tattoos."

"Mmm hmm," he licked up her throat and nipped her chin. "We all have them."

"Do I?"

"You did." He started massaging one breast with his hand. "You don't now though."

Fuck, with him touching her this way, it was getting difficult to string two words together, much less have a coherent thought. "Where," *fuuuck*, "Why..." *Holy hell, that feels good*, "Why don't I have them anymore?"

Tanner pulled his mouth off her breast and began to run his hands up and down her sides again, "We were hoping that was something you'd be able to remember."

"Do the tats mean something?"

"Oh yeah," he kissed her neck again, "They're real important."

"Tanner," she whacked him on the top of the head to make him stop, "What do they do?"

He pulled back and met her level stare with one of his own.

120

"They're our brands. They bind us as one. If someone was in trouble, we'd feel it down our spines and instinctively know who it was that needed our help."

"And I had them?"

"Yes."

"Then how did they go away?"

"I'm guessing probably the same way it was put on you, to be honest." When she cocked an eyebrow he shrugged, "Dark magic."

"Dark. Magic. Like some kind of what, bad juju shit?"

Tanner laughed, his head tilting back, "God no. Lucifer would be so pissed if we tried to cross those lines. No, Beautiful, these tats were something Lucifer gave us when our pack was made. When it became whole."

"So how do I get mine back? How do I become one with the pack again?"

"It's not going to be easy." Tanner sighed and leaned back, "and it kills me that yours are gone."

"So help me get them back!"

"I can't. Getting them back is all on you."

"What the fuck does that mean?"

"Trust, Sara. You have to trust every single one of us."

"I do!" she shrieked.

Tanner lifted her off his lap and put space between them. "You don't. Not yet."

"Well I must! Here I am," she waved her jazz hands at him. "I'm literally living in a house with the four of you."

"Yeah, the four of us whom you can't remember, so how are you supposed to trust us?"

She bit back her rebuttal because he had a point. She was going about this whole thing moment by moment with more questions than answers. And all because they had done things sexually with each other didn't mean she trusted them. She lusted them. That most certainly included the breakfast/kitchen table situation earlier and her sexcapades with Jack. If she was going to be honest, her sexual appetite had more to do with filling herself with something she needed.

What had she needed? *Them.* The answer was a gonging bell in her bones. She needed *them.* Her pack. Her Hounds…

But need and trust weren't the same, were they?

"You have to trust us with more than your life, Sara. You have to trust us with your soul." Tanner leaned forward and tucked a stray piece of hair behind her ear. "Love only goes so far. Without trust, love dies out. Everything can fade away and burn to hate and resentment when trust is broken."

"What happens if I don't get my tattoos back?"

"You'll stay vulnerable. There's no way we're gonna let you out of our sight until your tats are back. Someone will always have to be with you until you trust us again. And that could take a while."

Sara slumped back on the couch and crossed her arms. She was getting a raging headache.

"Hey," Tanner knelt down in front of her, "This isn't a race, Sara. We love you, and deep down, you love us. Once you get your memories back, when things begin to snap back into place for you, I'm sure your tats will reappear. You'll see. It's just going to take time."

"Time we might not have."

"What does that mean?"

She shut her trap. She didn't know what she was talking about, it just slipped out. Something told Sara that time was of the essence, but that might just be her impatience talking. "It means nothing, let's just watch a show."

Tanner rocked back and glared at her. "Fine."

"Fine."

He scooped her up and threw her over his shoulder. "We'll watch a show after I give you a bath and wash your hair. I can't believe you made me take a shower before you tonight. Not cool, Beautiful. Not. Cool."

Sara kicked and hit his back, playfully. "You stunk like a pig! And you had black gunk all over you!"

"And you think you smell like roses after sparring all day?" He cracked her ass with his big hand and got a squeak out of her.

"I don't stink!"

"Didn't say you did."

"And I don't sweat, I glisten!"

Tanner rumbled in laughter, "Don't I know it, Beautiful. Don't I fucking know it."

122

CHAPTER 24

Kalen's boots pounded the concrete. The air in his lungs felt like frozen razor blades. Two *malanum* were just ahead of him, moving effortlessly through the alleyway. He felt, before he saw, Jack and Eli at the other end. Like wolves, they surrounded their prey and closed in.

Eli's blade gleamed under the street light and Jack's teeth were a lovely pearly white as he smiled greedily and snarled at their targets.

The souls hissed and screeched. They were so old they'd lost their function to talk all together. Now they were both mindless violence and mayhem trapped in a warped-once-was-human soul.

Pity, really. It was souls like these that made it hard to decipher if they had escaped Hell or been infected because they stayed around too long and became contaminated by another dark spirit.

Kalen jerked his head to the right and moved left, just as Jack came straight ahead and Eli brought up the rear. They cornered the two *malanum* against a wall. Eli switched into true Hound form – a spirit himself, in a sense - and he scaled the wall, waiting for the next move.

Jack snarled like an animal and lunged for the one on the left,

Kalen took the one on the right, while Eli opened up a Hell hole in the brick wall. They made quick work of immobilizing their prey and tossing them back to Hell.

Like stabbing fish in a bucket, that's what Sara would have said. *Oh God*, Kalen braced his body against the wall, *Sara*.

All day and all night he'd done nothing but run himself ragged in an effort to shake her off his mind. And just like the real deal, the Sara in his head clung to him like Velcro.

"You need to go home, Kalen." Jack's voice broke through the fuzz in Kalen's brain.

"I'm fine."

"Then be fine at home. You need to rest, Hound. You aren't doing us any favors running yourself into the ground like this."

"I can't."

"You can and you will," Jack grabbed Kalen by the neck and snarled. "Lucifer gave us time off to be with Sara and fix what's broken. You have no business out here."

"And yet here you are, and Tanner before you. Scouring and hunting." Kalen jerked out of Jack's grip and tucked his knife back where it belonged.

Eli stepped between the two, "You're going to have to face her sooner or later, Kalen."

"I'll take later, then." No way was he going back to the farm to sit across from her at the dinner table and pass around the mashed potatoes and laugh at jokes and feel her vibes sink into him with the look she always used to save for Kalen and Kalen only.

Ohhhh they had history alright. An incredibly long history...

"I can't," Kalen's voice cracked and he hated that his weakness was showing. "We're all doing our part in our own ways, okay? Even Tanner came out here earlier to hunt. He didn't care that Luce gave us time off. And since when the fuck did Satan ever grant us vacation time?"

The *malanum* had been thick in the area for over a month as it was. Now wasn't the time to slack off, it was the time to reinforce, put in some overtime.

"He has a point, Jack." Thank fuck Eli was leaning more towards Kalen's thinking. "The malanum are thick as ever around here. We can't just drop our duties. Besides, it's not just the city that needs our protection now, Sara does too. We need to eliminate as

124

many *malanum* as possible in the area. It's not just population control anymore, we need to eradicate all we can for Sara's sake. At least until she gets right again."

"Fine," Jack growled. "Hunt every day if you wish." He grabbed Kalen's shoulder and spun him around, practically frog marching his ass out of the ally, "but you will do it in twelve hour rotations. You're about ready to drop, Kalen. We can't lose a Hound. And Sara can't lose you now; she's suffered enough as it is."

Suffered? SUFFERED? Kalen's anger roared like electric fire in his veins. *She* suffered?

"How do you think it'll go if we lose you just when we've gotten our girl back?" Jack kept shoving him forward. And, well, Jack man-handling Kalen was probably a good thing. It was most likely the only way Kalen was going to get anywhere. Between exhaustion, fury, and fear, his damn legs were useless now.

"She's better off without me," Kalen whispered in a low voice.

Jack shoved him against the wall and snarled. "Don't you fucking go there, Kalen."

"I'm already there, Jack."

Too numbed out, Kalen didn't even register the fact that he was being shoved into the back of Jack's Camaro until the engine roared to life. Guess his motorcycle parked six blocks over would have to stay put for now. Someone could pick it up later... or they could have it towed home. He was too tired to give a shit.

Leaning his head against the window, it took all of ten seconds for exhaustion to sweep Kalen into darkness. Guess sleep was going to be his only escape... for now.

Sara had definitely died and this was definitely Heaven. She sat in a bathtub, hot water steaming up the place, while Tanner shampooed her hair. It should not feel this good to have a man's hands massage her scalp the way he was right now. Something this amazing would soon lead to an addiction. Pretty sure her arms were already going on strike, refusing to ever wash her own hair again after tonight.

"How did we meet?" she said, breaking their comfortable silence.

"In Hell."

Oh. Well, that wasn't quite the answer she was hoping for.

"I died after murdering my stepfather."

Careful to not react too much to his confession, Sara just nodded her head and kept her eyes closed, hoping he continued talking with that incredibly deep voice of his.

"He beat my mom a lot."

Her heart clenched. "I'm sorry."

"Don't be, it wasn't your fault. My mom had the worst taste in men. My dad was a fucking bastard, and, after he died, she up and married another asshole who treated her like a piece of shit. I never understood it." *Rub, rub, rub, massage the scalp, suds the hair.*

"I always carried guilt with me for leaving the house once I turned eighteen. I didn't want to leave her alone with him, but didn't want to stay there, either. No matter how many times I asked her to, she wouldn't leave him. I have no idea why. Even after I offered to move her out of state and get her a fake I.D. and promised we could start a new life as new people, she refused. So I kept close. I got my own place, started a job at a tattoo shop in town." Tanner continued to slowly massage her scalp. Then his hands stopped moving all together.

"One day the phone rang at the shop and I answered it." Silence engulfed the room. Tanner cleared his throat, "My mom was on the other end. I couldn't make out anything other than her saying my name and this... gurgling noise." He dunked his hands underwater to rinse them. "I raced home and blew every red light along the way. But I was too late. I ran into the house and saw her lying face down in her own blood and piss, the phone still in her hand. My stepfather came up behind me with a crow bar. Guess he figured the damn thing did a good job on my mom so he'd use it on me next. He was drunk and crazed."

Tanner began rinsing Sara's hair and stayed quiet for a little while. She didn't push him either. This was such a painful story, if he didn't want to speak more on it, she wasn't going to make him. God, she was regretting ever having asked now. After rinsing her long hair out, he continued to sit on the side of the tub and stare at the floor.

126

"We went blow for blow. He cracked my skull in two places before I was able to disarm him and turn the tables. I saw red. Started swinging. We made it into the kitchen and destroyed it in our attempts to kill each other. Everything started getting wobbly. Then he pulled a gun out from the top of the fridge. I didn't even know he had one there. He shot me in the stomach just as I tackled him to the ground. I snatched the gun from him. My only mission was to kill him before I died."

"Did you?"

Tanner sighed, "I shot him in the face."

"Oh God," Sara turned around to look at him. Holy Hell, she seriously wished she hadn't asked for this story. It was obvious this was difficult for him to talk about.

"My last thought before dying was at least he'd rot in Hell and my mother was at peace. No one was going to beat her and treat her cruelly in Heaven."

Sara pulled him close to her. "I'm so sorry you had to go through that."

"S'all good, Beautiful. In the end it worked out, right?"

"Did it?"

"Fuck yeah. I laid there dying and the next thing I knew, I was someplace else and Lucifer was offering me a deal. 'Be a Hound,' he said, 'live forever, and protect the living from evil.' I didn't have to think about it. I'd just done that very thing killing my stepfather. I might not have saved my mom from his evil ass, but I know I saved someone else who would eventually become his next victim. If the Devil was offering to give me an eternity to do something similar, I was damn sure gonna take it."

"Was I there, too?"

"Not at first," he started working on conditioning her hair. "Lucifer brought me into another room and that's when I first saw you. You were waiting for Luce, angrily throwing blades against one of his precious paintings." Tanner's laugh bubbled out of him and he rinsed her hair again. "I thought for a second maybe he wasn't the Big D and you were. You seemed to own that place, Sara. And when Lucifer gave you hell for destroying his painting, you rolled your eyes and tossed your knife one more time into the canvas just before you shred it to ribbons. Then you saw me and raised your hand slowly until you were pointing right at some invisible bullseye on my chest and you said, 'That one'." Tanner grabbed a towel from the linen closet and helped Sara stand. "I was your Hound right then and there."

Sara stepped out of the tub and wrapped herself in the soft terry cloth. "You don't regret it?"

"Why the fuck would I?"

"Because it sounds like you didn't really have a choice. I just demanded you be in the pack and you had no say."

Tanner pulled the plug on the tub and looked up from where he was sitting. "Beautiful, you were worth dying and going to Hell for. I didn't need to make a choice. One look at you and I was a goner."

"Love at first sight?"

"Nahhh, love came later. I just seriously wanted to fuck your brains out on top of that shredded painting." Tanner cracked a laugh so loud she felt it in her bones. "Watching you piss the Devil off, to this day, is the hottest thing I've ever seen."

Before she could figure out if he was joking or not, Tanner kissed the hell out of her and she forgot all about asking anything else.

A door slammed shut and there was shouting down below, in the kitchen. Tanner broke away from her and he rushed out the door. Sara scrambled for something to wear, grabbed a shirt from the hamper, and put it on. It was Eli's shirt. How she knew that, she couldn't tell you, but it was definitely Eli's.

"Open his door," Jack barked as he and Eli practically dragged a half-conscious Kalen up the steps.

"Oh my God," Sara whispered, "What happened to him?"

"Nothing that wasn't self-inflicted," Eli said.

Tanner opened the bedroom door and the Hounds got Kalen into his room. Sara didn't have the nerve to move forward. Her feet were glued to the hallway floor and she just stared at Kalen's door.

Moments later, Jack, Eli and Tanner came out and shut the door with a *snick*.

"What's going on?" she asked, heart hammering.

"It's what he does," Eli began escorting her down the steps. "Kalen doesn't like to sleep, so he pushes himself into an exhaustion so fierce his body is forced to shut down."

"Why?"

They all looked at one another, then Eli shrugged, "It's just how it is with him."

Sara knew they were keeping something from her and she grew angry. "You talk of trust and yet you don't give me any."

"What the bloody hell?" Jack scowled. "No one's telling lies, Sara."

"Yeah, but you're deliberately watching your words. All of you."

"No we're—"

"Save it," she shoved her hand up in the air to silence them. Then she stalked down the steps and landed in the living room. Yanking a blanket off the chair in the corner, she curled up on the couch with her face stuffed into the cushion. She was dog tired and pissed off and had no place to run.

The couch dipped down by her feet and Tanner rubbed her leg, "Sleep in one of our beds, Sara."

"No. Thank you."

"We won't sleep in it with you. One of us will take the couch."

"I said No. Thank. You." She didn't want to be in a bed that smelled like one of them. It would have been too much for her. All their belongings and memories on display for her to study, the desire to dig around, search for clues to help her clear the fog in her brain would drive her bonkers. The desperate need to find something that would truly link her to them was already doing a job on her. If she was to lie in one of their beds now, she'd never sleep.

The sofa was at least neutral territory.

Besides, it was bad enough that her gut was saying this was where she belonged, especially when it all felt foreign and strange to her still. Add to that her lusty needs and the smell of their skin and the feel of their hands and she had no damn sense left in her. Any bed was a bad fucking idea.

"Come on," Jack huffed. "Leave her be. It's been a long fucking weekend for all of us."

After the Hounds left her alone, Sara clung to the blanket and cried herself to sleep.

CHAPTER 25

Some kind of terrible animalistic screech woke Sara. It was pitch black in the house and—

There it was again. A noise so devastating, it chilled her bones. Immediately, Sara perked up, alert and paranoid.

The animal made the noise again.

Sara popped to her feet and searched for a weapon. Footsteps started pounding down the hallway above her and she took the steps two at a time. All bedroom doors were wide open and she felt like the hallway stretched for ten miles.

"Fuck! Grab his arms!"

"Get his legs!"

"Bloody Hell."

Sara slowly made her way down the hall. Past the bathroom and Jack's room. Past Tanner's room. Past Eli's. She stopped in Kalen's doorway just as another sonic roar boomed its way through her body.

"Oh my God," she whispered, clutching the door jamb.

Kalen was the animal screaming. Back arched, he fought and yelled as he tried to kick his legs free from Jack and Tanner who were struggling to hold him down. Eli was straddling Kalen's torso, pinning his arms down. Kalen's eyes were wide open, as another horrible scream ripped its way out of his throat.

"It's not real. It's not real," Eli chanted. "See me, Kalen. Know where you are."

Kalen ripped one leg free and kicked Jack in the mouth as he screamed again.

"FUCK!" Eli barked as he lost his hold on Kalen's left arm. With a tremendous amount of strength, they managed to pin him down again. "Kalen! It's not real!" Eli yelled. "Wake up! WAKE THE FUCK UP!"

He was dreaming with his eyes wide open. Kalen was nothing more than a possessed man in desperate need of escaping a hell no one but him could see. Sara's entire body froze as she watched in horror.

"SARA!" Kalen roared her name like it was the last word he'd ever fucking say. "SSSSSSSAAAAARRRRAAAAAA!"

She almost fell to her knees. No man should scream like that. Nothing on this earth should ever scream like that. Sara moved into the room but she hadn't realized it until she was at the side of Kalen's bed.

"It's not real. It's not real." Eli kept saying. Then he turned to Sara and the look he gave her said, *Help us.*

Automatically, Sara placed her hand on Kalen's chest, right on the tattoo of her goddamn name over his goddamned heart. She was going to remember this moment for the rest of her life. "I'm here," she said.

"I'm here."

The memory came slowly… soooo slowly….

"Let go, Kalen. Be with me."

"Let go, Kalen. Be with me." She repeated the words she remembered saying once - long, long ago.

"Sara!" he yelled again. This time it was emphasized with a harsh cry.

She kept her one hand on his chest and used the other to grab one of his hands. "I'm here, I'm right here."

"Let go, Kalen. Be with me."

She looked at their clasped hands and saw red. *Blood dripped down and the world was dark and cold and miserable and –*

Sara blinked and there was no blood at all. Just two hands clinging to each other.

Kalen's body began to relax. He stopped kicking, stopped screaming. His unseeing eyes closed again. "Sara," he called out, only now his voice box was shredded and it sounded like another kind of pain. "Sara... run."

"There's no more running."

"There's no more running," she repeated from her memory.

Kalen let out one more ragged cry and stilled. His body went slack and his breathing grew more even and steady.

Sara looked up at the painting above Kalen's bed. It was all dark shadows and trees at night. In the middle of the black forest was a wolf with long, sharp teeth. The animal's head was down, ready to attack. Next to the wild animal was an impish looking thing with the same hair and eyes as Sara. The woman's fingers were buried deep into the wolf's fur, clutching him fiercely, and they both stared out of the painting with looks that said, "Try us if you dare."

"Bloody. Fucking. Hell." Jack leaned against the foot of the bed and tried to catch his breath. "Do you remember him?"

"Almost." Sara kept her eyes on the painting and tried to summon the rest of the memory that was on the verge of revealing itself. "Almost."

The four Hounds left Kalen to sleep and headed down stairs, into the kitchen. On the way, Tanner slipped into his bedroom real quick and snatched a shirt for himself and a pair of pants for Sara.

"Here," he tossed her his black sweatpants that were way too big and she shimmied into them while Tanner put on a shirt that said, *I would cuddle you so hard.*

Once in the kitchen, Eli got coffee brewing and Jack dropped into a chair. "You can take one of our beds, love. None of us are sleeping after that."

As if *she* could? There was no curling up and going nighty-night after hearing those screams. Shit, Sara doubted she would ever sleep again after tonight. Slumping down in a chair, she buried her head in her hands and tried to focus on that memory. No matter how hard she tried to snatch the damn thing, it eluded her. It was like catching fog with a butterfly net.

"Tell me what just happened up there." She wasn't asking. She was demanding. "And before you all go looking at each other to see who's gonna speak up, I want to hear a piece of it from each of you until the whole fucking story is out."

Eli and Tanner brought over the coffee mugs, cream and sugar, and then sat down, too.

"Jack. You start." Sara crossed her arms over her chest and didn't accept her coffee. "Why did he scream my name like that?"

"Why do you think?"

"NO!" she slammed her fist down on the table. "I'm tired guys. I'm tired of running. Tired of fighting. Tired of trying. Tired of failing to remember. Tired of everything right now. Just answer me with the truth. Why did he scream MY name?"

"Why. Do. You. Think." Jack's eyes bore into hers to the point she thought he was going to burn a hole through her damned skull.

"I... think..." she focused on Jack's glare, "I think he helped me somehow."

"Yes, he did." Jack reached for his black coffee. "He was there when you died."

"Which time?"

"Both." The three men said in unison.

"Tell me about the first one," Sara waited for someone to speak.

Eli dropped two sugars into his coffee and stirred it slowly. "Your village was under attack. Kalen used himself as bait to keep your enemy focused on him so you'd have a chance to escape."

Sara swallowed the grapefruit sized lump in her throat.

"Only it didn't work and he didn't know it," Tanner added.

Jack shifted in his seat, "Kalen was used to draw you out. They gutted him, quartered him, and tortured him in ways you can't imagine. All the while, keeping him alive, just barely, hoping to call you out from hiding."

Sara felt numb.

"They pulled him apart, piece by piece." Eli sighed, "Every time they asked him a question about where you were, he wouldn't answer and they'd take another pound of flesh off him."

"Literally," Tanner added.

"He sacrificed himself so you could run," Jack's eyes were still

133

drilling into hers. "So you'd have a shot at escaping."

"*Sara... run!*" Kalen's voice echoed in her head.

"They kept him alive for three days. Just meat on a stone slab." Jack just kept fucking staring at her. "He didn't know you'd already been caught. None of them did."

"Oh god," Sara whispered.

"He wouldn't die. If he did, they'd abandon him and hunt you down and kill you, so Kalen kept clinging to life, no matter how much it hurt, so you'd have a chance to escape."

Tears fell freely down her face. Her hands shook. She couldn't swallow.

"And then he heard you," Eli's voice was soft and deep, "He heard you say, 'I'm here.'"

"Let go, Kalen. Be with me." She repeated the words she remembered saying.

"You're the reason he's a Hound. And he's the reason you're a Hound." Tanner dumped extra cream in his coffee and stared at the mug intently while he stirred. "You followed each other straight into Hell."

She didn't know what to say. She didn't know...

"He never sleeps." Eli sliced through the dreaded silence. "He's always been like that. When he does, he's stuck on repeat in the last moments of his life before turning into a Hound."

"He must hate me," she whispered. Again, she looked at the table and thought of the one he'd cracked when he first saw her. It was the only reason she could think of that would make him so volatile when he saw her.

"How could you think that?" Jack leaned forward. "He'd never hate you, Sara."

"If it weren't for me, he never would have died that way." She swiped her cheeks again. Kalen's death was on her hands. "Wait. You said he was there *both* times I died?"

"He was with you in New Orleans," Tanner got up and grabbed a napkin for Sara. "Here, your face is leaking."

"Thanks," she began mopping up her tears. "What happened in New Orleans?"

"We don't know." They all said together.

Maybe... just maybe... Kalen had taken revenge on her there. Killed her, stripped her of her tats and left her there to rot.

She wouldn't blame him one bit if he had. To suffer, every time he slept, for all eternity and all because of her? Sara shivered. She'd caused him to break like that. Her freedom from whenever they were both alive the first time around had cost him an eternity of nightmares she couldn't even begin to fathom.

And the worst part was she felt like she died all over again hearing him scream her name just now. "He needs help," she whispered.

"He needs *you*, Beautiful."

She tucked her legs under her ass as if trying to be as small physically as she felt spiritually at the moment. "Why would he do that? Why... why would anyone do that? Let themselves hurt so badly, let someone torture them beyond repair just to hope to give another person a chance at life?"

Tanner chuckled, "What wouldn't we do for the one we love, Sara?"

Jack's voice was soft, "It was his choice, love."

"And he's never regretted it." Eli deadpanned her.

Sara looked down and stared at her hands. God, she would have sworn there was blood dripping all over them. Closing her eyes, she saw the entire story play out – the memory settled over her like a sheet draped over an antique piece of furniture...

"Sara!"

"I'm here."

Kalen's body jolted and jerked as they removed another organ. They cracked open his ribs, pulled out a lung. Blood spilled out of his mouth. He only had one arm left, his other limbs had been tossed into the far corner of the room. They tied the stumps to constrict blood flow just long enough to keep him from dying too fast. So much blood. So much gore. So much pain.

"Tell us where she is and it all ends."

"Sara!" His voice remained the last thing intact because it sure wasn't his mind or his body anymore. "SSSSSAAAAARRRRAAAA!"

"I'm here. I'm here." She grabbed Kalen's remaining hand and squeezed while she placed the other over his opened chest. They'd flayed him – his ribs, heart, intestines were all exposed. "Let go, Kalen. Be with me."

He looked over, his eyes moving slowly until they made contact with hers. "Sara."

"Let go, Kalen." She squeezed his hand tighter, "Be with me."

"Sara," Kalen's mouth turned up just a fraction at the corners as he exhaled his last breath.

The memory faded into mist on that sad note. Sara shot up from the table and puked in the sink.

CHAPTER 26

Kalen wasn't going to wake up for a while; they'd all told her that. Feeling trapped in a house with men who were equal parts familiar and foreign to her, Sara didn't know what to do.

Dressed in a pair of tube socks hiked up past her knees, cotton short-shorts, and a black hoodie, she pace, pace, paced. Her hair tied into a messy bun, she was currently listening to music Tanner uploaded onto his phone. The headphones did wonders to block out the world so she could focus.

Sara loved every single track that played. The songs stirred things inside her. Emotions, echoes. The playlist was carefully selected, Tanner said, but he didn't tell her anything past that.

Hours. Hours she spent listening to the songs.

At some point in the afternoon, Jack leaned against the wall and said something she couldn't hear. Yanking the headphones off she asked for a repeat, "What?"

"I said you're going to wear a hole in the floor if you keep this up much longer." He strolled over to the couch and took a seat, patting the cushion next to his.

Warily, she complied and sat beside him.

"Have you remembered anything, love?"

She shook her head.

Sighing, Jack grabbed both her feet and placed them on his lap. Then he began to massage them and she practically purred with how good it felt.

"I don't want to wait for things to fall back into place for me, Jack. I want to be what I was. I want to know what happened. And why." She wasn't sure if this unknowing bullshit was better or worse than being dead and unseen. Both made her feel so empty. To have had a life – and from the looks of it a damned good one – and have no recollection of it made her emptiness feel a thousand times worse. It was like she was wasting a good thing. Letting her blank mind hold her back from enjoying her second, or was that now *third* chance, at life.

She wanted to talk with Kalen. If her life started and ended with him, then he would be the best source to go to. But there was no way in hell she was going to wake him up.

Jack continued to massage her feet. He was purposefully not looking at her. Instead, he focused on her ankles.

"How did we meet, Jack?"

His hands slowed for a couple seconds, then picked back up the relaxing rhythm again. "I lived in London and was the eldest of seven boys. My father got into debt with the British firms, gambling."

"Like the mafia?"

"Mmm hmmm." He rubbed the soles of her feet harder, "My mother flipped out and left him. Left us, too – me and my brothers. My father's debt was beyond that of currency by then and these thugs threatened to kill us, one-by-one, if he didn't do as they said and work off his debt in a more… how do I say it?"

"Without filters?"

"They wanted my father to be a hit man. Kill, without question." Jack moved his hands from her left foot to her right foot. "My father was an excellent shot and a damned good fighter. He was strong, skilled, and had a moral compass that barely worked on his best of days. He was perfect for the job."

She waited for Jack to continue and melted more and more under his seriously dynamite foot rub.

"He refused to do it. Said he would fight in the underground clubs, which was how he'd lost all his money to begin with, but he wouldn't kill just to kill. Fighting to the death in the ring and killing

138

outright were different for him."

"Not you?"

Jack's smile was wicked and hot as fuck. "I eventually learned there was a fine line between the two." He went back to focusing on her feet. "They ignored both his refusal and his offer and put my father into service for them immediately. His first mark was a woman and her two small children."

"Why?"

"Her husband killed himself to get out of paying his debt. Guess he figured his family would be left alone since the debt was owed by him and only him. That wasn't the case, though. Once you got involved with those guys, it became a family affair. So, if the husband took the easy way out, they still made an example of those left behind. My father was in the same boat. There was no easy way out for us either."

"What happened?"

"When my father refused to do it, they killed one of my brothers. He was seven."

Sara stilled, her gut clenching.

"My father had a heart attack when he walked in and saw Sam dangling from our balcony for all of London to see."

"Oh my God, Jack."

"We buried them both on the same day and then I went after them. Offered to be the assassin they wanted my father to be. I worked my way into their trusted circle. Became the go-to guy for any deeds too dirty for the rest of them. I lost my humanity at some point. I just... turned it off like a light switch." He went back to massaging her other foot as if to keep his hands busy as he poured out his confession. "I would become the monster they needed so long as it kept my brothers safe and alive. I didn't care if it cost me my soul. And if ever I found myself hesitating, all I had to do was close my eyes and see Sam swinging from that rope and I found my purpose again."

"Your purpose?"

"I wanted justice. Though I never wanted to kill an innocent to get it. After I'd accept a new hit job, I did my homework on the target, studied their habits, their families, everything I needed to know about them to get the job done. Never did I follow through with killing a single person I was told to. Instead, I set up ways to get them out of harm's reach. I'd fake their deaths - even if it meant paying off the crypt keepers to steal cadavers to use as props. I always needed some kind of proof that the job was complete - a ring still attached to a finger, an eye, a severed dick. Something that would show the target suffered and got the message. Sometimes I needed a whole body."

Jack let go of her feet and leaned back, still not looking at her.

"Eventually they caught on to what I was doing. Someone had spotted a target who was supposed to be dead in Leeds, yet they were at a café in Paris – not dead. To teach me a lesson, the bastards went after my brother, Riley. I just happened to walk in while they were halfway through their handiwork and I saw red. It was like... I shut down and became a killing machine. I literally went in-fucking-sane."

Sara sat up straighter and waited.

"I didn't just beat them to a bloody pulp. I shredded them like an animal. And I couldn't stop. I couldn't see, couldn't hear, couldn't think. I just... killed." Jack scrubbed his face and his voice cracked with his next words, "I didn't even recognize that I'd killed them all until my brother shot me in the leg when I went after him next. It was like I was possessed, Sara. My only goal was to kill anything in the room that moved. So I just kept at it until nothing fucking moved anymore."

"Your *brother* shot you?"

Jack shrugged, "He was trying to slow me down. Get me to snap out of it. Or at least buy himself time to run out of there. I was too crazed to decipher who was on my side and who was my enemy. Everything was just... red."

"Jesus."

Jack sighed. "I think I had a second of clarity when I told Riley to run and then I lost my shit again. I got so bloody lost in my head, there was nothing but darkness in me at that point. I don't know how long I sat in the middle of the flat with all those dead bodies, but eventually I got up, set a match to the curtains and took a seat on the couch."

Sara's breath caught in her throat.

"I let the place go up in flames with me in it. I think I figured if I was that mad, I needed to be put out of my own misery. It had been a long time coming, really. But at least I'd taken out the bloody

140

bastards who'd been a constant threat to my family. My brothers would be safe, I'd be free, and my sins would be ashes."

Jack was quiet for a moment and then, "As my body burned it was agony unlike anything I've ever felt. And then," he snapped his fingers, "I was in Hell. Where I knew, damn well, I belonged."

She swallowed and continued to stare at him.

"And then there you were, love. Clapping like you'd watched the entire show with a bucket of popcorn. Lucifer came into the room and I thought I was still going insane because why else would I be hallucinating you – the most beautiful angel in the world – point right at me and say 'I want him.' Hell, my skin was still smoking from the fire I'd died in. And Lucifer, like a father doting over his baby girl, gave you just what you asked for. He brought me into a room, shoved me into the transformation fires, and I came out a Hound. I was yours from that day on."

Sara looked down at her hands, "So you went from one kind of killing service to another."

"One was hell, love. This is heaven."

"I don't see how."

"That's because you weren't in my Hell so you can't compare the two." Jack leaned in closer to her and smiled. "Life without you, Sara, was more painful than being burned alive. At least then I had breath to scream through my pain and death came swiftly. Living these past five years without you was like suffocating with no mercy in sight."

"And what about now?"

He moved in, his mouth getting closer and closer to hers. "Now, love, I'm breathless in an entirely different way." He slanted his lips to hers and she fell into his kiss effortlessly. He tasted sweet and divine and she wanted more, so more she took.

"Fuck, love." He began to nibble her earlobe, "We said we'd give you space, but you make it hard for a man to behave after he's been forced to bare his soul."

Jack dropped to his knees, swerved her body so it was half on the couch, half draped over his shoulders, and he began kissing up her inner thigh. "Jack," she sighed, shoving her hand into his short-cropped hair.

He tossed her another wicked smile and licked her inner thigh.

"I want you," she forced him to keep looking at her, "to take me to Hell."

He froze. *"Now?"*

"Yes."

Ohhhh the look on his face was adorable. He was almost pouting. "Fine."

He stood up and tried to tuck his enormous erection in a way that his pants didn't tent so obviously. With a grumble, he grabbed her hand and they headed to the basement.

"Thank you," she said as he unlocked the door.

"For what?"

"Everything." She kissed him good and hard before stepping back into Hell for the second time in a week.

Only when they crossed the threshold, she really wished she'd dressed more badass for this trip. Guess tube socks were going to have to do.

CHAPTER 27

Jack and Sara entered Hell without invitation or notice. Yanking down her hoodie, Sara tried to feel confident and get her ass in gear. If she was going to go interrogate Lucifer, she needed some kind of plan, right?

Shit.

She followed Jack's lead down the hall. This place was just as familiar and foreign as everything else in her new/old life. Just as they came to the big double doors, they opened of their own accord and Sara almost ran smack into a big dude with more piercings than she thought one eye brow could have.

"Sara?" the big guy gawked with wide eyes.

"Reggie?" His name just spilled out of her mouth automatically.

"Holy shit, woman," he looked like he was seeing a ghost. "You're back?"

"I am." Geez she wished this wasn't so awkward.

"I can't believe it!" Reggie gave her a huge bear hug. "This is incredible. Where have you been?"

"Around," she was shooting for light and nonchalant. "Just came to talk to Luce."

Reggie's smile was slow to take over, but once it did it was contagious and Sara found herself beaming one right back at him. She liked this guy. He scooped her into another bear hug.

"Can't… breathe…."

He set her back down on her feet, laughing. "Damn, it's good to have you back, baby girl."

Jack grabbed Sara's hand and pulled her away from Reggie. "We better get going, don't want to keep his Lordship waiting."

"Right," Reggie moved out of the way and marched down the hall.

Sara whispered, "Is he a Hound, too?"

"No," Jack's voice was low and controlled, "He's a Gate Keeper. One of the finest in the group."

"Oh."

"You remembered him?"

Sara shrugged, "His name popped into my head."

Jack's eyes narrowed, "Nothing else?"

"Nope." It was weird, but the truth. "I'm telling the truth, Jack. I don't know how I knew his name, it just popped out of my mouth."

"I believe you," he said. His harsh glare melted into a hopeful one, "You're getting your memories back. This is good."

She didn't know what to say. Remembering some random Gate Keeper's name didn't feel like a big deal, but seeing Jack look at her like that, she was willing to take some of his hope for herself. Maybe this was a start to discovery.

"Come on, love." He yanked her forward and they went into the Devil's room again. Déjà vu slapped her ass when she stood in the big room and looked around. She had just been here a few days ago, but it felt like a lifetime had passed since then.

It also strangely felt like home.

"I didn't expect to see you again so soon, Darling." Lucifer came out of nowhere. "Care for a drink?"

"No, thank you."

Lucifer glanced at Jack, who bowed and turned to leave.

"I want him to stay." Sara shuffled her feet, keeping her eyes pinned on Lucifer.

The Devil shook his head. "No, you don't."

"Don't tell me what I want." She turned towards Jack. "I don't want you to go, Jack."

Lucifer didn't budge, but his voice slid over her skin and slipped into her mind. *"Yes... you do."* His words weren't a command. They were... a warning maybe?

"Jack." Sara jolted at the Hound's name on the Devil's tongue. "Leave. Now."

She and her Hound exchanged looks. She didn't want him to go. He had no choice but to obey.

"We won't be long, Hound." Lucifer said. "And you know she is safe with me."

"I'm right outside, love." Jack turned and left.

God, hadn't Jack said that the last time she was here?

Lucifer waited for Jack to leave, then turned his attention to Sara, "You're back too soon."

"I have questions."

"Have your memories returned?"

"Only a few."

"What of your tattoos?"

"No."

Lucifer tsked. Strolling over to a large chair, he took a seat and practically melted into the leather. "Why are you here, Sara?"

"How did we meet?"

His face was stoic. Controlled. Void of all emotion. "You'll remember eventually."

"I want to remember NOW." She almost stomped her foot. Hands balled into fists, she was positively fuming. "Tell me, Luce."

His brow arched. She bit her lip.

The Devil stood back up and gracefully made his way over to her again. "Are you sure you don't have your memories?"

"I'm not sure of anything anymore. But," she huffed and crossed her arms over her chest, "I feel things that make no sense."

"Have you told the others?"

"No."

"Why?"

She shrugged. "I want to figure this out on my own."

The growl that erupted from his throat almost made Sara piss herself. In a blink of an eye, his hand wrapped around her throat and he began backing her up against the wall. She was pinned, but not hurt. The threat was there, though.

"Let go of me."

"Why did you just call me *Luce*?"

"Because it's what I've always called you." She'd have gasped in surprise at her automatic answer if her windpipe wasn't being squeezed.

"You need your Hounds, Sara. And you need your tattoos."

"Why do I need them?"

"Because you cannot survive without them."

There was no distinction between whether they were talking about the tattoos or the Hounds, which meant both. She needed both.

Lucifer inched forward, his big hand still wrapped around her delicate throat. He squeezed tighter, letting her see how easy it would be for him to kill her with just one hand. "Are you not scared, Sara?"

"No." There was no hesitation in her voice.

"*NO?*" He squeezed harder.

Sara kicked her feet out and wrapped her hands around his arm. "You won't... kill me."

Again with the eyebrow arch. "So confident, are you?"

"Yessss," she hissed.

"Why won't I kill you?"

"Because," she struggled, "You... need... me."

"So do your Hounds." Lucifer dropped her to the ground. She landed with a yelp.

Coughing and sputtering, Sara stood up slowly. Air, she just needed a couple good gulps of air. Finally, she was able to get a lungful and the world stopped spinning. Next, her temper rose to match the heat in the room. She took three steps forward and clocked the Devil with a mean right hook. "Don't you ever do that to me again, asshole."

Lucifer laughed. His humor roared and vibrated around them. "That's a start."

"What the fuck is the matter with you?" She rubbed her throat, coughing again.

Lucifer grabbed her wrist and held it up between them. Sara's mouth would have hit the floor had she not been gritting her teeth in fury. They both looked at her wrist. No not her wrist, her ink. They both stared at the tattoo that had just appeared. A simple, intricate design with sharp edges was inked in all black on the

146

underside of her wrist.

Lucifer let go of her arm and cupped her face in his big hands. "Let this be a lesson, Sara."

"I didn't come here for a lesson. I came here for answers."

"Everyone has a truth, Darling," his voice sharpened, "Do you think you can handle yours?"

"Yes."

Lucifer licked his lips, his gaze pinning her to the point where she started to squirm. She wanted to know her truth, but the way he was looking, maybe she shouldn't.

"You're not ready, Sara. When you are, come back." He left before she could force him to answer her gazillion new questions. Damnit.

CHAPTER 28

Time flies when you're in Hell. You'd think it would be the opposite. That the minutes spent down there would be agonizingly slow and torturous, but instead time had gone by in a blink. Jack and Sara had left around lunch time and returned in the middle of the night.

Up above them, the sounds of deep voices and footfalls let them know the kitchen was occupied and everyone must still be awake. When they got to the top of the steps and Jack opened the door, all the bustling stopped.

Sara took one look at Eli – who was the first face she saw – and just about melted.

She couldn't explain the feeling that overwhelmed her. It was as if she'd been gone for forever and was finally back home and the whole world was right and good and nothing but nothing could strip the joy that danced under her skin. Whatever this emotion bubbling out of her was, it turned her into a spider monkey of a woman. She practically jumped into Eli's arms and wrapped her legs around his waist.

"Woah," he stumbled back, catching her, and before he could say another word, Sara kissed him hard enough to knock the earth off its axis. When she broke away, Eli chuckled, "Welcome home, baby."

Blushing, she didn't know how to explain herself so she didn't bother trying. Whatever had gotten into her just now felt too good to fight or deny.

"Got one of those for me?"

Sara dropped down from Eli, spun around, and grabbed Tanner by the shirt. Dragging him down to her mouth, she used her other arm to clutch the nape of his neck, holding him to her while she kissed the ever loving shit out of him. Thing was, he was a little more prepared and returned the favor with some serious heat behind his tongue. When they finally broke away, both were panting.

"I think Lucifer did something to her," Jack teased as he took a seat at the table.

Jack might have said it as a joke, but Sara knew it was also the truth. She rolled up her sleeve and showed-off the tattoo on her wrist.

The Hounds rushed towards her all at the same time, but Jack was the fastest. He grabbed her wrist and stared at the mark for a few seconds before cupping her cheeks with his hands, much like the devil had done earlier. "Why didn't you say anything to me?"

"I wanted to show you all together."

He kissed her. Not with hungry greediness, but with a gentle confidence that felt like relief. "This is good, love."

He backed away so Eli and Tanner could have a closer look. Eli held her hand and rubbed the tattoo softly with his thumb. "Did the others come back, too?"

"Let's see." Tanner grinned, "Beautiful, take off your shirt."

Sara laughed. Tanner's command wasn't just because he wanted to see if her other ink was back. She pulled off the hoodie, anxious to know the answer herself.

As she pulled her hoodie up and off, her neck became fully exposed and they all growled. "WHAT THE FUCK IS THAT?"

She didn't know who yelled it, because they were all yelling now. Instinctively, Sara placed a hand over her throat. It felt a little bruised. She probably had the Devil's entire handprint on her neck right now. "It's fine, don't freak out."

"Don't freak out, she says," Jack vibrated with anger. "You want to explain why Lucifer's handprint is wrapped three quarters of the way around your neck?"

"He was teaching me a lesson?" Yup, she'd asked it. Like, maybe they would have a clue because she still wasn't sure what had happened between her and Lucifer just now.

"What the hell happened in that room Sara?" Jack was furious.

Now, here's the thing. Whatever happened behind those closed doors with Lucifer was a private matter. What happened there, stayed there. That was a rule that he "reminded" her about when Jack had brought her to him a few days ago.

Eli moved forward, "Answer us, Sara."

Her hands rose to her throat and she rubbed the bruises the Devil's fingers had left on her neck. They would heal soon, since she was a Hound, but right now it probably looked terrible. "I'm fine, Hounds. Really." What a dick, strangling her like that to help her. How twisted were the Devil's methods of teaching a lesson? "Lucifer said I need you and my tattoos to survive."

The men all exchanged looks and then turned their gazes back to her. "So he strangled you?" Tanner took a step forward and tilted her head back gently so he could see how extensive the damage was. A hiss slipped through his teeth.

"It was... not what you think," she said quietly.

She felt Tanner's hand shake when he gently ran his finger over the bruises. He was likely not dealing well with another woman in his life being hurt by the hands of a man and then her saying some poor excuse like *it's not what you think.*

"Besides," she stepped back for some space, "I decked him for it afterwards."

"Tell us exactly what happened." Eli's voice was so controlled it didn't sound real. He was shaking with fury. She saw his arms tremble as he gripped his knife with a serious case of white knuckle fever. "Sara, tell me right now what the fuck happened before I go into Hell and kill that fucker with my shiny new chef's knife. I know we can't talk about what happens behind closed doors with Lucifer, but right now I don't give a flying fuck what the rules are. Break them. Now."

She sat down at the kitchen table and told them everything. Why she'd gone down to Hell to speak with Lucifer. What he said. What he did. How she felt. Sara even told them about the conversation she had with Lucifer when Jack brought her into Hell a few days ago. That conversation was supposed to be private, too. And so, she'd kept it as such. Not now, though. Sara left nothing unsaid. No secret hidden. Big, little, stupid, unworthy, mysterious, didn't matter what it was… she told her Hounds all of it. Including what just happened when she went to Hell to speak with Lucifer.

Tanner got up and started pacing. "He threatened to kill you and his mark reappears."

Sara's happy meter went down a notch. "This isn't one of your marks?"

"No," Jack leaned back and crossed his arms over his chest. "Ours are down your spine."

"Which we still haven't checked for," Eli reminded them.

Her Hounds had gotten distracted with her throat and they'd yet to check her back. Sara stood up and yanked off her tank top. Spinning around so they could see her back, she trembled with anticipation. "Well?"

Silence engulfed the kitchen.

"No," one of them whispered.

"Damnit." She pulled her shirt back down and fell into her chair. She wasn't going to cry. There would be no crying. No cr—

Sara squeezed her eyes shut and began to sob.

Arms wrapped around her from all angles and she caught three distinct scents of her Hounds. They felt amazing and smelled like home and her brain was fried and she was exhausted and everything felt like too fucking much.

"Come on, baby," Eli's scooped her into his arms and took her out of the kitchen.

"I can't stand this," she cried into his neck.

"Neither can we." Eli carried her up the stairs, down the hall, and into his bedroom. When he placed her on his bed, Sara's senses were filled with nothing but the scent and feel of Eli and it was amazing and comforting and scary and confusing. He started rubbing her lower back in small circles, "We'll get through this like we do everything, okay?"

"How?"

"Together. That's how we work through shit. We do it together." He leaned down and kissed her head. "I'll be back okay? Try to sleep."

The words *don't leave me* were on the tip of her tongue, but she didn't say them. Instead, she watched him go. Sara knew he'd be back soon.

It wasn't her head that told her that… it was her heart.

Eli practically flew back into the kitchen and shoved a finger in Jack's face, "You don't go down there without me."

He knew Jack and Tanner were going to confront Lucifer. There would be no way they were going to let someone strangle their woman without some serious consequences. Devil be damned, that fucker had no right. No. Right.

All because Lucifer owned their asses didn't mean it was okay to lay a hand on Sara like that. And knowing Jack so well, Eli figured there was about thirty seconds left to stop and cut him off at the pass. "We go together, got it?"

"Fine," Jack growled. "Let's go."

"Not yet," Tanner stopped them both. "We can't just leave Sara."

"Put her in with Kalen." Eli didn't give his words a second thought. It had been so easy to fall back into old ways these past few days. If ever Sara needed a wolf to guard her, Kalen was always the chosen one.

"Kalen?" Tanner jerked back like Eli had spoke in tongues, "Are you forgetting that he's not dealing well with life right now?"

Eli waved away the concern, "He'd never hurt her."

"But his head isn't in the game yet, Eli."

"Putting her in bed with him might help with that."

"No," Jack intervened. "Not yet."

What's the big deal? It's not like Kalen was going to wake up. Sara wanted a warm body she could cling to for the night, and even though Eli wanted to be that body, he'd give his spot up to Kalen no questions asked. Eli needed her, but Kalen needed her more and she needed them both equally.

"Then we wait." Eli stared at the Hounds and dared them to argue. "We wait until Kalen is ready, too." He was just as much a part of this as the rest of them. And once he learned about Sara's neck, he was going to be livid – more so if he found out they went without him to seek justice.

Jack's shoulders rounded, his jaw muscles flexing while he ground his teeth in frustration. "Fine."

"WHAT?" Tanner was pissed and turning red. Eli deadpanned the Hound, hoping he'd obey and wait. The two started growling at each other and then Tanner flung his arms up in the air. "Fine. We'll fucking wait."

Satisfied, Eli headed back upstairs, taking the steps two at a time and rushed down the hall. Pausing at Kalen's door, he cracked it open and saw the sleeping Hound face-down, one arm stretched across a pillow, the other dangling off the edge of the bed. Relieved, Eli closed the door quietly and went back to his own room. He arrived just in time to see Sara pull on one of his t-shirts and the sight of her wearing his old Metallica shirt just did things to him.

She spun around, hiding her perfect ass but now gave him a great frontal view. Hey, no complaints there. Sara was spectacular at all angles.

She climbed back into the bed, watching him almost cautiously. Without saying a word, he met her gaze and slowly reached behind and pulled his t-shirt off. Then he unbuckled his pants and shimmied out of those, too. He went commando, sooooo…

Sara made a sound. One a woman makes when she sees something she likes. Eli's jaw clenched and he stood ramrod straight. Her gaze raked down his body. And yeah, he was hard as stone and didn't bother hiding his arousal. He wanted her to see it. Wanted her to know just what wearing one of his t-shirts did to him. He could smell her desire from ten feet away. Hounds had incredibly sharp senses.

And voracious appetites.

Eli crawled into the bed and told himself he was only going to make a move after she made the first one. He didn't want to push her too far tonight. No matter how badly he wanted her. No matter how much he wanted to bury himself deep and howl as he came inside her, he wouldn't make a move unless she initiated it.

Nothing mattered tonight except giving Sara what she needed. And she might not need him like that right now.

His breath caught when she nuzzled up against him. Sara fit

so perfectly in his arms, just like she always had. And they laid there, half entwined, with her hair tickling his nose and her leg immediately riding up his thigh, just like it always used to do. Old habits. Old memories. Old feelings that never died, bubbled up and out of him. Eli wondered if Sara realized this was how they always laid together. He kissed the top of her head and waited to see if she'd say it…

"Rub my butt?"

He got dizzy. He seriously felt like the world had just gone all topsy-turvy. "Absolutely."

He reached down and gave her a booty rub. Just like he always used to do. She fell asleep in his arms within minutes. Just like she always did with him.

His Sara was coming back. Whether she realized it was happening or not, Eli could see it. And that was all that mattered.

CHAPTER 29

Kalen rolled over. Mother of God, his body felt like it weighed an extra thousand pounds. Rubbing with both hands, he gave his eyes a good massage before opening them. Laying in the quiet bedroom, the curtains drawn tight, he felt like he was in a cave. He preferred it that way. Darkness, after all, was something he was well acquainted with.

He could hear the sounds of dishes clanking, voices, music, mumbles, the heat kicking on, the water running. The house was alive.

And so was Sara.

Kalen needed to speak with her. It was time. But shit, what would he say? What would she say when he said whatever he would say?

Now his head hurt. Maybe he should wait a little longer.

No, he couldn't wait anymore. It wasn't like he could avoid her forever. The *malanum* were swarming around their district and with Sara back, he figured she would want to go out and take some down as soon as possible. That woman lived to hunt. Maybe she was out hunting now...

Sara preferred hunting in the day time. Her nights, however, she liked spending in other ways.

Kalen rubbed his aching chest. She was back. She was alive. She was here and the pack was whole again. Dread consumed his relief. Ate it up like breakfast. Sara would have a lot of questions for him. Questions, Kalen wasn't sure he was ready to answer yet.

Fuuuuuck.

Stumbling out of bed, Kalen managed to pull on some pants and shuffle into the hallway. Bacon. He smelled bacon. Before following the scent, he went into the bathroom and brushed his teeth, then pulled his long hair back into a pony tail. Shit, his arms hurt. What did he expect though, after having cut and split three cords of wood by hand? In one day. They had a wood splitter but Kalen needed to burn off his energy so he hadn't used it. Add to that a night of hunting, chasing, and capturing some *malanum* and his body was screaming for a respite. He'd been wiped out completely.

Rotating his shoulder, Kalen winced at how sore his muscles were. It was all good though, by the end of the day, his Hound powers will have fixed him right up. Until then, the pain would be a comfort to him. A little *Fuck you, Kalen, you deserve to hurt* that he could ride on all day.

He stared into the mirror. Christ, he looked like shit. Dark circles under blood shot eyes, his cheeks hollow, and eyes all puffy. It didn't matter. He slept like the dead last night and it was the first time in a long fucking while that he could claim that victory.

Coffee would be good. Coffee would perk him right up.

He didn't glide, so much as bumble, his groggy ass downstairs. Staind was playing on the radio in the living room and as he entered the kitchen, he saw Jack cooking. Not Eli. What the Hell? Had he entered an alternate universe or something?

"Rise and shine, motherfucker." Jack poured him a cup of coffee and Kalen took the black elixir of life and plopped his ass into a seat. "You feeling better?"

"Mmmph," Sip, sip. Sigh. "Where..." he had to clear his throat, his voice still not up for much after all his night-terror screaming. He tried to speak again, "Where is everyone?"

"Tanner threw more wood in the furnace and then ran to the store for some things Sara's going to need."

Kalen's heart stopped beating. Annnnd then slowly picked up again. "How..." he had to clear his throat again, damnit. "How is she?"

"Better." Jack plopped two pieces of toast on the plates scattered across the counter. In an assembly line, he made BLT sandwiches. "Sara and Eli are still sleeping."

Kalen stilled and then relaxed once more. "That's... good."

Jack placed three plates on the table and grabbed a bag of chips from the pantry. "We need to talk, Kalen."

The groggy Hound took a bite of his sandwich and tried to swallow. It tasted so damn good but dread had taken up all the space in his gut and he was worried he wouldn't be able to choke the bite down.

In perfect timing, Tanner came in through the back door carrying two plastic bags. "Oh man, I'm starving." He dropped the bags on the table and took a seat next to Kalen. Diving into his sandwich, he took three huge bites. "I had a run in with two *malanum* outside the store. One almost poked my damn eye out."

"You took care of them?"

Tanner gave Jack a *what the fuck* face. "No, we played ring around the rosy and then I bought them milkshakes. Yes, I took care of them."

Jack shook his head and smirked. "Dick."

"You're one to talk."

The three of them went back to eating their lunch. Eli entered the kitchen with his dark, curly hair a total mess. Yanking on a shirt, he shuffled towards the coffee pot and assembled his own BLT.

"Where is she?" Jack asked.

"Still sleeping."

They all seemed to collectively sigh in relief.

"Then while she's up there, let's talk." Jack waited for Eli to have a seat before continuing. "Kalen, we need your head in the game."

"My head is always in the game."

"No," Jack focused on him, "I mean we need you all in. Whatever you and Sara need to do to be better, do it. Because she fucking needs us. All of us."

Kalen shuffled in his seat and pushed the plate of food away. Leaning back, he crossed his arms over his broad chest and pegged Jack with a dangerous glare. "Don't fucking tell me what to do, Jack. Not when it comes to Sara."

It was stare down time. "Whatever happened, you need to bloody fix it."

"Nothing is broken."

Jack's brow arched. "She remembers things, Kalen. We're hoping that after what just happened between her and Lucifer, she's going to remember the rest. That means whatever happened in New Orleans will be figured out."

Kalen looked down at the tablecloth while Jack continued his warning.

"You know how we've been saying that the *malanum* seemed to have swarmed this area lately?"

"Yeah."

"We think it's because of Sara."

Kalen's head jerked up, brow furrowing, hands balling into fists. "What makes you think she has something to do with them?"

Jack took a sip of whatever he had in his glass – probably bourbon – and looked around the table before saying, "In a nutshell, here's what we've got: Sara was stripped of everything. Her power, her tats, her memories. She became a shell. A hollow fucking spirit."

"A wisp," Eli murmured.

Kalen felt his blood drain down to his feet. "Jesus. Christ."

"She said something pulled her here. She woke up dead in New Orleans and fought, every single day, against a barrage of *malanum*. They've been gunning for her. And when I found her, she was half-turned already."

Kalen was going to puke. He was absolutely going to upchuck his coffee.

"She didn't recognize me when I found her. All she said was something had pulled her here."

"Us," Tanner chimed in. "It was us. She had to feel us and just didn't know what it was."

"Maybe," Jack nodded, "And her ability to fight wasn't taken from her."

"It never would be," Kalen's deep voice rumbled. "She was always a fighter." Jesus, his chest hurt.

"She's been on her own for five years. I brought her into Hell after she tried to convince me to make her a Hound. She seriously had no idea she already was one. And when I brought her to Lucifer, she went behind the doors with him and I had to stay outside."

"Great," Kalen huffed. Closed door meetings with Big D meant they weren't to be shared later.

"She told us everything," Tanner smiled. "She also went back to Luce yesterday and told us all about that, too."

Kalen couldn't help but smile. Sara, his Sara, was coming back. That woman was the only creature alive that would go against the Devil himself if she wanted to and break his rules.

"There's more," Eli grumbled. "Luce made her a Hound again. She has all her magic back. And she can use it like it was never lost."

"So what's the problem?"

"Her tats still aren't back."

Kalen frowned. "Her spine is bare?"

"Mmm hmm."

Kalen leaned in and gawked, unable to comprehend this at all. "You're telling me our marks have completely disappeared from her body?"

"All but one." Eli nodded. "And you're not going to like how she got it to return."

"Just fucking tell me, god damnit. I hate it when you guys give me shit in pieces." Kalen would rather take the entire thing all at once. Get slammed hard and deal. But ever since Sara had vanished, they'd treated him like a landmine – tip-toeing cautiously at all times around him.

Tanner was the one to say, "Lucifer nearly choked her to death. It got his mark back on her, though."

Kalen popped out of his chair and slammed his fists on the table as he literally roared in fury.

Red. He was seeing red. Without hesitation, Kalen bolted for the basement door and flew down the steps. Jack and Eli snatched his arms and forced him to halt, which led to another problem. Kalen didn't want to fight his pack, but damn if he was going to be stopped either. "Let me GO!" he roared.

"What's going on?"

They all froze. Sara stood at the top of the steps, hair in a serious state of bed head, wearing Eli's Metallica shirt, no pants on, and she looked… pissed off.

"Get off of him. All of you." She descended the steps slowly, her eyes locked on Kalen. "Leave us alone, for a minute, please?"

Jack, Eli and Tanner obeyed.

God, it was like no time had passed at all. Everyone just went back to the way it was before Sara had ever vanished from their lives.

Kalen stiffened as she padded her bare feet over to him. His breaths came out in punches. Eyes burning, heart racing, he was going to explode. The pack had been right to treat him so delicately. Kalen was an explosive weapon. A grenade, pin out.

"Thank you," she whispered.

Kalen's nostrils flared and he flinched when she brought her hand up and put it over his heart. Right over her name that was tatted on his pec. His eyes closed so he could focus on the feel of her hand on him. So small. So strong. So Sara.

"I remember," she said. "I heard you screaming my name in your sleep. And I... remembered."

His eyes popped open, all of him suddenly shaking, and he tried to force his knees to *not* buckle. He didn't know what to say. She heard him have a night terror. It wasn't something he was proud of nor capable of hiding. He'd had them so long, it was just his way of life now. But... if Sara didn't remember him, remember this part of his life, then it would have been a new experience for her and she was probably terrified.

"I'm sorry," Kalen's knees gave out and he crashed onto the concrete floor. "Oh God, Sara. I'm so fucking sorry." Dropping his head, he fought the tears that threatened to spill out. He hadn't cried over her in five years. He wouldn't allow himself the weakness. But it seemed she was doing a fine job of turning him into an emotional disaster with just her scent. Her touch. Her voice.

"I'm the one who's sorry Kalen." She dropped to her knees too and cupped his face, forcing him to look at her. "You sacrificed yourself for me. You tried to save me."

His hand went up to her cheek and he swiped away her tears with his thumb. "I love you," his voice was barely audible, "There's nothing I wouldn't do for you. Then or now."

They held each other like that for several heartbeats. "I love you, Wolf."

The air rushed out of him. *Wolf.* He was always her Wolf. If she was saying it now, it meant she remembered that part of him,

160

too. And if she remembered, then… "Please forgive me, Sara."

"For what?"

"For what I did in New Orleans."

CHAPTER 30

This morning, when Sara had awoken in Eli's bed, she was ready for anything. Lying there, listening to the sounds of deep voices in the kitchen, she felt like she was home. Truly home. Things were coming back to her. Memories. Feelings. Urges.

And now here she was, face-to-face with the man who'd died for her. "*I love you, Wolf*," she'd said to Kalen. The words tumbled out of her mouth automatically as if she'd said them for a thousand years.

"Please forgive me, Sara."

She grew confused, "For what?"

"For what I did in New Orleans."

Sara froze, still embracing Kalen as he gently held her face. For an instant, she wondered if they had the strength to decapitate each other. *Yes*, she thought. *We're both capable of that.* Acknowledging the power they both shared was half the battle, the other half was going to take some serious concentration... to not Freak. The. Hell. Out. Sara tried to calm the panic rising within her. She noticed Kalen wasn't hurting her, he was caressing her cheeks gently, and the look he gave her spoke volumes about his intentions. He wanted forgiveness, not revenge. "What did you do in New Orleans, Kalen?"

He stopped touching her and rocked back on his haunches.

"You don't remember."

"I will when you remind me." Her voice was steady and she prayed it stayed that way.

Kalen swallowed. She watched his Adam's apple bob twice and then he stood up. Sara had no choice but to stand as well. Immediately, her feet spread about shoulder-width apart. Sara hadn't realized she was going into attack mode until she was already in it. "Refresh my memory, Kalen."

She was scared shitless. Everything she felt was the complete opposite of how she should have been feeling. Her heart said Kalen was hers. Her soul seconded that notion. But her head? That clusterfuck was screaming that she should tread carefully because she died in New Orleans and Kalen had something to do with it. "What did you do?"

Carefully keeping his distance he said, "It was the beignets."

"What?"

"You sent me out for fucking beignets, Sara. And like a fool, I left you alone."

Her hands fell to her sides and she gawked in confusion. "I don't understand."

"We were on a mission for Lucifer," he continued. "We were staying in the French Quarter and you were getting dressed for the night. I was pacing around because, like always, you took forever to get ready. I hated the wait and we still had three hours left before the party so I went down to the restaurant in the hotel to grab us food and you called asking for beignets." Kalen began to pace like a caged wolf on his side of the basement. "I should have known. I should have *known*."

Now Sara was the one gulping.

"I came back to the hotel and you were gone."

Sara shook her head but he didn't see it. He was too lost in sorrow.

"You never came back." Kalen took a single step towards her. Then another. "You literally vanished and abandoned the pack that night."

Sara took a step back. "Why would I do that?"

"You tell me. You were the one so dead-set on none of us going with you."

They glared at each other.

163

"Cat got your tongue, woman, or is your memory still shoddy?"

It was and it wasn't. His story held a faint caress of truth, but she wasn't sure. Not entirely. "What mission were we on?"

"Luce thinks there's a traitor amongst us."

"*Thinks.* As in there still is?"

Kalen's eyes glowed like hot embers. Dangerous... the Hound was deadly. "There is definitely still a traitor on the loose."

Sara's blood drained from her head. She took another step back. "Annnnd, who might that traitor be?"

"You tell me, woman." He took another step closer to her.

Panic flooded her system and Sara spun around, booking it up the steps just as Kalen tried to snatch her.

They both burst through the kitchen, into the living room, and he caught her on the steps. Yanking her ankle, she fell with a scream.

"What the hell is the matter with you?" Kalen twirled her leg, forcing Sara to roll over. She kicked at him with her other foot and he caught it, yanking her down two of the steps and pinning her there. "Stop it, Sara!"

She screamed again, and then, as if someone hit her pause button, Sara froze, mouth gaping open and she stared past Kalen into... nothingness. Her eyes widened as pure terror took over every single molecule in her body while another memory slammed into her hard enough for Sara to lose her breath...

Kalen answered her call on the second ring, "Yes, Darling?"

"Can you pick up two orders of beignets?"

"What?"

"Pleeeeeease?"

"Sara, I'm in the lobby with our dinner. Are you seriously going to make me go out for that?"

"If you love me, you'll go."

"I do love you."

"Enough to go get me the beignets?"

He growled.

"I'll make it worth your trouble, Wolf." He was totally gonna get her what she wanted. "Banana ones."

"BANANA?" he practically yelled.

"From the café we went to, yesterday."

"That's ten miles out! Damnit, Sara."

"I love you sooooo much."

He growled again and hung up.

Sara went back to applying her face paint. They were going to a ceremony in hopes to get some answers. All they had to go on were a few pieces of magic and a Devil's hunch. Nevertheless, Lucifer insisted New Orleans was the place to be. Sara secured an invitation to a closed gathering slated to take place on All Hallows Eve. Wishing she could go alone, because she didn't want to jeopardize her pack, Sara was in a shit mood. Her Wolf insisted he join her. Always the vicious one, Kalen would keep her guarded during the party and her other Hounds had all agreed to stay back only if Kalen was her escort. She had no choice but to comply. She would never want one of her Hounds to go on a solo mission this dangerous, she should have known they'd feel the same way about her going on this mission by herself.

She and Kalen had kept busy at the French Quarter, if only to keep her mind off the dreaded mission. And now it was time to complete this hunt and end this shit once and for all.

A couple more details with a flick of a brush and her skull face was done. Satisfied, Sara turned her head to inspect her artwork, double-checking to make sure she hadn't left out a single detail. Yeah, this was good work. She really loved her face paint. Almost made her look like an actual skeleton. Once she was dressed, Sara figured she'd look like a sexy ass voodoo priestess – except with biker boots.

Ohhhh she couldn't wait to ride Kalen's motorcycle later. She loved that thing and insisted they'd take it instead of a plane to New Orleans.

Next, she started buckling her favorite corset. She could stuff the knives in all the pockets later. A knock on the door kicked her heartrate up. Food always got her excited. Grabbing her cane with the skull of their dead goat, Georgie, on it and snatching the top hat – that belonged to Jack – off the bed, Sara wanted to answer the door in full costume and show Kalen her awesomeness in its full glory. He loved this corset. It was his favorite, too. And her skull paint job was dynamite.

Another, much louder knock made her eyes roll. "I'm coming, Wolf!"

"Little pig, little pig, let me in."

Sara cracked a laugh as she swung open the door, "Are you calling me a p – "

Her world went black as the blade sunk into her throat.

Annnnd, just like being dowsed with ice water, Sara snapped out of it. "I remember," she gasped. "I remember."

Kalen let go of her ankles immediately. "Tell me what you know, Sara."

"I'm not the traitor. I haven't traitored." Was traitored a word? Fuck, she couldn't think.

"Who said *you* were the traitor?" Tanner barked from somewhere to her right. She saw him through the spokes of the railing and realized all the Hounds were in the room.

"Kalen," she sputtered.

"What the FUCK, Sara! I never said that!"

"But you're thinking it!"

Kalen stumbled back like she'd kicked him in the face. "I can't be here." He stormed out of the room and no one tried to stop him.

"Explain yourself, love."

"He thinks I'm the traitor, Jack. He thinks I tricked him with the beignets."

"He said that?"

"Sort of." Hadn't he? Oh god, her head. Sara's blood pressure was going through the roof.

Jack leaned down to help her up. "Kalen would never have called you a traitor."

"Maybe Luce fucked her brain up. You know, the brain needs oxygen. Maybe he cut off her supply for too long yesterday and it caused damage?" Tanner crossed his arms over his chest and stared at her. "Crazy talk like this can be explained no other way."

"She doesn't trust us," Eli huffed. "She doesn't get it, Tanner."

Sara waved jazz hands at them. "Ummm SHE is right here, listening."

"Good," Jack poked a finger in her face, "You need to tread carefully, love. To say a Hound in this house would turn against the pack," Jack shook his head in disappointment, "there's no lower blow, Sara."

"But he—"

"Said there was a traitor. And there is." Tanner cut her off. "But we never once thought it was you."

"But I—"

"Just vanished? Didn't want us to go with you? Yeah, we

166

know all that." Eli shoved his hands in his pockets. "And the traitor is still out there."

Sara's ass hit the steps and she buried her head in her hands.

Jack leaned against the banister. "Lucifer suspects a traitor in Hell. Something is going on. The walls are cracking faster. More *malanum* are escaping. The Gate Keepers can only control the gates, but the cracks are coming from something else."

"We were put on a mission to find who the traitor could be," Eli said quietly, "And we were picked not only because we're the strongest pack in Hell, but Lucifer trusts you, Sara. Implicitly. That's what that tattoo on your wrist means, baby. That mark is the Devil's sign that you are one of his favorites. You're... untouchable."

"Not true." She shook her head, "that can't be true. I was killed."

"By who, love?" Jack squatted down to be more at her eye level. "Give us the name and we'll have justice."

Sara tried to remember. Truly. But the memory didn't come. "I don't know who it was. I don't remember."

"Then what do you remember?" Tanner came over and stood behind Jack.

"I remember opening the door, thinking it was Kalen. And... something stabbed me in the throat," she placed her hand around her neck, "and then everything went black."

Silence blanketed the room.

"Shit, I'll go speak with Kalen." Eli spun to leave and Sara stopped him.

Sara tried to stand. "No. I better be the one."

"Not now, Sara." Eli held his hand up to stop her, "He has blamed himself for your death all this time. If he hadn't left you alone, you'd have never disappeared. When he came back to the room that night, he said you were gone. That you'd vanished. He thought someone kidnapped you because there was no other way you would have vanished like that. He refused to believe you'd turn your back on the pack and go on the mission alone. But there was no evidence of a struggle. Nothing at all that helped us figure out what happened that night. You were gone, along with your stupid staff with Georgie's skull and Jack's old top hat. Kalen spent six months scouring New Orleans, killing *malanum*, interrogating people, ghosts, and Mediums, doing all he could to get answers, to

167

sniff out a single clue that might bring us closer to finding you."

Sara's chin trembled and she started crying. God, to have been Kalen in that moment. To come home and find the love of your life gone without a trace? It wasn't just Kalen who'd suffered that fright, all four of her Hounds had.

"He would never say you were the traitor, Sara. Never. Because he *trusts* you. Trust," Tanner jabbed a finger in the air at her, "Remember what I told you about that."

Eli and Tanner turned away from her and Jack followed. Sara sat on the steps and tried to pull herself together. Someone had murdered her. Someone had stripped her down to a hollow shell and left her worse than dead. And that someone had caused her Hounds to mourn terribly over her for five years.

That someone was going to pay dearly. Sara would make sure of it.

CHAPTER 31

Kalen was in the barn. He couldn't bring himself to do anything but sit. Drained of all energy and emotion, he was a lump on the floor, back against the wall, eyes staring blindly. His heart was crushed.

"Wolf?" Jack's voice didn't really register. "Wolf, where are you?"

He clenched his jaw, not answering.

"He's over here." Tanner was suddenly in his line of view.

Kalen's voice sounded dead, "What do you want?"

"She's trying, Wolf," Tanner crouched down and frowned, "Give her a chance."

Kalen shot daggers with the look he gave. "She accused me of calling her a traitor. How would you feel after everything..." his heart rate sped up, "after everything she and I have been through?" Kalen leaned back and stared at the ceiling. "Down in the basement she was scared of me, I could see it. She ran away from me. She thought I was going to *hurt* her."

He squeezed his eyes shut. There was no denying the look of pure fear in Sara's eyes earlier. She was scared of him. Jesus, she wasn't his Sara at all. His Sara would never be fearful of him. Everyone else in the world would cower before him, but not his

Sara. Never his Sara.

Trust was what glued this pack together. She didn't have that. Not with Kalen anymore. Not with any of them. It was scary as shit to realize their pack was in jeopardy of unraveling.

If one pack member didn't have trust, then slowly, it could spread doubt among the rest of the Hounds and the entire pack could break apart. It would be the ultimate ruination for each of them.

"She just needs time. And our patience." Eli picked up a blade and started tossing it at the target hanging on the far wall. "We gotta give her what she needs. It's the only way. Right now, she needs time to figure herself out."

"And time is what we don't have," Jack leaned against the wall, scowling. "I'm worried."

"About what?"

"Everything." Jack started tossing knives at another target. "Too many *malanum* are here. They're following Sara. I know it."

"Then we keep her here until she's back to normal."

Kalen shook his head, "And what do you think she'll have to say about that, Tanner? Sara hates feeling trapped. Her memories have faded, but not the rest of her ways. She'll get cabin fever in T-minus two days and bolt."

"Then we keep her occupied."

Eli laughed at Tanner's implied remedy. "I'm so down with that."

"Me too," Jack smirked, "but she might not be. Sara's not ready for all of us like that. She's scared and confused right now."

"But she's hungry," Kalen said. "She needs us. You can smell it."

Eli groaned in response. "So it's not just me that senses it?"

"Nope," they all said in unison.

Jack nodded, "Then we start slow. And add a little at a time."

Kalen's teeth ground together. He wanted to be part of it, but didn't. Would she even allow him to touch her after what just happened?

Jack looked around the room at each of the Hounds. "If she says no, we back off immediately. Got it?"

"Absolutely."

"No problem."

"Kalen?" Jack arched a brow, waiting for his answer. "You with us, Hound?"

Jack extended his hand to help Kalen stand. Ultimately, they all knew Kalen wouldn't deny Sara. Whatever she needed, he'd give her. Whatever she wanted him to be, he'd be for her. It was always this way in the pack. She'd do the same for each of them.

"Okay," he clasped Jack's hand and rose to his feet. "Let's do this."

Sara went upstairs. The hallway was dimly lit, not that she even noticed. She went into the bathroom and shut the door. No way was she going into one of the guys' bedrooms. She had no space of her own here and it sucked. Maybe on another day, under other circumstances, it wouldn't be a big deal. Today, however, was a different story. She needed a place to hide. To be alone. To escape.

Facing the mirror, she tilted her head back and stared at the bruises that were a perfect imprint of Lucifer's right hand. She closed her eyes and relived that moment one more time...

"Are you not scared, Sara?" He squeezed her throat tighter, letting her see how easy it would be for him to kill her with just one hand.

There was no hesitation in her voice when she replied, "No."

"NO?" he squeezed harder.

Sara's feet kicked out as she struggled. Wrapping her hands around his arm she said, "You won't kill me."

Again with the eyebrow arch. "So confident, are you?"

"Yessss," she hissed.

"Why wouldn't I kill you?"

"Because," she struggled, "You... need me."

"So do your Hounds." Lucifer dropped her to the ground. "Let this be a lesson, Sara."

She popped her eyes open as his meaning dawned on her. Yes, he could have killed her. Yes, it hurt like a bitch when he kept squeezing. But she wasn't scared of him. She knew, in her very bones, that Lucifer would go only so far and then he'd relent because he loved her and she loved him and they had complete trust in each other. He hadn't done it to hurt her or be a dickhead because he wasn't abusive like that.

He'd done it for another reason.

"Let this be a lesson, Sara."

She could have fought him. She could have run. She could have given up. But she didn't. Instead, she'd cocked back and slugged him for his bullshit stunt. She had complete confidence in calling his bluff because she knew better than to think the Devil would ever kill her.

His tattoo reappeared on her wrist within seconds of that stunt.

What a dick, she thought. Couldn't he have proven their bond some other way that didn't involve a near death experience? *Fucker.*

So what was she going to do now? How could she prove to the guys she trusted them? Wait... *did* she trust them? Actions spoke louder than words. So, no, she really didn't trust them. Not yet. Her running scared from Kalen proved she wasn't ready to let go of her doubts.

But she wanted to.

Deep down, something stirred in her. Like a caged beast desperate for release. And that – whatever it was – wanted the Hounds with her.

Okay, okay, okay. She could do this. She could figure this out.

"I need to make a list," she said to herself. "Number one, get the guys to make me trust them somehow." Okay, yeah, that was going to be tricky. If it required what she was thinking, none of them would like it. The Devil had to threaten her life in a very real way for his tat to reform on her wrist. She was starting to suspect the Hounds might have to go to the same extreme and she doubted Tanner and the others would be willing to almost kill her to get her trust back.

That was just fucked up.

"Number two," where was a pen and paper when she needed one? "I need to figure out who killed me. Number three, get one of those pretty little slicey-dicey blades like Jack has."

Numbers four, five, and six would be find the traitor, take them out of the equation on a permanent level, and take a hot bath.

Not necessarily in that order.

Sara shrugged out of Eli's shirt and held it to her nose. Damn

172

he smelled so good. Like wood smoke and chocolatey yumminess. It made her feel warm and gooey and sexy and sultry. Eli was decadent. Yeah... decadent and hot as sin.

She'd spent the entire night with him and hadn't made a single move. She thought for sure he would have tried something. After all, he was naked. Except he hadn't and she realized she was grateful. Her head was too filled last night for anything fun. It felt perfect to curl into his arms and get a booty rub until she conked out.

Now though? With all these new revelations spinning in her head, she could use a distraction. Sara was already feeling too trapped in the house and was desperate for some kind of escape.

Or release.

Turning on the faucet, she waited until the tub was half-filled and then sank into the hot water while it continued to rise. She eyed the door. There was no lock, but after what just happened, she doubted any of them would come looking for her so soon.

Sara slid one hand down to the joining of her thighs. Parting her folds, she began rubbing herself. Closing her eyes, she let the fantasies dance... Eli standing naked in his bedroom, Jack's face as he pounded into her the other night, Tanner suckling her breasts at the kitchen table, and Kalen... she locked on the vision of his green eyes and long, dark hair.

The orgasm came fast and furious. With a gasp, she let a flood of desire rush through her. Her body spasmed, water sloshed out of the tub. Her ears were ringing. Not ready for it to be over, Sara arched her back and gripped the side of the tub as her other hand moved faster and faster. She caught a second wave of ecstasy and cried out this time. Slipping, she slid under the water, completely submerging herself in the process.

The entire bathroom disappeared and she was suddenly surrounded by animal masks. Sara kicked out, feet and fists thrashing as she fought the hands that held her down.

Gasping she flew out of the tub and spewed out a mouthful of water.

"Fuck, Sara! Are you okay?" Tanner's eyes were wild.

Sara looked around the bathroom, panting.

"Hey, Beautiful. You're alright. You're alright. I got you."

She swiped the water off her face and clutched Tanner's arms for dear life. "I was being held down."

"What?"

"I was..." she looked around the room, including up at the ceiling, trying to grasp where she was, "I was being held down by people with animal masks. They put me in water and I was drowning."

Tanner yanked a towel from the shelf and quickly wrapped it around her. "I heard you yell and came in to make sure you were okay. You were thrashing in the tub like you couldn't swim."

She stood up just in time to not get the towel wet. He helped her out of the tub and called for reinforcements, "HOUNDS!"

The door opened again and the others piled into the room. All except for Kalen. He stood in the doorway, taking up all the space, but didn't cross the threshold. "What's going on?"

"She's had a flashback, I think."

Jack moved forward, "What was it, love?"

"I... I was just..." words seemed to fail her. She just couldn't believe her current situation. Four men were standing before her, ready to kill, ready to protect, ready for anything.

And they were all hers.

Surrounded by her Hounds, a sense of completeness rocked her to the core. She could feel it. The strength of the pack. It was like a warm rush of electricity coursing through her body. Then something else seemed to overrun her. The walls closed in, the air was vacuumed out of the room, and everything got wonky. She couldn't breathe. Couldn't move. Couldn't—

"Sara?" Eli reached out and tilted her chin up. "Guys."

"On it." Tanner backed up and pulled Sara with him. He plopped down on the tiled floor, holding Sara between his legs. The other Hounds all held some part of her body - an ankle, a hand, an arm.

"Breathe, Beautiful. Breathe through it."

"Come on, love. We're right here."

"We got you." Kalen's face was suddenly the only thing she could see. He squatted down and took up her entire line of sight. "Eyes on me, Sara. Eyes on me."

"Kalen," she panted, losing control.

Tanner tensed when her hands slammed onto his legs. Sinking her fingers into his thighs, she grabbed fistfuls of denim and didn't let go for nothing. Shaking, she was gasping and choking and –

"Can't… breathe…"

Kalen was right there, keeping his eyes locked on hers. "Yes, you can. Look at me, Sara. In and out." His nostrils flared as he showed her how to inhale and exhale.

Eyes wild, Sara thrust her hand out and grabbed a hold of Kalen's shoulder, digging her nails into his flesh.

"In and out," he said again. "Come on, I can't do it alone, I need you to breathe with me, too. Be with me, Sara. In and out."

Collectively, they all started breathing in the same rhythm. Big deep breath in and long exhale out. It took a few more tries but Sara finally got with the program.

The lights in the bathroom brightened, her head stopped swimming, her cheeks no longer felt tingly, and she was able to calm the hell down. "Thank you," she whispered. "Thank you so much."

Tanner gave her a hug from behind, Jack squeezed her hand, Eli rubbed her leg. Kalen continued to stare at her. "Move."

That command from Kalen was all it took for Jack and Eli to get out of the way. Kalen leaned in and pressed his mouth to hers. It was a solid impact kiss. The kind that wasn't crushing but demanded attention. It felt warm. It felt right.

Sara wrapped her arms around Kalen's neck and Tanner released his embrace so she could be picked up by her Wolf. Again, as if her legs knew how to handle a guy this size, they instantly wrapped around Kalen's waist and he carried her out of the bathroom.

No one argued. No one bitched or whined or threw a hissy fit.

Kalen claimed this moment as his and that was all there was to it. Not even Sara stopped him.

CHAPTER 32

Kalen pushed his door open and gently laid Sara on the bed. Call him a bastard, but if it took a panic attack for her to want him, he was glad it happened.

She would get them from time to time. Everyone had their hang ups, and Sara's panic attacks were just like his night terrors - A lifelong affliction.

Was it any wonder? They've been through a lot. Some wounds healed while others left scars. Worth it, though. Soooo worth it when she focused on him and he and the rest of the pack were able to help her climb back to the reality of the situation, which was Sara was safe. She was home. Her Hounds had her surrounded.

Nothing but nothing got better than that.

"Kalen," she sighed when he leaned forward to take her mouth with his again. "I'm so sorry."

"Shhhhh," he didn't need her to apologize for shit. Not for what happened in the basement between them, not for what happened five years ago between them, not for anything. Kalen and Sara's relationship had no apologies.

He kissed down her neck and made it all the way to the edge of the towel that was still wrapped around her sweet body. "May

I?"

She nodded and bit her lip.

Fuck, he loved that look on her. It was the side of Sara he doubted the others got to see as often as he did. With the Hounds, she was in control and she was fierce and she was confident. Kalen knew because he'd been the one to watch. But in the moments when it was just the two of them and no other Hound was in the room, he saw the Sara that he'd fallen in love with over three hundred years ago when she was brought to his village from another clan. He'd fallen in love with her on the spot. Hard, fast, and completely, when she stood before his clan members – a prized possession and key to uniting two sides. She was brave yet a wee bit nervous. Confident but cautious. And she had a habit of biting her lip at the sweetest of times.

Those things about her never changed. He loved all her little quirks but his favorite was when she bit her bottom lip, like she was doing right now while he unwrapped her like a present.

Merry motherfucking Christmas to him. Or what was the next holiday coming up? Thanksgiving? Yeahhhh, Kalen thought, he had a lot to be grateful for right about now.

"You want to stop, say the word." He kissed her again. She moaned in response, a glorious sound he happily swallowed. "God damn I've missed you."

Kalen allowed the world to fall away until all that remained was him and Sara. Palming one breast, he bent down and suckled on her. Then he let go only to have his hand sail south. She spread her legs enough for him to have access to what he desperately wanted. Sinking his finger inside her, Kalen unraveled right along with her.

Moving his head down, Kalen kept pumping his finger in and out as his tongue joined the party. Sara let out a yip and grabbed a fistful of his hair. "Stop," she said.

He froze immediately. Ohhhh fuuuucckk. That look on her face was so priceless and hot he almost came in his pants.

"I want you inside me, Kalen." *Of course she would*, he thought. Sara was a Hell Hound. And being a Hound came with a few prices - one of which was the need for touching. Lots and lots and lots of sexual stimulation. Kalen bit back a smile as he climbed back on top of her.

"You sure about this?"

Sara nodded. "I want to feel you come inside me. I want to remember how you feel, Kalen. How... *we* feel."

She did not have to repeat that twice. Kalen ripped off his clothing and got back into position. "We stop if it gets to be too much, okay?"

Sara bit her lip again and nodded. Gripping his shoulders, she braced herself. Kalen watched her eyes roll back in her head when he pushed his way inside her. They both groaned with how good it felt. Kalen pulled out nice and slow and then pushed in, balls deep, taking his good ol' time. He wanted to drink in every ounce of this pleasure. Feel all of it. Memorize it.

"More," she urged. "Harder."

He quickened his pace and gently bit down on her neck. It seemed to be the thing that sent her over the edge. The scent of her arousal was fucking intoxicating. "More," she said again.

Kalen bit down harder on her neck, pinned her arms above her head, and started thrusting inside her like it was his last act on this earth.

"Oh God, don't stop!"

"Never." Kalen began pounding, knowing exactly how she liked it. Her hips met his every thrust, her back arched and she screamed his name when her orgasm hit. He let her ride it alone, nowhere near ready to seek his own pleasure. Not until she came a few more times and begged him to stop. "Hold on to me."

He let go of her hands so she could wrap them around his neck. When she latched on, he picked her up, still buried deep inside her, and moved them over to the dresser. One swipe of his hand and everything that was on it crashed to the floor. He put her sweet ass on the dresser, perched on the edge, and continued thrusting inside her. "Touch yourself," he coaxed.

He continued pumping his hips while Sara reached between them and began to work herself into a frenzy of desires again.

"That's it, Darling. Come for me. I want to see my cock coated with you."

She let out a guttural noise and he felt her inner walls squeeze him. With a roar, Kalen slammed into her again and again, making sure to wring every ounce of pleasure from her. "Hold on to me," he grabbed her by the ass and brought them back to the bed. This time, he pulled out long enough to flip her over onto her stomach. Instinctively, Sara lifted her hips and arched her back, giving him what he wanted – a perfect entrance.

He plunged inside her again and knew damn well this was going to be a mix of pleasure and pain for her. His Sara liked this almost as much as she enjoyed having someone watch her unravel.

Gripping her shoulders, Kalen had her almost immobile and then he slowly started to build another orgasm for her.

"Oh God, Kalen!"

He slammed into her again and again, "There is no God here."

Kalen let out a roar as they both came together.

Sara's head was going to explode. Nope, scratch that, ALL of her was going to explode. Kalen rocked her body, and she was absolutely certain she would never be able to walk again. Once completely satisfied, Kalen froze, suspended above her, and then slowly eased out of her.

She missed him instantly.

Kalen shifted to her right side and ran a lazy finger across the small of her back. "I feel alive again," he said in the moonlit bedroom.

She wasn't sure what to say, or even what to say first. "I remember." Tears filled her eyes and she let them come. "I remember you. Us."

His eyes widened, "How much?"

"All of it, I think." It was hard to tell. "Or... at least, I remember a long time ago."

Kalen curled his arm around her waist and slid her in close, pressing her body flush against his. "Jesus Christ, Sara." His voice cracked. And then she felt a heat roll off him and his chest jolt. It was then she realized he was quietly crying with her. "I don't have words for this."

"Sometimes words aren't necessary, Wolf." She craned her head and looked up at him. He was staring at the ceiling. "Kiss me?"

Kalen shifted his big body around and kissed her like his sanity depended upon it. His tongue swept into her mouth, caressing her, coaxing her, melting her. Next thing she knew, they were going for another round. "Are you too sore?"

"No," she smiled. "And even if I was I don't think I'd care. I want you."

The air whooshed out of him as he pushed his way back into her body. "I'm not ever going to get enough of you."

"Good," she gasped as he started to rock their bodies gently. "'Cause I plan to never get enough of you."

Kalen dipped down and kissed her again. Their mouths stayed pressed together as he picked up his pace and they both climaxed – first her, then him. He pulled out before she was able to beg for more. "You need to be able to walk, Darling."

"Walking is over-rated."

Kalen cracked a laugh. He looked so heartbreakingly beautiful when he was happy. After laying tangled in each other's arms for a little while longer, Sara's stomach growled and Kalen said, "You need to eat."

"I'm not very hungry."

"You say that, but if I had a cheeseburger in my hand right now, you'd probably inhale the whole thing in three bites."

Sara laughed, "That does sound yummy."

"Come on," he slapped her ass playfully, "Let's get you some food."

Sara groaned in protest. She really wanted to lay there and relive her old memories of Kalen but he was already stuffing those thick, muscular thighs of his into some pants. "Your hair is so much longer now," she said.

"I let it go." *After you disappeared*, wasn't said, but they both knew what he meant.

"I like it this way." She reached over and ran her hand through it. Then she gathered a fistful and gave it a tug, yanking his head back as far as it would go, before she kissed him. "I like this a lot, Wolf."

"Gonna use it for a leash, are you?"

"Maybe," she bit his bottom lip and was rewarded with a growl.

"It's good to have you back, woman."

Sara climbed off the bed and pulled her long hair into a knot on the top of her head. The air rushed out of her body when she felt Kalen's finger trail down her spine the same way Tanner had earlier.

"It's back," he whispered. His voice was low and controlled to the point where she wondered if he'd even said the words at all.

"What?"

"My mark is back on your spine, Sara."

She rushed over to the mirror hanging on the door of his closet. She couldn't see it though, but she trusted Kalen and if he said the tat was there, then it was.

Trust.

She trusted Kalen.

Sara tried to hold onto the idea that was half formed in her mind, but it faded away like mist before she was able to fully comprehend it. "Was it the sex?"

"I don't think so." Kalen kissed the top of her head.

Sara bit her lip and then it dawned on her… "It was the panic attack." She looked up at Kalen, her eyes big as saucers, "It was you helping me climb out of that mess."

"Maybe…"

"No, not maybe. The answer is yes, Kalen." She wrapped her arms around him and squeezed, "I knew I was okay with you. I knew you'd help me get out of that dark place. You just," she thought more about it, "You just focused and pushed your all into me, forcing me to breathe, to come back, to rise above the panic."

Kalen kissed her again. "We all helped you. It wasn't just me."

"No, I mean, yes, but I only focused on you. You were all I could feel. All I could see." She squeezed him again. "It was you. I knew if I kept myself focused on your eyes, your voice, I'd be okay. You'd make me okay again. You'd save me."

Kalen wrapped his arms around her and squeezed. "Fuck, Sara." He kissed the top of her head. "We all saved you together, but if you saw only me, then I'm glad I was what you needed. And I'm glad you trusted me in your darkness."

"Not the first time you've done that."

He pulled away and looked at her, shaking his head, verifying her statement. "Come on, let's go down and be with everyone."

Sara pulled on the t-shirt Kalen handed her. The damn thing

hit her knees because Kalen was as big as a Viking. She caught a whiff of his scent as she tugged the shirt on, and all of her lit up inside. He smelled like home.

And home was where the heart lived.

CHAPTER 33

Tanner grabbed three beers from the fridge and handed them out. He tried not to pout, but seriously, it was hard. Really fucking hard.

"If you can't play with the big dogs, stay on the porch, Tanner." Jack winked and tossed in a twenty.

"Says the fucker who's known for cheating." Tanner tossed his twenty into the pot the same time Eli did.

"I don't cheat; you just have the worst poker face in the entire world."

"No I don't." Tanner's leg bobbed up and down. He had three Aces. That was fucking awesome. "Raise."

Eli did a facepalm. "Dude."

"What?"

"Seriously man, you gotta work on containing your excitement."

"I have a lot to be happy for. I can't contain all this," Tanner waved his hand over his body. "This much awesome just cannot be tamped down."

Jack laughed and went all in. Tanner followed suit. Eli folded.

"Whatcha got?"

Tanner proudly displayed his three Aces. Annnnnd then Jack

tossed his cards on the table, showing off four Kings.

"Mother Fucker!" All Tanner could do was accept defeat and drown his sorrows in beer. Then he snatched Eli's and drank his, too.

"Hey guys," Sara padded into the kitchen with Kalen close behind her.

"Heyyyyy," Eli got up and offered Sara his chair.

Kalen grabbed two beers from the fridge and handed one to Sara. "You never learn do you, Tanner?"

The Hound shrugged his shoulders.

"What happened?" Sara tucked her legs under her butt and gave Tanner a poor baby face.

"Jack took all my money and now I'm so sad."

Sara slid out of her chair and sauntered over to the pouting Hound. She straddled him as if it was the most natural thing in the world to do. "Better?"

"A little."

She cupped his face and kissed him softly, "How about now?"

"Sort of." Fuck him sideways, she was hot like this. Tanner tried to keep his hands off of her, which meant he was clutching his drink so hard it was in jeopardy of shattering.

"What about now?" she nibbled that hot spot just below his ear.

"Fuck, Sara." Tanner couldn't help but gyrate his hips and rub against her. She smelled like sex and strawberries and he was totally down with sex and strawberries.

"We're trying to play a game here, love." Jack fussed, playfully.

"Don't listen to him, Beautiful. He tried to take all my money. It wasn't a game, it was a robbery."

"I hardly robbed you. You practically threw your money at me."

Sara's laugh bounced around the kitchen. "I have a feeling you're very transparent, Tanner. And Jack," she twisted around to look at him, "is very good at keeping his face unreadable."

"Twenty bucks says you can crack him, Beautiful." Tanner nipped her shoulder blade while he glared excitedly at Jack.

"I want in on that," Eli slapped his money on the table. "Kalen?"

The Wolf looked from Sara to Jack then back to Sara. "Fifty says he wins."

"WHAT!" Sara hopped off Tanner's lap with a snarl. "You have no faith in me?"

Kalen winked and sat back, arms crossed over his chest. He was enjoying every minute of this.

"Get him, Beautiful. Make him suffer for taking all my money." Tanner cracked her ass and took another sip of beer.

It was all eyes on Sara as she rose to the challenge. Sauntering around the table, she made her way over to Jack. He was at the far end, leaning back with a smirk. "I'm going to love spending your money, Hounds."

"Gonna spend some on me?" Sara ran her hand up his arm, across his shoulders and down his other arm.

"What would you like, love?"

"A puppy."

"You have Tanner. He's a puppy for your love."

Tanner didn't even try to scowl. It was the truth. If Kalen was Sara's wolf, Tanner was absolutely the puppy for her love. He didn't mind in the slightest either. Tanner was the fun one. The others took life too seriously and she came to Tanner when she was ready to let loose and be extreme. And silly.

"A night in the clubs, then. And you have to dance with me. All night."

Tanner bit back his smile. Did Sara remember Jack didn't dance? Well, he did, but only because Sara had forced him to take lessons. He hated it though and only did it for her.

"You have to make me crack first, love. And I'm far from losing this." Jack's face remained emotionless.

Sara looked at Tanner and winked, then she glanced at Kalen, then lastly Eli. "Hand me that knife over there, Eli."

He snatched his shiny new Chef's knife from the chopping block and placed it gently on the table. They all waited with bated breath.

"What the hell are you going to do with that, love?" Jack's face remained impassive.

"You'll see." Sara sat down on Jack's lap and wiggled her ass against him. "Eli? Be a dear and take that knife for a moment."

Tanner sat up straighter and leaned forward. What the fuck

was she up to?

Sara let her hair down, fanning all those beautiful waves across her back. Tanner stared at her, his eyes fixed on hers from across the way while she placed her hand on the table, fanning her fingers out.

She purred, "Eli?"

"Yeah, baby?"

"How good is your aim?"

"Spot on, why?"

"Let's play the knife game."

Tanner's breath caught. Sara hated that game. She hated playing or watching it be played. One wrong move and someone's finger would be cut clean off. Or their hand impaled.

"Sara," Tanner stood up and Kalen stopped him.

"Let her."

"But—"

"Let. Her."

Tanner wanted to scream. This wasn't right. This wasn't a game his Beautiful would ever play. Trusting Kalen wouldn't give the order unless she was truly going to be okay, Tanner did as he was commanded and sat back down. Vibrating with anticipation, his leg started bobbing up and down with wayyyy too much nervous energy.

"We're waiting, Eli." Sara smiled.

"Are you fucking serious, baby?"

"Yup. Do it."

Eli gripped the handle of his knife and Tanner noticed he was nervous as fuck. Eli looked down at her hand and she said, "Eyes on me, big boy. Eyes. On. Me."

Fuuuuck, Tanner didn't like this. *Bad idea! BAD IDEA!*

"Jack," she purred leaning into him a little. "Hold me."

"Don't do this, love."

"Eli," Sara ignored Jack's plea, "Now."

Eli's arm swung down hard and fast. They all flinched when the blade pierced the wood.

"Again," she barked.

He complied.

"Faster, Eli."

Tanner held his breath as Eli's speed picked up. *Boom, boom,*

boom, boom, boom! His knife hit the wood between each of Sara's delicate, long fingers.

"AGAIN!" she roared.

Eli stabbed over and over and over and over until she and Eli were both screaming. Not once, even for a fraction of a second, did they break their eye contact with each other. The knife pierced the table again and again. Faster, faster, faster, FASTER!

Tanner stood, hands gripping the top of his head, panic and fear choking his airway. Kalen sat still as a statue. Jack wasn't moving.

Eli's hand was a blur with that blade. The wood chipped away, splinters flying with every strike he made.

Tanner couldn't take it anymore. The pressure was too much. If Eli ended up hacking off one of Sara's fingers, she'd have trouble throwing a blade during a hunt. If he stabbed her hand, he could destroy her tendons for a while. FUCK! Tanner shook with fear. "ENOUGH!" he yelled.

Eli's hand halted, mid-swing, breath punching out of him. He slowly lowered the blade back onto the table and fell into his chair. Looks like Tanner's nerves weren't the only ones shot.

Sara turned around and they all looked at Jack. His face was still stoic as ever. "Nice show, love. But you'll have to do better than that. Eli's the best out of the five of us with a blade."

"But I didn't know that." She said calmly. "I don't remember that yet."

She stood up and turned around, giving them her back and she lifted her shirt up and over her head. Tanner fell into his chair. He gave her sweet, bare ass no attention, which said a lot for him. But he was currently staring at something far more spectacular than Sara's ass at the moment.

She swept her hair over her shoulder and looked over at Tanner, tossing him a wink. "One or two?"

"Two," Tanner gasped. She had two of their tats on her spine again. Kalen's and Eli's.

"How's Jack's poker face doing now?"

Tanner's gaze swung over to Jack.

VICTORY!

"Holy fuckety fuck!" Tanner popped up on his feet and rushed her. Slamming Sara against his chest, he found her mouth

187

and ravished her.

"Holy shit," Eli gasped. "How did this happen?"

Tanner broke away from Sara and jabbed a finger in Jack's face. "Pay up, Voodoo Man."

The Hound made no moves at all. Jack just sat there, statue still, with his mouth slightly agape. He clamped it shut once he realized they were all gawking at him. "Well played, love. Well, fucking, played."

Sara smiled and shimmied back into her over-sized shirt. "Trust," she winked at Tanner.

Well wasn't that enough to make him howl. Tanner threw his head back and howled like the happiest fucking Hound this side of Hell. Then he picked Sara up and twirled her around. "God damn, Beautiful, that was such a risk."

"One I had to take."

Eli buried his face in his hands, unable to grasp what had just happened. "I think I'm going to puke."

"You?" Jack ran his hands through his short hair, "I just lost to Tanner! TANNER!"

"Annnnnd you liked it," Tanner snatched the money from the table and stuffed it into his back pocket. "Admit it. That was a helluva way to lose."

Jack chuckled nervously as he smiled over at Sara.

"This calls for a celebration!" Tanner snatched the bottle of whiskey from the cabinet above the fridge and five shot glasses.

Sara sat back down on Jack's lap and Tanner frowned. "Hey, I'm the winner."

"Which is why I'm now sitting on pouty Jack's lap." Sara leaned back and kissed his cheek. "Are you mad?" she whispered in his ear.

Jack's face was impassive again as he ground his molars. "No, love." His hot breath tickled her ear when he said, "You never cease to amaze me. It's what I've always loved most about you."

Two down and two to go. Tanner and Jack would have their tats back on her spine soon enough. They both just hoped it wouldn't take a blade to do it.

CHAPTER 34

The sun was rising by the time the pack settled down. Still sitting around the kitchen table, they spent the rest of the evening, and the dawn, telling old stories, reminiscing, and hoping Sara would remember the moments they told her about.

It was all in good fun. No pressure, of course. But Sara felt a desperate need to recall the memories they were tossing around like fun stories. She felt a pang of guilt for not being able to do so.

"Hounds," Kalen's hoarse tone cut through their laughter, "As nice as this evening has been, we need to focus again."

"Agreed," Jack sipped his coffee, dodging Sara's quizzical look. "I hate to be the one to ask, but…"

"Can we talk about what happened in the tub?" Eli butted right in and took the burden off Jack.

The entire atmosphere changed in the kitchen. The Hounds were turning cautious around her.

Sara shrugged, "I can't really explain it. I was…" Yeah, maybe she shouldn't get into the specifics of what she'd been doing in the tub, "I slipped and submerged completely under the water and then it was like—"

Her breath hitched and Kalen's hand wrapped around hers and he squeezed it. "You're okay."

"I was drowning."

Tanner cursed under his breath, as did Jack. Eli, however just stared at his mug.

"There were these people holding me down. And they had animal faces. Masks or something."

"How many?" someone asked.

Sara closed her eyes, trying to recall her vision. "Three, maybe? Or there could have been more. It felt like there was more." She clutched Kalen's hand tighter. "There was a crow, a big thing with horns, a pig, and maybe some others? I'm not sure. I feel stupid even saying this much. It was like National Geographic, horror edition."

"Ring any bells?" Jack asked the room.

They all shook their heads.

"I was in the same clothes as when I died." She hurried to add, "But I was naked when they were holding me down, which makes me more confused." That didn't make any sense at all. "At some point, I drowned. I..." Sara looked at Kalen and then it dawned on her that maybe her memories were crossing her deaths, mixing them all up.

Her memories about her and Kalen were ones she hadn't examined too closely yet. She just hadn't had a chance to. But now that she thought about it... yes, she drowned at some point in her life. "Did I drown the first time I died, Kalen?"

His face was carefully masked. Slowly, he started shaking his head. "No, darling."

Damnit, she was so confused again.

"They drowned me the second time I died then. I think." Disappointment practically choked her because she thought she remembered everything about Kalen, which should have included how she died three hundred years ago. Now, she was realizing she didn't remember it all.

Double damnit.

"Don't worry," Kalen caressed her arm, "it'll come back to you, eventually."

Going by the pain in his eyes, she wasn't sure she *wanted* to remember.

"What's your earliest memory of one of us, love?"

Sara looked down at her mug that said *Poe me a cup* with

Edgar Allen Poe's face on it. "I remember seeing Kalen with grass in his hair. He was over by the horses." She looked at him and frowned, "Why don't we sound Scottish?"

Kalen erupted in a fit of laughter, "We shed our brogue forever ago, Sara."

"Why?" she was rather fond of a Scottish accent. It sucked to have had one and lost it.

"We didn't stay in Scotland after we died."

She paused, focused super hard... "Yeah," she mumbled. "It wasn't safe to go back, was it? We stayed in Hell for a long time and then we started building our pack."

"That's right," Kalen beamed a smile and if she was wearing panties, they would have melted off her right then and there.

"And then..." her gaze sailed to Eli, "We met Jack and then Eli," her gaze spun around to the other end of the table, "Then our Sunshine Boy, Tanner."

Tanner grinned, "Saved the best for last, if you ask me."

"I won't argue with that logic."

The question of how she died the first time was on the tip of her tongue, but she stopped herself from asking. She had a feeling it was a gruesome death. Still, something... some piece of a memory or concern fluttered in her head. She spilled out the words in a rush, "Did I get the rest of our clan killed?"

"Don't worry about that clan, Sara." Kalen's voice had a sharp edge to it.

"How about some breakfast?" Eli popped up and began banging pots and pans around. "Tanner, grab the bacon."

Jack stood up and stretched. "I'll go put wood in the furnace so we can have hot showers in a bit." Their furnace didn't just heat the house, it was used for the hot water, too. The damn thing was the only bit of efficiency in the otherwise old, creaky house.

Sara silently watched everyone get busy. It was obvious what they were doing – distraction sometimes looked like bacon and home fries. "Can we go out for breakfast instead?"

She was sick of being in the house. She wanted fresh air badly.

Eli shrugged, "I'm down for getting out of the house."

"I'll grab some weapons," Tanner vanished into the other room.

Sara looked down at her bare legs. "I guess I should get

dressed." She wandered up the steps and into Jack's room. He came in soon after and shut the door with a soft click.

She pulled on some yoga pants and a bra and was now trying to find a comfy shirt by rummaging through her one and only drawer in his room. Jack stepped closer to her and trailed his finger down her spine. It made her shiver. Snatching a white v-neck, she tugged it over her girls and turned to face him. "I'm sorry," she said quietly.

Jack leaned in slowly, "What would you have to be sorry about?"

She tried to swallow around the lump of guilt wedged in her throat. "That your tattoo isn't on me."

"Yet," his mouth grazed her earlobe. "It'll be there soon enough, love. I'm not worried." His hands wrapped around her waist and he felt good and strong and confident. It was something she seriously loved about this Hound. Nothing rattled him.

"I feel like time is ticking."

"It is," his gravelly voice sent another shiver down her limbs.

She put her hands on his shoulders to steady herself. Seriously, Jack had a way about him that just made her mush. "Are we in danger?"

"Not so long as we're together, love." He raised her chin with his finger, "and I have no intentions of getting separated ever again."

She blushed. "Gonna chain me to you with handcuffs?"

"Now there's a thought." His eyes glinted with mischief. Jack leaned around and opened his top, middle drawer. "Take your pick, love."

Sara looked down and her mouth hit the floor. The entire drawer was filled with –

"What the hell is this for?" she picked up something that looked like big silver tweezers with balls on the end.

Jack laughed and took it from her. Then he ran it over her breast, circling her nipple with it. "That's for later. Right now, the Hounds are hungry and we can't let them starve." He tossed the whatever the fuck it was back into the drawer and snatched a shirt from his closest while Sara stood there dumbfounded, hot, and curious.

Jack opened his bedroom door and held it for her, "After

you."

Sara practically stumbled out of the bedroom. She was seriously hungry but it wasn't for pancakes.

CHAPTER 35

They took Jack's Camaro. He insisted on driving. Kalen sat up front with him because he was the biggest. Although, seriously, Eli was a close second and Tanner was crazy tall, sooooo yeah, Sara just sat in the back, sandwiched between two yummy Hounds.

"Can I ask about going off-grid?"

Kalen turned down the volume on the radio and nodded.

"How does that work, exactly?"

"Magic," they all said together.

Kalen twisted around so he could look at her while he said, "We have certain powers as Hounds. Like opening up the Hell holes, scaling walls, that kind of thing. But when we're all together and need a recharge, we can put up a field that makes us unable to be detected."

"Does that work when we're separated?"

"Yes, individually we can go undetected by the living."

"The living?"

"We're Hounds, Sara. We're not dead, but we've died."

Tanner joined in the convo, "We got a second chance at life. Did Lucifer not explain any of this to you?"

"No," Sara grimaced, "not really. He said you guys would guide me."

"Dick." Tanner had such a way with words.

"So I can be undetectable now?"

"Yes, but it'll cost you energy since you're outside the house. And it's not something that can always be spared." Jack parallel parked in front of a diner and turned off the ignition. "The reason we can do it at home is because our house is attached to Lucifer. The doorway to Hell is literally in our basement."

"Do all Hounds have a doorway like that in their house?"

"Yeah," Jack said, "Each pack has a portal into Hell and that kind of power has no bounds, so we could technically go undetected forever and not get our energy levels dinged for it. But out and about, individually? It costs us."

"You'd think it wouldn't matter," Sara tried to wrap her head around the whole concept. "Lucifer's power he gave us to go undetected should be strong no matter if we're home or not without it costing us a damn thing."

Eli shrugged. "He likes his Hounds on a tight leash."

"Clearly," Sara climbed out of the back seat and smoothed down her shirt. "Do all energy transfers drain you like that?"

"Yes," they all answered in unison.

Jack held the door open for everyone as they filed into the small diner, "Thank you," she said. "Not for being the door man, but for giving me so much of your energy when we met. I didn't realize what it had cost you. Or how much danger you'd put yourself into doing that for me."

Jack smiled, "Think on it no more, Sara. You're worth any price."

Okay, now she was blushing. As she moved passed him, Jack slapped her ass and let the door close behind them. They sat down at a corner booth and packed in tight.

"I'm ordering the entire right side of this menu," Tanner announced.

"Then I'll order the left side," Eli closed his menu and placed it in the middle of the table.

Moments later, the waitress came and took everyone's orders, which also included the lumberjack special for Jack, the sunshine platter for Kalen, and Sara's order of baked oatmeal and fruit.

She was midway through her meal when something caught her attention over by the kitchen. "Shit," she hissed. "There's a *malanum* over by the coffee station."

They all casually looked over in that direction, "Where?" Eli asked.

"Right. There." Sara stopped herself from pointing at it. "You don't see it?"

Kalen slid out of his seat, palming a small blade against his arm. He casually walked over to the counter, snatched the black spirit and dragged it unceremoniously out from behind the counter. Jack sprinted towards the door and opened it, like the polite doorman he was today, and Sara watched through the window as they dragged the *malanum* around the corner and out of sight. Kalen and Jack hadn't even bothered concealing themselves. They just dragged an evil entity right out of the diner and slung it back into a Hell hole in broad daylight.

Moments later, they returned with matching scowls on their faces.

"Only like .01% of the living population can see *malanum*," Tanner explained as if he read Sara's confused little mind. "So long as we're calm, cool and collected about it, we don't have to pull the go-into-ghost-form stunt."

Her eyebrows popped up in surprise. "So if Kalen had pulled some magic out and ghosted, would we still see him?"

"Yeah, 'cause we're Hounds. All Hounds can see each other. No matter what state we're in." Tanner grabbed the ketchup and dumped it all over his hashbrowns. Sara shivered and called him a monster for it. He laughed and snarled viciously when he took the first bite.

They left the diner with full bellies and Sara tried to convince them to go shopping. "I need more clothes."

"You have plenty," Jack grumbled.

"No, I don't. My drawer in your room is almost empty and I haven't even been back a week."

Jack smiled wickedly, "Clothes are overrated."

"But necessary when I'm hunting."

"You're not hunting anytime soon, so clothes are a non-issue."

Regardless, he opened the door for them and the Hounds filed into a boutique.

Sara looked around and put her hands on her hips, "Seriously?"

"Clothes are overrated, love. But this," he held up a tiny sliver of lace lingerie, "is most definitely a necessity."

She felt her cheeks get hot. Her Hounds did the divide and conquer routine – moving around the store like they were well acquainted with the place.

Sara crossed her arms over her chest, "I'm sure I have some of this crap in one of your drawers at home."

"Nope," Tanner answered while digging through a rack of lacey strappy things. "These little gems don't last past one wear with us."

She arched an eyebrow. "Well that sounds like a waste."

"Not for us. Money well fucking spent," Eli winked. "What say you, Hounds?"

They all let out a half-growl, half-bark.

Holy Hell Hounds…their animalistic sound sent a searing heat straight to the joining of her thighs. How was that even possible? Dear God. She felt dizzy.

Hot. It was so hot in here all of a sudden.

Eli steered her over to a lounging area and handed her a glass of champagne from a silver tray. "Stay here until we're done. You're distracting."

Helpless, Sara obeyed and tried to tame the lust surging in her body. This was crazy. Stupid crazy. Beautifully, wonderfully deliciously crazy.

Chugging her bubbly, Sara started fanning herself. Shit, it was really, really getting way too hot in here.

"Make it fast, gentlemen," Jack tossed a bunch of things onto the counter and a woman started ringing up the merchandise.

"Is she okay?" the cashier asked.

"Just hot," Jack smiled.

"And bothered," Tanner tossed his stuff on top of Jack's.

"And needy," Eli added more to the tab.

Kalen was over in the far corner grumbling about never having the right size in the color he liked. Finally, he showed up at the counter with his choices. The cashier began carefully folding each piece separately and wrapping them in tissue paper.

"That's really not necessary," Jack grabbed handfuls of the lace and satin and started stuffing the things into the bag. "Just toss it in."

"I'll take Sara out for fresh air," Tanner shoved off the counter and headed towards their woman.

"That'll be Two thousand, three hundred forty-two dollars and eleven cents."

Sara squeaked when she heard the amount as Tanner rushed her out of the boutique. "Are you guys crazy?"

"Just for you, Beautiful."

She slapped his shoulder. "You all just spent over two grand on dumb lace."

"And satin," he grinned. "We got off cheap this time."

"Cheap!"

"Yeah, last trip to a place like this cost us a smidgeon under ten grand."

Sara rocked back on her feet and gawked. "WHAT?"

"We were just in a hurry this time because you know," he motioned his hand over her like she was the cause of their shopping excursion being cut short.

"Can we go home now?" Eli asked as Jack and Kalen carried the bags out of the shop.

"I need clothes, damnit!" Sara actually stomped her foot. "Not straps and silk!"

Tanner grabbed her hand and dragged her towards the car. "I'll order you outfits online. Come on."

She had no choice but to go with them. Not only was the Camaro her only ride home, but she was seriously in need of something... and that something was best done in the privacy of her own house.

With her own Hounds.

"Oh dear God," she gasped, "Am I in *heat*?"

The Hounds all burst into laughter and Jack's engine revved so loud it vibrated her bones.

That wasn't really a yes or a no answer though, now was it?

CHAPTER 36

They pulled up to the farmhouse and Jack parked in the detached garage. Everyone got out of the car and Sara's mind was still trying to wrap around her current situation. They opened the back door to a high-pitched alarm going off and Tanner rushed past everyone and booked it up the steps.

"What is that?" Sara asked.

Just before he could answer, Jack's cell phone rang and he reached into his pocket, pulled it out and frowned. "Yeah?" Jack answered his phone and moved out of the kitchen and into the living room to talk.

The alarm finally stopped but Sara wasn't dropping the subject, "Kalen, what was that noise?"

"That alarm is one of Tanner's. It signals us when there's been a huge power outage somewhere or an unusual surge."

Made sense. If they were Hounds who hunted evil spirits, and said evil spirits had a nasty habit of fucking with electronics, then it would be smart to have something that could alert the Hounds when the *malanum* were up to no good. Sara thought back to how often she'd seen those fuckers mess with traffic lights, blow fuse boxes, that kinda thing. Once, when she was haunting an apartment in Virginia, the entire basement was filled with *malanum* and they managed to not only short-circuit the whole building, but let the electric box catch fire.

Sara had depleted her very limited supply of energy that night waking up those who were still asleep so they could have a chance to evacuate. The firefighters were able to rescue the remainders, thank goodness. It was a mess, though. And afterwards, Sara had run as fast as she could to get away from the swarm that had taken over the building she'd been in.

"What's wrong?" Kalen reached out and rubbed her cheek, "You look pale."

"Nothing."

"You're safe, Sara." Eli said.

"I know I am, but," she looked back and forth between the two. "I think those dark spirits have been gunning for me. Like I was a target, not just another soul to infect."

Kalen sat straighter. "I'm listening."

"The entire time I was a ghost, they kept trying to get at me. Not like they would another ghost, it was like they wanted to... possess me." Well now she felt stupid saying it out loud. Egotistical maniacs sound like this. "The night Jack found me, I was attacked. By then, I'd almost turned anyway."

Their impassive expressions had her assuming they already knew about it.

"Jack said they run from Hounds. It's why we have to hunt them down, right? Except I didn't have to hunt them. They came right at me. Like I had a big fat 'Come and get me' sign on my ass."

Eli and Kalen looked at each other and she grew anxious. "Talk out loud, guys. I don't speak mental-man."

Eli rubbed his thumb across his bottom lip, thinking. "Do you remember anything about the mission you were on, baby?"

"Not really." She sat back and let go of Eli's hand, "I know we were on a hunt for a traitor. I was getting dressed for a party we were going to work, undercover. All I remember is opening the door, thinking it was Kalen, and getting my throat pierced with a big knife."

She didn't look over at Kalen. He was being so damn still she figured he turned into stone. Heat radiated off him and it wasn't a good heat, it was dangerous.

Eli nodded, "Luce suspects a traitor."

Kalen cleared his throat and took a seat at the kitchen table. "Someone seems to have the capability to conjure the *malanum*, they're cracking Hell's prison walls big enough so the fissures don't mend swiftly."

"Wait, what do you mean? This is still happening?"

"Oh yeah, and it's gotten way worse." Eli looked from Sara to Kalen then back to Sara. "We've been trying to catch them, working with Hounds in the other districts to take as many as we can down."

"This has gone beyond keeping the balance, Sara. We're on the brink of war."

Well shit, she thought. "Have you seen a pattern or anything?"

"In the past five years, we've noticed these massive power surges that move from city to city. Tanner set up a sort of tracking system by tapping into the power company databases."

"Hacking, you mean."

"He's also got certain online sites flagged to watch for posts on increased death rates in major cities, leaked footage, police scanners. Jack has Mediums all around the world keeping him updated on anything strange they're able to sense, too." Eli looked over at Kalen, "Anything we're missing here?"

Kalen fixed his eyes on Sara and smiled, "Not anymore."

Her cheeks were getting redder. Damnit. Why was she a blusher? She was a grown woman. Grown women shouldn't blush all the time like this. "So have you found anything strange with the power surges or anything?"

Eli shook his head, "No, it started in Jackson, Mississippi, then Georgia, then, what was it Kalen?"

"Charleston."

Sara covered her mouth with her hand before saying, "What about Charlotte? Greensboro?"

"Yeah, I think." Eli's brow furrowed.

"Virginia after that?"

"Yeah," Kalen leaned in and was making a similar face as Eli. "What are you thinking, Sara?"

"I'm thinking that's the same trail I was on during my death. That was the direction and cities I stayed in during the past five years."

Kalen leaned back and swiped a hand over his mouth.

"And if they're now happening here," Sara tossed her hands up in a *ta-da* way "maybe it's because I'm here." It was a bit narcissistic to think an entire species of evil was tailing her because she was just that extra special, but the dots were there and easy to connect.

"She might be on to something, Kalen."

Tanner ran into the kitchen. "East side just went out, but it's back up now. No damage." He plopped into a chair.

"Eastside of Philly?" Sara asked.

"Yeah."

"Fuck," Kalen scrubbed his face with both hands before popping up and going into the living room just to drag Jack back in with him seconds later.

"We got a serious problem," Kalen announced once they were all together. "Sara's been followed."

Jack crossed his arms over his chest, "I'm listening."

"You said they attacked her when you found her the other night," Tanner looked absolutely vicious. All that cute blonde, blue-eyed sweetness was suddenly replaced with a viper attitude and piercing eyes. "And that she was turning into one of them."

"Yeah."

"What if she wasn't just turning. What if she was *turning*."

Eli cracked a fist on the table. "Tanner, talk normal, not all Tannery."

Okay, with how they were being all testy and snarly, clearly the Hounds had gone into protective-mode, ready to attack whoever took what was theirs away. Or maybe Sara was fantasizing that?

"Here's my theory," Tanner's knee started bobbing up and down. "She was stripped of our tats, which means—"

"She no longer had our protection. And the pack was weakened." Kalen let out an involuntary growl.

"And she was stripped of her power. All Lucifer's magic was gone, right?"

Jack nodded.

Kalen's next growl was louder. Okay, that one was totally voluntary. Probably.

"She was a hollow shell, Jack. You said it yourself." Tanner's knee started to rock the table at this point. "She was empty, guys."

The idea hit Eli like a sledgehammer. "Empty and in need of filling."

Tanner's knee just kept bobbing. "They could have possessed her entirely. They could have taken her over and make her come back to us. Trick us."

"Kill us."

"And get to Lucifer. She's his favorite. He'd never suspect her being the traitor."

"Woah, woah, woah, guys." Sara stood up and backed away, "I'm not the traitor. I haven't traitored at all." Traitored was officially a word now.

"How would that even be possible?" Jack ignored Sara's outburst, "That doesn't make sense. I mean, yes, they were after her, but what good would it have done to use her to get to Lucifer?"

"Makes sense to me. Kill the man in charge; get a new man in charge."

"No one bloody wants that bastard's job!"

Tanner tapped the table. "Listen, it fits, Jack. And whoever is in charge can open the gates and let everything out instead of chipping away at the walls like they're currently somehow doing."

"Which would do nothing but cause total Armageddon and no one would bother with that bullshit. There'd be nothing left to play with."

They all leaned back in silence as if Jack had just made an excellent point.

"Regardless of the why, the bottom line is the traitor's still out there. We have to find out who it is and stop them before they realize Sara is whole again and try for round two with her." Eli sat down and sighed. "It's only gotten worse lately. We all know it. The Gate Keepers are struggling to keep Hell intact. Lucifer's hands are tied because he can't do much topside. All the Hounds are busy as fuck hunting all the goddamn time. The packs have done nothing but be at each other's throats." Eli huffed as he realized something. "It's turning into anarchy, isn't it? Everything is falling to pieces. And fast. At least Sara is now back, unharmed."

"And hunted!" Kalen slammed his fist on the table and the damn thing cracked.

"Two tables in one week? Really Kalen?" Eli pushed out of his chair and started pacing.

"Let's focus on the good, guys," Tanner's knee was still bounce-bounce-bouncing. "Sara's back, our pack is whole, and we've always been the best Hell Hounds. We're only stronger with our girl back. Until she gets all her tats again, which," - he silenced Jack before he could butt in - "she's already halfway there in just the few days she's been with us. Add to that the fact that she will eventually, hopefully sooner rather than later, get her memories back, then she'll be able to tell us a little more about what the fuck happened in New Orleans. Only when that happens can we move forward with the grand hunt. Meanwhile, she stays here with us and we stay off the fucking grid. Call in favors, have the other Hounds hunt our district. Luce said we had off until Sara was back in full force. Make it be under his orders, not ours. Right now, our top priority is Sara. Hell's problems can wait a little longer."

Jack's arms dropped to his sides, "Well damn, Tanner."

"What?"

"That's bloody brilliant."

Tanner cocked his head annoyed, "Seriously fucker? Now you give me compliments. What about when I had that genius plan about the Voodoo Games?"

Eli dropped his head and groaned, "He was so close." Looking over at Sara, he explained, "About two years ago, Tanner wanted the Hounds to run a Voodoo Games contest, kinda like the Hunger Games, but with magic."

"And roosters." Tanner added, "I still think it would have been awesome."

Sara started giggling. The giggles turned to laughter which grew into hilarious cackles. Tears started streaming down her cheeks and she held her stomach, continuing to laugh her ass off.

"Beautiful, I love your laugh and all, but it hurts a little when you're laughing this fucking hard at me."

Sara made her way over to Tanner and sat on his lap, "I'm not laughing at you, I'm laughing because I'm so fucking happy right now."

"Great," Jack threw his hands up in the air, "She's been infected with Tanner's crazy."

"Like that would be so bad," Tanner rolled his eyes and kissed Sara's nose, "Crazy people have the most fun."

"No offense Sara, but what about this entire situation could possibly be making you happy enough to cry?" Eli was truly fuming.

Sara sobered up when she realized how upset he still was. "I don't care what happens. I don't care if there's a war, I don't care if Hell busts open, I don't care if every traffic light in Philly goes out and the entire power grid on the East Coast blows up. I don't care about what creepy crawly piece of shit is out there right now and I don't care if they're hunting me." She stood up and swiped her cheeks, "I'm so happy because I've spent five years trying to fight by myself. Trying to find my way to where I needed to be."

Now she was starting to cry for real, "I spent five years scared and angry and holding onto my little sliver of light. I wanted someone to see me." Now her voice rose, sounding more desperate, and she looked over at Jack. "I just wanted someone to listen. To notice. To fucking CARE." Sara sniffled a couple times. "And now here I am, with four guys who half the time I feel like I've just met and the other half I feel like I've known and loved all my life. And here you all sit, talking about me, freaking out and breaking tables because you're scared for me, planning how you're all going to keep me safe and you all fucking care…. About me."

"Of course we do, love." Jack cupped her face in his hands. "We fucking love you, woman." He claimed her mouth and kissed her slow and sweet. Next thing she knew, Eli pulled her away and took her mouth with full lips and a wicked tongue, and then Kalen was tugging her into his arms. He ran his hand through her hair, kissing her breathless. She stumbled forward, knees weak and body turning to hot lava. She was suddenly nose-to-nose with Tanner who picked her up and those damn legs of hers wrapped around his waist.

"Saved the best for last again, I see," he winked just before kissing her good and stupid.

Sara let their love wash over her. This was her home, these were her Hounds, and nothing was taking her away from them ever again. She was going to make sure of it.

CHAPTER 37

"We can't just stay locked up in here," Sara took a swig of her beer.

"We can until you're ready to go out again."

She deadpanned Jack. "I'm going to go crazy if I'm cooped up."

"We'll keep you occupied."

"I'm down for that. I'm great at distraction," Tanner winked.

"This doesn't seem right. Why can't Lucifer just fire me up or something?"

Eli started laughing, "Fire you up? He barely knew what to do with you the first time you showed up on his doorstep. I don't think anyone, even the Devil, can fire you into something you're not ready to be."

"But I am ready," she fussed. "I'm a Hound. I'm so ready to go out there and kill."

Kalen shook his head. "Not without your tats, Sara."

"I've survived five years without my tats, Kalen." Well now she felt bad. The whole kitchen grew quiet, "Look, all I'm saying is, I can fight. I have my powers back, and I clearly never lost my memory when it came to taking down a threat. I don't see why we have to stay here all holed up like bears in a cave."

"Wolves, you mean." Kalen leaned in and glared at her, "I'm not a fucking teddy bear."

Her smile grew a mile wide. "Wolves, then."

"We're already under direct order from Lucifer to sit tight." Jack said. "Our priority, and Lucifer's, is for you to get your spine re-inked with our marks again. Even Hell can wait. The Devil's made that clear."

"I only need two more. That can't be hard. I trust you. I do. Seriously." She was half tempted to pull her shirt off and see if the tats were already there.

"You need *three* more, love. You need your own mark back as well."

"What kind of bullshit is that? I trust myself. That should have been there all along."

Eli shook his head. "You have to trust us all together. If we move as one unit on the field, you have to trust that all actions are taken for the good of the pack. You can't second guess one of us. It's not about trusting just yourself in a tight spot, its trusting us as a whole when in a tight spot."

"It's harder than you think, love."

Dropping her head back, Sara wanted to scream. "This feels impossible."

"We'll get there," Kalen said. "You did it once, you'll do it again."

"I'm going to go lie down," she grumbled.

"Take my bed." Jack insisted and she didn't argue.

Pushing away from the table, she dragged her ass up the steps ready to lie down in Jack's bed. But first, she stopped in the bathroom to wash her face and brush her hair. She would have taken a shower had it not felt like too much trouble at the moment.

Shutting the door behind her, she rubbed her eyes and looked at her reflection. Good grief, she looked like shit. When was the last time she'd slept?

Even with exhaustion looming over her, she was still riding some kind of buzzy-feel-good high. Maybe it was the house? The energy? The tie to Hell that kept them all going when a crash-and-burn was long overdue?

Or maybe she was too restless for sleep.

Regardless of the why, now that Sara was taking a good look

in the mirror, she wanted to brush her teeth, shave her legs, and make everything all pretty and smooth and shiny and happy.

Running the shower, she made sure the water was blazing hot before stepping in. The spray felt good and when she turned to grab the guys' shampoo, she smiled. Someone had restocked the place with all her things. Strawberry-scented shampoo, a loofa, a new razor, apricot face scrub, even body wash.

She was about to get clean and smell like a fruit salad. This. Was. Awesome.

Halfway through the suds and rinse was when shit got real. She dunked her head under the spray of water to rinse off her face when a flashback bitch slapped her. Jerking her eyes open, the image was still there and she braced herself against the tiled wall.

"Breathe, Sara. You can do this." Nope, she fucking couldn't. The water was going to take her down. She was going to die.

Sara dropped to the floor and froze on her hands and knees. Water sprayed on her back, hot and sharp. The shower floor filled with water. The drain wasn't working fast enough.

Sara roared with fear. Was she making a sound at all? Her breaths grew shallow until she couldn't breathe at all.

She was going to die!

Her spine burned as if it was splitting wide open. Warm blood rushed down her back, pooling around her. Sara's hands were bound. She couldn't scream past the gag in her mouth.

Body jolting, she fought so hard she felt sick and knew there was no hope. She couldn't escape this. But damned if she was gonna go quietly into the night. "HOUNDS!"

Her throat didn't work. It was shredded. Blood flowed down her chest. "HOUNDS!"

Still nothing. And then a new burn blasted through her veins. The pig-faced man was standing in front of her. She was surrounded. The crow. The horned animal. She tried to scream again, "HOUNDS!" Tears blurred her vision.

"Stop fighting, dog."

She wasn't a dog. And she wasn't going to stop fighting. Sara chewed the gag, her wrists were bleeding. Everything was bleeding. The water sloshed around her and was turning red. "HOUNDS!"

"BLOODY FUCKING CHRIST!"

Sara gasped in horror. Her mouth was wide open, her eyes

darting around the room. Jack's mouth was moving but she couldn't hear a damn thing he said. All she could do was clutch him and hope he kept her afloat.

Inhaling again, Sara screamed so loud her voice cracked from the strain. "HOUNDS!" Can they hear her even though she couldn't hear them? "HOUNDS!"

"SARA!"

"HOUNDSSSS!" she just kept screaming it. If she screamed it loud enough they'd hear her. They had to hear her. They had to save her!

"SARA, LOOK AT ME!" Jack's face came into view and she was no longer surrounded by shadows and masks. "SARA, CAN YOU HEAR ME!"

Eyes bugging out of their sockets, she grabbed his face to make sure it was really him. He shook her shoulders hard, rocking her body back and forth. "Bloody hell, woman. I'm here. It's me. I've got you."

She started wailing, clinging to him. "Oh my god," she cried. "I can't do this, Jack. I can't live like this."

Sara buried her face into his shirt and continued to cling. She hadn't even noticed her entire pack of Hounds was in the bathroom with her. She just stayed focused on Jack. Jack her Hound. Jack her mate. Jack the one who found her just in time.

Jack. Jack. Jack.

"I'm okay," she croaked. "I'm okay." No she wasn't, but she was getting there. Slowly.

"Where are you, love?"

"With you."

"Where?"

"In the bathroom."

"That's right," Jack stroked her wet hair, "And who am I?"

"My Hound," she cried.

"Say my name. Let's hear you say who I am."

"Jack."

"There she is… say it again for me."

"Jack."

"And you are?"

"Sara."

"Good," he peeled her off his chest long enough to meet her

eyes, "You did good, love."

She collapsed back into his embrace and didn't stop crying for several minutes.

"The others are going to touch you, Sara. They need to touch you. Okay?"

She nodded her head but didn't move from where she'd buried herself inside Jack's arms.

"Fuck guys, that was scary." Eli put his hand on her back, rubbing in small circles.

Sara blindly reached out and someone took her hand. Jack kept petting her head and was squeezing the life out of her. It felt good. It felt safe.

"Where's Kalen?" her voice was muffled.

"Right here, Darling." She felt his finger trace the invisible line down her spine. Immediately, she jolted and whimpered. "What's wrong, Sara?"

"I still feel it."

"Feel what, Beautiful?"

"The burn." She pulled away from Jack and turned to look at her Hounds. "I don't know what they used to remove the tattoos, but it burned. It felt like they flayed my back wide open." Okay she needed to stop talking. Just saying those words made her feel ill.

"It's done, baby. It's never going to happen to you again."

"Don't say that, Eli," Kalen growled. "Don't say shit like that when you can't truly know."

Eli shoved a finger in Kalen's chest, "Never. Fucking. Again. Let that vow be heard by everything and everyone."

Kalen growled like a vicious animal. "I made that vow, once. Look how well it served us."

Sara sniffled. "What are you talking about?"

"Nothing, love." Jack glared at the two arguing Hounds. "Not now, gentlemen."

"Then when?" Kalen yelled.

Sara stepped back, "What's going on?"

Jack scowled at Kalen and Eli. Tanner took her hand and started for the door, "Come on. Let's get you dressed."

She followed him out of the bathroom and down the hall. Tanner's room was the last door on the left. She was dripping water down the hallway, not that she cared.

"Here," he grabbed one of his shirts and pair of sweatpants and handed them to her.

Of all the men, Tanner was the most slender. He stood just over six feet tall without an ounce of fat on him, but he lacked Kalen's broad chest or Eli's thick arms. Tanner was built long and lean like a swimmer. His t-shirt smelled like him, and his sweatpants were too big but comfy as all get out.

He helped her get dressed, one foot at a time, into his sweatpants. And then silently he pulled the t-shirt over her head and got her arms through the right holes. The shirt had a little devil on it and said *Cute As Hell*. She'd laugh if she wasn't still so upset.

"I feel like a big baby," she sniffled.

"Come here," Tanner brought her over to a curtain. Pulling it back, she realized it was his cave. There was a series of computer screens sitting on a long table, a chair, and some other stuff.

Tanner sat down in the swivel chair and patted his lap, "Have a seat."

She complied. "What is all this?"

"It's mostly surveillance bullshit, but," he tapped a few buttons and turned on a monitor, "This is what I think you might like." He turned a movie on one of the screens. The Lord of the Rings.

Sara smiled. She loved these movies. Hobbits were awesome.

"Here, put these on." Tanner handed her a headset and she immediately put them over her ears. Then he kissed her cheek and leaned back in the chair. Sara, in turn, leaned forward and was lost in Middle Earth for the first time in a long while. At some point between Gandalf setting off fireworks and the Wraiths making their way to the Shire, Sara had grabbed Tanner's hand and held it.

Right now she could not have been more grateful for Samwise Gamgee, Aragorn, Frodo... and Tanner.

CHAPTER 38

Tanner sat back in the chair with Sara on his lap, Frodo on his computer screen, and a lot of *what the fuck* on his brain. He rubbed her back in slow, small circles, being mindful of her spine. He wasn't sure if the sensation she talked about earlier was still there or not and he wasn't about to risk it.

Besides, her lower back was just as fun to touch as the rest of her.

It was good to get some alone time with his Beautiful. He'd missed their movie nights. Missed the feel of her ass in his lap. Missed that strawberry-scented shampoo of hers, too.

Earlier, he went out and bought all the stuff he knew she would want - bath stuff, mostly, plus a few things he tucked away for later in each of their rooms. Her wet hair made the entire space they were in smell delicious as fuck.

A loud rumble vibrated through the floorboards. Tanner's lips made a thin, tight line as he listened to the other Hounds argue downstairs. He was all too glad he removed Sara from the situation before shit hit the fan. The pack didn't argue often, so when they did, it was ugly.

Now that he and Sara were tucked away in his computer cave, Tanner focused on keeping her distracted and content while the others battled out their issues.

He understood both sides of the war that was quickly escalating downstairs – Eli's vow to Sara that nothing would ever happen to her again, and Kalen's fury that Eli would say such a thing.

Kalen made Sara that same promise once, right after she died the first time. Sara's death, they all learned when first entering the pack, was almost as brutal and ugly as Kalen's had been.

Tanner shivered just thinking of what it must have been like for her. And it killed him to know she didn't remember it. That meant when the memory came back it was going to be so painful for her. He'd do anything to keep her away from that kind of torture – memory, flashback, real life situation. Fuck, however it wanted to present itself, Tanner wanted to save her from it.

Now she had two deaths to deal with.

Or did she?

Was she really dead that second time? Like for real dead? She wasn't a human when those assholes took her and did whatever the fuck they'd done to strip her of Hell's magic and her special tats. Hounds don't die easily like a human. They could be killed, but it would take something really severe or a shit ton of magic to take one of them out permanently.

Lucifer made Hounds special. They were tailored for one specific reason: HIS purpose. Hounds were to help keep the balance in the living world and make sure there wasn't too much good or too much evil lingering in the land of the living. Thus securing a steady stream of energy, both negative and positive, flowing from one realm to the next.

It was a sweet job, really. One Tanner was extremely good at. Except now that things were going sideways, the hunts were no longer fun, they were stressful. The *malanum* weren't just evasive, they were downright manipulative. Tanner was really starting to believe that the traitor and Sara's killer were the same person and he wanted to know why they'd chosen her specifically to go after.

Fuck his head hurt.

Leaning back, Tanner scrubbed his face and itchy eyes. On the computer screen, he saw that shadow dragon thing spitting fire, about to take Gandalf into the darkness with it.

"Run you fools!" Sara said along with the wizard.

He smiled. She probably didn't even realize she'd said it out loud. The headset he gave her to wear was top of the line, she would hear nothing else but what was on the screen, which would explain why she'd said it so loudly. Fuck, he loved her so much.

With a sigh, Sara leaned into him like he was nothing more than a big Tanner lounge. He didn't mind in the slightest. To have the length of her body pressed solidly against his? Psht, who the fuck would say no to something that fantastic?

She grabbed his free hand and laced her fingers with his. Then she wrapped his arms around her. Damn it was so easy to fall back into a routine with this woman. Did she know this was how they worked together? Perfect. This was just so damn perfect.

Moving his head to the left a little, he kissed the shell of her ear and nuzzled his cheek against hers. Cuddling with Sara was one of his favorite things to do. She was warm and wonderful - like holding sunshine in his hands.

Sitting in silence, he watched the images on the screen, not needing the headphones to know what they were saying. He had that movie memorized years ago. So had Sara.

"Oh God," she said much later.

Ah yes, he thought, *here's the part where Boromir dies.*

Tanner brought one of her hands up and kissed her knuckles. She turned her body just enough so she could see him, tears shining in her eyes. "I hate this part," she said loudly.

"I know," he mouthed back and kissed her temple.

Tanner ran his hands up and down her sides and the world just kinda fell away for a minute. With the curtain drawn, they were in the dark. The only light shining on them came from the monitor.

"Tanner," Sara breathed into his ear, causing him to get all hot and hard. Then she twisted her body around even more so she could straddle him. Their gazes locked onto one another and he put up a finger, silently asking her to give him a minute.

Quickly, he hit a few buttons and turned the movie off and started playing music instead. Seether's *Broken* began playing. Tears slowly slid down Sara's face and he wiped them away, kissing them. This song always moved her. Moved him, too.

"Tanner," she whispered again.

He spoke with his eyes, hoping they conveyed everything he wanted her to know. Funny, in moments like this when it was him, her, and a whole lotta nothing else, it was hard to breathe. She consumed him entirely - his heart, his mind, his soul.

His vision began to blur, the tears that he always kept from coming were now seeking their freedom. He never cried over Sara. He refused to mourn her. If he did that, it meant he accepted her death and that just wasn't ever going to happen. Each of the Hounds had their own way of dealing with Sara's disappearance, and Tanner's was to refuse acknowledging that she was seriously gone for good. He'd have gladly lived in denial for the rest of his days because it meant deep down he still had hope that a miracle would happen and they'd find her again. The alternative was too much to bear.

Tilting his head, Tanner pressed his mouth to hers, nice and gentle. Hand-to-God that little bit of contact in his suddenly fragile state was enough to bust him wide open. Emotions he'd buried and locked into a dark room in the pit of his soul were now running rapidly through him.

Every bit of his body tensed up and started to shake. She cupped his face in her hands and he held her wrists.

Frozen. He was totally fucking frozen right now.

They clung to each other. Then her gaze softened and she started giving him little tiny kisses all over his face. She pressed her mouth against his again, this time, with a little more heat behind it.

Taking the cue, Tanner opened up and took what she was giving him. Her tongue was like candy. Her little noises only made him harder. Just as it started to get hotter, Sara pulled away with a wicked smile and pulled her headphones off. "This one's yours," she said cheekily.

He put the headphones on and grinned. Fucking right this song was his. Nickelback's *Something in Your Mouth* was one of his faves.

She crushed her mouth against his and cranked that kiss up another notch. Then she slid down off his lap and kneeled between his legs. Grabbing the waistline of his sweats, she slowly started pulling down his pants. He jacked his ass up off the chair to make it easier for her.

Hungry. That look she was rocking was a hungry one. She grabbed his cock with both hands and started to pump it nice and slow with her hands. Tanner refused to look away. He wanted to watch her do whatever she had planned. He wanted to burn that look of hers into his brain and file it away with all the other moments they've shared.

But then she took the head of his cock into her mouth and he was a fucking goner. Tilting his head back, he squeezed eyes shut and gritted his teeth. "Fuuuuck."

His dick was pierced. Sara tried to contain her excitement. Not only was he pierced on the top, he had another down at the base. Holy shit, how did she not remember this part of him? It felt like an important thing to remember and looked too hot to ever be forgotten.

"Fuuuuck," he said when she took him further down her throat.

Tanner tasted delicious. He looked so hot right now with his head tilted back, that sharp jaw line gleaming from the reflection of the computer screen. The headphones made his blonde tufts all wild looking. His thigh muscles were ridiculously sexy, too, when he flexed them.

She positioned herself for a better angle and took him all the way down as far as she could without gagging. Determined to go further, Sara relaxed her throat and inched him all the way down. This wasn't about anything more than having a taste of something she desired. Yes, it was for Tanner's pleasure too, but Sara felt like it went deeper than that. She craved this guy.

He let out a hiss of pleasure which turned into an all-out growl when she slowly grazed her teeth against his taut skin. Tonguing his tip, Sara began toying with his balls and smiled against him when Tanner let out another growl.

Okay, hearing a man make these sounds did wonders for a woman. To have it be Tanner who was making those noises though, brought Sara's confidence up ten notches in the sexy department. She could listen to him groan all day long and never get tired of hearing it.

"Sara," his voice sliced through the darkened space.

She quickly got back to making him squirm. Sucking him off

hard and fast at first, then easing up to lick and flick her tongue over his head again. He began to pant and tense up. Soooo what else was she to do but go more wild with him.

Sucking him hard, she took him all the way and bit down at his base. Tanner gasped, hips jerking, his hands delving into her hair. He started to fuck her mouth and it was dirty and messy and exciting. His fingers stayed tangled in her hair, her hands dug into his thighs, the piercings grazed her tongue and every once in a while, she applied more pressure with her teeth, pull a little harder on his balls, squeezing them until he cried out.

Deep throating Tanner was thrilling. But watching him lose control and roar as he came down her throat was fucking exhilarating. He was so beautiful like this. Raw. Hot. On the edge. Spilling over. Unraveled and animalistic with his growls.

What would fucking him be like?

Mind-blowing, that's what.

Tanner yanked the headphones off and tossed them onto the desk. "Fuck, Sara." A sheen of sweat glistened across his brow. "You're going to make my heart explode doing that."

She licked her lips, purposefully trying to savor every last drop of him.

Tanner crushed his mouth to hers, kissing her right off her feet. He picked her up and moved them out of the computer area. Laying her gently on the bed, she was expecting him to do all kinds of dirty things to her. So imagine Sara's surprise when he walked back over and grabbed his pants and started putting them back on.

"Wait," she said.

Tanner crawled onto the bed like a big cat and slowly made his way up to her mouth again. "Shhhhhh, I'll be right back."

Without further explanation, he left her in the bed alone and shut the door behind him. Moments later, he came back with a tray laden with food and some drinks. "You need food, Beautiful."

"I'd rather eat more of you."

Tanner's face lit up. "I'm going to hate myself for saying this, but not tonight, Sara. You aren't ready."

"What the hell's that supposed to mean?"

He sat on the edge of the bed and put the tray of food between them. Well, food wasn't the word for what he was serving which was Tootsie Pops, strawberries, fun-sized chocolate bars, cookies, cherries, and whipped cream. They were all her favorite sweet things. Her mouth watered.

Tanner held a strawberry out for her and she bit down on it, suddenly craving all the sugar. "Are you trying to distract me, Tanner?"

He smiled. "Maybe."

He repositioned himself so he was sitting across from her and the food was between them. "It's good to have you back."

"How good?" she baited.

"Really, really, really good." His deep voice was extra low and gravely.

Picking out a cherry Tootsie Pop, Sara unwrapped it and started sucking it slowly to remind him how good she was with her mouth.

"You do look good with something in your mouth." Winking, Tanner popped the top off the whipped cream and shot a bunch of it into his mouth before giving her the same treat.

He laughed when some of it fell out and onto her leg. Bending down, he licked the good stuff off her and then groaned like he was in pain.

"What's wrong?"

"It's my fucking dog jaw."

"Your what?"

Tanner ran the back of his hand over his jaw line and winced, "Right here. It fucking hurts all the time."

Sara leaned in to see what he was talking about.

He whipped his head around fast and started barking and snapping his teeth like an animal, scaring the hell out of her and she yipped. The son-of-a-bitch almost fell off the bed laughing so hard.

"So not funny, Tanner!"

"Yes it was!"

"Nope." She couldn't hide her smile. He was right, it was hilarious. And how gullible was she to have fallen for that crap? Dog jaw. Seriously?

"It's good to hear you laugh, Beautiful." Tanner popped one of the chocolates in his mouth next.

Loud noises rose from the first floor and Tanner smoothly reached over to his bedside table and grabbed a remote. Turning on a stereo that was sitting on his dresser, he pumped the volume up

218

and grabbed the whipped cream again.

"You're trying to distract me."

"Is it working?"

"A little." She sucked on her Tootsie Pop some more and they fell into silence.

"I want you, Sara. Don't think otherwise."

It was as if he'd read her mind. "Then why all this?" she waved her hand over all the wrappers and cookies and junk food he brought in.

"You're not ready for me yet."

Her eyebrow arched, "How do you know what I'm ready for, Hound?"

Tanner maneuvered across the bed with a wicked glint in his eyes, "We get extremely passionate, Beautiful. I don't think you need more intensity in your life tonight."

Why the fuck did that have to sound so good? "What do you think I need, then?"

Tanner answered by pulling her into his arms and forcing her to lie down with him. "You just need a break."

She hated to admit it, but maybe Tanner was right. The instant he started to nuzzle against her, Sara felt calm and content.

"I'm going to cuddle you so hard tonight, woman."

Sara giggled. "And then what?"

"When you're ready, I'm going to fuck you hard enough to maybe make up for the past five years of not having you in my arms."

"Sounds fun."

"Fun it will be, too. And intense. And wild."

She twisted her head around to look at him. "You talk a mean game, Tanner."

"I don't make promises I can't keep, Sara. I have every intention of making you bedridden for days."

Her thighs clenched and she grew hot again. "No one answered my question earlier."

"About?"

"Am I in heat?"

Tanner chuckled and squirted more whipped cream into his mouth. "Good night, Beautiful."

Damnit. Why won't anyone answer that question!

219

CHAPTER 39

Sara was awake but didn't open her eyes. Between his black painted walls and his drawn curtains, Tanner's room was crazy dark, which made it very easy to fall asleep and stay asleep. It also made it super easy to lie in bed and pretend it was still night. Sara snuggled against Tanner more and realized he was still out cold. His breathes were deep and even, his body giving off a lovely heat. He was still holding her, his arm draped across her chest and keeping her close to him.

Man oh man, did this feel amazing.

They had fallen asleep with the music on, and, at some point in the night, he must have turned it down because it was more like background noise now. She appreciated his attempts at distracting her. He'd done a helluva job. That didn't mean she was going to let the subject drop, though. Sara would just have to approach it cautiously when the time was right.

Sara slowly peeled her eyes open. Annnd she was instantly staring into a green gaze. *Kalen.* He was sitting against the wall, ass on the floor, knees bent and arms wrapped around his legs. He looked like a gigantic gargoyle.

Silently, he placed a finger over his mouth, making a "shhhhh" gesture. Then he crawled across the floor in lithe, predatory movements, and got into bed with her and Tanner. He wasted no time kissing her mouth. That touch, coupled with Tanner still holding her tightly against his body, was enough to awaken Sara in all the ways. Her body felt like a bell ringing, all vibrations and resonating gongs, singing loudly.

She literally squealed with delight.

Kalen smiled at her with a wicked glint in his eyes. *God, did he ever* not *look sexy as sin?* He nuzzled her neck and nipped that sweet spot of hers just below the ear. She moaned against him.

"Shhhhh," Kalen hissed in her ear.

She did anything but shush. Sara wiggled against Tanner, grinding her ass into his hardness and coaxed Kalen back in for another kiss. "Let him sleep, darling. He finally crashed about an hour ago." Kalen got out of the bed and motioned for her to follow.

Sara slid out of Tanner's embrace and missed him terribly the moment their bodies no longer touched. She padded her bare feet across the room and realized Jack and Eli had crashed on the floor, soft snores coming out of both of them.

Kalen grabbed her hand and led her out of Tanner's room and into his. "We can't seem to leave you alone, can we?"

Sara shrugged, "I don't mind. It's nice to not be alone anymore." She rubbed her eyes and stretched.

"Want to go downstairs and workout with me?"

The sun wasn't even up yet, and this guy wanted to work out? Oh good Lord. Sara was about to respectfully decline the offer when she remembered that Kalen barely slept and he probably wanted some alone time with her, same as Tanner had. She could get down with that.

"Sure," she went over and pulled open the top drawer of his dresser. "Let me just put on something else." Sara grabbed some decent workout clothes and changed fast. "Ready when you are, Wolf."

Kalen grinned. "Come on."

They headed into the basement and he quickly flicked all the lights on. "I normally workout in silence, but if you prefer music, be my guest," he motioned over to a stereo that was identical to the one in Tanner's room.

"Quiet is good."

Kalen nodded and got on the floor, "Stretch?"

"Sure."

She went down on the ground, opposite Kalen, and they began a partner stretch routine that felt so fucking good she could have done it for hours. He'd pull, she'd give. She'd pull, he'd give. Then he stood up and tapped his abs. "Hop on." He reached around and pulled his t-shirt off.

Yeah, Sara could hop onto that.

Wrapping her arms around his neck, Kalen held her ass and she locked her ankles together around his middle. "Ten reps of ten, Sara. Go."

She began doing sit ups on Kalen's body. He stood stiff as a board, knees slightly bent, and supported her weight like she was no heavier than a book bag. "One, Two, Three," he kept count while she crunched and released, crunched and released. She was sweating in no time but it felt really good.

Next, he sat on the floor for his sit ups. Sara held his ankles and counted for him. Every time Kalen popped up and touched elbows to knees, he kissed her.

This was the best workout ever. All mornings should start this way.

After several more core strength routines, she was seriously feeling the burn. "What next?"

"You, squats. Me, weights."

She started working on her thighs while Kalen took up the barbells. They were both huffing and puffing halfway through it. "How long were you all in Tanner's room?"

"He let us in around three."

She hid her smile. "And you and Tanner stayed awake?"

"Yeah,"

"Doing what?"

"Watching you sleep." Kalen's arms flexed as he pumped the weights up and down.

"Sounds boring."

"Not for us," he huffed. Up. Down. Up. Down. "We've missed you, Sara. All the pieces of you. That includes the way you make little noises in your sleep."

"I make little noises?"

Kalen put the bar back on the rack and wiped his brow, "You snore sometimes too."

222

She rolled her eyes.

"And drool."

Sara's head lashed back and she laughed. "I do *not* drool."

Kalen shrugged, then jumped up to a handle bar attached to the ceiling, and started doing pull ups.

Fuck, this guy was ripped. Sara stood there gawking until he said, "You're drooling right now, Darling."

So? Could you blame her? Shaking the lust fog out of her head, Sara sat down and gave up on working out. She really just wanted to watch the *Kalen Show*. "Wanna tell me what last night's argument was about?"

He was quiet for a few reps then, "Nope."

"Why not?"

"Because it's done and over with. Let sleeping dogs lie."

"It was about me. I think I have a right to know."

He dropped down, landing like a big cat and stretched his arms. "Eli and I had a disagreement about making promises that can't be kept."

"I'm sure he meant well."

"It doesn't matter now. It's done."

She bit back her next words. If Kalen didn't want to discuss it, then fine. She wouldn't push it with him. She'd just have to push it with Eli instead.

Stomps above signaled that at least one other Hound was awake now.

"Come on," Kalen held his hands out and hoisted her up. "We need showers and coffee."

No argument there. Sara followed Kalen into the kitchen where she said good morning to Jack before heading up to the second floor. Not gonna lie, she was nervous about taking a shower, but she seriously needed one after how hard their workout had been. Risking a flashback was worth it if she could get clean and not go the rest of the day smelling like a sweaty farm animal.

Kalen followed behind her. "We've decided no more being alone in the tub or shower for you."

"What?"

"One of the Hounds will be with you when you shower, just in case something happens."

Her face grew red. She didn't have a bedroom of her own,

and now the bathroom wasn't hers anymore either? This fucking sucked ass. But she got it. She did. Honestly, she didn't want to be alone in the tub either. Not after yesterday. "Do you think the water has something to do with it?"

Kalen shrugged, "I don't know, but that's twice you've had a flashback in water, Sara. We don't want you alone if there's a third time. You could get hurt falling. And if you end up having a panic attack again, we want to be able to help you through it quickly so it's not so hard on you."

Now she felt a little embarrassed. And weak. She hated feeling weak.

"Hey," he lifted her chin up, "it's temporary alright? We all need a little help every now and then."

"I don't want to keep being like this."

"You won't." He turned on the shower and kept his hand under the water, testing the temp. A few heartbeats later he opened the shower door, "Ladies first."

You're not taking a shower with me? She thought. Sara didn't ask it out loud. If Kalen wanted to join, he would. After Tanner denying her the pleasure of more sexy time yesterday, she didn't think her ego could handle another shutdown so soon anyways.

Sara peeled off her clothes and stepped in.

Ahhhhh instant relaxation. The glass door closed and she stood there by herself with the hot water beating on her back.

Then the shower door opened again and she smiled like the Cheshire Cat.

Sweaty Workout Kalen was hot. Wet-in-the-Shower Kalen was much hotter. He knew it too, damn him. Her smile said all the things that Sara was thinking. *Yes, I want to touch him. Yes, I want to lick him. Yes, I want to fuck his brains out against the tiled wall.*

Kalen dumped a load of shampoo into his hands then slathered her head with it and started massaging her scalp. Having a man wash your hair had to be in the top ten of most awesome things a guy can do for a girl. Tanner had been Hound number one to do it and now Kalen.

Sara could totally get used to this life.

"Turn."

She obeyed and bit her bottom lip as he ran soap all over her body, lathering her up. She could do nothing but return the favor.

Kalen growled teasingly when she squirted apple-scented body wash onto her loofah. "I hate smelling like fruit."

"But you'll smell sooo delicious." She ran the loofah across his chest and pecs, down his abs and swirled it over his massive thighs. Good God, the man was built like a Viking warrior. "Turn," she commanded. It was so hard to contain her delight when he did. She was now staring at his glorious ass. It was totally squeal-worthy. The Hound was built like a statue of chiseled perfection.

Fuck her six ways to Sunday, Sara was not going to get out of this shower without combusting into flames first.

She scrubbed his back and made sure to get all the special places before having him spin around again. She decided to scrub a few spots a second time. Kalen's eyes stayed pinned on hers. He reached behind her and pulled the shower head off the wall, spraying her down. Soaking her. Rinsing her. Then he did the same for himself and let her watch.

A man dripping wet was a beautiful thing.

Her legs were starting to turn to mush again. Heat bloomed over her skin that had nothing to do with the hot shower. "Wolf?" Kalen's dark brow arched in response. "Make me howl."

The smile he gave her was slow to come and delicious to watch. "How many times, Sara?"

"Three."

He turned the water off and hung the shower head back up. "*Three?*"

"Too many?"

"Too few."

She stepped onto the mat and didn't bother reaching for a towel. Was she being bold? Yup. Did she care? Nope. Sara needed to be touched like flowers need the sun and fish need water. She had to be in heat. It was the only explanation that fit her current situation.

Kalen licked his lips as he stepped out of the shower and dropped to his knees, immediately sealing his mouth over her core. Sara's ass hit the large vanity, hands braced against the countertop, and she cried out.

Holy mother of God, Sara thought, *that was one.* Her head spun. It might have been the fastest orgasm of her life, but it was also one of the hardest. She came within seconds – SECONDS – of his

225

tongue's quick moves. She should have been embarrassed but there just wasn't time for it. Kalen pulled away and turned her around to face the mirror. Bending her over, he lifted one of her legs onto the sink and plunged deep inside her.

"Oh fuck," she whimpered.

He was showing no mercy here. "Touch yourself, Sara."

She reached down and started making small circles over the spot Kalen's tongue had just been. The buildup was steady and strong. Kalen quickened his pace, their bodies smacking each other. His hands wrapped around her waist and she looked at their reflection, "Let go, Sara. Let me see you go wild."

She pushed into him, meeting his thrust until they were both groaning loudly. Steady, steady, steady, the pressure built until she reached a point of no return. The second orgasm was like opening a flood gate. She saw stars.

Just when the high of her climax began to ebb, Sara reached down and grabbed his balls. Kalen growled and she squeezed harder. "I like that noise," she purred. "I want to hear more of it."

"Fuck, woman." Kalen's head tilted back as he rammed into her harder. Knocking her hand out of the way, he rubbed her clit in time with his thrusts. Biting down on her shoulder, he got her to yip, then he pulled out so they could get into another position.

Sara hopped up on to the counter and spread her legs wide as an invitation.

"Mother of God, Sara. You're killing me right now." He slid into her entrance nice and slow. He made sure the ride along the edge of pleasure was just enough to keep the bliss steady, but not too much that she'd lose her control so quickly again. "I haven't heard you howl, Sara." Kalen nipped her ear. "I want to hear it."

She held back from giving him what he desired. It was so hard to do, too, because Kalen was no stranger to her body. She had zero control and he had it all. He knew just when to ease up, go slow, go fast, go hard, go soft. He rode her into a frenzy, hitting all her erogenous zones along the way.

Kalen lifted both her legs over his shoulders, causing Sara to lean back against the mirror. Mind reeling. Body melting. Sara went up in flames.

"Howl, Sara. Howl for us."

It was getting impossible to hold back. Sara bit her lip so hard she drew blood.

"Let them all hear you scream your pleasure. Release it, Sara. Give me all you have."

Kalen deepened his strokes and started circling his thumb over her sensitive bundle of nerves. She was going to shatter apart at any moment now. Sex like this made her feel as though Kalen was a storm and she was the sea. The force of his nature colliding with hers caused the ultimate Tsunami. The last orgasm built, built, built and then crashed over her.

Sara screamed like she never thought possible. Digging into Kalen's shoulders, she writhed and howled. Only then did Kalen seek his own release and join in on her final ride. She felt him fill her. Felt his cock pulse inside her body and he howled right along with her.

Slowing down and finally stopping, Kalen rested his head on her shoulder as he caught his breath. Her ears were ringing. Her thighs burned. She ached in ways that were glorious.

With a low chuckle, Kalen nipped her chin and said, "Let's go get coffee."

CHAPTER 40

Sara went into Jack's room to get some clothes. For whatever reason, she felt most comfortable in his space. Maybe it was because out of all of the bedrooms, Jack's was the sparsest. It was as if he didn't have many attachments. Or perhaps he was a minimalist.

The only things out were his weapons, a pair of boots, a couple belts, and some candles. The only bit of décor that hung on his wall was the painting above his bed. It was very simple in here, which was something she could totally appreciate.

Shimmying into a pair of jeans and a hoodie, Sara stepped back to take a look at herself in his mirror and her foot hit something, causing her to trip. She caught herself before falling over. Damn box. Who would leave a box out on the floor like that?

Oh, it was her box. Oops.

Tucking some loose hair behind her ear, she bent down and opened it again. Was she a minimalist like Jack and all her earthly possessions had been so easily packed away?

Maybe.

Sitting on the floor, she carefully began pulling out the objects. Before now, she'd not been ready to dig into her past, but now she was almost desperate to fill in her blanks.

The black and white photo of her and Jack was on the top.

Next was the photo of all of them at the beach. Under that was the small painting of a village. It was mostly yellows and browns with some blue and green highlights. If it had a smell, the fragrance would have been burning peat and straw.

Next she pulled out a bundle of white lace. The fibers were brittle and yellowing. Laying that down carefully, she pulled out a small rabbit with floppy ears and black bead eyes. Her stomach stirred, clenching and fluttering all at once. For whatever reason, she brought it up to her nose and inhaled the stuffed animal. It had no scent that rang bells. Actually, it had no scent at all.

Next, she pulled out a bundle of paint brushes that were bound together with a rubber band. They were old and had been used a lot at some point. She ran her hand over the bristles, the fibers tickling her palm. Carefully placing them next to the other objects, Sara tipped the box and peered in. There was a small wooden chest with an engraved top. She pulled it out and knew that Kalen had made this object…

"Happy Anniversary, Darling."

As the words came to her, so had the image of his face….

He winked and she slapped his arm, playfully. "Stop calling me 'Darling'."

"Good enough for the Devil but not me?"

"I don't know why Lucifer calls me that either. Nothing about me is darling."

"Amen to that," Kalen chuckled.

The Devil had called her his darling since the first day they met and Kalen loved to tease her about it. The name stuck and probably would forever. She'd grown used to it over the years. "So long as Lucifer and you are the only ones who call me that, I guess I can live with it."

She unwrapped the package and gasped. Her hands traced the beautifully engraved picture on the lid. Five wolfish looking beasts howling together at the moon. Hell Hounds weren't wolves, or even shapeshifters, but they ran in packs and were devoted to one another in a fierce way. Wolves were predatory, loyal, and beautiful creatures, much like how she always thought of her Hounds.

"Kalen," she whispered, "this is amazing."

"You might be the Devil's Darling, but you're our moon."

She stared at the box again. "Wait. There are five Hounds here AND the moon, who's the fifth Hound?"

"Tanner insisted you were both the Hound and the Moon."

She grinned big and bright. Well now she felt extra special since she got to be two cool things.

He leaned in and kissed her. "You're our everything, Sara."

"Sara?" the sound of her name brought her back to the here and now. Exhaling a shaky breath, Sara turned towards whoever just said her name.

Jack stood in his doorway holding a cup of coffee and a bowl. "It didn't seem like you were coming down and we didn't want this to grow cold." He placed the bowl of oatmeal and cup of coffee on the floor. His eyes coasted along the belongings she'd emptied from the box and he sighed. Without another word, he left and closed the door quietly behind him.

Her stomach growled as the scents of warm brown sugar and black coffee hit her nose. Taking a break from memory lane, she devoured her breakfast and chugged half the coffee.

One can never truly appreciate how good food is until they can't eat it anymore. Sara had gone five years without the taste of cream and cinnamon and Tootsie pops and beer and oranges. It was hell, she'll tell ya. Pure. Hell.

Bracing herself, she opened the lid and peered into the carved wooden chest. There was a small book which looked like a journal, some jewelry, a small blade, a passport, stones, a couple vials of oil, and a ring.

Her fingers hovered over the journal first, but she wasn't ready to read it. Just staring at the objects that were significant in her life felt strange enough without reading excerpts. Instead, she grabbed the ring and slid it on her left ring finger, as if knowing that's where it belonged. Then she hooked the necklace around her neck and sighed at the familiar comfort the weight of the pendant brought her.

It was a crescent moon with four stars to the left, all linked as part of the chain, not pendants. *This was a gift,* she thought. Closing her eyes, she held onto the moon and exhaled slowly. *This was from Eli.* She didn't know how she knew that, but she did.

Tipping the cardboard box to its side, she saw the last of the contents. They were CDs or DVDs in cases, all labeled in black ink. The handwriting was both meticulously neat, yet wild and off center.

Tanner. That was Tanner's handwriting.

Inspecting the first disc, she saw it had several dates listed as well as places. Italy, Vermont, Key West, Ireland. And each was labeled, 1, 2, 3, 4. All the way up to 13.

"Those are old videos," Eli said from the doorway.

She jumped at the sound of his voice. She had no idea he'd been standing there watching her.

Pushing away from the door jamb, Eli came into the room quietly, cautiously. "We would sometimes make videos and over time, Tanner was able to collect and convert them all to DVD's."

She gulped. Would he want her to watch them now? She wasn't sure she was ready.

Eli's gaze coasted down to her necklace. Sorrow danced across his handsome face. He cleared his throat before saying, "I love seeing you wear that." His hand sailed up to her neck and he fingered the four stars. "I gave that to you on the Anniversary of –"

"The day you became my Hound," she said quietly. The memory of that day was bold and bright and took up her whole mind as he touched her…

Sara stood over the pot of jambalaya, shaking hot sauce into the mix. She liked seven dashes, her Hounds preferred twelve. She settled on ten. Dancing to some Creedence Clearwater Revival, she was shaking her ass while stirring the pot.

Two arms wrapped around her middle and she didn't need to turn around to know who it was. Only Eli ever came up behind her and nibbled her earlobe like this.

Without facing each other, he put his hands out, both fists closed. "Pick one."

Excited, she chose the right. He opened his hand and revealed nothing. Soooo, she picked the other one. He opened his other hand and revealed nothing. Spinning around to give him hell for teasing, she saw he was only wearing one thing. A new necklace. The chain so delicate and tight around his thick neck, she was shocked the chain hadn't snapped.

"Happy Anniversary, baby." He reached around and unclasped it, only to put it around her neck instead.

"It's so beautiful." Her fingers slid down the chain. The moon was delicate, the stars smooth and sharp, the chain felt good on her. "I am never taking this off."

His eyes darkened for a moment and then he lifted her chin. "Take it off when you hunt."

"Okay," she smiled. Of course, she should have known he'd say that.

The memory receded and Sara's hands shook as she clutched the necklace.

Eli cupped her face. "You remember that day?"

"I do now." She felt her cheeks warm. "My memories are returning. Looking at some of this seems to help."

"That's good," his smile grew wider. "That's really good, Sara."

She wasn't sure if she agreed. It felt strange and exhilarating and scary and encouraging all at the same time. "I need to do this slowly," she warned. "I just…"

"I get it. Seriously." Eli sat back on his haunches and sighed. "You're dancing between worlds right now. The one you used to know and the one you're in now. You love us, but you don't know why. You remember, but you don't want to let go of rediscovery."

He could have knocked her over with a feather. That's exactly how she felt.

"How about you and I go out for a bit?" He stood up and stretched his hand out towards her. "Just the two of us."

"What will the others say?" She wasn't going to lie. Getting out of the house would be nice. She was getting too restless and the things she desired to occupy herself with weren't what she felt she should be doing at the moment.

"They aren't going to mind, Sara. You're not a prisoner. And I'll be with you so no one is going to worry about your safety."

"Okay," she grabbed her empty bowl and cup from the floor and downed the rest of her coffee. "Lead the way."

After telling the other Hounds he was taking Sara out for a little bit, Eli grabbed a few more blades from his room and tucked them away where they'd be easily accessible but not obvious. With Sara's magic not fully intact yet, he wasn't about to risk her safety by not having enough weapons on him.

Grabbing his leather jacket off the hook in the hallway, he poked his head into the kitchen, "You ready, baby?"

"Yeah," Sara kissed each of her Hounds good-bye. "See you guys soon."

Eli's heart skipped a beat. She was falling so naturally back into their way of life it was moments like these that made it feel like she'd never gone missing. Especially when she walked behind Tanner, ran her hand down his spine and he turned with sleepy, happily content eyes and kissed her goodbye. "See you in a little while, Beautiful."

She pulled her hood over her head and Eli grabbed her hand. They headed outside. Clicking his key fob, Eli unlocked the doors to his Jeep and opened the door for her. Two minutes later, they were heading down the road, towards the city.

Sara's voice rose over the music blasting through his speakers, "Where are we going, Eli?"

He turned down the volume, "You'll see."

His left hand steered the wheel while his right reached over the console and rested on Sara's thigh. He just needed to touch her. Make sure she was real. Shit, it had been hell to keep his control and not force her to sit on his lap during meals or wrap his body around hers while they slept, or at least tether her to him somehow.

There had already been three moments since she'd come home that his panic rose to the point where he felt like blowing chunks because she would be in the living room one minute and then leave without him realizing it.

One minute there, next minute gone.

The last time that happened was just this morning. He awoke in Tanner's room and there was no Sara in the bed. He broke out in a sweat immediately, heart slamming into his chest, blood draining from his goddamn head. He bolted out of the room and searched the entire house.

Then he heard her voice down in the basement and everything in him just kinda… broke down.

She was working out with Kalen in the basement. Laughing. Breathing hard. Grunting as she pushed past her limit on squats. Eli hadn't joined them. His panic had zapped his energy and he was so fucking weak from it, he doubted he would have been able to curl a motherfucking can of soup. Instead of interrupting their flow, he'd gone back up to his room to collect himself.

Eli chanced a glance and looked over at Sara now. She was staring out the window, her hood covering most of her face, except for the tip of her nose and her luscious lips. "Whatcha thinkin', baby?"

Sara shrugged, "Too much. My thoughts are jumbled."

He squeezed her leg, reassuring her. "That hood won't hide you from the world, Sara."

"Or the truth," she muttered.

His brow furrowed. Driving in silence the rest of the way, he finally pulled up in front of their destination. "Look familiar?"

Sara turned to him with confusion. "This is Jack's apartment."

His smile was tight. Turning off the ignition, they both got out and met on the curb. She pulled her hood down and stuffed her hands in her pockets. "Why are you bringing me here?"

"You'll see." He hoped.

Eli opened the lobby door and they went to the elevator. She was the one to hit the number seven button, and he bit back a smile. Was that by memory or because she saw Jack do it?

He knew Jack had brought her here when he'd found her. According to the Hound, she made no signs of knowing the place. Eli wanted to test her again.

When they reached their floor, *ding-ding* went the elevator as the doors reopened. He placed a hand over the sensor, forcing the doors to stay open, so she had time to get out and then he followed her to the correct apartment. Jingling keys was the only sound in the hallway. That, and his heart pounding. Unlocking the door, he held that one open for her too and she stepped inside. Sara's pace slowed as they entered the living room. He held his breath and waited.

Please, please, please.

He wanted her memories to come back. He wanted her whole. He wanted her...

"This... isn't Jack's place, is it?" She slowly walked around. Turning to Eli, her cheeks had lost a little bit of their color. "It was mine."

"*Is,*" he corrected, "Is yours."

Sara ran her hand across the small table against the left wall in the living room. A bouquet of flowers, half wilted, sat in a purple vase. "I don't understand," she whispered.

Eli made his way over to her slowly. "You loved the city as much as you loved the country. As Hounds, we rotate districts every ten years or so. And each time we move, we have a house for us and something small for you."

She shook her head, still not getting it.

"You'd grow restless with us. Too much testosterone, I guess. Sometimes you'd break off and need your own space for a while." He lifted her head with his finger on her chin and placed a soft, gentle kiss on her lips, "And other times you'd bring one of us here with you for some alone time."

She tugged out of his reach and continued to look around. "Why don't I just have a room for myself at the farm?"

"You didn't want that."

"Do I always get what I want?"

Eli laughed. "Yes."

She meandered out of the living room and into the small kitchen. "Why didn't you sell this place? If you thought I was dead, why didn't you guys just get rid of it?"

"We couldn't."

She came back into the living room. "Everything's so clean," she whispered, "And there are fresh flowers. Who put them there?"

"Kalen," Eli sighed. "He refused to give this place up. After he finally came back from New Orleans, he shoved all his grief down and refused to give up your apartment. Instead, he worked through his emptiness by keeping this place alive. He comes here and cleans, changes the unused sheets, and brings new flowers. In five years, he's never missed a week."

She stifled a sob.

"He refused to let you go." Eli cleared his throat, "We all refused to believe you were really gone."

Sara's shoulders drooped and she turned to go down the hall. Opening the door to the right, she stumbled into the bathroom. There was no need to follow her. Eli knew there was soap in a silver pump on the sink. The shower curtain was black with a white Cheshire cat smile on it.

Next, Eli watched her go down the hall and she opened the bedroom door. The sheets would still be messed up from her and Jack using the bed. Eli's soul burned with the knowledge that Jack had been the lucky son-of-a-bitch to find her. He wasn't jealous of

Jack. He was grateful.

Eli would have never survived seeing Sara for the first time after all these years, dancing and enjoying herself in a club like the world hadn't crashed down and left them all in despair. He could only imagine how hard it had been for Jack that night. To keep his cool, to not crumble, to bring her in nice and slow and not crush her with five years of tormented grief and a ton of questions.

Sighing, Eli scrubbed his face with both hands and diverted his thoughts.

Sara opened the last door and gasped at what was in the tiny second bedroom. "Holy shit."

Eli's palms grew sweaty and he followed her into the room.

Everything was the same. From the canvases to the mason jars to the last drop of paint. Sara touched the painting sitting on the easel, unfinished. The brushes were in mason jars, bristles dry and clean. The large window brought in late morning light, which cast a bright glow over the canvases stacked up against the wall.

There was a photo in a frame over by the bins of paint. It was of Sara and a group of little kids. Her hands shook as she touched it. He watched her throat work hard to swallow. Did she remember? Did she recognize those little eyes and big smiles?

"Did... are they... have... we..." she couldn't string together her words coherently. "Eli, who are they?"

"Try to remember, baby." It was a plea. He was begging now. Begging God, Lucifer, something, someone, *anything,* to help his woman remember her life faster.

Tears filled her eyes and she panicked. "Are they ours?"

The question was so unexpected, Eli stumbled on his answer. "*Ours?*" He looked down at the picture and it dawned on him. "No, baby."

Her lungs punched out ragged breathes. "Then..."

"You taught art to preschoolers." Eli's hands immediately ran down her back and he brought her in for a hug. God, he had no clue she'd think those kids would be hers. To make it worse, Sara's reaction was... devastating. He rubbed her back and kissed the top of her strawberry-scented head. "We all do things to feel normal, Sara. Painting was your outlet. Just like I have my cooking, Jack works on rehabbing old cars, Kalen carves wooden furniture, and Tanner writes music."

She sniffled in his chest, "I didn't remember that. I didn't know that."

"You will, I promise." The words came out like they had earlier. *I promise.*

"You keep making me promises, Eli."

He chuckled and shook his head. Of course she'd pick up on that. "And I intend to keep them, baby."

She swiped away her tears and looked at him, "Tell me why making me promises made you and Kalen fight yesterday."

She wasn't asking. She was demanding. Eli rocked back on his heels. "After you died the first time," he had to take a moment to collect himself, "your first death was awful, baby. And Kalen, who'd sworn to protect you, felt as if he failed."

"That's not true though. He died giving me a chance to escape. My getting caught wasn't his fault."

Eli froze. "You remember that?"

"Only a little. I was told the rest of the story," she shrugged. "I remember coming to him when he was dying and I was already dead."

He shook his head. "The two of you stayed in Hell for a really long time. It took a lot for you guys to recover – not physically, because Lucifer took care of that – but, mentally and emotionally the two of you were a wreck." There was no point in sugar coating Sara's truth. "Kalen made you a promise in Hell that nothing would ever happen to you again. When you went missing in New Orleans and it seemed like you were dead and gone from us … Kalen lost it, Sara. What bit of sanity he had was shredded with guilt from failing you for the second time."

Her chin trembled and tears flowed freely down her face.

Eli felt awful for speaking on Kalen's behalf, but she needed to know. "He's not going to speak of it to you. He's not ready. I don't know if he will ever be ready. Perhaps Kalen will be content with having you back and holding you close… but he lost his shit with me because I did what he'd done. I promised you, yesterday, that nothing would happen to you ever again. I was wrong to say that."

"You were just trying to reassure me that I was safe, Eli."

"No, I was trying reassure all us Hounds that we wouldn't lose you again."

She gulped and folded her arms over her chest.

"I can't make that promise," he admitted. "Especially right now with you so vulnerable and not yet whole."

"I understand," she whispered, "I get both sides."

"But I'm serious," he cupped her cheeks, "I will do everything in my power to protect you, Sara. Never again will we be tricked or you pulled away from us. I won't allow it. I can't... I can't fucking stand the thought of you not with us."

"I'm not going anywhere," she pushed up on her tippy toes and kissed him softly. "We're in this together. No repeating our mistakes."

Guilt lifted from his shoulders. Kalen and Eli had gone head-to-head over his misstep last night, but he wanted to explain things to Sara too. And he was grateful she was listening with her heart. Just as he was about to squeeze her harder, Sara pushed back a little from his embrace and he let her.

"Can I have a moment?"

"Absolutely." He backed out of the room even though every step that put distance between them hurt like a bitch, "Take all the time you need, baby. I'll be outside guarding the door."

He left only after double checking the locks on the windows and making sure the entire apartment was locked up tighter than a frog's ass. For extra protection, Eli grabbed the canister of blessed salt from the kitchen and poured it onto the weaker points of the place like the windows and tub. Finally, Eli sat out in the hallway of the apartment building. There, he prayed. He chanted. He pushed his energy around until it was a maelstrom of hope and sorrows. He had nothing else left in him but fragile tendrils of what once was his soul. And his soul was currently trying to recollect her memories.

Eli pulled out one of his daggers and stared at the blade. He doubted anything would come near her apartment with him guarding it, but he wasn't about to take any risks.

He meant what he'd said: Nothing was going to happen to his woman ever again.

CHAPTER 41

When Sara asked to be alone for a moment, she hadn't expected Eli to leave the apartment, but when she heard the front door click shut, she sighed in relief. Was that wrong of her? She didn't know.

Eli seemed to have a natural ability to understand what she was saying, even when she wasn't saying anything at all. He read her like an open book. Heard the meaning behind her silence. And the Hound made her feel safe and secure, even when he was just standing with his hands behind his back. Had he just double-checked the entire apartment, making sure it was safe and secure for her to be in? Yes. Yes he had. The Hound was protective. He was also incredibly understanding since he gave her as much space as she needed.

Sara knew he wasn't far. She could feel him. The returned tattoo on her spine – Eli's mark – almost tingled with magic. That, too, gave her a sense of security.

Walking around the small bedroom, she tried to collect her thoughts. Reel in her emotions. She pulled the half-painted canvas off the easel and leaned it against the closet door to get it out of the way. Next, she unwrapped a fresh 24X36 inch blank beauty and propped it on the easel. Some piece of her itched to get paint out. To smell it. Create. Indulge. She wanted to lose herself in the peace and freedom of brushes, cerulean blue, burnt sienna, and cadmium red.

She didn't realize she was an artist until this moment. The scent of acrylic paint awoke something inside her. Whatever was sleeping, dormant or knocked out unconscious inside her soul, was awake and vibrant and energetic now. Sara's heart fluttered, her mind running a mile a minute.

Pulling her hair back, she twisted it into a bun and shoved a paintbrush in to secure it. Yanking another brush from the mason jar, Sara held it between her teeth while she walked over to the bins of paints. Hand hovering over the variety of colors, she scanned the stash and started making choices. Some were too old to use now, but others had a little bit of life in them. Next, she snatched a palette and began squeezing tubes of paint onto it.

Popping her ass up on the stool, she closed her eyes and let her mind go. Images, loose, detached, bright and hypnotic, were dancing in her head. Dipping the brush into the paints, Sara started with small strokes. Speckling the canvas all over the place as if her hand wasn't sure how to work the brush or make sense of what she was trying to paint. After a few moments, a fever seemed to spike in her and the strokes that had no meaning started coming together. More paint. More brushes. More time. More images.

Small strokes grew bigger. Wilder. Extreme. Passionate. Details started to emerge.

Sara had no idea how long she stayed in that room, or if her lungs drew breath even once while she painted, but by the time she came back to reality, the sky was a warm pink and she realized the sun was setting.

Sara stared at the image she'd painted. Biting her lip, she pulled the canvas off the easel and set it aside. Was she ready to paint more? Yes and no. Some kind frenzy had been unleashed within her and she wanted to run with it. She intended to keep painting, but wanted to ride this high a little longer before starting a new one. Nothing felt better than this - To create something out of nothing, literally pluck an image out of your head and be able to recreate it for the world to see. It was an amazing feeling, this kind of accomplishment.

Rubbing her hands over her jeans, Sara didn't care that she'd wrecked her outfit. Paint was all over her and it felt so damn good.

240

She wanted to share this feeling with Eli. After stepping out of the small bedroom, she shut the door. That room was private and she didn't want Eli to see what she'd just painted. Not yet, at least.

Opening the front door, she practically ran smack into a huge wall of muscle. Eli was standing guard in the hallway, blade in hand, his face etched in hard lines. His intensity softened the moment he saw her.

"I'm sorry," she spoke softly, "time got away from me in there."

She loved that his smile was a little crooked, the right side of his mouth tilting up just a wee bit higher than the left. "I figured that would happen." He reached up and plucked dried paint out of her hair. "It's good to see you this way."

"It's good to be seen in any way." For the life of her, Sara was still so grateful to have her body back and the Hounds could all see her. Being an invisible ghost for so long had been awful. She took a step back into the apartment knowing Eli would follow. After they crossed the threshold, he shut and relocked the door.

Her eyes fluttered when his fingertip traced a hot line from her forehead, down the slope of her nose and across her mouth. "You have paint all over you."

She smiled, "Not everywhere."

His hand traced the curve of her neck, "Prove it."

Eli couldn't stop his hand from shaking when he touched Sara. To see her covered in paint was a vision he'd clung to in his dreams over the past five years. She loved painting. Loved it so much, in fact, she practically wore as much as the canvas she was tackling.

He never thought he would see her like this again.

Blues and reds speckled her hair. White, yellows, and black were all over her cheeks and the tip of her nose. She had orange on her forehead. Some on her chin, too. Her jeans were destroyed. Her hoodie looked like it had a battle with Jackson Pollack and lost.

He reached up and slowly pulled the paintbrush from her hair. The bun fell loose and her dark hair curtained her sweet face.

Eli watched her reaction to his every move. He didn't want to push her, but he didn't want to give this moment up either. "Can I kiss you, Sara?"

Her eyes seemed to darken. "You don't need to ask me that, Eli Carter Jenson."

Eli stiffened. "You... remember my full name?" His heart pounded so hard his eardrums had a pulse.

"Yes," she whispered. "I remember more of you now."

His eyes squeezed shut as she wrapped her arms around his neck and hugged him tightly. Every fiber of his being seemed to explode. The feeling of being lost in the dark was ebbing away as the bright light at the end of his tunnel was finally coming into view for the first time in a long fucking while. It was a miracle that they had their Sara back, but for her to not remember what they had was a new kind of loss that he'd not been prepared for. They were going through the motions, falling back into old habits, but it wasn't the same. Not yet.

Sara still wasn't quite right and Eli was desperate to find some way for her to reconnect. Now, she was truly coming back.

"Say my name again."

"Eli."

"All of it."

"Eli," she kissed his chin, "Carter," she kissed the tip of his nose, "Jenson," she sealed her mouth over his and he knew this was what flying apart felt like.

Eli roared to life again. "I've been so lost without you, baby." He ran his hands through her hair, desperate to feel every inch of her.

"Me too," she met his touches with fervor. Pulling her hoodie over her head, she tossed it onto the couch. "Touch me."

No need to ask twice. Eli ran his hands down her body and cupped her ass. Lifting her up, she wrapped her legs around his waist and he found a solid wall to pin her against. He ravaged her neck, nipping, kissing, licking his way down to her breasts. She arched her body so more of her could go into his mouth. The taste of her was unreal. The smell, feel, sound of her... Fuck, he'd never get enough.

She released her legs from him and slid down the wall until her feet hit the floor. Sara started unbuttoning her jeans and he followed suit, doing the same with his pants. In no time at all, they were both naked.

"See?" she teased as her hand ran over her stomach, "No paint here. Or here," she turned and rubbed her ass cheeks.

Fuuuck. This woman knew all the ways to send a man to his knees. Goddamn, he loved her more with every breath he took.

Eli snatched her by the waist and in less than a second, had her on the floor. She yipped when he slung her legs over his shoulders and dove down. He buried his face in her sweet spot and she moaned immediately.

"There's a bed just over there, you know."

Eli tilted his head and glared at her. "If you can make it there, I'll fuck you there. If you can't... then I'll fuck you here."

Her eyes glinted with humor and desire. She was the most beautiful woman in the world.

Sara pressed a bare foot on his pec and gently kicked away from him. Crab crawling backwards down the hall, her sweet spot totally exposed for his viewing pleasure and also an incredibly effective lure, she slowly made her way towards the bedroom.

He crawled on his hands and knees after her. Just as slow. Just as enticing. Eli was the predator, playing with his prey.

Their eyes locked onto each other. She was challenging him, luring him where she wanted him to go. All she had to do was ask and he would have carried her into the bedroom. But crawling worked too.

He'd go on his knees any day of the week for Sara.

Her back finally bumped into the foot of the bed. Eli took that moment to attack her again. Crawling up her body, he landed between her legs and pressed his mouth to hers, unable to get enough of her taste. His hard cock pressed against her wet opening and he groaned at the feel of her warmth. Moving fast, he scooped her in his arms and placed her on the bed, all the while being sure to keep their bodies pressed together.

"I need you, Eli."

He melted, right then and there. "I'm here, baby."

She ran her hands through his hair, her nails lightly digging into his scalp. "I miss all my Hounds."

"We're here. We're all fucking here. We're not going to let you go again." The head of his cock pressed against her opening, begging entrance.

She hooked her leg around, her heel pressing into the small of his back and nudged him, urging him to enter her.

Eli kept his eyes locked on hers and slid in nice and slow. Her body welcomed him with pulsing heat. She gasped when he finally buried himself, balls deep, into her. Knowing she was going to need a moment to acclimate to his size, he held her close for a few seconds and then he began the slow and steady retreat. He roared to life all over again as he plunged back into her.

No matter how many times he said he wanted to take it slow and easy with her, it never worked out that way. But damned if he was going to speed things up just yet.

Sara whimpered in bliss under his body. Normally she liked to be on top with him, but not today. Today, he was in control. Today he was going to make sure she got everything she fucking needed and not have to work for it, either.

He quickened his pace marginally, swirling his hips as he buried himself as deep as possible. Fuck, she felt incredible.

"Eli!" she cried out.

He knew she was close to coming. He wanted to watch her. Bracing his hands on either side of her head, Eli moved his body like a big wave. Thighs clenching, ass tensing, back arching, arms flexing. His pace quickened a little more.

Sara started panting. Her eyes fluttered shut.

He wanted to make her look at him, but loved that she was already lost in ecstasy. Her entire body was practically blushing. Eli kept her on the edge of a climax for as long as he could stand it and then he swirled his hips and began to pound into her. Her orgasm was earth shattering for both of them. Sara clawed his back to ribbons while she screamed his name to the heavens.

Eli dipped his head down and ate her screams. His tongue slid against hers and she wrapped both legs around his body, squeezing him against her harder. Her fingers dug into his back and he roared with his own release. He spilled over the edge and filled her with everything he'd been holding back.

One orgasm wasn't enough. Not for her. And not for him.

They were going to be here a while.

CHAPTER 42

Jack was in the kitchen when the call came through. He quickly gathered Tanner and Kalen and the three of them headed into the basement.

"We need to make this fast. I don't want to leave Eli and Sara on this side without us." Tanner looked antsy and annoyed.

Jack didn't blame him. Eli and Sara had left hours ago, and even though Eli kept sending updates and assured them she was all good, they would have felt better had she been home at the farm with all of them.

But, as Jack said no less than three times that afternoon, Eli was a helluva guard. Nothing would get past him.

"What does he want?" Kalen pulled on a shirt as Jack unlocked the door in the basement that led straight to Hell.

"I have no bloody idea. Let's just get it over with."

Jack's gut coiled with dread. It was rare for Lucifer to call them in ahead of schedule. And the split in realms meant if something were to happen to Eli and Sara, Jack, Kalen and Tanner wouldn't feel it if they were on the other side of the door. Again, Jack steeled himself and assured the others that Eli and Sara would be fine. They were at her apartment. Eli would keep her safe.

More dread clenched his gut. Twisting, squeezing, ripping

him from the inside out. It was guilt, of course. Guilt for making assurances that might not be true. After all, Jack thought for sure he and Sara would be safe in the apartment the other night and look how wrong he'd been about that.

The image of Sara being literally torn away from him by those *malanum* fuckers had his hands balled into fists. He shook off the urge to growl and snap his teeth. Eli would double-check the locks. He was aware of what had happened to her and Jack. Eli would take the extra precautions to keep her safe. He'd not leave her side.

Knowing that Hound, Eli probably dumped all the salt they kept in the cupboard above the fridge around the perimeter of the apartment just to be extra careful.

Fuck, he loved that Hound.

"Let's go. The sooner we're there, the sooner we're back."

"And hopefully Sara and Eli will be home by then," Tanner added. "I'm texting him so he knows where we are."

"Good idea." Jack opened the door and waited for Tanner to hit send. With a nod, they headed into Hell.

The heat of Lucifer's chambers seemed extra heavy. Jack's muscles tensed but he kept his expression blank.

"Fuck, you feel that?" Tanner cracked his neck and then his knuckles.

Kalen, like always, kept to himself and didn't say shit.

Rounding the corner, they were just about to enter Lucifer's main room when a loud roar brought their attention to the opposite end of the hall. Heading towards the noise, they rushed forward and turned down another hall. There, Reggie was going head-to-head with another Gate Keeper. Both were snarling and fists were flying.

Jack jumped in to break up the fight. Tanner and Kalen joined – Kalen tackling Reggie to the ground, while Tanner had the other Gate Keeper up off his feet and locked in his arms.

"Easy," Tanner hissed, "What the fuck is going on?"

"He's trying to pin the blame on me!"

Reggie jerked, trying to get out of Kalen's hold. "You were the one in charge for the day."

"That doesn't mean I did it!"

Jack's arms thrust out, silencing everyone in the hallway. "Explain yourselves. Reggie, you first."

The large Gate Keeper panted heavily. "The walls have cracked more."

Jack cursed. They needed to get out of here as soon as possible. Sara might be in danger. No, not might. *Definitely*. It was only a matter of time before the *malanum* came after her again. Fuck, fuck, fuck.

"Why are you fighting Micah about it?" Tanner let go of the other Gate Keeper, Micah, but kept his body between the two feuding fools.

"Micah was the one on duty at the time." Reggie glared, "He could damn well be the traitor."

"I'M NOT THE TRAITOR!" Micah lunged forward and swung out to clock Reggie. He'd have made contact too, had Tanner not pulled him back in time.

"Knock it the fuck off. All of you." Lucifer's voice boomed down the hallway. Everyone behaved immediately. "Hounds, get in here right now. Reggie and Micah, get the fuck out of here and guard those MOTHERFUCKING GATES! Bump up security in there, Reggie. NOW."

The Gate Keepers rolled their shoulders back and left without protest.

Silently, the Hounds followed Lucifer into his main chamber and the doors closed behind them with an ominous *thud*. Lucifer was tense, the corded muscles in his neck straining. He paced back and forth and they all waited for him to say something.

"How is Sara?"

Jack spoke first. "She's getting better."

"But she's not complete?"

"Not yet," Tanner answered. "But she's close. Two of our marks are back on her already."

Lucifer ran a hand over his mouth. "You need to try harder."

"We are," Kalen interjected. "Broken things take time to repair."

The Devil cast a cool glare towards Kalen. "Fine," Lucifer finally grumbled. "Work harder for her, Hounds. Make her whole as soon as possible. Whatever it takes, you hear me?"

Jack took a step closer, "What's going on, my lord?"

"The walls have cracked more. I can feel the storms of darkness brewing. Someone has a great amount of power. And that

247

someone is fucking with me."

"So kill them," Tanner shrugged.

"Would if I could, Hound, but as it stands, I cannot leave this place – as you all very well know – and I have no idea who this person is. I need Sara to regain her memories so she can tell us who killed her and stripped her soul. It's my only fucking lead at this point."

"But that was years ago," Jack interjected. "With the exception of the intermittent flurry of these fuckers coming and going, everything else died down after Sara disappeared that night."

Lucifer's mouth was a tight line. He crooked a finger and silently ushered them into a back room. It was a place only Kalen had stepped into before. "You're right, Jack. The walls have steadily weakened for years. And, we've always been able to repair and reinforce them. But this started up a few days ago," the Devil opened the door and they all peered inside the room.

"Holy shit."

Jack only thought he knew what dread felt like before that moment. Lucifer slammed the door shut. "I'm calling a meeting. Gathering all my Hounds. I called you here separately so you can prepare Sara. The meeting is in two hours."

"Alright," Jack nodded. "Hounds, let's move."

They took off, boots pounding on the hard floor as they left Hell.

"This is bad," Tanner said, slamming his hand against their door and opening it. "This is really fucking bad."

Jack couldn't say anything. Only one word played in his head over and over and over.

SARA.

Eli was on his back, one arm draped over Sara's luscious ass, the other across his forehead. What a fucking work out, man.

His cell went off. Then it went off again, and again, and again. He was going to have to answer the damned thing. It was the other Hounds. He had kept them updated on Sara the whole time she'd been painting, but then things got a little hectic and he hadn't checked in with them for... ohhh going on six hours now.

Guilt tickled his gut, but he wasn't sorry. Rolling over, he carefully slid out of the bed, not wanting to wake the beauty beside him. Fuck, his limbs were sore. In a good way. No, scratch that. In a glorious way.

He dug his cell out of his pocket and saw several messages and missed calls. All the Hounds, of course. He clicked on the messages and read them, gripping the cell harder and harder. It was a miracle the screen didn't crack under the pressure. Snatching his clothes, he stuffed his legs in a pair of jeans and gathered the rest of their stuff up in his arms. He hated waking her up, but they had to get home. Now.

"Sara," he gently shook her shoulder. "Come on, baby. Wake up."

"Mmph," she rolled over, her eyes still closed.

He shook her harder. "Come on. Wake. Up." When she still didn't respond, Eli cracked her ass hard with his palm. The slap forced her eyes to pop wide open and a wicked smile curled her lips. She stretched and arched so her ass went high in the air, begging for another spanking.

Damn her sexy self. Eli bit the inside of his cheek and wished like hell he could indulge, but now was definitely not the time. "We have to go." His voice was deep and dark and his cock had its own heartbeat all of a sudden. "The Hounds need us home. Now."

She sat up and rubbed her eyes. "Are they okay?"

"Yeah, but we need to hurry back."

She crawled off the bed and he moaned at the sight of her ass with his red handprint taking up her entire right cheek. Only the call of Lucifer could break Eli away from this moment. Damn that motherfucker.

"Here," Eli handed Sara her clothes and the two got dressed almost as fast as they'd gotten undressed earlier. "Let's roll."

Keeping her behind him, his hand firmly gripping hers, Eli poked his head out and scanned the hallway of the apartment building. *Malanum* usually steered clear of Hounds, but since they seemed to be drawn to Sara, he didn't want to assume they were safe.

"All clear," he announced, then ushered her into the elevator.

"What's going on, Eli?"

"I don't know yet, but Lucifer has called a meeting and we need to prepare you."

"Prepare how?"

"I'm not entirely sure. Jack will know." His gaze bounced around, constantly scanning the area.

"You'll fight better with two hands, Eli."

"I'm not letting go of you." The elevator *ding-dinged* and he scanned the lobby. Coast was clear. The two of them beat feet out into the cold night and he quickly got her into his Jeep. Just as he slammed his door shut and locked them in, he saw shadows lurking on the edge of the brick building. "Fuck."

He was torn between duty to the Devil and duty to Sara. The Hound in him said HUNT. The man in him screamed to PROTECT. Eli revved his engine and peeled rubber down the road.

In all things, he'd choose Sara.

CHAPTER 43

Jack was standing in the driveway, his arms crossed over his chest, when Eli and Sara pulled up to the farmhouse. Jack's eyes pinned Eli through the windshield with a look that said he was really pissed. Sara hopped out of the Jeep and walked over to her other Hound.

Jack cupped her face with both hands and he stared at her, doing a silent inventory of her features, scanning for marks of having run into trouble.

"I'm fine, Eli kept me safe."

He didn't respond with words. Instead, Jack kissed her soundly on the mouth and the sigh of relief was visible in the way his shoulders dropped some tension and a groan slid up his throat. "Get inside, love."

Gracefully, she headed into the house. Kalen held the door open for her and slammed it shut once she crossed the threshold.

Eli and Jack stayed outside. "What's going on, Jack?"

The fact that he didn't respond immediately with his usual barking orders and weapon distribution told Eli one thing: Jack was not in control.

Eli's spine tingled. This was bad. This was really fucking bad. It raised his hackles. Figuratively speaking, since he wasn't an actual canine.

"Where were you that you didn't receive our calls?" Jack's question was paired with a lot more growling.

"Sara and I were busy. She was safe the entire time. You know I'd take every precaution."

"You ran into no trouble at all?"

"Nope," Eli rubbed the back of his neck, "There were a few shadows on the side of her building, but I laid down the salt and kept my hand on her the entire time when we left. None of the *malanum* tried to come at her."

"Did you take them out?"

"No, I got our girl home instead."

Jack squared his shoulders and sighed. "Good."

Yeah, Eli thought, *this must be really fucking bad.* Under normal circumstances, he would be in deep shit for not hunting the *malanum* that were so obviously standing there as if they'd wanted to be caught. "What the fuck is going on?"

"Come inside and we'll catch you two up on things." Jack led the way and Eli followed.

Sara went into the living room. Kalen hadn't kissed her, but his eyes stayed locked on her no matter where she went. Tanner, however, planted a half dozen kisses all over her face.

"You okay, Beautiful?"

"Yeah, I'm fine. What's gotten into all of you?"

Jack and Eli stepped inside. The Hounds' magic locked into place once they were all together. Sara could feel it like a deep vibration in her bones. The sensation lasted all of three seconds and was gone. They must have gone off-grid, she realized.

"Lucifer has called a meeting with everyone," Jack sat on the couch. "The walls have weakened more."

Tanner sat next to Jack and leaned over, his elbows resting on his knees. "Luce called us in and we walked in on Micah and Reggie fighting over who was to blame."

Eli scoffed, "How could it possibly be either of their faults? They're the two best Gate Keepers in Hell."

"Which is why they are both so angry, I suspect." Jack rubbed his chin. "Hounds are the same way if a *malanum* gets away from the pack. They start pinning the blame on each other instead of either admitting their personal failure or considering the *malanum* had a lucky break."

Kalen leaned back in his chair. "Doesn't matter. Reggie trained Micah. He'd feel the failure either way."

They all nodded silently in agreement. Tanner looked around the room, "Reggie's been working non-stop. He looks exhausted."

Jack nodded, "His loyalty is commendable, but it seems Lucifer needs more than loyalty to get through this."

Sara sat up. She was sitting on the other side of Tanner and his hand was rubbing her thigh like it brought him comfort to touch her. She got that. She totally fucking got that. "So what do we need to do, Jack?"

"We need to roll with the act that you're back and in full swing. No one can know that you don't have all your memories."

"Alright."

"And we need a way to divert any questions to one of us."

"Alright."

"We've got to go in strong. It's been a while since a meeting like this was called. To have every pack there, it's going to be tough to keep our leadership in line." Jack turned to look at Sara, "You've always been our leader, Sara. When you... left us... I took over as Alpha at these meetings. Things will now need to shift back to you so we can keep the illusion that you've not changed in any way."

She saw it kill Jack a little to say that last bit. She wasn't offended. She was sad for him. "I'm better every day, Hounds. We'll get through this."

"Atta girl," Tanner squeezed her thigh.

She quickly smiled and addressed Jack again. "When do we go?"

"In forty-five minutes. Jump in the shower and get dressed." They all stood up to break apart and prepare.

Sara figured her outfit, albeit splattered with paint, wouldn't really matter to anyone. She had just gone down to Hell in short-shorts and tube socks for crying out loud. This outfit was a little nicer than that, at least. "Why can't I go like this?"

Jack's eyes hardened. "You smell like sex, Sara. And you're

about to go into Hell and sit in a closed room with all male Hounds. I am not in the mood to fight them all for desiring a chance to mount you."

Oh What. The. Fuck.

"I'm the only female Hound?" Didn't that seem stupid? Cliché? Abnormal?

"Lucifer has never allowed a female to be a Hound before or after you. Some days you give him such a run for his money, we've all wondered if he regrets his choice."

She scowled until Jack added, "God created only one of you, love. I imagine Lucifer, who chose to rule over Hell, was likely very pleased with his decision once he was able to call you *his* creation."

"Are you saying the Devil has a crush on me, Jack?"

"No, love. I'm saying you're a rare breed of miracle that even the Devil knows better than to try to recreate. Had he been just a fallen angel, maybe he would have tried to make a million of you. Instead, he kept the only one that existed—"

"And fixed her broken pieces," Kalen whispered.

"And spoiled her for a couple centuries," Eli winked.

"And then let us lucky sonsabitches have her to hold and love and cherish forever." Tanner walked over and kissed her again.

Sara stood there stunned for a few heartbeats. What the hell were they telling her?

"Come on, Darling." Kalen placed his hands around her waist and started steering her around the couch and over to the steps. "Time to wash up."

"Are you coming with me again?" she asked.

"No," he said, a slight smile softening his features. "Eli is."

"But... I thought I'm supposed to wash Eli off of me. Isn't that being counterintuitive?"

"Nope," Kalen deadpanned Eli now, "He just has to be in there while you wash that sweet body of yours. He won't be touching you, so his scent and your arousal will not cling afterwards."

She heard a growl rumble from behind her and knew, instinctively, that it was Eli. She ascended the steps, her mind trying to put all these pieces together. For some reason, it felt a little like Eli was getting punished. But... that could just be her ego talking.

Or maybe it was the grumbles of laughter from the other three

Hounds as they watched the two of them go up the steps.

Eli stayed out of the shower the whole time, but the sink was definitely groaning under the strain of his iron grip. When she stepped out of the shower to snatch a towel, he looked so hard she thought he'd snap. Thankfully, the small bit of panic Sara had under the water, she was able to tamp down all by herself. Whether it was because of Eli being there and she felt safe, or she had grown stronger and her mind was coping better, she wasn't sure. Nor did she care.

Drying off, she left Eli alone to collect himself in the bathroom. She braided her hair back so it was out of her face and Tanner had her dress in leather pants and a corset, which seriously annoyed the hell out of her.

"I've spent every moment of my dead life in a corset and leathers. Why are you boys torturing me?"

"I'd say we're the ones being tortured, Beautiful." Tanner stuffed small blades into different areas of her outfit. "This is the standard garb for Hounds."

"So you have a corset, too?"

He laughed. "Not exactly." He continued to tug and strap more things into her body. "Why am I armed so much? We're going into Hell. That's a safe place."

"But you always strapped up like this. To do anything less might spark curiosity and we'll have enough of that tossed in our direction as it is."

She watched the lump in his throat bob up and down. "What aren't you Hounds telling me, Tanner?"

His gaze flicked to hers and then back down to her chest where he was putting together the last buckle. "The stakes of the situation have escalated." His voice was soft and low, as if he didn't want anyone else to hear him speak of it.

"How so?"

"Sacrifices are being made."

"Like chickens and stuff?"

Tanner's baby blues pinned her, "Children, Sara."

She tensed, "Oh my God."

Tanner nodded and an ominous silence engulfing the room. After a few more minutes he said, "There. All done." Tanner grabbed Sara's shoulders and spun her around to look in the mirror.

"Holy shit," she mumbled. Sara looked... vicious. Savage. Fierce.

Tanner ran his finger down her spine as he stared at her in the mirror. Even with the leather between her skin and his touch, she felt it as if she were naked. "You made love to Eli." His voice betrayed his smile.

She regarded his reflection. "I lost myself to painting." She gulped when Tanner's emotions danced across his face. "And... I remembered more things." She spun around to face him. "I remember more about Eli now. And Kalen... and you, Tanner Lee."

Her belly fluttered when he smiled. "You remember my full name?"

"Well, not your full name. You hate your middle name and never gave it to me."

The air rushed out of him. "Oh my God," he rested his forehead on hers. "I could totally fucking kiss Eli for this."

She smirked, "I would not object to watching that."

He chuckled and shook his head. "Fucking hell, Sara." He pressed his lips to her forehead. "I've missed you so much, woman."

"I'm here now."

He opened the door and gestured for her to head out because it was time to go. "So," he cleared his throat, "Old habits die hard, huh?"

"Why do you say that?"

"Because you're still saving the best for last." Tanner cracked her ass as she walked by him.

"Well, obviously."

They both laughed and headed back to Hell.

CHAPTER 44

Sara found herself in a strange place. Mentally, physically, emotionally. Here she sat, in a room that put the Taj Mahal to shame. Not that she'd ever spent quality time at the Taj Mahal, but … well, this place was just breathtaking.

Annnnd not at all something she remembered being in before today. Damnit. Why couldn't her memories just come back so she could move the fuck on to her next big problem?

"The others will be here soon," Lucifer warned from his chair at the opposite end of the round table. "Remember, act like a bitch."

Sara rolled her eyes. "Got it."

"And don't answer a question with a lie. Evade."

Talk about walking a fine line. "Got it."

She sat stiffly, her hands clasped in her lap. Then she gave up the pose and rested her elbows on the table. Eli and Jack were to her left. Kalen and Tanner were on her right. She smiled, feeling Tanner's leg bouncing up and down, nervously. He was making the table tremble a little bit.

"Tanner," Lucifer growled, "knock it off or I cut it off."

The vibration stopped immediately.

Why were they here before everyone else? That was the first question out of her mouth when they arrived twenty minutes ago.

The answer was not what she expected, but also not surprising.

Apparently they were the strongest pack. As such, Lucifer had more meetings with them than the others. Also, Lucifer was stricter on them, and forced them to work harder, so as to not look as though he played favorites.

Totally false, by the way. Sara knew that like she knew snow was cold and the sun was hot. She was Lucifer's favorite. Her pack was, too.

"It begins." Lucifer sat back in his chair looking as if he'd been waiting for too long and everyone was late. The scowl perfected the irate look. "Hurry the fuck up and get in your seats."

Every Hound was clad in leather pants, black shirts, boots and blades. The moment their eyes hit Sara, they all seemed to forget how to walk. Or talk. So they stumbled to their seats with uneasy looks on their faces.

"What the fuck is the matter with you?" Lucifer slammed a fist on the table. "Sit."

Like well trained dogs, the Hounds all took their designated seats.

"Forgive us, sire, but..." one redheaded Hound four seats down from Sara gulped, "How is this possible?"

"What are you talking about, Fin?"

"Sara!" he jabbed a finger in her direction. "We were told she was dead."

"You were never told that by me," Lucifer cocked a dark brow.

"But... we all searched for her. She was dead."

"I'm right here, you know." Sara waved jazz hands at Fin.

"Where have you been?"

"Around."

A couple Hounds on her other side guffawed.

"I don't see what's so fucking funny," Sara immediately tossed the laughing hyenas a nasty look.

Fin crossed his arms over his chest, looking angry as Hell. "We've been played, Hounds. The stupid bitch played us."

Kalen stood up, his chair tilting back until it crashed to the floor. He was on the offending Hound within seconds. Jack and Tanner pulled him off only after Lucifer demanded order in the room.

Fin wiped the blood off his face, and was otherwise unfazed by Kalen's fury. "We were all sent to hunt you down and no one could find you, Sara."

"Then you *failed*. Some Hounds you are." Sara snapped her words. Her teeth ground together as she narrowed her gaze and met the eyes of every Hound in the room.

She was suddenly furious. Hounds were made to hunt and she'd been left stranded with nothing and no one and they had all stopped looking for her? Left her? The packs abandoned their search.

Maybe she was taking things too far, but she didn't care. A sudden burst of outrage threatened to erupt from her lips and she swiftly moved her hands to her lap so no one could see her shake. "You didn't look hard enough."

"We searched for months!" This coming from a blonde with a pierced lip.

"I was right under all your noses."

"You were gone!" another argued.

"I was HERE!" Sara slammed her fist on the table and screamed. "I WAS HERE, DAMN YOU! You didn't bother to look hard enough! You all gave up because you didn't give a shit. The female was gone. Ding dong the bitch is dead, am I right?"

Where the fuck those words came from she didn't know. Was she being possessed? Was she dreaming this? Was she drunk? Lucifer had offered them all drinks earlier and she accepted hers no questions asked. She was thirsty. The Devil had water. What could be wrong there? But… maybe he spiked it with something.

Or maybe old grudges and nasty feelings were resurfacing. It felt natural to argue and snap her teeth at this crowd.

"Sara's right," Lucifer's deep voice cut through her anger. "She was here and you all failed to find her."

"Including her own Hounds!" Fin jabbed a finger in Jack's direction.

Sara seethed, "My Hounds found me, you fucktard."

"Oh how convenient." Fin leaned back with a shit eating grin on his puss. "So this was all a fucking ruse?"

"Hardly," Sara hissed.

"Then what was it?"

"It's over with," Lucifer growled. "And now that we're over

the shock and awe of Sara's inevitable return, we have bigger problems than the disappearance of our Darling Sara."

Ohhh that bastard. Sara glared at Lucifer. Was he trying to pit the entire room against her and her Hounds? What the fuck was the matter with him?

Motherfucker.

Our Darling Sara. She wasn't theirs and she wasn't darling.

Jack's hand gripped hers under the table and he squeezed. Not in an *It'll be alright* way, but in a *Shut the fuck up and keep your shit together* kinda way.

Sara obeyed. For now.

Lucifer's voice boomed, "Every pack is on high alert from now until I say otherwise. This means working around the clock, no breaks, and you split your packs into two teams. Day and Night."

"No offense, sire, but where's the fire? Our territories haven't had any problems lately. As a matter of fact, our numbers are all down," Fin said.

"I speak for all of London when I say our numbers are low, too," said a Hound with tattoos all over his hands.

"Our areas have been swept clean as well, sire," said a big burly guy with a Hells Angels feel to him. "And where are the missing Hounds?"

Sara, too, had noticed four chairs sitting empty.

"That pack is on an errand for me. They've been excused."

Fin's eyes cut to Sara again. "Well isn't that interesting. Another pack is *excused.*"

She tried to not squirm. What the hell gives with this dick?

"Shut your mouth, Fin," Lucifer's voice grabbed their attention again. "There's a lot of work to do."

"What's going on?" asked a Hound with jet black hair.

"The walls are weakening worse than ever." Lucifer gave them all a moment to bark and growl over it then he stood up and casually walked around the room. "So, my trusted dogs," he punctuated each world with the thump in his boots. "You think I'm lying to you?"

"No," a blue hair Hound who could have been no more than eighteen when he died spoke up. "It just… all seems peaceful in our districts."

"Yeah," said Tattoo Hands, "I seriously thought this was

going to be a celebration. The world around us has been so quiet."

Tanner snickered.

"Got something to add, Tanner?" Lucifer's gaze didn't fall on Tanner though; he was watching every other Hounds' reaction.

"Power grids have gone out in a pattern. I can't be the only one to notice that. The electrical failures are now on the East Coast. Philly was the last to go down a couple days ago."

"That's your territory, so it's your problem."

"You know what, Fin, I'm about ready to shove this pretty little blade into a special place of yours." Lucifer ran the threatening weapon across his tongue as if the damn thing was gonna need lubrication for wherever Lucifer planned to stick it.

"We aren't asking for your help, Fin." Jack leaned back but kept his hand in Sara's. "We're just sharing knowledge."

"Oh so now you're into sharing, Hound?" Fin shoved away from the table and stood up. "You all hole up and basically fall off the face of the earth these past few years. You don't answer our calls. You don't show up for meetings. And now here you are, with your bitch in tow, and you act like you're doing us all a favor? Fuck that and fuck you."

Lucifer slung his blade. The business end nailed its target. Or… well… Sara assumed that was where Lucifer was aiming.

All she thought was Fin better like pirates, because he's going to be wearing an eye patch for the rest of his days. He'll have to change his name to Captain Fin Fuckhead.

Sara gawked at the Hound as he roared in pain. Jesus, how had the blade not killed him? It was buried to the hilt, straight through the eye socket and most likely into the brain. Maybe Fin didn't have a brain? It would explain so much.

To her astonishment, Fin silently pulled the blade out of his eye socket. The sickening wet suction noise made Sara squirm and Jack clenched her hand again.

"Sorry," Fin said quietly.

Lucifer's voice was deadly. "Say it again. Louder."

"Sorry."

"Did you hear him speak, Darling?" Lucifer stood behind Sara. His big hands gripped the top of her chair and the wood groaned under his fingers.

"Nope. Maybe his tongue isn't working right." Good God, she

261

was being a callous little woman. But it was fun. Besides, clearly there was a rejuvenating quality to Hell; Fin's eye was healing already. Or maybe he had a secret ability to regrow body parts?

"Shall I cut his tongue out next, Sara? If it doesn't work properly, it should be extracted. Same as any Hound who does not pull his weight in one of my packs."

The clear warning fell over the room and several Hounds shifted nervously. Sara, however, sat back in her seat and got comfy. Letting go of Jack's hand, she crossed her arms over her chest and cocked her head to the side, debating. "I don't know, Luce, now I'm curious to see if his tongue is forked."

Jack interjected and tried to tame the tempers flaring, "She has enough tongues to hold her attention already."

Lucifer laughed, "Of that, I have no doubt." He moved away from the table. "You have your orders. All are dismissed except, you." He pointed at Sara.

She felt her face redden as all eyes turned to her.

"Your Hounds can wait out in the hall, Sara. The rest of you, Do. NOT. Disappoint me. There are enough souls leeching through the cracks now to keep you busy. I expect results." As they started pushing away from the table, Lucifer added, "You all failed to find our Hound, Sara. You will not like what I will do to you should you fail twice. Hell is too precious to lose. Your lives depend on its survival more than anything else in the world."

As they all filed out of the room, Sara held her breath. Finally, the door shut and she was closed in with the Devil. Again.

"Well done, Darling."

She hadn't really pulled anything off. In fact, she sort of felt like she made a mess with her temper. "I got carried away."

Lucifer sat down in the chair beside hers and rubbed his forehead. "You did exactly what I knew you'd do."

"Fuck it up?"

"Split them up."

Sara didn't get it. "How?"

"You were right to be angry, Sara."

She crossed her arms over her chest again. It did nothing but bump her breasts up higher, damn her corset. So she released her arms and leaned on the table. Massaging her temples, she clamored for the right words. "Do they all hate me?"

"Some, yes. Others… they are envious but not a threat."

"So that's it, hate or jealousy? No friendship?"

"You have friends amongst some of the packs. Today proved it."

"How?"

"That's for me to see, not you." He reached over and grabbed her hand, rubbing his thumb over her knuckles. "How are you now?" Suddenly, his voice was softer and lighter. It made her nervous.

"I'm good."

"Are you whole?"

"Not sure what you mean by that."

"Don't play coy with me, Sara." He placed a kiss over the tattoo on her wrist - his mark. "Your pack is my strongest weapon. Envy is no stranger to you and your Hounds. Neither is fear or revenge. Someone in my domain is a traitor."

"You think it's a Hound?"

"I think it's not you or your Hounds." He released her hand and stood up. "That is all I know."

She watched him walk in circles. "Why are you confiding in me?"

"Old habits I suppose," he shrugged and kept pacing.

"Why don't I remember my time with you?" She watched his pace slow down and she used it to fuel her courage. "Why can't I remember much of you, Luce? Kalen said we spent a long time in Hell. Surely I have more memories of you than I'm recalling. Are you keeping them from me?"

"No, darling. Your time with me was…" he struggled to find the words and finally sighed in defeat, "not pleasant." He went over to his stash of liquor and glasses and poured himself a drink.

"Not pleasant because it's Hell or because of what was done to me when I was killed?"

"Both." He took a sip of dark red liquid. "You now know you are my only female Hound."

"Yes."

"Why do you think that is?"

"Because…" she tried to lighten up the mood because she was growing more nervous and didn't know why. "You were madly in love with me?"

Okay, that was not the right thing to say. Soooo not the right thing. Can she do a take back? *Take back! TAKE BACK!*

"You're not far off, Darling." He seemed to avoid her stare. "I was in love with humanity. Yours, especially. After what happened to you... what they did to you... it broke my heart, black as it may be." He flicked a half-hearted smile.

"What did *they* do to me?" She had no other way to refer to the ones who'd killed her the first time.

"Awful things," he whispered, "And coming from the Devil, that's saying a lot." He chugged the rest of his drink and poured another.

"Can I have some?" she needed liquid courage at this point.

"Absolutely," he poured her a healthy dose of whatever it was and handed her the glass. "You were so broken, Sara. When your spirit traveled to Kalen, it was your strength that I admired so much. Not even death fazed you. No matter how bad it was."

"I love him," she said quietly. "I love all of them."

"And they love you." He sat in silence before clearing his throat. "My Hounds cannot die easily. It's almost impossible, actually. After that shit in New Orleans, to have thought you dead, Sara... it was a sickening nightmare. Whatever they did to you was..."

"As bad as my first death?"

"Even worse, I fear."

She shivered at the thought.

"To have stripped your power, your tattoos, your memories. They didn't just empty you, Sara. You were nothing more than a wisp, an easy to use vessel with no reason to fight it. You wouldn't, shouldn't, have known better. A blank canvas, that's what they turned you into. Wiped clean, poised for their purpose. They could repaint you however they pleased."

Her belly coiled. "But I wasn't so easily caught, was I?"

"No," he grinned, "You certainly were not."

The pride radiating from him made Sara all warm and gooey on the inside.

"When you first came to me," Lucifer sipped his drink, "you and Kalen were both the definition of a broken soul. It took so long to mend you two. Your bodies healed instantly with my fires, but your minds... they took a lot longer. All the while, you never

264

backed away from fighting. As if your life was still in your hands and not mine." He licked his lips, a smile slowly turning up his mouth. "So I used your fight, your anger, your hurt, and forged you to be a killer. A Hound in the most glorious sense of the word. Nothing stood in your way, Sara. You were fearless then, just as you are fearless now. You were so restless here, but no pack I had would suit you. You wanted your own, with Kalen, and I was inclined to indulge." He began chuckling, "I've never regretted my decision to let you select your own pack. Yours was always the strongest by far."

"Then what do you regret?"

"That everyone knew I loved you and doted upon you." He took another sip, "In hindsight, I now think that wasn't the smartest move I've made. The Devil's Darling was a target that would ensure the hardest blow. Not just to me, but to my strongest pack."

"Then why did you put on that show just now with everyone?"

"Because no one can hide from the truth Sara. You *are* my favorite. You will always be the one who sank her teeth into me and changed me." He laughed boldly, "Literally. I still carry the scar." He held his arm up to show her teeth marks.

"How can you scar when Fin's eye healed so cleanly?"

"I *chose* to keep this mark." He leaned forward and kissed the top of her head. "Let that be your second lesson, Darling."

He stood up and headed towards the door like the conversation was over. But it wasn't. Not yet.

"Why didn't you save me, Luce?"

He stopped dead in his tracks. Without turning around he answered, "Even the Devil has his limits."

Her breath hitched. Sara had no doubt in her mind that the Devil would burn the earth down trying to find her. Same as her Hounds. There was only one reason why Lucifer wasn't able to get to her when she was a wisp. "You can't leave this place, can you?"

His shoulders dropped a fraction of an inch. "Get yourself back together, Humpty Dumpty. We have souls to hunt and Hell to fix."

CHAPTER 45

No one said a word as they marched down the Halls of Hell towards the entrance that led them home. Filing through their basement door, Jack locked it up and Sara felt the wards click back into place.

More magic.

She was either acutely aware of every little thing or she was getting stronger and more sensitive – didn't matter to her because both meant she was getting better at being the Hound Lucifer and her pack needed.

"That didn't go the way I thought it would," Tanner said as they took the steps and headed into the kitchen. He rummaged through the fridge and pulled out a six pack and placed it on the table. "You okay, Beautiful?"

"I'm fine," she said quietly. It felt good to have Tanner sit next to her. He reached behind her and started rubbing her back.

Suddenly, a heavy rock landed in her stomach. A big, icky, burning hunk of awfulness, pressed in her gut. She didn't want to let Lucifer down. She didn't want her pack to be broken. She didn't want Hell to burst and the earth to be eaten alive by the evil that was escaping, bit by bit.

She needed to get herself back together. This Humpty

Dumpty was gonna pick up her pieces and get right again, damnit.

"Take off your shirts." Her command seemed to stun them all and her Hounds just stared at her. "Take them off. All of you."

Tanner pulled his off first, leaning back from the table, he just ripped the rolling stones t-shirt clean off his body. Jack unbuttoned his with nimble fingers, rotating his shoulders as he peeled his black dress shirt off. Eli reached behind his back and yanked his Henley over his head. Kalen pulled his faded black t-shirt off from the bottom up – his big, sinewy arms with a full sleeve of tats crossing over as he grabbed the hem and lifted the shirt over his head.

Her mouth watered.

They were all shirtless and in black leather pants. There had to be laws against this much sexiness.

Sara stood up slowly and walked around each of them. She went to Tanner first. Running her hand down his spine, her breath hitched when she saw the effect her touch had on not just him, but the ink on his spine. Each of the five symbols lit up as her finger touched them. His back arched, like the magic sent a ripple of electric fire down his spine, and he moaned.

Every time one of the guys would run their finger down her spine, her body would react much the same way as Tanner just did. Seeing the tattoos respond, though, was a lightshow that was mesmerizing.

Exquisite.

Next, she moved to Jack. He groaned as she ran her finger down his backbone. Then she did the same to Eli. He braced for her touch, but still, when she ran her finger over his vertebrae, the ink lit up and he shivered as his back arched. Kalen was last. With a wicked gleam in his eyes, her Wolf leaned over to give her access to his bare back. She scored him with a fingernail, leaving a pink line down his spine, slicing right through each of the symbols. Kalen's rumbling growl was all pleasure. Goosebumps covered his arms.

"Do me." Sara started yanking on the buckles of her corset. What the fuck kind of torture device was this shit? How many buckles and straps were truly necessary to hold up a piece of leather?

"Here, let us help." Tanner pushed away from the table and he and Jack started making fast work of her leather straps and silver buckles. They got the corset off of her in no time.

Now they were all topless and in leather pants.

"Do me," she urged again. Sara pulled her long hair over her shoulder, exposing her back for them. Closing her eyes, she waited for the first touch.

Kalen. She'd know his rough hands anywhere. Warm, gentle, perfect. Next it was Tanner who ran a nimble finger down her spine. Sara's composure crumbled a little and she gripped the back of a chair to stay steady.

Heat flooded her system, pooling between her thighs.

Next, Eli pressed his finger on the nape of her neck and held it there for a moment before sending a trail of tingles down her back. Jack was last. His confident hand pressed hard against her skin as he sailed his middle finger down the ridges of her backbone.

"Together," her voice was deep and sultry, "Do it together, now."

Four hands pressed against her, and, as one unit, they sailed down her body and she felt like she was going to explode.

"Fuck me sideways," Tanner cursed. "Do you guys see what I'm seeing or have I lost my mind?"

"We see it," Kalen answered.

"See what?" Sara looked back at them.

"You have another symbol." Kalen seemed a little undone. "It's yours. The one that represents your trust with the pack."

Her eyebrows knit together. "What about Jack and Tanner's symbols?"

"Not yet," Tanner answered, his voice edgy and weak.

"Well that doesn't make any fucking sense. How can I trust you all as a whole but not separately?"

"Trust is a complicated thing, love." Jack sighed and crossed his arms over his chest. His scowl would have looked so deadly to anyone else, but she thought he looked adorable.

"You're disappointed," she whispered. "I'm so sorry." Scrambling to cover herself up, she snatched Kalen's shirt and wiggled into it. No sense in having her tats exposed if it was going to upset her Hounds.

"I'm not disappointed, love." Jack pressed a light kiss on her mouth. "You'll get there."

"I want to be there now."

Was she pouting? Yeah, a little bit.

"You need to do something thrilling. Lose all control and give it to someone else." That piece of advice came from Eli.

"Go on," Sara urged. "I'm willing to do anything to get myself back to normal. We can't let Lucifer down and he needs his strongest pack right now."

Tanner chuckled, "You want to hunt, don't you?"

She shrugged, unable to lie, "Yes." She felt her cheeks redden when two of the Hounds started laughing quietly. "What? I have five years of revenge to get on those stupid things and I'm all..." she waved her hands through the air, searching for the right word.

"Wound up?"

"Frustrated?"

"Restless?"

The words just kept coming and she stomped her foot. "YES. All of that, damnit."

"She's getting more like herself every day," Kalen smirked.

"SHE is right here," Sara's hands were on her hips. "SHE would appreciate you remembering that."

"Well, SHE," Jack grabbed her hand and started luring her out of the kitchen. "How about we see what we can do to relieve some of your stress."

She followed Jack and felt the other Hounds behind her. Their individual scents filled her nose, muddling her thoughts until she was nothing but desires. Whatever they had planned, she just hoped she could handle it.

CHAPTER 46

Jack brought her into his room and waited, expecting her to say something. When she didn't, he asked, "How many Hounds, love?"

His question caught her off guard. Sara looked across the room at her entire pack. Suddenly, Jack's intentions became clear and her mouth ran dry. "I... I don't think I know."

Stupid, stupid, stupid. She should have said *All of you*, but she wasn't ready for that yet. She wasn't sure if she'd ever be ready for that much. Sara's mind swirled around thoughts of each of them naked, bringing her pleasures she was suddenly desperate for. Her eyes met Tanner's and a piece of her panicked. He said they were passionate in bed. He said she wasn't ready for him yet.

Was she ready for him now?

Sara gulped. No, she didn't think so.

Next, her eyes shifted to Kalen. For whatever reason, her stomach clenched. She didn't want to share him. Not yet. Not even with Jack.

Eli? *Yes,* she thought. Eli was good at reading her. Whatever they were about to do, Eli would be a wise choice.

"Eli," her voice was thin and trembling. "Just Jack and Eli."

Shockingly, neither Kalen nor Tanner looked disappointed in

her decision. As a matter of fact, the two Hounds seemed relieved. Tanner winked and walked out of Jack's room quietly and Kalen followed.

Her focus swung around to Eli, her cheeks felt so hot Sara reached up and pressed her hands on them. "What do you have planned?"

Jack came up behind her and whispered, "A little exercise in trust, love." With that, he blindfolded her.

Plunged into darkness, Sara's heart slammed into her chest. She was two parts thrilled and one part nervous as fuck. Jack guided her to the bed and she sat, perched on the edge of the mattress. A cold, hard object ran down her skin between her breasts.

"What is that?" she asked nervously.

"A knife," Eli growled. "Spread your legs, Sara."

Eli's voice was calm and controlled, she trusted him. Trusted Jack, too. Now was the time to prove it. Legs spread, the leather pants she wore felt tight on her thighs.

"Are you frightened, love?"

"No." Her hands began to shake in anticipation.

Eli's voice was deeper than normal. "Stay still and do not move a muscle."

Sara obeyed and her breath hitched when she sensed movement between her legs.

"Jack's going to cut a slit open in your pants."

She was so turned on now, it hurt to breathe. There was a tug and then a small *ffft* sound, followed by cool air hitting her sex. The air *whooshed* out of her. This shouldn't have felt so thrilling, but it did. Goddamn, she was so aroused right now.

A warm wetness engulfed her right breast. She reached forward, holding someone's head to her as they suckled. Immediately, the mouth released from her skin. "No touching, Sara." Eli grabbed her hands and pulled them backwards, having her fall back on the mattress. He tied her wrists to something, most likely the middle of the headboard.

She allowed it, her sensations heightening even more. Now her sight and capability to touch were gone. But she could still feel, and right now Sara was feeling a lot of things. Shit, this was incredible…

271

Sara hissed as something cold and hard clamped onto her nipples next. Her hands grappled for something to cling to but the restraints wouldn't allow her much movement. She laced her fingers together tightly and bit her bottom lip.

With the help of her Hounds, Sara's hips rose into the air. Someone tugged her pants off.

"Fuck, love. You smell so good when you're like this." Jack bent down and licked her wet slit, making her moan. "I could bury my face in here and never come up for air."

Sara's body tensed when Jack went in for a second taste. Suddenly Eli's hot breath was tickling her ear. "Do you like that, Sara?"

"Yes," she whispered.

Jack stopped immediately and Sara snarled. Before she could get a word in, hands grabbed her ankles and she felt something bind around them, spreading her legs wider.

A bar, she realized. Her ankles were strapped to a bar. There'd be no running with that thing. No way out. "What's the safe word?" she asked.

"There isn't one, love." Jack nipped her earlobe.

It was a lie. Right? She's had sex with Jack before and nothing about it was scary or too rough. Of course, he hadn't used these methods of pleasure on her then. Would they stop if she needed them to?

Yes. Her Hounds would never hurt her.

Sara's head spun when they flipped her over. She was truly at their mercy like this. They hoisted her into a new position and she whimpered. Ass up high in the air, her sex completely exposed and her head face down on the sheets, Sara's arms were stretched over her head. With her legs still spread wide, her Hounds were getting the best view right now.

The idea of them seeing her sex like this turned her on even more than she was ten seconds ago.

"Do you want me to watch you or fuck you?" Eli's question had her panting again. "Your choice."

"Watch me," she moaned. "I want you to watch me, Eli."

"Funny thing about your current situation right now, love," Jack's voice tickled her other ear, "You aren't really in a position to make demands, are you?" he slapped her ass hard. The sting made her yip and then a big hand rubbed the burn away.

She gulped, her body eager for more.

Jack's hand snaked between her thighs and he plunged a finger inside her. "So wet already and I haven't even started."

"Get the other things."

"What other things?" Sara tried to not sound desperate. It didn't work.

"We're going to take your senses away, one by one, Sara. You will not see us. You will not hear us. And by the end, you will not have enough energy to even scream." The whip in Jack's hand slapped her ass and she squeaked. It didn't hurt like she thought it was going to. "Hear no evil." *Crack.* "See no evil," *Crack.* "Speak no evil." *Crack.*

Focusing on their caresses, Sara couldn't help but find her current state a little humorous. For five years she'd been furious that no one could see her, hear her, or touch her. Now she was rendered blind, deaf and immobile and she was in fucking heaven. The touching was what she craved the most during her solitary ghost days, and right now her Hounds were making up for lost time. She wished she had asked for all four of them to join her at this point.

Something hard slapped her sex and she cried out. It surprised her... not hurt her. Within moments, Sara had a gag in her mouth, a damn effective head set cuffed her ears that made it impossible to hear anything, and she was rendered totally helpless and at the mercy of her Hounds.

Not gonna lie, she was a little scared. Her curiosity was peaked though. Sara wanted this and she trusted them. Her heartbeat swished in her ears as she waited with bated breath for their next move.

Someone pulled the headphones off of one side and whispered, "Good-bye," before putting the headphones securely back onto her head.

Wait... what?

Seconds passed.

Then minutes....

What the hell? Had they left her?

Sara tried to make sense of what the fuck was going on.

The silence became deafening and there was a horrible

ringing in her ears. Her arms began to ache, her leg muscles clenched. She grew beyond frustrated. Yanking at her restraints, Sara was reminded of how stuck she was.

A new panic rose in her. The feeling of abandonment and vulnerability started to suffocate her rationale. Desperate to escape, she started pulling harder, whimpering as she tried to free herself.

Her mind was set on one objective: FREEDOM.

Her body was honed in on one goal: RELEASE.

Every molecule she owned was screaming now. Lost in darkness, locked in restraints, she was floating with no tethers. She wasn't going to survive this torture. Panic rose and bubbled out in tremors. Time ticked by slowly… or had it stopped completely? How long has she been lying like this, alone and deprived? Minutes. Hours. Days?

Nothing made sense. Her mind played unwelcomed visions and she went wild trying to find her Hounds with no means to see, hear, or move. Sara sobbed into her gag, confused and torn between reality and nightmare.

She yanked her restraints harder. If she could, she'd have gnawed off her hands to get free. Darkness consumed her. She was lost. Scared. Abandoned! SHE WAS ALL ALONE!

"HELP!" she cried around her gag. "HELP ME!"

No one answered. She jerked and twisted, unable to move more than a few inches. Sweat trickled down her temples. Her tears soaked the blindfold.

Sara let out a devastatingly sad howl. She choked on the gag, on her sorrow, on her rising panic. She didn't know who she was anymore. Or where she was. Had this entire thing been a dream? Was she not really found and saved? Was she still being killed by the crow, the pig and the antlered man?

She howled again.

Jack would find her. Was there ever a Jack to begin with?

Find me, she pleaded. *Jack, find me. Save me.*

He must exist. This can't have all been a dream. Jack was real, right? RIGHT?

JACK! Sara screamed in her head. She yanked harder to free herself, all to no avail. After several more tries, Sara cried louder and began snarling like a vicious animal.

Then… a calmness took hold of her and she felt as though she were sinking into a black abyss. She would wait... He *will* come for her. In this, she had no doubt. Jack. Will. Come. For. Her.

Sara's mind shut down. Her fear, her anxiety... every ounce of doubt faded into mist. She continued to lay there and cling to her fraying sanity.

Out of nowhere, hands grabbed and caressed her skin. The sudden contact was a shock to her overworked system.

The scent of her Hounds filled her nose. They were close, covering her, caressing her. She twitched away a second before she pushed into the hand that was now running over her thigh. Her hips jutted out as another hand caressed her sex, plunging a finger inside her again.

Sara knew where she was. She knew who she was with. There was no darkness here, only her and her Hounds. Safety was no longer a concern. Her fears of abandonment vanished. Her need for release was all she could focus on now. She wasn't surprised Jack had come for her. She knew damn well he would. Like the sun set in the west, Sara had absolute confidence that her Hound would find her.

And here he was.

A hand sailed down her back and her body arched, heaving her chest forward. She groaned, her head tilting back.

Her sex was so swollen with need now she was beyond desperate for more touching. Four hands were on her at once, moving, caressing, slapping, tickling. Then she felt the press of something warm and hard against her opening. Four hands held her waist, rendering her immobile as someone pushed into her body. She cried out again. *Jack*, she thought, wishing she could speak his name out loud. Stars burst behind her eyelids as he buried himself deep within her body.

As he rocked in and out of her, something new pushed into her backside, teasing, circling, tempting. It never penetrated her though, and she couldn't tell if she was disappointed or not.

Next, a vibration slid between her thighs. A cock ring? A vibrator? Shit, she couldn't tell, and it didn't matter. Everything felt like too much and not enough. More, she wanted more. Sara was so close to coming, her body was tightly coiled and threatening to implode.

She had no control. She had no say. She had no senses left.

Her only form of communication was the way she moved her hips and even that was minimal. Sara swayed back as her body was forced into a new position. Some slack was given on the ties around her wrists and she was now able to hold herself up on hands and knees. The nipple clamps were released and she hissed at the sting and surge of her blood rising to the tips. Next, the gag was removed from her mouth and she was finally able to cry out for all she was worth. "Jack!"

The reprieve was short lived. The gag was replaced with something warm and thick. She accepted the offering, licking the head of her Hound's cock. His hand plunged into her hair but didn't force her head forward to take more than just the tip of his incredibly hard erection. His other hand stroked in time with her licks and she sucked him harder, turned on by the idea of being filled at both ends.

The Hound behind her picked up pace and Sara bit down on the cock between her teeth. She was so lost in the moment now, her climax riding her closer and closer to the point of do or die.

Jets of hot liquid poured into her mouth and she swallowed it all. It was sweet, like pineapples.

More pressure built within her. Something pressed against her backside again, teasingly, and she leaned into it, not giving a fuck what it was. Slowly, it was pushed inside her tightest hole. Beads? Maybe. Whatever it was, it was doing something fantastic to her.

"I'm so close." She couldn't tell how loud she was with the headphones over her damn ears.

Jack's pace quickened, his hips thrusting, his body slamming into hers with a brutal force of pure pleasure. Swaying backwards, she encouraged him to fuck harder and bring her to the point of explosion. "Don't stop, don't stop. Fuck! Don't stop!"

Sara roared as her body detonated. The world crashed down all around her, sweeping her up and tossing her into space.

A mouth found hers and she melted into the kiss, realizing Eli had to be upside down to pull it off. Or was she upside down? She stroked his tongue with hers, and the taste of him was enough to keep her orgasm going. Sara convulsed, the Hound behind her pulled out the beads nice and slow and she came again, all the while kissing her other Hound.

She'd never felt so alive in all her life. Breaking the kiss, Sara half-laughed, half-cried. Her body continued to jerk and writhe from the aftershocks of what they'd done. Finally, the blindfold was pulled off and she gasped.

Jack was lying on his back, his head directly under hers, which meant...

Eli was the one who'd taken her from behind.

Holy. Shit. Sara tried to catch her breath but there seemed to be no air in the room.

"You found me," she whispered. "I knew you would... I knew you would come back for me."

"Always, love." Jack's gaze glassed over.

They made quick work of releasing all the restraints and she collapsed onto the bed in a heap of lust and confusion. Dear god, what a rush.

Sara was dumbfounded. In the midst of their chaos, it hadn't mattered who was doing what to her. Sara's trust was absolute with both of them.

She had assumed it was Jack behind her, pushing her limits, but at some point they were just her Hounds. It hadn't mattered who did what to her, because it had all felt so good and so right and so incredible. The lines had blurred. The Hounds had become one. She didn't lean on one or the other, she depended on both. Trusted them with her life. Her safety.

Holy Hell, she thought. They'd taken her beyond her limits and...

"Did it work?" Sara's voice cracked. Everything felt tingly and her limbs felt boneless.

She met Eli's eyes first. He looked... torn. "I'll give you two a minute," he said quietly. Eli left the room and shut the door without answering her question.

Their reactions scared her and tears filled her eyes. What they'd just done together was incredible, why were they acting like this? "Jack?" Panic slammed into her. "Did it work?"

She saw him swallow hard. He cautiously started folding the straps and blindfold around his whip and tucked them back into his drawer. He looked raw and undone ...

"JACK!" she shouted, "DID IT WORK?"

His gaze rendered her immobile. "Yes."

CHAPTER 47

Tanner was at the kitchen table, his knee bobbing up and down so hard the table had shifted a little to the left. Kalen leaned against the counter, his face buried in his hands. Eli walked in and didn't meet either of their eyes. Instead, he went over to the sink and splashed cold water on his face.

"Well?" Tanner stood up, his blonde hair as disheveled as Eli felt.

"It worked."

Tanner fell back into his chair. "Jesus."

Kalen's head popped up, eyes red-rimmed. "Are you serious?"

"Yeah," Eli took a seat, his legs weak and ready to give out on him. It had taken all his strength to get back into a pair of pants. It wasn't his muscles that were drained, it was his emotions.

What they'd done to Sara was nothing they would have ever considered doing before. She never allowed them to take away every bit of her control. As a matter of fact, Sara was more often on the other side of that whip.

Not today though.

"What did you do?" Kalen's deep rumble brought Eli's head around to meet a cold stare.

"We took away everything from her. Her sight. Her hearing.

Her mobility. Her voice. And we abandoned her, long enough for her mind to push her into a tailspin." Eli braced for the impact a second before Kalen locked his hand around his throat.

"You went too far," the Wolf growled.

"She liked it."

"Jesus," Tanner said again.

Kalen's hold loosened. "How could you take a risk like that?"

Sara, as they all damn well knew, didn't like restraints. Her first death had involved too many of them.

"Tell us everything from the beginning, Eli." Tanner jabbed the air between them, "How the *fuck* did you just pull that off?"

Eli knew they could hear her screams. Could feel her panic and fear in the air. Now that her pack symbol was on her once more, they could all feel each other if they chose to concentrate hard enough, or if one of them pushed energy into it as a call sign.

"I gave her the choice of me being the one to watch or the one to have sex with her. She chose to have me watch." They'd given her a false sense of control. "We got her all worked up, ready for sex, and then we restrained her, blindfolded and deafened her with headphones. Then... we left her for forty three minutes. Alone." *Alone* was the key word. Shit, his hands were still shaking.

"Mother. Fucker." Tanner scrubbed his face with his hands, his knees bouncing in triple-time.

They never actually left the room, but Sara was too gone in her head to notice. Eli and Jack stood at the far end of the bedroom and watched her unravel, one breath at a time, until they couldn't stand it anymore. When she went stiff as a board, and stopped fighting her restraints, they relented and returned to her.

Jack had reached her first.

"She was also gagged," Eli admitted.

Kalen's head lolled back and he stared at the ceiling. He was silently counting to ten in an effort to control his temper.

Eli cleared his dry throat. "When we saw it was getting to be too much for her to handle, Jack nearly went mad. Then... she just calmed down. She stopped freaking out and just... waited. It was like she knew, without a doubt, she'd be saved. Sara stilled on the bed, her breath controlled and she seemed to almost be determined that if she waited long enough, she'd be rescued and freed. I've never seen her so resolved. That's when we surrounded her.

Touched her. Soothed her. And Jack and I switched positions. She didn't know for sure who was doing what, and she didn't care. By then she was nothing but desperate desire."

"Holy fuck," Tanner whispered.

"She was so trusting," Eli shook his head, "she let us do anything we wanted to her."

Kalen growled like an animal, "I can't believe you went that far."

"She'd have gone further," Eli looked over as Jack came into the room. "I've never seen her like that in all our days together."

They all knew she liked it a little rough, but never was sex out of her control. They used plenty of toys and restraints before, but not so much all at once and never without a safe word or a way for Sara to tap out.

"Lesson number two," Sara said from the doorway, surprising them with her sudden appearance, "Choose which scars you keep."

She sat down gingerly at the table. Eli melted a little seeing she had chosen one of his shirts to wear. "Are you okay, baby?"

"I'm better than okay." She reached over and grabbed his hand. "I keep putting you two in situations together, don't I?" she winked at Jack. "I can't figure out why, but I like you two together scaring the shit out of me. And both times seem to have blades involved." Guess her leather pants were trashed now.

"Never again, love. I'm bloody thrilled my symbol is back on you, but I'll never put you through that again."

"Because of my first death?"

Jack's face fell, "Yes."

"I remember it."

Kalen pushed away from the table and fell to his knees at Sara's feet. "You remember that?"

She shook her head. "I painted it when I was at the apartment with Eli."

"You didn't say anything." Eli knelt by her other side.

"There was nothing to say. Some things are still slowly coming, but I remember... that."

Eli reached out and squeezed her leg, "Does Lucifer know?"

"I'm not sure," she shrugged, "I played it off after the meeting, acted like I didn't remember and asked him to tell me. That's when he gave me my second lesson: *Choose the scars you keep,* he said. I'm not keeping that one anymore."

Kalen's head fell into her lap and he squeezed her tight. "I'm so fucking sorry."

"There is nothing to be sorry about, Kalen. I have you. Isn't that what we always wanted? To be together, forever?"

"But the cost was so great."

"And worth it," Sara cooed. "I love you," her eyes met each of her Hounds. "I love you all. And what you've done for me? Words can't come close to explaining how your love makes me feel."

"You always had your painting for that," Tanner smiled from across the table. "I've ordered more art supplies, by the way. The delivery should be here in about a week or so."

"Nice," Eli grinned. "We can set you up a place to paint in the farmhouse if you want."

Kalen nodded, "The barn."

"It's too cold in there right now," Tanner argued.

"It doesn't matter, I don't feel anything when I paint," she shrugged, "I only seem to feel on the inside." No one argued with her. "I'm starving," she said, breaking through the last of the tension in the kitchen.

"I ordered pizza," Tanner said.

Her eyebrows arched, "Cheese?"

"Of course. And nine extra-large meat-lovers for the rest of us."

"I'll make a salad to go with it." Eli stepped over to the fridge and started pulling out ingredients.

The house started moving around again, everyone getting back to their lives. Sara reached out and grabbed Jack's hand. He still looked upset but wasn't saying anything, "Hey," her voice was soft, "You okay?"

"Mmm hmm." He kissed her nose and tried to move away.

She stopped him. "Talk to me, Jack."

Too many emotions danced across his face. "I just..." he struggled to collect his thoughts, "I don't think I'm going to get the sounds of your cries out of my head for a long time. Seeing you struggle through your hell in my bed. It was cruel to do."

"It was necessary."

"I should have found another way to get you to trust me." Jack's head dipped down in shame, "I abandoned you. I let you believe you were lost and alone. It's your greatest fear and I used it against you... paired it with things that you could have easily misconstrued as pain, not pleasure. I crossed a hard line, Sara."

"And that's why it was necessary. I needed to trust you. I needed you to bring me to rock bottom and trust you to get me out again."

"I'm never going to forgive myself for this."

"Hey," she grabbed Jack's arm and rubbed it, "I'm glad you did what you did. Both you and Eli brought me to my limit and gave me the choice to give you all I have or let my past hold me hostage."

"We didn't know you could remember though."

"Eli did," her head turned towards the Hound. "He saw the painting when he thought I was sleeping."

Eli's shoulders stiffened as he swallowed the massive lump in his throat and nodded silently.

"And he knows what I need, when I need it." Sara wasn't at all upset with him for snooping. She was relieved he saw the painting. It saved her the trouble of presenting the devastating canvas to him later. "Thank you."

"So," Tanner swerved the conversation back to something lighter. "Once again, you've—"

"Saved the best for last." They all said in unison.

"Exactly!" the blond Hound beamed a big cheesy grin.

Just then, the doorbell rang. "Pizza's here!" Sara kissed Jack in a last attempt to reassure him everything was alright. Then she grabbed the cash someone had laid on the counter and headed for the front door.

"Sara, wait!"

Too late. She opened the door and froze in fear. The man on the other side of the door was not holding pizzas. He was holding a knife.

"Hello, Sara. Long time no see."

Sara backed up, tripping over her own two feet in the process. She knew the man at her doorstep. He was the bastard who had watched her die.

As the man took another step closer, a scream ripped out of her throat, "HOUNDS!"

Other Books By This Author

Hell Hounds Harem Series:

Restless Spirit
The Dark Truth
The Devil's Darling

Hard to Find
Hard to Love
Hard to Kill

Sins of the Sidhe Series:
Shatter
Shine
Passion
Bargains
Ignite
Awaken
Rise
Exile

For information on this book and other future releases,
please visit my website: www.BrianaMichaels.com

If you liked this book, please help spread the word by
leaving a review on the site you purchased your copy, or
on a reader site such as Goodreads.

I'd love to hear from readers too, so feel free to send me an
email at: sinsofthesidhe@gmail.com or visit me on
Facebook: www.facebook.com/BrianaMichaelsAuthor

Thank You!

ABOUT THE AUTHOR

Briana Michaels grew up and still lives on the East Coast. When taking a break from the crazy adventures in her head, she enjoys running around with her two children. If there is time to spare, she loves to read, cook, hike in the woods, and sit outside by a roaring fire. She does all of this with the love and support of her amazing husband who always has her back, encouraging her to go for her dreams. Aye, she's a lucky girl indeed.

Made in the USA
Middletown, DE
31 January 2020